the Vampire
Diaries

Also by L. J. Smith:

Vampire Diaries

Volume 1 (Books 1 & 2) – *The Awakening* and
The Struggle
Volume 2 (Books 3 & 4) – *The Fury* and *The Reunion*
Book 5 – *The Return: Nightfall*
Book 6 – *The Return: Shadow Souls*

Coming soon:
Book 7 – *The Return: Midnight*

Night World

Volume 1 (Books 1–3) – *Secret Vampire, Daughters of
Darkness* and *Enchantress*
Volume 2 (Books 4–6) – *Dark Angel, The Chosen*
and *Soulmate*
Volume 3 (Books 7–9) – *Huntress, Black Dawn*
and *Witchlight*

Coming soon:
Book 10 – *Strange Fate*

Secret Circle

Volume 1 – *The Initiation* and *The Captive* Part I
Volume 2 – *The Captive* Part II and *The Power*

the Vampire Diaries

The Return – Shadow Souls

L. J. SMITH

Hodder
Children's
Books

A division of Hachette Children's Books

For my wonderful agent, Elizabeth Harding

CHAPTER

1

"**D**ear Diary," Elena whispered, "how frustrating is this? I left you in the trunk of the Jaguar and it's two o'clock in the morning." She stabbed her finger on the leg of her nightgown as if she had a pen and was making a full stop. She whispered even more softly, leaning her forehead against the window, "And I'm *afraid* to go outside – in the dark – and get you. I'm afraid!" She made another stab and then, feeling tears slip down her cheeks, reluctantly turned her mobile on to record. It was a stupid waste of the battery, but she couldn't help it. She *needed* this.

"So here I am," she said softly, "sitting up in the backseat of the car. This has to be my diary entry for today. By the way, we made a rule for this road trip – I sleep in the Jag's backseat and it's the Great Outdoors for Matt and Damon. Right now it's so dark outside that I can't see Matt anywhere . . . But I've been going crazy – crying and feeling lost – and so lonely for Stefan . . .

"We have to get rid of the Jaguar – it's too big, too red,

too flashy, and too memorable when we're trying *not* to be remembered as we travel to the place where we can free Stefan. After the car is sold, the lapis lazuli and diamond pendant Stefan gave me the day before he disappeared will be the most precious thing I have left. The day before . . . Stefan got tricked into going away, thinking he could become an ordinary human being. And now . . .

"How can I stop thinking about what *They* might be doing to him, at this very second – whoever 'They' are? Probably the kitsune, the evil fox spirits at the prison called the Shi no Shi."

Elena paused to wipe her nose on her nightgown sleeve.

"*How did I ever get myself into this situation?*" She shook her head, hit the seatback with her clenched fist.

"Maybe if I could figure that out, I could come up with Plan A. I always have a Plan A. And my friends always have a Plan B and C to help me." Elena blinked hard, thinking of Bonnie and Meredith. "But now I'm frightened that I'll never see them again. And I'm scared for the entire town of Fell's Church."

For a moment she sat with her clenched fist on her knee. A small voice inside her was saying, "So stop whining, Elena, and think. *Think*. Start from the beginning."

The beginning? What was the beginning? Stefan?

No, she had lived in Fell's Church long before Stefan came.

Slowly, almost dreamily, she spoke into her mobile. "In the first place: who am I? I'm Elena Gilbert, age eighteen." Even more slowly, she said, "I . . . don't *think* it's vain to say that I'm beautiful. If I didn't know I was, I'd have to have never looked in a mirror or heard a compliment. It's not something I should be proud of – it's just something that was passed down from Mom and Dad.

"What do I look like? I have blonde hair that falls in sort of waves past my shoulders and blue eyes that some people have said are like lapis lazuli: dark blue with splashes of gold." She gave a half-choked laugh. "Maybe that's why vampires like me."

Then her lips tightened and, staring into the utter blackness around her, she spoke seriously.

"A lot of boys have called me the most angelic girl in the world. And I played around with them. I just used them – for popularity, for amusement, for whatever. I'm being honest, all right? I considered them to be toys or trophies." She paused. "But there was something else. Something that I knew all my life was coming – but I didn't know what. I felt as if I were searching for something that I could never find with boys. None of my scheming or playing around with them ever touched my . . . deepest heart . . . until one very special boy came along." She stopped and swallowed and said it again. "One *very* special boy.

"His name was Stefan.

"And *he* turned out not to be what he looked like, a normal – but gorgeous – high school senior with rumpled dark hair and eyes as green as emeralds.

"Stefan Salvatore turned out to be a vampire.

"A real vampire."

Elena had to pause to take a few choked breaths before she could get the next words out.

"And so did his gorgeous older brother, Damon."

She bit her lips, and it seemed a long time later that she added, "Would I have loved Stefan if I'd known he was a vampire from the beginning? Yes! Yes! *Yes!* I'd have

3

fallen in love with him no matter what! But it changed things – and it changed me." Elena's finger traced a pattern on her nightgown by touch alone. "You see, vampires show love by exchanging blood. The problem was . . . that I was sharing blood with Damon, too. Not really by choice, but because he was after me constantly, day and night."

She let out a sigh. "What Damon *says* is that he wants to make me a vampire and his Princess of the Night. What that translates into is: he wants me all to himself. But I wouldn't trust Damon on anything unless he gave his word. That's one quirk he has, he never breaks his word."

Elena could feel an odd smile curling her lips, but she was speaking calmly now, fluently, the mobile almost forgotten.

"A girl involved with two vampires . . . well, there's bound to be trouble, isn't there? So maybe I deserved what I got.

"I died.

"Not just 'died' like when your heart stops and they resuscitate you and you come back talking about almost going into the Light. I *went* into the Light.

"I *died*.

"And when I came back – what a surprise! I was a vampire.

"Damon was . . . kind to me, I suppose, when I first woke up as a vampire. Maybe that's the reason I still have . . . feelings for him. He didn't take advantage of me when he could have easily.

"But I only had time to do a few things in my vampire life. I had time to remember Stefan and love him more than ever – since I knew, then, how difficult everything was for him. I got to listen to my own memorial service. Ha! Everybody should get a chance to do that. I learned to always, *always* wear lapis lazuli so I wouldn't become a vampire Crispy Critter. I got to say goodbye to my little four-year-old sister, Margaret, and visit Bonnie and Meredith . . ."

Tears were still sliding almost unnoticed down Elena's face. But she spoke quietly.

"And then – I died again.

"I died the way a vampire dies, when they don't have lapis lazuli in the sunlight. I didn't crumble into dust; I was only seventeen. But the sun poisoned me anyway. Going was almost . . . peaceful. That was when I made Stefan promise to take care of Damon, always. And I think Damon swore to take care of Stefan, in his mind. And that was how I died, with Stefan holding me and Damon beside me as I simply drifted away, like going to sleep.

"After that, I had dreams I don't remember, and then suddenly, one day everyone was surprised because I was talking to them through Bonnie, who is very psychic, poor thing. I guess I had landed the job of being Fell's Church's guardian spirit. There was a danger to the town. They had to fight it and somehow, when they were sure that they had lost, I got dumped back to the world of the living to help. And – well, when the war was won I was left with these weird powers I don't understand. But there was Stefan, too! We were together again!"

Elena wrapped her arms around herself tightly and held on as if she were holding Stefan to her, imagining his warm arms around her. She shut her eyes until her breathing slowed.

"About my powers, let's see. There's telepathy, which I can do if the other person is telepathic – which all vampires are, but to different degrees unless they're actually sharing blood with you at the time. And then there are my Wings.

"It's true – I have Wings! And the Wings have powers you wouldn't believe – the only problem being that I don't have the faintest idea how to use them. There's one that I can feel sometimes, like right *now*, trying to get out of me, trying to shape my lips to name it, trying to move my body into the right stance. It's *Wings of Protection* and *that* sounds like something we could really use on this trip. But I can't even remember how I made the old Wings work – much less figure out how to use this new one. I say the words until I feel like an idiot – but nothing happens at all.

"So I'm a human again – as human as Bonnie. And, oh, God, if I could only *see* her and Meredith right now! But all the time I tell myself that I'm getting closer to Stefan every minute. That is, if you take into account Damon's running us up and down and everywhere to throw off anybody trying to track us down.

"Why would anyone want to track us down? Well, you see, when I came back from the afterlife there was a very big explosion of Power that everyone in the world who can see Power saw.

"Now, how do I explain Power? It's something that everybody has, but that humans – except genuine psychics like Bonnie – don't even recognise. Vampires definitely have Power, and they use it to Influence humans to like them, or to think that things are different from reality – oh, like the way Stefan Influenced the high school staff to think his records were all in order when he 'transferred' to Robert E. Lee High School. Or they use Power to blast other vampires or creatures of darkness – or humans.

"But I was talking about the burst of Power when *I*

dropped down from the heavens. It was so big that it attracted two horrible creatures from the other side of the world. And then they decided to come see what had made the burst, and if there was any way they could use it for themselves.

"I'm not joking, either, about them being from the other side of the world. They were kitsune, evil fox spirits from Japan. They're something like our Western werewolves – but much more powerful. So powerful that they used *malach*, which are really plants but look like insects that can be no bigger than a pinhead or big enough to swallow your arm. And the malach attach themselves to your nerves and feather out along your entire nervous system and finally they take you over from inside."

Now Elena was shuddering, and her voice was hushed.

"That's what happened to Damon. A tiny one got into him and it took him over from inside so that he was only a puppet of Shinichi's. I forgot to say, the kitsune are called Shinichi and Misao. Misao is the girl. They both have black hair with red all around the tips, but Misao's is long. And they're supposed to be brother and sister – but they sure don't act like it.

"And once Damon was fully possessed, that's when Shinichi made Damon's body . . . do terrible things. He made him torture Matt and me, and even now I know that sometimes Matt still wants to kill Damon for it. But if he'd seen what I saw – a whole thin, wet, white second body that I had to pull out with my fingernails from Damon's spine – with Damon finally passing out from the pain – then Matt would understand better. *I* can't blame Damon for what Shinichi made him do. I *can't*. Damon was . . . you can't imagine how different. He was crushed. He *cried*. He was . . .

"Anyway, I don't expect to ever see him like that

again. But if I ever get my Wings' powers back, Shinichi is in big trouble.

"I think that that was our mistake last time, you see. We finally were able to fight Shinichi and Misao – *and we didn't kill them*. We were too moral or too gentle or something.

"It was a bad mistake.

"Because Damon wasn't the only one who got possessed by Shinichi's malach. There were girls, young girls, fourteen and fifteen and younger. And some boys. Acting . . . crazy. Hurting themselves and their families. We didn't know how badly until after we'd already made a bargain with Shinichi.

"Maybe we were too *immoral*, making a bargain with the devil. But they had kidnapped Stefan – and Damon, who was already possessed by then, had helped them. Once Damon was unpossessed, all he wanted was for Shinichi and Misao to tell us where Stefan was, and then for them to leave Fell's Church for ever.

"In exchange for that, Damon let Shinichi into his mind.

"If vampires are obsessed with Power, kitsune are obsessed with memories. And Shinichi wanted Damon's memories for the last few days – the time that Damon was possessed and torturing us . . . and the time when my Wings made Damon realise that he had done it. I don't think Damon himself wanted those memories, either of what he'd done or of how he'd changed when he had to face that he'd done it. So he let Shinichi take them, in exchange for Shinichi putting Stefan's location into his mind.

"The problem is that we were trusting Shinichi's word that he would leave then – when Shinichi's word meant nothing at all.

8

"Plus, ever since then he's been using the telepathic channel that he opened between his mind and Damon's to take more and *more* of Damon's memories without Damon even knowing.

"It happened just last night, when we were pulled over by a policeman who wanted to know what three teenagers in an expensive car were doing that late at night. Damon Influenced him to go away. But just a few hours later Damon had forgotten the policeman completely.

"It frightens Damon. And anything that frightens Damon – not that he would ever admit it – scares me to *death*.

"And, you might ask, what *were* three teenagers doing out in the middle of nowhere, in Union County, Tennessee, according to the last road sign I saw? We're heading toward some Gate to the Dark Dimension . . . where Shinichi and Misao left Stefan in the prison called the Shi no Shi. Shinichi only put the knowledge into Damon's mind, and I can't get Damon to say much about what kind of place it is. But Stefan is there and I'll get to him somehow, even if it kills me.

"Even if I have to learn how to kill.

"I'm not the sweet little girl from Virginia I used to be."

Elena stopped and blew out her breath. But then, cuddling herself, she went on.

"And why is Matt along with us? Well, because of Caroline Forbes, my friend since kindergarten. Last year . . . when Stefan came to Fell's Church, she and I both wanted him. But Stefan didn't want Caroline. And after that she turned into my worst enemy.

"Caroline was also the lucky winner of Shinichi's first visit to any girl in Fell's Church. But more to the point: she was Tyler Smallwood's girlfriend quite a while before she was his victim. I wonder how long they were together and where Tyler is now. All I know is that, in the end, Caroline hung on to Shinichi because she 'needed a husband'. That was how she put it herself. So I assume – well, what Damon assumes. That she's going to . . . have puppies. A werewolf litter, you know? Since Tyler is a werewolf.

"Damon says that having a werewolf baby turns you into a werewolf even faster than if you're bitten, and that at some point in the pregnancy you gain the power to be all wolf or all human, but before that point you're just a mixed-up mess.

"The sad thing is that Shinichi scarcely gave Caroline a second glance when she blurted it all out.

"But before *that* Caroline had been desperate enough to accuse Matt of–of assaulting her – on a date that went wrong. She had to have known something about what Shinichi was doing because she claimed her 'date' with Matt was at a time when one of the arm-swallowing malach was attacking him, making marks on his arm that looked like a girl's fingernail scratches.

"That sent the police after Matt, all right. So basically I just *made* him come with us. Caroline's father is one of the most important people in Fell's Church – *and* he's friends with the district attorney in Ridgemont and the leader of one of those men's clubs where they have secret handshakes and other stuff that makes you, you know, 'prominent in the community'.

"If I hadn't convinced Matt to run instead of facing Caroline's charges, the Forbeses would have *lynched* him. And I feel the anger like a fire inside me – not just anger and hurt for Matt, but anger and the feeling that Caroline has let all girls everywhere down. Because most girls aren't pathological liars, and wouldn't say something like that about a boy falsely. She's shamed all girls by doing what she did."

Elena paused, looking at her hands, and then added, "Sometimes when I get angry at Caroline, cups shake or pencils roll right off the table. Damon says all this is caused by my aura, my life force, and that ever since I came back from the afterlife it's been different. First of all, it makes anyone who drinks my blood incredibly strong.

"Stefan was strong enough that the fox demons could never have forced him into their trap if Damon hadn't tricked him in the beginning. They could only deal with him when he was weakened and surrounded by iron. Iron is bad news for any eldritch creature, plus vampires need to feed at least once a day or they get weak, and I'll bet – no, I'm *sure* that they used that against him.

"That's why I can't stand to think about what shape Stefan might be in right this minute. But I can't let myself get too afraid or angry or I'll lose control of my aura. Damon showed me how to keep my aura mostly inside, like a normal human girl. It's still pale gold and pretty, but not a beacon for creatures like vampires.

"Because there's one other thing my blood – maybe even just my aura – can do. It can . . . oh, well, I can say anything I want to here, right? Nowadays, my aura can make vampires want me . . . the way human guys do. Not just to bite, get it? But to kiss and all the rest. And so, naturally, they come after me if they sense it. It's as if the world is full of honeybees and I'm the only flower.

"So I have to practise keeping my aura hidden. If it's just barely showing, then I can get away with seeming like a normal human, not somebody who's died and come back. But it's hard to always remember to hide it – and it hurts a *lot* pulling it in suddenly if I've forgotten!

"And then I feel – this is absolutely private, all right? I'm putting a curse on you, Damon, if you replay this. But it's then that I feel like I want Stefan to bite me. It eases up the pressure, and that's good. Being bitten by a vampire only hurts if you fight it, or if the vampire wants it to hurt. Otherwise, it can just feel good – and then you touch the mind of the vampire who's done it, and . . . *oh, I just miss Stefan so much!*"

Elena was shaking now. As hard as she tried to quiet her imagination, she kept thinking about the things that Stefan's jailers might be doing to him. Grimly, she gripped her mobile again, letting tears fall on it.

"I *can't* let myself think of what they might do to him because then I *really* start to go crazy. I become this useless shaking insane person who just wants to scream and scream and never stop. I have to fight every second *not* to think about it. Because only a cool, calm Elena with a Plan A and B and C is going to help him. When I have him safe in my arms, I can let myself shake and cry – and scream, too."

Elena stopped, half laughing, her head bent against the passenger's seatback, her voice husky with overuse.

"I'm tired now. But I have a Plan A, at least. I need to get more information from Damon about the place we're going, the Dark Dimension, and anything he knows about the two clues Misao gave me about the key that will unlock Stefan's cell.

"I guess . . . I guess I haven't mentioned that at all. The key, the fox key, that we need to get Stefan out of his cell, is broken into two pieces that are hidden in two different places. And when Misao was taunting me about how little I knew about those places, she gave me flat-out clues about where they were. She never dreamed I'd actually *go* into the Dark Dimension; she was just showing off. But I still remember the clues, and they went like this: The first half is 'in the silver nightingale's instrument'. And the second half is 'buried in Bloddeuwedd's ballroom'.

"I need to see if Damon has any ideas about these. Because it sounds as if once we get to the Dark Dimension we're going to have to infiltrate some people's houses and other places. To search a ballroom, it's best to somehow get invited to the ball, right? That sounds like 'easier said than done', but whatever it takes, I'll do. It's simple as that."

Elena lifted her head in determination and went still, then said in a whisper, "Would you believe it? I looked up just now and I can see the palest streaks of dawn in the sky: light green and creamy orange and the faintest aqua . . . I've talked all through the darkness. It's so peaceful now. Just now the sun peeked up o—

"What the *hell* was that? Something just went **BANG** on the top of the Jag. Really, really loud."

Elena clicked off the recorder on her mobile. She was scared, but a noise like that – and now scrabbling sounds on the roof . . .

She had to get out of the car as fast as possible.

CHAPTER

2

Elena burst out of the backseat of the Jaguar and ran a little way from the car before turning to see what had fallen on top of it.

What had fallen was Matt. He was in the process of struggling to get up off his back.

"Matt – oh, my God! Are you all right? Are you hurt?" Elena cried at the same time as Matt was shouting in tones of anguish:

"Elena – oh, my God! Is the Jag all right? Is it hurt?"

"Matt, are you *crazy*? Did you hit your head?"

"Are there any scratches? Does the moonroof still work?"

"No scratches. The moonroof is fine." Elena had no idea if the moonroof worked, but she realised that Matt was raving, off his head. He was trying to get down without getting any mud on the Jag, but he was handicapped since his legs and feet were covered with mud. Getting off the car without using his feet was proving difficult.

Meanwhile, Elena was looking around. She herself had once fallen from the sky, yes, but she had been dead for six months first and had arrived naked, and Matt fulfilled neither requirement. She had a more prosaic explanation in mind.

And there it was, lounging against a yellowwood tree and eyeing the scene with a very slight, wicked smile.

Damon.

He was compact; not as tall as Stefan, but with an indefinable aura of menace that more than made up for it. He was as immaculately dressed as always: black Armani jeans, black shirt, black leather jacket and black boots, which all went with his carelessly windblown dark hair and his black eyes.

Right now, he made Elena acutely aware that she was wearing a long white nightgown that she had brought with the idea that she could change her clothes underneath it if necessary while they were camping. The problem was that she usually did this just at dawn, and today writing in her diary had distracted her. And all at once the nightgown wasn't the correct attire for an early-morning fight with Damon. It wasn't sheer, being more akin to flannel than to nylon, but it *was* lacy, especially around the neck. Lace around a pretty neck to a vampire – as Damon had told her – was like a waving red cloak in front of a raging bull.

Elena crossed her arms over her chest. She also tried to make sure that her aura was pulled in decorously.

"You look like Wendy," Damon said, and his smile was wicked, flashing and definitely appreciative. He cocked his head to the side coaxingly.

Elena refused to be coaxed. "Wendy who?" she said, and at just that moment remembered the last name of the young girl in *Peter Pan*, and winced inwardly. Elena had always been good at repartee of this kind. The problem was that Damon was better.

"Why, Wendy . . . *Darling*," Damon said, and his voice was a caress.

Elena felt an inward shiver. Damon had promised not to Influence her – to use his telepathic powers to cloud or manipulate her mind. But sometimes it felt as if he got awfully close to the line. Yes, it was definitely Damon's fault, Elena thought. She didn't have any feelings for him that were – well, that were anything other than sisterly. But Damon never gave up, no matter how many times she rejected him.

Behind Elena was a thump and squelch that undoubtedly meant Matt had finally gotten off the roof of the Jag. He jumped into the fray immediately.

"Don't call Elena, Elena *darling*!" he shouted, continuing as he turned to Elena, "Wendy's probably the name of his latest little girlfriend. And–and–and do you know what he *did*? How he woke me up this morning?" Matt was quivering with indignation.

"He picked you up and threw you on top of the car?" Elena hazarded. She talked over her shoulder to Matt because there was a faint morning breeze that tended to mould her nightgown to her body. She didn't want Damon behind her just now.

"No! I mean, yes! No *and* yes! But – when he did, he didn't even bother to use his hands! He just went like this" – Matt waved an arm – "and first I got dropped into a mud hole and next thing I know I got dropped on the Jag. It could have broken the moonroof – or *me*! And now I'm all muddy," Matt added, examining himself with disgust, as if it had only just occurred to him.

Damon spoke up. "And *why* did I pick you up and put you down again? What were you actually *doing* at the time when I put some distance between us?"

Matt flushed to the roots of his fair hair. His normally tranquil blue eyes were blazing.

"I was holding a stick," he said defiantly.

"A stick. A stick like the kind you find along the roadside? That kind of *stick*?"

"I did pick it up along the roadside, yes!" Still defiant.

"But then something strange seems to have happened to it." From nowhere that Elena could see, Damon suddenly produced a very long, and very sturdy-looking stake, with one end that had been whittled to an extremely sharp point. It had definitely been carved from hardwood: oak from the look of it.

While Damon was examining his "stick" from all sides with a look of acute bafflement, Elena turned on a sputtering Matt.

"Matt!" she said reproachfully. This was definitely a low point in the cold war between the two boys.

"I just thought," Matt went on stubbornly, "that it might be a good idea. Since I'm sleeping outdoors at night and a . . . *another* vampire might come along."

Elena had already turned again and was making appeasing noises at Damon when Matt burst out afresh.

"Tell her how you actually woke me up!" he said explosively. Then, without giving Damon a chance to say anything, he continued, "I was just opening my eyes when he dropped *this* on me!" Matt squelched over to Elena, holding something up. Elena, truly at a loss, took it from him, turning it over. It seemed to be a pencil stub, but it was discoloured dark reddish-brown.

"He dropped that on me and said 'scratch off two'," Matt said. "He'd killed two people – and he was bragging about it!"

Elena suddenly didn't want to be holding the pencil

any more. "Damon!" she said in a cry of real anguish, as she tried to make something out of his no-expression expression. "Damon – you didn't – not really—"

"Don't beg him, Elena. The thing we've got to do—"

"If anybody would let me get a *word* in," Damon said, now sounding truly exasperated, "I might mention that before I could explain about the pencil *someone* attempted to stake me on the spot, even before getting out of his sleeping bag. And what I was going to say next was that they weren't people. They were vampires, thugs, hired muscle – but these were possessed by Shinichi's malach. *And* they were on our trail. They'd gotten as far as Warren, Kentucky, probably by asking questions about the car. We're definitely going to have to get rid of it."

"No!" Matt shouted defensively. "This car – this car means something to Stefan and Elena."

"This car means something to *you*," Damon corrected. "And I might point out that I had to leave my Ferrari in a creek just so we could *take* you on this little expedition."

Elena held up her hand. She didn't want to hear any more. She did have feelings for the car. It was big and brilliantly red and flashy and buoyant – and it expressed how she and Stefan had been feeling on the day that he bought it for her, celebrating the start of their new life together. Just looking at it made her remember the day, and the weight of Stefan's arm around her shoulder and the way he'd looked down at her, when she'd looked up at him – his green eyes sparkling with mischief and the joy of getting her something she really wanted.

To Elena's embarrassment and fury, she found that she was shaking slightly, and that her own eyes were full of tears.

"You see," Matt said, glaring at Damon. "Now you're making her cry."

"*I* am? I'm not the one who mentioned my dear departed younger brother," Damon said urbanely.

"*Just stop it! Right now!* Both of you," Elena shouted, trying to find her composure. "And I don't want this *pencil*, if you don't mind," she added, holding it at arm's length.

When Damon took it, Elena wiped her hands on her nightgown, feeling vaguely light-headed. She shivered, thinking of the vampires on their trail.

And then, suddenly, as she swayed, there was a warm, strong arm around her and Damon's voice beside her saying, "What she needs is some fresh air, and I'm going to give it to her."

Abruptly Elena was weightless and she was in Damon's arms and they were going higher.

"Damon, could you please put me down?"

"Right now, darling? It's quite a distance . . ."

Elena continued to remonstrate with Damon, but she could tell that he had tuned her out. And the cool morning air *was* clearing her head a bit, although it also made her shake.

She tried to stop the shivering, but couldn't help it. Damon glanced down at her and to her surprise, looking completely serious, began to make motions as if to take his jacket off. Elena hastily said, "No, no – you just drive – fly, I mean, and I'll hang on."

"And watch for low-going seagulls," Damon said solemnly, but with a quirk at the side of his mouth. Elena had to turn her face away because she was in danger of laughing.

"So, just when did you learn you could pick people up and drop them on cars?" she enquired.

"Oh, just recently. It was like flying: a challenge. And you know I like challenges."

He was looking down at her with mischief in his eyes, those black-on-black eyes with such long lashes that they were wasted on a boy. Elena felt as light as if she were dandelion fluff, but also a little light-headed, almost tipsy.

She was much warmer now, because – she realised – Damon had enfolded her in his aura, which was warm. Not just in temperature, either, but warm with a heady, almost drunken appreciation, as he took her in, her eyes and her face and her hair floating weightlessly in a cloud of gold around her shoulders. Elena couldn't help but blush, and she almost heard *his* thought, that blushing suited her very well, pale pink against her fair complexion.

And just as blushing was an involuntary physical response to his warmth and appreciation, Elena felt an involuntary emotional response – of thankfulness for what he had done, of gratitude for his appreciation, and of unintentional appreciation of Damon himself. He had saved her life tonight, if she knew anything about vampires possessed by Shinichi's malach, vampires who were thugs to begin with. She couldn't even imagine what such creatures would do to her, and she didn't want to. She could only be glad that Damon had been clever enough and, yes, ruthless enough to take care of them before they got to her.

And she would have to be blind and just plain stupid not to appreciate the fact that Damon was gorgeous. After having died twice, this fact did not affect her as it would most other girls, but it was still a fact, whether Damon was pensive or giving one of those rare genuine smiles that he seemed to have only for Elena.

The problem with this was that Damon was a vampire and could therefore read her mind, especially with Elena being so close, their auras intermingling. And Damon appreciated Elena's appreciation, and it became a little cycle of feedback, all on its own. Before Elena could quite focus she was melting, her weightless body feeling heavier as it moulded itself to Damon's arms.

And the other problem was that Damon wasn't Influencing her; he was as caught up in the feedback as Elena was – more so, because he didn't have any barriers against it. Elena did, but they were blurring, dissolving. She couldn't think properly. Damon was gazing at her with wonder and a look she was all too used to seeing – but she couldn't remember where.

Elena had lost the power to analyse. She was simply basking in the warm glow of being cherished, being held and loved and cared for with an intensity that shook her to the bone.

And when Elena gave of herself, she gave completely. Almost without conscious effort, she arched her head back to expose her throat and closed her eyes.

Damon gently positioned her head differently, supported it with one hand, and kissed her.

CHAPTER

3

Time stopped. Elena found that she was instinctively groping for the mind of the one who was kissing her so sweetly. She had never really appreciated a kiss until she had died, become a spirit, and then been returned to earth with an aura that revealed the hidden meaning of other people's thoughts, words, and even their minds and souls. It was as if she had gained a beautiful new sense. When two auras mingled as deeply as this, two souls were laid bare to each other.

Semi-consciously, Elena let her aura expand, and met a mind almost at once. To her surprise, it recoiled from her. That wasn't right. She managed to snag it before it could retreat behind a great hard stone, like a boulder. The only things left outside the boulder – which reminded her of a picture of a meteorite she had seen, with a pocked, charred surface – were rudimentary brain functions, and a little boy, chained to the rock by both wrists and both ankles.

Elena was shocked. Whatever she was seeing, she

knew it was a metaphor only, and that she should not judge too quickly what the metaphor meant. The images before her were really the symbols of Damon's naked soul, but in a form that her own mind could understand and interpret, if only she looked at it from the right perspective.

Instinctively, though, she knew that she was seeing something important. She had come through the breathless delight and dizzying sweetness of joining her soul to another's. And now, her inherent love and concern drove her to try to communicate.

"Are you cold?" she asked the child, whose chains were long enough to allow him to wrap his arms tightly about his drawn-up legs. He was clothed in ragged black.

He nodded silently. His huge dark eyes seemed to swallow up his face.

"Where do you belong?" Elena said doubtfully, thinking of ways to get the child warm. "Not inside *that*?" She made a gesture toward the giant stone boulder.

The child nodded again. "It's warmer in there, but he won't let me inside any more."

"He?" Elena was always on the lookout for signs of Shinichi, that malicious fox spirit. "Which 'he', darling?" She had already knelt and taken the child in her arms, and he was cold, ice cold, and the iron was freezing.

"Damon," the little ragamuffin boy whispered. For the first time the boy's eyes left her face, to glance fearfully around him.

"*Damon* did this?" Elena's voice started loud and ended up as soft as the boy's whisper, as he turned pleading eyes on her and desperately patted at her lips, like a velvet-clawed kitten.

This is all just symbols, Elena reminded herself. It's Damon's mind – his soul – that you're looking at.

But are you? an analytical part of her asked suddenly. Wasn't there – a time before, when you did this with someone – and you saw a world inside them, entire landscapes full of love and moonlit beauty, all of it symbolising the normal, healthy workings of an ordinary, extraordinary mind. Elena couldn't remember the name of the person now, but she remembered the beauty. She knew that her own mind would use such symbols to present itself to another person.

No, she realised abruptly and definitively: she was *not* seeing Damon's soul. Damon's soul was somewhere inside that huge, heavy ball of rock. He lived cramped inside that hideous thing, and he *wanted* it that way. All that was left outside was some ancient memory from his childhood, a boy who had been banished from the rest of his soul.

"If Damon put you here, then who are you?" Elena asked slowly, testing her theory, while taking in the black-on-black eyes of the child, and the dark hair and the features she *knew* even if they were so young.

"I'm – Damon," the little boy whispered, white around the lips.

Maybe even revealing that much was painful, Elena thought. She didn't want to hurt this symbol of Damon's childhood. She wanted him to feel the sweetness and comfort that she was feeling. If Damon's mind had been like a house, she would have wanted to tidy it up, and fill every room with flowers and starlight. If it had been a landscape she would have put a halo around the full white moon, or rainbows amongst the clouds. But instead it presented itself as a starving child chained to a ball that no one could breach, and she wanted to comfort and soothe the child.

She cradled the little boy, rubbing his arms and legs

hard and nestling him against her spirit body.

At first he felt tense and wary in her arms. But after a little time, when nothing terrible happened as a result of their contact, he relaxed and she felt his small body go warm and drowsy and heavy in her arms. She herself felt a crushingly sweet protectiveness about the little creature.

In just a few minutes, the child in her arms was asleep, and Elena thought that there was the faintest ghost of a smile on his lips. She cuddled his little body, rocking him gently, smiling herself. She was thinking of someone who had held her when she'd cried. Someone who was—was not forgotten, never forgotten – but who made her throat ache with sadness. Someone so important – it was desperately important that she remember him now, *now* – and that she . . . she had to . . . to *find* . . .

And then suddenly the peaceful night of Damon's mind was split open – by sound, by light, and by energies that even Elena, young as she was in the ways of Power, knew had been kindled by the memory of a single name.

Stefan.

Oh, God, she had *forgotten* him – she had actually, for a few minutes, allowed herself to be drawn into something that meant forgetting him. The anguish of all those lonely late-night hours, sitting and pouring out her grief and fear to her diary – and then the peace and comfort that Damon had offered had actually made her *forget Stefan* – to forget what he might be suffering at this very moment.

"No–no!" Elena was struggling alone in darkness. "Let go – I have to find – I can't believe that I forgot—"

"Elena." Damon's voice was calm and gentle – or at least unemotional. "If you keep jerking around like that you're going to get free – and it's a long way to the ground."

Elena opened her eyes, all her memories of rocks and little children flying away, scattering like white dandelion silk in every direction. She looked at Damon accusingly.

"You – you—"

"Yes," Damon said composedly. "Blame it on me. Why not? But I did *not* Influence you, and I did *not* bite you. I merely kissed you. Your Powers did the rest; they may be uncontrollable, but they're extremely compelling all the same. Frankly, *I* never intended to get sucked in so deeply – if you'll forgive a pun."

His voice was light, but Elena had a sudden inner vision of a weeping child, and she wondered if he were really as indifferent as he seemed.

But that's his speciality, isn't it? she thought, suddenly bitter. He gives out dreams, fancies, pleasure that stays in the minds of his . . . donors. Elena knew that the girls and young women that Damon . . . preyed on . . . adored him, their only complaint being that he didn't visit them often enough.

"I understand," Elena said to him as they drifted closer to the ground. "But this can't happen again. There's only one person that I can kiss, and that's Stefan."

Damon opened his mouth, but just then there was the sound of a voice that was as furious and accusing as Elena had been, and which didn't care about the consequences. Elena remembered the other person she'd forgotten.

"DAMON, YOU BASTARD, BRING HER DOWN!"

Matt.

Elena and Damon came to a twirling, elegant stop, right beside the Jaguar. Matt immediately ran to Elena and snatched her away, examining her as if she had been in an accident, with particular attention to her neck. Once again Elena was uncomfortably aware of being dressed in a lacy white nightgown in the presence of two boys.

"I'm fine, honestly," she said to Matt. "I'm just a little bit dizzy. I'll be better in a few minutes."

Matt let out a breath of relief. He might not still be in love with her as he once had been, but Elena knew he cared deeply about her and always would. He cared about her as his friend Stefan's girlfriend, and also on her own merits. She knew he would never forget the time they had been together.

More, he believed in her. So right now, when she promised that she was all right, he believed that. He was even willing to give Damon a look that wasn't completely hostile.

And then both of the boys headed for the driver's side door of the Jag.

"*Oh*, no," Matt said. "You drove yesterday – and look what happened! You said it yourself – there are vampires trailing us!"

"You're saying it's my fault? Vampires are tracing this fire-engine-red-paint-job giant and it's somehow my doing?"

Matt simply looked stubborn: his jaw clenched, his tanned skin flushed. "I'm saying we should take turns. You've had your turn."

"I don't recall anything ever being said about 'taking turns'." Damon managed to give the word an inflection that made it sound like some rather wicked activity. "And if I go in a car, I *drive* the car."

Elena cleared her throat. Neither of them even noticed her.

"I'm not getting into a car if you're driving!" Matt said furiously.

"*I'm* not getting into a car if *you're* driving!" Damon said laconically.

Elena cleared her throat more loudly, and Matt finally remembered her existence.

"Well, Elena can't be expected to drive us all the way to wherever we're going," he said, before she could even suggest the possibility. "Unless we're going to get there today," he added, looking at Damon sharply.

Damon shook his dark head. "No. I'm taking the scenic route. And the fewer people who know where we're going the safer we're going to be. You can't tell if you don't know."

Elena felt as if someone had just lightly touched the hairs on the back of her neck with an ice cube. The way Damon said those words . . .

"But they'll already know where we're going, won't they?" she asked, shaking herself back to practicality. "They know we want to rescue Stefan, and they know where Stefan is."

"Oh, yes. They'll know we're trying to get into the Dark Dimension. But by what gate? And when? If we can lose them the only thing we need to worry about is Stefan and the prison guards."

Matt looked around. "How many gates are there?"

"Thousands. Wherever three ley lines cross, there's the potential for a gate. But since the Europeans drove the Native Americans out of their homes, most of the gates aren't used or maintained as they were in the old days." Damon shrugged.

But Elena was tingling all over with excitement, with anxiety. "Why don't we just find the nearest gate and go through it, then?"

"Travel all the way to the prison underground? Look, you don't understand at all. First of all, you need *me* with you to get you into a gate – and even then it isn't going to be pleasant."

"Not pleasant for who? Us or you?" Matt asked grimly.

Damon gave him a long, blank look. "If you tried on your own it would be briefly and terminally unpleasant for you. With me, it should be uncomfortable but a matter of routine. And as for what it's like travelling for even a few days down there – well, you'll see for yourselves, eventually," Damon said with an odd smile. "And it would take much, much longer than going by a main gate."

"Why?" Matt demanded – always ready to ask questions that Elena really, really didn't want to know the answers to.

"Because it's either jungle, where five-foot leeches dropping from the trees are going to be the least of your worries, or wasteland, where any enemy can spot you – and *everyone* is your enemy."

There was a pause while Elena thought *hard*. Damon looked serious. Clearly, he really didn't want to do it – and not many things bothered Damon. He *liked* fighting. More, if it would only waste time . . .

"All right," Elena said slowly. "We'll go on with your plan."

Immediately, both boys reached for the driver's side door handle again.

"*Listen*," Elena said without looking at either of them. "*I* am going to drive *my* Jaguar down to the next town. But first I am going to get in it and get changed into real clothes and maybe even catch a few minutes of sleep. Matt will want to find a brook or something where he can clean up. And then I'm going to whatever town is closest for some brunch. After that—"

"—the bickering can begin anew," Damon finished for her. "You do that, darling. I'll meet you at whatever greasy spoon you've selected."

Elena nodded. "You're sure you'll be able to find us? I *am* trying to hold my aura down, really."

"Listen, a fire-engine-red Jaguar in whatever flyspeck of a town you find down this road is going to be as conspicuous as a UFO," Damon said.

"Why doesn't he just come with . . ." Matt's voice trailed off. Somehow, although it was his deepest grievance against Damon, he often managed to forget that Damon was a vampire.

"So you're going to go down there first and find some young girl walking to summer school," Matt said, his blue eyes seeming to darken. "And you're going to swoop down on her and take her away where no one can hear her screaming and then you're going to pull her head back and you're going to sink your *teeth* into her *throat*."

There was a fairly long pause. Then Damon said in a slightly injured tone, "Am not."

"That's what you – people – do. You did it to *me*."

Elena saw the need for really drastic intervention: the truth. "Matt, Matt, it wasn't Damon who did that. It was Shinichi. You *know* that." She gently took Matt by the forearms and turned him until he was facing her.

For a long moment Matt wouldn't look at her. Time stretched and Elena began to fear that he was beyond her reach. But then at last he lifted his head so that she could look into his eyes.

"All right," he said softly. "I'll go along with it. But you know that he's going off to drink human blood."

"From a willing donor!" Damon, who had very good

hearing, shouted.

Matt exploded again. "Because you *make* them willing! You hypnotise them—"

"No, I don't."

"—or 'Influence' them, or whatever. How would you like it—"

Behind Matt's back, Elena was now making furious go-away motions at Damon, as if she were shooing a flock of chickens. At first Damon just raised an eyebrow at her, but then he shrugged elegantly and obeyed, his form blurring as he took the shape of a crow and rapidly became a dot in the rising sun.

"Do you think," Elena said quietly, "that you could get rid of your stake? It's just going to make Damon completely paranoid."

Matt looked everywhere but at her and then finally he nodded. "I'll dump it when I go downhill to wash," he said, looking at his muddy legs grimly.

"Anyway," he added, "you get in the car and try to get some sleep. You look like you need it."

"Wake me up in a couple of hours," Elena said – without the first idea that in a couple of hours she was going to regret this more than she could say.

CHAPTER
4

"**Y**ou're shaking. Let me do it alone," Meredith said, putting a hand on Bonnie's shoulder as they stood together in front of Caroline Forbes's house.

Bonnie started to lean into the pressure, but made herself stop. It was humiliating to be shaking so obviously on a Virginia morning in late July. It was humiliating to be treated like a child, too. But Meredith, who was only six months older, looked more adult than usual today. Her dark hair was pulled back, so that her eyes looked very large and her olive-skinned face with its high cheekbones was shown to its best advantage.

She could practically be my babysitter, Bonnie thought dejectedly. Meredith had high heels on, too, instead of her usual flats. Bonnie felt smaller and younger than ever in comparison. She ran a hand through her strawberry-blonde curls, trying to fluff them up a precious half inch higher.

"I'm not scared. I'm *c-cold*," Bonnie said with all the dignity she could muster.

"I know. You feel something coming from there, don't you?" Meredith nodded at the house before them.

Bonnie looked sideways at it and then back at Meredith. Suddenly Meredith's adultness was more comforting than annoying. But before she looked at Caroline's house again she blurted, "What's with the spike heels?"

"Oh," Meredith said, glancing down. "Just practical thinking. If anything tries to grab my ankle this time, it gets *this*." She stamped and there was a satisfying clack from the pavement.

Bonnie almost smiled. "Did you bring your brass knuckles, too?"

"I don't need them; I'll knock Caroline out again bare-handed if she tries anything. But quit changing the subject. I can do this alone."

Bonnie finally let herself put her own small hand on Meredith's slim, long-fingered one. She squeezed. "I know you can. But I'm the one who *should*. It was me she invited over."

"Yes," Meredith said, with a slight, elegant curl of her lip. "She's always known where to stick in the knife. Well, whatever happens, Caroline's brought it on herself. First we try to help her, for her sake and ours. Then we try to make her *get* help. After that—"

"After that," Bonnie said sadly, "there's no telling." She looked at Caroline's house again. It looked . . . skewed . . . in some way, as if she were seeing it through a distorting mirror. Besides that, it had a bad aura: black slashed across an ugly shade of grey-green. Bonnie had never seen a house with so much energy before.

And it was cold, this energy, like the breath out of a meat locker. Bonnie felt as if it would suck out her own life-force and turn it into ice, if it got the chance.

She let Meredith ring the doorbell. It had a slight echo to it, and when Mrs Forbes answered, her voice seemed to echo slightly, as well. The inside of the house still had that funhouse mirror look to it, Bonnie thought, but even stranger was the feel. If she shut her eyes she would imagine herself in a much larger place, where the floor slanted sharply down.

"You came to see Caroline," Mrs Forbes said. Her appearance shocked Bonnie. Caroline's mother looked like an old woman, with grey hair and a pinched white face.

"She's up in her room. I'll show you," Caroline's mother said.

"But Mrs Forbes, we know where—" Meredith broke off when Bonnie put a hand on her arm. The faded, shrunken woman was leading the way. She had almost no aura at all, Bonnie realised, and was stricken to the heart. She'd known Caroline and her parents for so long – how could their relationships have come to this?

I won't call Caroline names, no matter what she does, Bonnie vowed silently. No matter what. Even . . . yes, even after what she's done to Matt. I'll try to remember something good about her.

But it was difficult to think at all in this house, much less to think of anything good. Bonnie knew the staircase was going up; she could see each step above her. But all her other senses told her she was going *down*. It was a horrifying feeling that made her dizzy: this sharp slant downward as she watched her feet climb.

There was also a smell, strange and pungent, of rotten eggs. It was a reeking, rotten odour that you *tasted* in the air.

Caroline's door was shut, and in front of it, lying on the floor, was a plate of food with a fork and carving knife on it. Mrs Forbes hurried ahead of Bonnie and Meredith and quickly snatched up the plate, opened the door opposite Caroline's, and placed it in there, shutting the door behind her.

But just before it disappeared, Bonnie thought she saw movement in the heap of food on the fine bone china.

"She'll barely speak to me," Mrs Forbes said in the same empty voice she'd used before. "But she did say that she was expecting you."

She hurried past them, leaving them alone in the corridor. The smell of rotten eggs – no, of *sulphur*, Bonnie realised, was very strong.

Sulphur – she recognised the smell from last year's chemistry class. But how did such a horrible smell get into Mrs Forbes's elegant house? Bonnie turned to Meredith to ask, but Meredith was already shaking her head. Bonnie knew that expression.

Don't say *anything*.

Bonnie gulped, wiped her watering eyes, and watched Meredith turn the handle of Caroline's door.

The room was dark. Enough light shone from the hallway to show that Caroline's curtains had been reinforced by opaque bedspreads nailed over them. No one was in or on the bed.

"Come in! And shut that door fast!"

It was Caroline's voice, with Caroline's typical waspishness. A flood of relief swept over Bonnie. The voice wasn't a male bass that shook the room, or a howl, it was Caroline-in-a-bad-mood.

She stepped into the dimness before her.

CHAPTER
5

Elena got into the backseat of the Jaguar and put on a plush aquamarine T-shirt and jeans underneath her nightgown, just in case a police officer – or even someone trying to help the owners of a car apparently stalled by a deserted highway – stopped by. And then she lay down in the Jag's backseat.

But although she was now warm and comfortable, sleep wouldn't come.

What do I want? Really want right now? she asked herself. And the answer came to her immediately.

I want to see Stefan. I want to feel *his* arms around me. I want to just look at his face – at his green eyes with that special look that he only ever shows to me. I want him to forgive me and tell me that he knows I'll always love him.

And I want . . . Elena felt herself flush as a warmth went through her body, I want *Stefan* to kiss me. I want Stefan's kisses . . . warm and sweet and comforting . . .

Elena was thinking this as for the second or third time

she shut her eyes and shifted position, tears once again welling up. If only she could cry, really cry, for Stefan. But something stopped her. She found it hard to squeeze out a tear.

God, she was exhausted. . . .

Elena tried. She kept her eyes shut and turned back and forth, trying not to think about Stefan for just a few minutes. She *had* to sleep. Desperate, she gave a mighty heave to try to find a better position – when everything suddenly changed.

Elena was comfortable. Too comfortable. She couldn't feel the seat at all. She bolted upright and froze, sitting on air. She was almost hitting her head against the Jag's top.

I've lost gravity again! she thought, horrified. But, no – this was different than what had happened when she had first returned from the afterlife, and had floated around like a balloon. She couldn't explain why, but she was sure.

She was afraid to move in any direction. She wasn't sure of the cause of her distress – but she didn't dare move.

And then she saw it.

She saw *herself*, with her head back and her eyes closed in the backseat of the car. She could make out every tiny detail, from the wrinkles in her plush aquamarine shirt to the braid she'd made from her pale golden hair, which, for the lack of a hair tie, was coming unbraided already. She looked as if she were serenely sleeping.

So this was how it all ended. This is what they'll say, that Elena Gilbert, one summer day, died peacefully in her sleep. No cause of death was ever found . . .

Because they could never see heartbreak as a cause of

death, Elena thought, and in a gesture even more melodramatic than her usual melodramatic gestures, she tried to fling herself down on her own body with one arm covering her face.

It didn't work. As soon as she reached out to begin to fling herself, she found herself outside the Jaguar.

She'd gone right through the ceiling without feeling anything. I suppose that's what happens when you're a ghost, she thought. But this is nothing like the last time. Then I saw the tunnel, I went into the Light.

Maybe I'm not a ghost.

Suddenly Elena felt a rush of exhilaration. I know what this is, she thought triumphantly. This is an out-of-body experience!

She looked down at her sleeping self again, searching carefully. Yes! Yes! There was a cord attaching her sleeping body – her real body – to her spiritual self. She was tethered! Wherever she went, she could find her way home.

There were only two possible destinations. One was back to Fell's Church. She knew the general direction from the sun, and she was sure that someone having an O.O.B. (as Bonnie, who had once gone through a spiritualist fad and had read lots of books about the subject, familiarly called them) would be able to recognise the crossing of all those ley lines.

The other destination, of course, was to Stefan.

Damon might think she didn't know where to go, and it was true that she could only vaguely sense from the rising sun that Stefan was in the other direction – to the west of her. But she'd always heard that the souls of true lovers were connected somehow . . . by a silver string from heart to heart or a red cord from pinky to pinky.

To her delight, she found it almost immediately.

A thin cord the colour of moonlight, that seemed to be stretched taut between the sleeping Elena's heart, and . . . yes. When she touched the cord, it resonated so clearly to her of Stefan that she knew it would take her to him.

There was never a doubt in her mind as to which direction she would take. She'd been in Fell's Church. Bonnie was a psychic of some impressive powers, and so was Stefan's old landlady, Mrs Theophilia Flowers. They were there, along with Meredith and her brilliant intellect, to protect the town.

And they would all understand, she told herself somewhat desperately. She might not ever have this chance again.

Without another moment's hesitation, Elena turned towards Stefan and let herself go.

Immediately she found herself rushing through the air, far too quickly to take note of her surroundings. Everything she passed was a blur, differing only in colour and texture as Elena realised with a catch in her throat that she was going *through* objects.

And so, in just a few instants, she found herself looking at a heart-wrenching scene: Stefan on a worn and broken pallet, looking grey-faced and thin. Stefan in a hideous, rush-strewn, lice-infested cell with its *damned* bars of iron from which no vampire could escape.

Elena turned away for a moment so that when she woke him he wouldn't see her anguish and her tears. She was just composing herself, when Stefan's voice jolted through her. He was awake already.

"You try and try, don't you?" he said, his voice heavy with sarcasm. "I guess you should get points for that. But you always get *something* wrong. Last time it was the little pointed ears. This time it's the clothes. Elena wouldn't wear a wrinkled shirt like that and have dirty, bare feet if her life depended on it. Go away." Shrugging his shoulders under the threadbare blanket, he turned from her.

Elena stared. She was in too many kinds of distress to choose her words: they burst from her like a geyser. "Oh, Stefan! I was just trying to fall asleep in my clothes in case a police officer stopped by while I was in the backseat of the Jag. The Jag *you* bought me. But I didn't think you'd care! My clothes are wrinkled because I'm living out of my duffel bag and my feet got dirty when Damon – well–well – never mind that. I have a real nightgown, but I didn't have it on when I came out of my body and I guess when you come out you still look like yourself *in* your body . . ."

Then she threw up her hands in alarm as Stefan swung around. But – marvel of marvels – there was now a tinge of blood in his cheeks. Moreover, he was no longer looking disdainful.

He was looking deadly, his green eyes flashing with menace.

"Your feet got dirty – when Damon did *what*?" he demanded, enunciating carefully.

"It doesn't matter—"

"It damn well *does* matter—" Stefan stopped short. "Elena?" he whispered, staring at her as if she had only just appeared.

"Stefan!" She couldn't help holding out her arms to him. She couldn't control anything. "Stefan, I don't know how, but *I'm here*. It's me! I'm not a dream or a ghost. I was thinking about you and falling asleep – *and here I am*!" She tried to touch him with ghostlike hands. "Do you believe me?"

"I believe you . . . because I was thinking about *you*.

Somehow–somehow that brought you here. Because of love. *Because we love each other!*" And he spoke the words as if they were a revelation.

Elena shut her eyes. If only she could be here in her body, she would show Stefan how much she loved him. As it was, they had to use clumsy words – clichés that just happened to be uniquely true.

"I will always love you, Elena," Stefan said, whispering again. "But I don't want you near Damon. He'll find a way to hurt you—"

"I can't help it," Elena interrupted him.

"You have to help it!"

"—because he's my only hope, Stefan! He's not going to hurt me. He's already killed to protect me. Oh, God, so much has happened! We're on our way to—" Elena hesitated, her eyes flicking around warily.

Stefan's eyes widened for an instant. But when he spoke his face was deadpan. "Someplace where you'll be safe."

"Yes," she said, just as seriously, knowing that phantom tears were now racing down her bodiless cheeks. "And . . . oh, Stefan, there's so much you don't know. Caroline accused Matt of attacking her while they were on a date because she's pregnant. But it wasn't Matt!"

"Of course not!" Stefan said indignantly, and would have said more, but Elena was racing on.

"And I think that the–the litter is really Tyler Smallwood's because of the timing, and because Caroline's changing. Damon said that—"

"A werewolf baby will always turn its mother into a werewolf—"

"Yes! But the werewolf part is going to have to fight the malach that's already inside her. Bonnie and

Meredith told me things about Caroline – like how she was scuttling on the floor like a lizard – that just terrified me. But I had to leave them to deal with that so that I could–could get to that safe place."

"Werewolves and were-foxes," Stefan said, shaking his head. "Of course, the kitsune, the foxes, are much more powerful magically, but werewolves tend to kill before they think." He struck his knee with his fist. "I wish I could *be* there!"

Elena burst out with mixed wonder and despair, "And instead here *I* am – with you! I never knew I could do this. But I haven't been able to bring you anything this way, not even myself. My blood." She made a helpless gesture and saw the smugness in Stefan's eyes.

He still had the Clarion Loess Black Magic wine she'd smuggled to him! She knew it! It was the only liquid that would – in a pinch – help keep a vampire alive when no blood was available.

Black Magic "wine" – non-alcoholic and never made for humans in the first place, was the only drink that vampires really enjoyed aside from blood. Damon had told Elena that it was magically made from special grapes that were grown in the soil at the edges of glaciers, loess, and that they were always kept in complete darkness. That was what gave it its velvety dark taste, he'd said.

"It doesn't matter," Stefan said, undoubtedly for the benefit of anyone who might be spying. "Exactly how did it happen?" he asked then. "This out-of-body thing? Why don't you come down here and tell me about it?" He lay back on his pallet, turning aching eyes on her. "I'm sorry that I don't have a better bed to offer you." For a moment the humiliation showed clearly in his face. All this time he'd managed to hide it from her: the shame he felt in appearing before her in this way – in a filthy cell, with rags for clothes, and infested with God knew what. He – Stefan Salvatore, who had once been – had once been—

Elena's heart truly broke then. She knew it was breaking, because she could feel it inside shattering like glass, with each needle-like shard skewering flesh inside her chest. She knew it was breaking, too, because she was weeping, huge spirit tears that dropped on Stefan's face like blood, translucent in the air as they fell, but turning deep red when they touched Stefan's face.

Blood? Of course, it wasn't blood, she thought. She couldn't even bring anything so useful to him in this form. She was really sobbing now; her shoulders shaking as the tears continued to fall onto Stefan, who now had one hand held up as if to catch one . . .

"Elena—" There was wonder in his voice.

"Wha – what?" she keened.

"Your tears. Your tears make me feel . . ." He was staring up at her with something like awe.

Elena still couldn't stop weeping, although she knew that she had soothed his proud heart – and done something else.

"I d-don't understand."

He caught one of her tears and kissed it. Then he looked at her with a sheen in his own eyes. "It's hard to talk about, lovely little love . . ."

Then why use words? she thought, still weeping, but coming down to his level so she could snuffle just above his throat.

It's just . . . they're not too free with the refreshments around here, he told her. *As you guessed. If you hadn't – helped me – I'd've been dead by now. They can't figure out why I'm not. So they – well, they run out before they get to me, sometimes, you see—*

Elena lifted her head, and this time tears of pure rage fell right onto his face. *Where are they? I'll kill them. Don't tell me I can't because* I'll find a way. *I'll find a way to kill them even though I'm in this state—*

He shook his head at her. *Angel, angel, don't you see? You don't have to kill them. Because your tears, the phantom tears of a pure maiden—*

She shook her head back at him. *Stefan, if anyone knows I'm not a pure maiden, it's you—*

—of a pure maiden, Stefan continued, not even disturbed by her interruption, *can cure all ills. And I was ill tonight, Elena, even though I tried to hide it. But I'm cured now! As good as new! They'll never be able to understand how it could happen.*

Are you sure?

Look at me!

Elena looked at him. Stefan's face, which had been grey and drawn before, was different now. He was usually pale, but now his fine features looked flushed – as if he had been standing in front of a bonfire and the light was still reflecting off the pure lines and elegant planes of his beloved face.

I . . . did that? She remembered the first tear droplets falling, and how they had looked like blood on his face. Not like blood, she realised, but like natural colour, sinking into him, refreshing him.

She couldn't help but hide her face again in his throat as she thought, *I'm glad. Oh, I'm so glad. But I wish we could touch each other. I want to feel your arms around me.*

"At least I can look at you," Stefan whispered, and Elena knew that even this is like water in the wasteland to him. "And if we *could* touch, I'd put my arm around your waist here, and kiss you here and here . . ."

They spoke to each other this way for a while – just

exchanging lovers' nonsense, each sustained by the sight and sound of the other. And then, softly but firmly, Stefan asked her to tell him all about Damon – everything since they'd started. By now Elena was cool-headed enough to tell him about the incident with Matt without making Damon sound too much like a villain.

"And Stefan, Damon really is protecting us as best he can." She told him about the two possessed vampires who had been tracking them and what Damon had done.

Stefan merely shrugged and said wryly, "Most people write with pencils; Damon writes people off with them." He added, "And your clothes got dirty?"

"Because I heard a great big crash – which ended up being Matt on top of the car," she said. "But, to be fair, he was trying to stake Damon at the time. I made him get rid of the stake." She added, in the barest of whispers: "Stefan, *please* don't mind that Damon and I have to–to be together a lot right now. It doesn't change anything between us."

"I know."

And the amazing thing was that he did know. Elena was bathed in the deep glow of his trust for her.

After that they "held" each other, Elena snuggling weightlessly above the curve of Stefan's arm . . . and it was bliss.

And then abruptly the world – the entire universe – shuddered at the sound of a gigantic slamming sound. It jerked at Elena. It didn't belong in here with love and trust and the sweetness of sharing every part of her *self* with Stefan.

It began again – a monstrous booming that terrified Elena. She clutched uselessly at Stefan, who was looking at her with concern. He didn't hear the clanging that was deafening her, she realised.

And then something even worse happened. She was torn out of Stefan's arms bodily, and she was rushing backward, back through objects, back faster and faster until with a jar she landed in her body.

For all her reluctance she landed perfectly on the solid body that until now had been the only one she'd known. She landed on it and melded into it and then she was sitting up and the sounds were the sounds of Matt rapping at the window.

"It's been over two hours since you went to sleep," he said as she opened the door. "But I figured you needed it. Are you all right?"

"Oh, Matt," Elena said. For a moment it seemed impossible that she was going to be able to keep from crying. But then she remembered Stefan's smile.

Elena blinked, forcing herself to deal with her new situation. She hadn't seen Stefan for nearly long enough. But her memories of their short, sweet time together were wrapped in jonquils and lavender and nothing could ever take them away from her.

Damon was irritated. As he flew higher on his wide, black crow's wings, the landscape beneath him unfolded like a magnificent carpet, the breaking day making the grasslands and rolling hills glow like emerald.

Damon ignored it. He'd seen it too many times. What he was looking for was *una donna splendida*.

But his mind kept drifting. Mutt and his stake . . . Damon still didn't see why Elena wanted to take a fugitive from justice along with them. Elena . . . Damon tried to conjure up the same irritated feelings for her as he had for Mutt, but just couldn't manage it.

He circled down toward the town below, keeping to the residential district, searching for auras. He wanted a strong aura as much as a beautiful one. And he'd been in America long enough to know that this early in the morning you could find three sorts of people up and outdoors. Students were the first, but this was summer, so there were fewer to pick from. Despite Mutt's assumptions, Damon seldom sank to high school girls. Joggers were the second. And the third, thinking beautiful thoughts, just like . . . *that* one down there . . . were home gardeners.

The young woman with the pruning shears looked up as Damon turned the corner and approached her house, deliberately hurrying and then slowing his stride. His very footsteps made it clear that he was delighted to take in the floral extravaganza in front of the charming Victorian house. For a moment the girl looked startled, almost afraid. That was normal. Damon was wearing black boots, black jeans, a black T-shirt and black leather jacket, in addition to his Ray-Bans. But then he smiled and at the same moment began the first delicate infiltration of *la bella donna*'s mind.

One thing was clear even before that. She liked roses.

"A full flush of Dreamweavers," he said, shaking his head in admiration as he looked at the bushes covered with brilliant pink bloom. "And those White Icebergs climbing the trellis . . . Ah, but your Moonstones!" He lightly touched an open rose, its petals moonlight-coloured but shading to palest pink at the edges.

The young woman – Krysta – couldn't help smiling. Damon felt the information flow effortlessly from her mind to his. She was just twenty-two, not married, still living at home. She had precisely the kind of aura he was looking for, and only a sleeping father in the house.

"You don't look like the type to know so much about roses," Krysta said frankly, and then gave a self-conscious laugh. "I'm sorry. I've met all sorts at the Creekville Rose Shows."

"My mother is an avid gardener," Damon lied fluently and without a trace of misgiving. "I guess I got my passion from her. Now I don't stay in one place long enough to grow them, but I can still dream. Would you like to know what my ultimate dream is?"

By this time Krysta felt as if she were floating on a delicious rose-scented cloud. Damon felt every delicate nuance with her, enjoyed seeing her flush, enjoyed the slight tremor that shook her body.

"Yes," Krysta said simply. "I'd love to know your dream."

Damon leaned forward, lowered his voice. "I want to breed a true black rose."

Krysta looked startled and something flashed through her mind too quickly for Damon to catch. But then she said in an equally hushed voice, "Then there's something I'd like to show you. If–if you have time to come with me."

The backyard was even more splendid than the front and there was a hammock gently swinging, Damon noted with approval. After all, he would soon need a place to put Krysta . . . while she slept it off.

But at the rear of the bower was something that caused his pace to quicken involuntarily.

"Black Magic roses!" he exclaimed, eyeing the wine-dark, almost burgundy-coloured blooms.

"Yes," Krysta said softly. "Black Magics. The closest anyone has ever gotten to a black rose. I get three flushes a year," she whispered tremulously, no longer questioning who this young man might be, overwhelmed by her feelings which almost took Damon with her.

"They're magnificent," he said. "The deepest red I've ever seen. The closest to black ever bred."

Krysta was still trembling with joy. "You're welcome to one, if you like. I'm taking them to the Creekville show next week but I can give you one in full bloom now. Maybe you'll be able to smell it."

"I'd . . . like that," Damon said.

"You can give it to your girlfriend."

"No girlfriend," Damon said, glad to get back to lying. Krysta's hands shook slightly as she cut one of the longest, straightest stems for him.

Damon reached out to take it and their fingers touched.

Damon smiled at her.

When Krysta's knees went boneless with pleasure, Damon caught her easily and went on with what he was doing.

Meredith was right behind Bonnie as she stepped into Caroline's room.

"I said, shut the damn door!" Caroline said – no, snarled.

It was only natural to look to see where the voice was coming from. Just before Meredith cut off the only sliver of light by shutting the door Bonnie saw Caroline's corner desk. The chair that used to sit in front of it was gone.

Caroline was underneath.

It might have been a good hiding space for a ten-year-old, but as an eighteen-year-old Caroline had curled into an impossible position in order to fit there. She was sitting on a pile of what looked like shreds of clothing. Her *best* clothes, Bonnie thought suddenly, as a twinkle of gold lamé flashed and was gone when the door shut.

Then it was just the three of them together in the darkness. No illumination came from above or below the door to the hall.

It's because the hall is in another world, Bonnie thought wildly.

"What's wrong with a little light, Caroline?" Meredith asked quietly. Her voice was steady, comforting. "You asked us to come and see you – but we can't see you."

"I said come and talk to me," Caroline corrected instantly, exactly as she always had in the old days. That should have been comforting, too. Except–except that now that Bonnie could hear her voice sort of reverberating under the desk, she could tell it had a new quality. Not so much husky as—

You really don't want to be thinking this. Not in the midnight darkness of this room, Bonnie's mind told her.

Not so much husky as *snarly,* Bonnie thought helplessly. You could almost say Caroline growled her answers.

Little sounds told Bonnie that the girl under the desk was moving. Bonnie's own breathing quickened.

"But *we* want to see *you,*" Meredith said quietly. "And you know that Bonnie's scared of the dark. Can I just turn on your bedside lamp?"

Bonnie could feel herself trembling. That wasn't good. It wasn't smart to show Caroline you were afraid of her. But the pitch-blackness was making her tremble. She could feel that this room was wrong in its angles – or maybe it was only her imagination. She could also hear things that made her jump – like that loud double clicking noise directly behind her. What had made that?

"All rrright then! Turrn on the one by the bed." Caroline was definitely snarling. And she was moving towards them; Bonnie could hear rustling and breathing getting closer.

Don't let her get to me in the dark!

It was a panicked, irrational thought, but Bonnie couldn't help thinking it any more than she could help stumbling blindly sideways into . . .

Something tall – and warm.

Not Meredith. Never since Bonnie had known her had Meredith smelled like rancid sweat and rotten eggs. But the warm something took hold of both Bonnie's upraised hands, and there were strange little clicking noises as they clenched.

The hands weren't just warm; they were hot and dry. And the ends poked oddly into Bonnie's skin.

Then, as a light by the bedside went on, they were gone. The lamp Meredith had found put out a very, very dim ruby light – and it was easy to see why. A ruby negligee and peignoir had been tied around the shade.

"This is a fire hazard," Meredith said, but even her level voice sounded shaken.

Caroline stood before them in the red light. She seemed taller than ever to Bonnie, tall and sinewy, except for the slight bulge of her belly. She was dressed normally, in jeans and a tight T-shirt. She was holding her hands playfully hidden behind her back, and smiling her old insolent, sly smile.

I want to go home, Bonnie thought.

Meredith said, "Well?"

Caroline just kept smiling. "Well, what?"

Meredith lost her temper. "What do you want?"

Caroline just looked arch. "Have you visited your friend Isobel today? Had a little talk with her?"

Bonnie had a powerful urge to slap that smug smile off Caroline's face. She didn't. It was just a trick of the lamplight – she knew it had to be – but it looked almost as if there was a red dot shining in the centre of each of Caroline's eyes.

"We visited Isobel at the hospital, yes," Meredith said expressionlessly. Then, with unmistakable anger in her voice, she added, "And you know very well that she can't talk yet. But" – with a triumphant little pounce – "the doctors say she will be able to. Her tongue will heal, Caroline. She may have scars from all the places she pierced herself, but she's going to be able to talk again just fine."

Caroline's smile had faded, leaving her face looking haggard and full of dull fury. At what? Bonnie wondered.

"It would do you some good to get out of this house," Meredith told the copper-haired girl. "You can't live in the dark—"

"I won't for ever," Caroline said sharply. "Just until the twins are born." She stood, hands still behind her, and arched her back so that her stomach protruded more than ever.

"The – twins?" Bonnie was startled into speaking.

"Matt Junior and Mattie. That's what I'm going to call them."

Caroline's gloating smile and impudent eyes were almost too much for Bonnie to stand. "You can't do that!" she heard herself shouting.

"Or maybe I'll call the girl Honey. Matthew and Honey, for their daddy, Matthew Honeycutt."

"You can't *do* it," Bonnie shouted, more shrilly. "Especially with Matt not even here to defend himself—"

"Yes, he did run away very suddenly, didn't he? The police are wondering why he had to run. Of course" – Caroline lowered her voice to a meaningful whisper –

"he wasn't alone. Elena was with him. I wonder what the two of them do in their spare time?" She giggled, a high, fatuous giggle.

"Elena isn't the only person with Matt," Meredith said, and now her voice was low and dangerous. "Someone else is, too. Do you remember an agreement you signed? About not telling anyone about Elena or bringing publicity around her?"

Caroline blinked slowly, like a lizard. "A long time ago. In a different lifetime, for me."

"Caroline, you're not going to *have* a lifetime if you break that oath! Damon would *kill* you. Or – have you already—" Meredith stopped.

Caroline was still giggling in that childish way, as if she were a little girl and someone had just told her a naughty joke.

Bonnie felt cold sweat break out all over her body at once. Fine hairs lifted on her arms.

"What are you hearing, Caroline?" Meredith wet her lips. Bonnie could see that she was trying to hold Caroline's eyes, but the copper-haired girl turned away. "Is it . . . Shinichi?" Meredith moved forward suddenly and grasped Caroline's arms. "You used to see and hear him when you looked in the mirror. Do you hear him all the time now, Caroline?"

Bonnie wanted to help Meredith. She did. But she couldn't have moved or spoken for anything.

There were – grey threads – in Caroline's hair. Grey hairs, Bonnie thought. They shone dully, much lighter than the flaming auburn Caroline was so proud of. And there were . . . other hairs that didn't shine at all. Bonnie had seen this brindled colouration on dogs; she knew vaguely that some wolves must look the same. But it was really something else to see them in your girlfriend's hair.

Especially when they seemed to bristle and quiver, lifting like the hackles of a dog . . .

She's mad. Not angry mad; insane mad, Bonnie realised.

Caroline looked up, not at Meredith, but straight into Bonnie's eyes. Bonnie flinched. Caroline was gazing at her as if considering whether or not Bonnie were dinner or just garbage.

Meredith stepped to stand beside Bonnie. Her fists were clenched.

"Don't starrre," Caroline said abruptly, and turned away. Yes, that was definitely a snarl.

"You really wanted us to see you, didn't you?" Meredith said softly. "You're – flaunting yourself in front of us. But I think that maybe this is your way of asking for help—"

"Harrrrdly!"

"Caroline," Bonnie said suddenly, amazed by a wave of pity that swamped her, "please try to *think*. Remember back when you said you needed a husband? I—" She broke off and swallowed. Who was going to marry this monster, who a few weeks ago had looked like a normal teenage girl?

"I understood you back then," Bonnie finished lamely. "But, honestly, it won't do any good to keep on saying Matt attacked you! No one . . ." She couldn't bring herself to say the obvious.

No one will believe something like you.

"Oh, I clean up rrrreal prrretty," Caroline growled and then giggled. "You'd be surprrrised."

In her mind's eye, Bonnie saw the old insolent flash of Caroline's emerald gaze, the sly and secretive expression on her face, and the shimmering of her auburn hair.

"Why pick on Matt?" Meredith demanded. "How did

you know he was attacked by a malach that night? Did Shinichi send it after him just for *you*?"

"Or did Misao?" Bonnie said, remembering that it was the female of the twin kitsune, the fox spirits, who had spoken the most to Caroline.

"I went out on a date with Matt that night." Suddenly Caroline's voice was a singsong, as if she were reciting poetry – badly. "I didn't mind kissing him – he's so cute. I guess that's when he got the hickey on his neck. I guess I might have bitten his lip a little."

Bonnie opened her mouth, felt Meredith's restraining hand on her shoulder, and shut it again.

"But then he just went crazy," Caroline lilted on. "He attacked me! I scratched him with my fingernails, all up and down one arm. But Matt was too strong. Much too strong. And now—"

And now you're going to have puppies, Bonnie wanted to say, but Meredith squeezed her shoulder and she stopped herself again. Besides, Bonnie thought with a sudden twinge of alarm, the babies might look human, and there might only be twins, as Caroline herself had said. Then what would they do?

Bonnie knew the way adult minds worked. Even if Caroline couldn't dye her hair back to auburn, they would say, look what stress she's been under: she's actually going prematurely grey!

And even if the adults saw Caroline's bizarre appearance and strange behaviour, as Bonnie and Meredith just had, they would dismiss it as being due to shock. Oh, poor Caroline, her whole personality has changed since that day. She's so frightened of Matt that she hides under her desk. She won't wash herself – maybe that's a common symptom after what she's been through.

Besides who knew how long it would take *these* werewolf babies to be born? Maybe the malach inside Caroline could control that, make it seem to be like a normal pregnancy.

And then suddenly Bonnie was snatched away from her own thoughts to tune into Caroline's words. Caroline was through growling for the moment. She sounded almost like the old Caroline, offended and nasty, as she said, "I just don't understand why you should take his word over mine."

"Because," Meredith said flatly, "we *know* both of you. We would have known if Matt had been dating you – and he wasn't. And he's hardly the kind of guy to just show up at your front door, especially when you consider how he felt about you."

"But you've already said that this monster that attacked him—"

"Malach, Caroline. Learn the word. You've got one inside you!"

Caroline smirked and waved a hand, dismissing this. "You said these things can possess you and make you do things out of character, right?"

There was a silence. Bonnie thought, if we have said it, we've never said it in front of *you*.

"Well, what if I admitted that Matt and I *weren't* dating? What if I said that I found him driving around our neighbourhood at about five miles an hour, just looking lost. His sleeve was torn to pieces and his arm was all chewed up. So I took him inside *my* house and tried to bandage his arm – but suddenly he went crazy. And I did try to scratch him, but the bandages were in the way. I scratched them off him. I even still have them, all covered in blood. If I told you that, what would you say?"

I'd say that you were using us as a dry run before telling Sheriff Mossberg, Bonnie thought, chilled. And I'd say that you were right, you probably can clean up pretty normal looking when you make an effort. If you'd just stop that childish giggling and get rid of the crafty look, you'd be even more convincing.

But Meredith was speaking. "Caroline – they've got DNA tests for blood."

"Of course I know that!" Caroline looked so indignant that for a moment she forgot to look sly.

Meredith was staring at her. "That means they can tell if the bandages you've got have Matt's blood on them or not," she said. "And if it flows in the right pattern to match your story."

"There isn't any pattern. The bandages are just soaked." Abruptly, Caroline strode over to a dresser and opened it, plucking out a length of what might have originally been athletic bandage. Now it shone reddish in the faint light.

Looking at the stiff fabric in the ruby light, Bonnie knew two things. It wasn't any part of the poultice that Mrs Flowers had put on Matt's arm the morning after he'd been attacked. And it was soaked with genuine blood, right to the stiff tips of the cloth.

The world seemed to be spinning around. Because even though Bonnie believed in Matt, this new story scared her. This new story might even *work* – provided that no one could find Matt and test his blood.

Even Matt admitted that there was time unaccounted for that night . . . time he couldn't remember.

But that didn't mean Caroline was telling the truth! Why would she start out with a lie, and only change it when the facts got in the way?

Caroline's eyes were the colour of a cat's. Cats play

with mice, just for amusement. Just to see them run.

Matt had run . . .

Bonnie shook her head. All at once she couldn't stand this house any longer. It had somehow settled into her mind, making her accept all the impossible angles of the distorted walls. She had even grown accustomed to the awful smell and the red light. But now, with Caroline holding out a blood-soaked bandage and telling her that it was Matt who had bled all over it . . .

"I'm going home," Bonnie announced suddenly. "And Matt didn't do it, and – and I'm never coming back!" Accompanied by the sound of Caroline's giggling, she whirled, trying not to look at the nest Caroline had made under her corner desk. There were empty bottles and half-empty plates of food piled in there with the clothes. Anything could be under them – even a malach.

But as Bonnie moved, the room seemed to move with her, accelerating her spin, until she had gone twice around before she could put out a foot to stop herself.

"Wait, Bonnie – wait, *Caroline*," Meredith said, sounding almost frantic. Caroline was folding her body like a contortionist, getting back under the desk. "Caroline, what about Tyler Smallwood? Don't you care that he's the real father of your – your kids? How long were you dating him before he joined up with Klaus? Where is he now?"

"Forrr all I know he's dead. You and yourrr friends killed him." The snarl was back, but it wasn't vicious. It was more of a triumphant purr. "But I don't miss him, so I hope he stays dead," Caroline added, with a muffled giggle. "*He* wouldn't marrrry me."

Bonnie had to get away. She fumbled for the doorknob, found it, and was blinded. She had spent so long in ruby dimness that the hall light was like the midday sun on the desert.

"Turrn off the lamp!" Caroline snapped from under the desk. But as Meredith moved to do it Bonnie heard a surprisingly loud explosion and saw the red-swathed shade go dark by itself.

And one thing more.

The hallway light swept across Caroline's room like a beacon as the door swung shut. Caroline was already tearing at something with her teeth. Something with the texture of meat, but not cooked meat.

Bonnie jerked back to run and almost knocked over Mrs Forbes.

The woman was still standing in the hall where she had been when they went into Caroline's room. She didn't even look as if she'd been listening at the door. She was just standing, staring at nothing.

"I have to show you out," she said in her soft, grey voice. She didn't lift her head to meet Bonnie's or Meredith's eyes. "You might get lost otherwise. I do."

It was a straight shot to the stairs and down and four steps to the front door. But as they walked, Meredith didn't say anything, and Bonnie couldn't.

Once outside, Meredith turned to look at Bonnie.

"Well? Is she more possessed by the malach or the werewolf part of her? Or could you tell anything from her aura?"

Bonnie heard herself laugh, a sound that was like crying.

"Meredith, her aura isn't human – and I don't know what to make of it. And her mother doesn't seem to have an aura at all. They're just – that house is just—"

"Never mind, Bonnie. You don't have to go there ever again."

"It's like . . ." But Bonnie didn't know how to explain the fun-house look of the walls or the way the stairs went down instead of up.

"I think," she said finally, "that you'd better do some more research. On things like–like possession of the American kind."

"You mean like possession by demons?" Meredith shot her a sharp look.

"Yes. I guess so. Only I don't know where to start listing what's wrong with her."

"I have a few ideas of my own," Meredith said quietly. "Like – did you notice that she never showed us her hands? That was very strange, I thought."

"I know why," Bonnie whispered, trying not to let the sobbing laughter out. "It's because – she doesn't have fingernails any more."

"What did you say?"

"She put her hands around my wrists. I could *feel* them."

"Bonnie, you're not making any sense."

Bonnie made herself speak. "Caroline has claws now, Meredith. Real claws. Like a wolf."

"Or maybe," Meredith said in a whisper, "like a fox."

CHAPTER

6

Elena was using all her considerable talents at negotiation to calm Matt down, encouraging him to order a second and third Belgian waffle; smiling at him across the table. But it wasn't much good. Matt was moving as if he were driven to rush, while at the same time he couldn't take his eyes off her.

He's still imagining Damon swooping down and terrorising some young girl, Elena thought helplessly.

Damon wasn't there when they stepped out of the coffee shop. Elena saw the frown between Matt's eyebrows begin and had a brainstorm.

"Why don't we take the Jag to a used-car dealership? If we're going to give up the Jaguar, I want *your* advice on what we get in return."

"Yeah, my advice on beat-up, falling-apart heaps has got to be the best," Matt said, with a wry smile that said he knew Elena was managing him, but he didn't mind.

The single car dealership in the town didn't look very promising. But even *it* was not as depressed-looking as the owner of the lot. Elena and Matt found him asleep inside a small office building with dirty windows. Matt tapped gently on the smudged window and eventually the man started, jerked up in his chair, and angrily waved them away.

But Matt tapped again on the window when the man began to put his head down once more, and this time the man sat up very slowly, gave them a look of bitter despair, and came to the door.

"What do you want?" he demanded.

"A trade-in," Matt said loudly before Elena could say it softly.

"You teenagers have a car to trade," the little man said darkly. "In all my twenty years owning this place—"

"Look." Matt stepped back to reveal the brilliant-red Jag shining in the morning sun like a giant rose on wheels. "A brand-new Jaguar XZR. Zero to sixty in 3.7 seconds! A 550-horsepower supercharged AJ-V8 GEN III R engine with 6-speed ZF automatic transmission! Adaptive Dynamics and Active Differential for exceptional traction and handling! There *is* no car like the XZR!" Matt finished nose to nose with the little man, whose mouth had slowly come open as his eyes flickered between the car and the boy.

"*You* want to trade *that* in for something on *this* lot?" he said, shocked into frank disbelief. "As if I'd have the cash to— Waitaminute!" he interrupted himself. His eyes stopped flickering and became the eyes of a poker player. His shoulders came up, but his head didn't, giving him the appearance of a vulture.

"Don't want it," he said flatly and made as if to go back into the office.

"What do you mean you don't want it? You were

drooling over it a minute ago!" Matt shouted, but the man had stopped wincing. His expression didn't change.

I should have done the talking, Elena thought. I wouldn't have gotten into a war from word one – but it's too late now. She tried to shut out the male voices and looked at the dilapidated cars on the lot, each with its own dusty little sign tucked into the windshield: 10 PER CENT OFF FOR XMAS! EASY CREDIT! CLEAN! GRANNY-OWNED SPECIAL! NO DOWN-PAYMENT! CHECK IT OUT! She was afraid she was going to burst into tears at any second.

"No call for a car like that around here," the owner was saying expressionlessly. "Who'd buy it?"

"You're crazy! This car will bring customers flocking in. It's – it's advertising! Better than that purple hippo over there."

"Not a hippo. S'an elephant."

"Who can tell, with it half deflated like that?"

With dignity, the owner stalked over to look at the Jag. "Not brand new. S'got too many miles on it."

"It was bought only two weeks ago."

"So? In a few more weeks, Jaguar will be advertising next year's cars." The owner waved a hand at Elena's giant rose of a vehicle. "Obsolete."

"Obsolete!"

"Yeah. Big car like this, gas guzzler—"

"It's more energy efficient than a hybrid—"

"You think people know that? They see it—"

"Look, I could take this car anywhere else—"

"Then take it. On my lot, here and now, that car is barely worth one car in exchange!"

"Two cars."

The new voice came from directly behind Matt and Elena, but the car dealer's eyes widened as if he had just seen a ghost.

Elena turned and met Damon's unfathomable black gaze. He had his Ray-Bans hooked over his T-shirt and was standing with his hands behind his back. He was looking hard at the car dealer.

A few moments passed, and then . . .

"The . . . silver Prius in the back right corner. Under . . . under the awning," the car dealer said slowly, and with a dazed expression – in answer to no question that had been asked aloud. "I'll . . . take you there," he added in a voice to match his expression.

"Take the keys with you. Let the boy test-drive it," Damon ordered, and the owner fumbled to show a key ring at his belt, and then walked slowly away, staring at nothing.

Elena turned to Damon. "One guess. You asked him which was the best car on his lot."

"Substitute 'least disgusting' and you'd be closer," Damon said. He flashed a brilliant smile at her for a tenth of a second, and then turned it off.

"But, Damon, why two cars? I know it's more fair and all, but what are we going to do with the second car?"

"Caravan," Damon said.

"*Oh*, no." But even Elena could see the benefits of this – at least after they held a summit to decide on a rotation schedule between the cars for Elena. She sighed. "Well – if Matt agrees . . ."

"Mutt will agree," Damon said, looking very briefly – *very* briefly – as innocent as an angel.

"What have you got behind your back?" Elena said, deciding not to pursue the question of what Damon intended to do to Matt.

Damon smiled again, but this time it was an odd smile, just a quirk of one side of his mouth. His eyes said it was nothing much. But his right hand came out and it was holding the most beautiful rose Elena had ever seen in her life.

It was the deepest red rose she had ever seen, yet there wasn't a hint of purple to it – it was just velvety burgundy, and open at exactly the moment of full bloom. It looked as if it would be plush to the touch, and its vivid green stem, with just a few delicate leaves here and there, was at least eighteen inches long and straight as a ruler.

Elena resolutely put her own hands behind her back. Damon wasn't the sentimental type – even when he got on his "Princess of the Night" soapbox. The rose probably had something to do with their journey.

"Don't you like it?" Damon said. Elena might be imagining it, but it almost sounded as if he were disappointed.

"Of course I like it. What's it for?"

Damon settled back. "It's for you, Princess," he said, looking hurt. "Don't worry; I didn't steal it."

No – he wouldn't have stolen it. Elena knew exactly how he would have gotten the rose . . . but it was so *pretty* . . .

As she still made no move to take the rose, Damon lifted it and allowed the cool, silky-feeling petals to caress her cheek.

It made her shiver. "Stop it, Damon," she murmured, but she didn't seem to be able to step backward.

He didn't stop. He used the cool, softly rustling petals to outline the other side of her face. Elena took a deep breath automatically, but what she smelled was not flowerlike at all. It was the smell of some dark, dark wine, something ancient and fragrant that had once made her drunk immediately. Drunk on Black Magic and on her own heady excitement . . . just to be with Damon.

But that wasn't the real me, a small voice in her

head protested. I love *Stefan*. Damon . . . I want . . . I want to . . .

"Do you want to know why I got this particular rose?" Damon was saying softly, his voice blending in with her memories. "I got it because of its name. It's a Black Magic rose."

"Yes," Elena said simply. She'd known that before he said it. It was the only name that fit.

Now Damon was giving her a rose kiss by swirling the blossom in a circle on her cheek and then applying pressure. The firmer petals in the middle pressed into her skin, while the outer petals just brushed it.

Elena was feeling distinctly light-headed. The day was warm and humid already; how could the rose feel so cool? Now the outermost petals had moved to trace her lips, and she wanted to say no, but somehow the word wouldn't come.

It was as if she had been transported back in time, back to the days when Damon had first appeared to her, had first claimed her for his own. When she had almost let him kiss her before she knew his name. . . .

He hadn't changed his ideas since then. Vaguely, Elena remembered thinking something like that before. Damon changed other people while remaining unchanged himself.

But *I've* changed, Elena thought, and suddenly there was quicksand under her feet. I've changed so much since then. Enough to see things in Damon I'd never imagined could be there. Not just the wild and angry dark parts, but the gentle parts. The honour and decency that were trapped like veins of gold inside that stone boulder in his mind.

I have to help him, Elena thought. Somehow, I have to help him – and the little boy chained outside the boulder.

These thoughts had trickled slowly through her mind while it seemed separated from her body. She was so involved with them, in fact, that she somehow lost track of her body, and only now did she realise how much closer Damon had gotten. Her back was against one of the sad, sagging cars. And Damon was speaking lightly, but with an undertone of seriousness.

"A rose for a kiss, then?" he asked. "It *is* called Black Magic, and I *did* come by it honestly. Her name was . . . it was . . ."

Damon stopped, and for a moment a look of intense bewilderment flashed across his face. Then he smiled, but it was the warrior's smile, the brilliant one he turned on and off almost before you were sure you had seen it. Elena sensed trouble. Sure, Damon still didn't remember Matt's name correctly, but she had never known him to forget a girl's name when he was really trying to remember. Especially within minutes of when he must have fed from that girl.

Shinichi again? Elena wondered. Was he still taking Damon's memories – only the highlights, of course? The thrills, good or bad? Elena knew that Damon himself was thinking the same thing. His black eyes were smouldering. Damon was furious – but there was a certain vulnerability about his fury.

Without thinking, Elena put her hands on Damon's forearms. She ignored the rose, even as he traced the curve of her cheekbone with it. She tried to speak steadily. "Damon, what are we going to do?"

That was the scene that Matt walked in on. Ran in on, actually. He came weaving through a maze of cars, and dashed around a white SUV with one flat tyre, shouting, "Hey, you guys, that Prius is—"

And then he stopped dead.

Elena knew what he was seeing: Damon caressing her with the rose, while she was practically embracing him. She let go of Damon's arms, but she couldn't back away from him because of the car behind her.

"Matt—" Elena began, and then her voice trailed off. She had been about to say *"This isn't what it looks like. We're not in the middle of a cuddle. I'm not really touching him."* But this *was* what it looked like. She cared about Damon; she had been trying to get through to him. . . .

With a small shock, that thought repeated itself with the force of a shaft of sunlight shooting through an unprotected vampire's body.

She cared about Damon.

She really did. It was usually difficult being with him because they were alike in so many ways. Headstrong, each wanting their own way, passionate, impatient . . .

She and Damon were alike.

Small shocks were going though Elena, and her entire body felt weak. She found herself glad to lean against the car behind her, even though it must be getting dust all over her clothes.

I love Stefan, she thought almost hysterically. He's the only one I love. But I need Damon to get to him. And Damon may be falling to pieces in front of me.

She was looking at Matt all the while, her eyes full of tears that would not fall. She blinked, but they stubbornly stayed on her lashes.

"Matt . . ." she whispered.

He said nothing. He didn't need to. It was all in his expression: astonishment turning to something Elena had never seen before, not when he was looking at *her*.

It was a sort of alienation that shut her out completely, that severed any bonds between them.

"Matt, no . . ." But it came out in a whisper.

And then, to her astonishment, Damon spoke.

"You do know it's all me, don't you? You can hardly blame a girl for trying to defend herself." Elena looked at her hands, which were shaking now. Damon was going on, "You *know* it's all my fault. Elena would never—"

That was when Elena realised. Damon was Influencing Matt.

"No!" She took Damon off guard, grabbing him again, shaking him. "Don't do it! Not to Matt!"

The black eyes that were turned on hers were definitely not those of a suitor. Damon had been interrupted in the use of his Power. If it had been anyone else, they would have ended as a small spot of grease on the ground.

"I'm saving you," Damon said coldly. "Are you refusing me?"

Elena found herself wavering. Maybe, if it was only once, and only for Matt's benefit . . .

Something surged up inside her. It was all she could do not to let her aura escape completely.

"Never try that on me again," Elena said. Her voice was quiet but icy. "Don't you *dare* ever try to Influence me! And leave Matt alone!"

Something like approval flickered in the endless darkness of Damon's gaze. It was gone before she could be sure she'd seen it. But when he spoke, he seemed less distant.

"All right," he said to Matt. "What's the game plan now? You name it."

Matt answered slowly, not looking at either of them. He was flushed but deadly calm. "I was going to say, that Prius isn't bad at all. And the dealer guy has another one. It's in OK condition. We could have two cars just alike."

"And then we could caravan and split up if someone

was following us! They won't know which to follow."
Normally Elena would have thrown her arms around
Matt at this point. But Matt was looking at his shoes,
which was probably just as well really, since Damon had
his eyes shut and was shaking his head slightly as if he
couldn't believe something idiotic.

That's right, Elena thought. It's my aura – or
Damon's – that they're homing in on. We can't confuse
them with identical cars unless we have identical
auras, too.

Which really meant that she should drive with Matt
the whole way. But Damon would never accept that.
And she needed Damon to get to her beloved, her one
and only, her true mate: Stefan.

"I'll take the ratty one," Matt was saying, arranging
it with Damon and ignoring her. "I'm used to ratty
cars. I already arranged a deal with the guy. We should
get going." Still speaking only to Damon, he said,
"You'll *have* to tell me where we're really going. We
might get separated."

Damon was silent for a long moment. Then,
brusquely, he said, "Sedona, Arizona, for a start."

Matt looked disgusted. "That place full of New Age
lunatics? You're kidding."

"I said we'll start out from Sedona. It's complete
wilderness – nothing but rock – all around it. You could
get lost . . . very easily." Damon flashed the brilliant smile
and instantly turned it off.

"We'll be at the Juniper Resort, off North Highway
89A," he added smoothly.

"I've got it," Matt said. Elena could see no emotion in
either his face or his expression, but his aura was
seething red.

"Now, Matt," Elena began, "we should really meet

every night, so if you just follow us—" She broke off with a sharply inhaled breath.

Matt had already turned around. He didn't turn back when she spoke. He just kept going, without another word.

Without a backward glance.

CHAPTER

7

Elena woke to the sound of Damon impatiently rapping on the window of the Prius. She was fully clothed, clutching her diary to her. It was the day after Matt had left them.

"Did you sleep all night like that?" Damon asked, looking her up and down as Elena rubbed her eyes. As usual, he was immaculately dressed: all in black, of course. Heat and humidity had no effect on him.

"I've had my breakfast," he said shortly, getting in the driver's seat. "And I brought you *this*."

This was a styrofoam cup of steaming coffee, which Elena clutched as gratefully as if it were Black Magic wine, and a brown paper bag that proved to contain doughnuts. Not exactly the most nutritious breakfast, but Elena craved the caffeine and sugar.

"I need a rest stop," Elena warned as Damon coolly seated himself behind the wheel and started the car. "To change my clothes and wash my face and things."

They headed directly west, which accorded with what

Elena had found by looking at a map on the Internet last night. The small image on her mobile phone matched the Prius's navigation system readout. They had both shown that Sedona, Arizona, lay on an almost perfectly straight horizontal line from the small rural road where Damon had parked overnight in Arkansas. But soon Damon was turning south, taking a roundabout route of his own that might or might not confuse any pursuers. By the time they found a rest stop, Elena's bladder was about to burst. She spent an unashamed half hour in the women's room, doing her best to wash with paper towels and cold water, brushing her hair, and changing into new jeans and a fresh white top that laced up the front like a corset. After all, one of these days she just might have another out-of-body experience while napping and see Stefan again.

What she didn't want to think about was that with Matt's departure, she was left alone with Damon, an untamed vampire, travelling through the middle of the United States towards a destination that was literally out of this world.

When Elena finally emerged from the restroom, Damon was cold and expressionless – although she noticed that he took the time to look her over just the same.

Oh, *damn*, Elena thought. I left my diary in the car.

She was as certain that he'd read it as if she'd seen him doing it, and she was glad that there was nothing in it about leaving her body and finding Stefan. Although she believed Damon wanted to free Stefan, too – she wouldn't be in this car with him if she didn't – she also felt that it was better that he didn't know she had gotten there first. Damon enjoyed being in charge of things as much as she did. He also enjoyed Influencing each police officer who pulled him over for blasting the speed limit.

But today he was short-tempered even by his own standards. Elena knew from firsthand experience that Damon could make himself remarkably good company when he chose, telling outrageous stories and jokes until the most prejudiced and taciturn of passengers would laugh in spite of themselves.

But today he wouldn't even reply to Elena's questions, much less laugh at her own jokes. The one time she tried to make physical contact, touching his arm lightly, he jerked away as if her touch might ruin his black leather jacket.

Fine, terrific, Elena thought, depressed. She leaned her head against the window and stared at the scenery, which all looked alike. Her mind wandered.

Where was Matt now? Ahead of them or behind? Had he gotten any rest last night? Was he driving through Texas now? Was he eating properly? Elena blinked away tears, which welled up whenever she remembered the way he had walked away from her without a backward look.

Elena was a manager. She could make almost any situation turn out OK, as long as the people around her were normal, sane beings. And managing boys was her speciality. She'd been handling them – steering them – since junior high. But now, approximately two and a half weeks since she had come back from death, from some spirit world that she didn't remember, she didn't *want* to steer anyone.

That was what she loved about Stefan. Once she'd gotten past his reflexive instinct to keep away from anything he cherished, she didn't need to manage him at all. He was maintenance-free, except for the gentlest of hints that she'd turned herself into an except on vampires. Not at hunting them or slaying them, but at loving them safely. Elena knew when it was right to bite or be bitten, and when to stop, and how to keep herself human.

But apart from those gentle hints, she didn't even *want* to manage Stefan. She wanted simply to *be* with him. After that, everything took care of itself.

Elena could live without Stefan – she *thought*. But just as being away from Meredith and Bonnie was like living without her two hands, living without Stefan would be like trying to live without her heart. He was her partner in the Great Dance; her equal and her opposite; her beloved and her lover in the purest sense imaginable. He was the other half of the Sacred Mysteries of Life to her.

And after seeing him last night, even if it had been a dream, which she wasn't willing to accept, Elena missed him so much that it was a throbbing pain inside her. A pain so great that she couldn't bear to just sit and dwell on it. If she did she might just go insane and start raving at Damon to drive faster – and Elena might hurt inside, but she wasn't suicidal.

They stopped at some nameless town for lunch. Elena had no appetite, but Damon spent the entire break as a bird, which for some reason infuriated her.

By the time they were driving again, the tension in the car had built until the old cliché was impossible to avoid: you could cut it with a folded napkin, much less a knife, Elena thought.

That was when she realised exactly what kind of tension it was.

The one thing that was saving Damon was his pride.

He knew that Elena had things figured out. She'd

stopped trying to touch him or even speak to him. And that was *good*.

He wasn't supposed to be feeling like this. Vampires wanted girls for their pretty white throats, and Damon's sense of aesthetics demanded that the rest of the donor be at least up to his standards. But now even Elena's human-sized aura was advertising the unique life-force in her blood. And Damon's response was involuntary. He had not even thought about a girl in *this* way for approximately five hundred years. Vampires weren't capable of it.

But Damon was – very capable – now. And the closer he got to Elena, the stronger her aura was around him, and the weaker was his control.

Thank all the little demons in hell, his pride was stronger than the desire he felt. Damon had never *asked* for anything from anyone in his life. He paid for the blood he took from humans in his own particular coin: of pleasure and fantasy and dreams. But Elena didn't need fantasy; didn't want dreams.

Didn't want *him*.

She wanted Stefan. And Damon's pride would never allow him to ask Elena for what he alone desired, and equally it would never allow him to take it without her consent . . . he hoped.

Just a few days ago he had been an empty shell, his body a puppet of the kitsune twins, who had made him hurt Elena in ways that now made him cringe inside. *Damon* hadn't existed then as a personality, but his body had been Shinichi's to play with. And although he scarcely could believe it, the takeover had been so complete that his shell had obeyed Shinichi's every command: he had tormented Elena; he might well have killed her.

There was no *point* in disbelieving it; or saying that it couldn't be true. It *was* true. It had happened. Shinichi was that much stronger when it came to mind control, and the kitsune had none of the vampires' detachment about pretty girls – below the neck. Besides which, he happened to be a sadist. He liked pain – other people's, that is.

Damon couldn't deny the past, couldn't wonder why he hadn't "awakened" to stop Shinichi from hurting Elena. There had been nothing of him *to* awaken. And if a solitary part of his mind still wept because of the evil he had done – well, Damon was good at blocking it out. He wouldn't waste time over regrets, but he was intent on controlling the future. It would never happen again – not and leave him still alive.

What Damon really couldn't understand was why Elena was pushing him. Acting as if she *trusted* him. Of all the people in the world, she was the one with the most right to hate him, to point an accusing finger at him. But she had never once done that. She had never even looked at him with anger in her dark-blue, gold-spattered eyes. She alone had seemed to understand that someone as completely possessed by the master of the malach, Shinichi, as Damon had been, simply had no choice – wasn't *there* to make a choice – in what he or she did.

Maybe it was because she'd pulled the thing the malach had created out of him. The pulsating, albino, second body that had been inside him. Damon forced himself to repress a shudder. He only knew this because Shinichi had jovially mentioned it, while taking away all Damon's memories of the time since the two of them, kitsune and vampire, had met in the Old Wood.

Damon was *glad* to have had the memories gone.

From the moment he had locked gazes with the fox spirit's laughing golden eyes, his life had been poisoned.

And now . . . right now he was alone with Elena, in the middle of the wilderness, with towns few and far between. They were utterly, uniquely alone, with Damon helplessly wanting from Elena what every human boy she'd ever encountered had wanted.

Worst of all was the fact that charming girls, deceiving girls, was practically Damon's own raison d'être. It was certainly the only reason he'd been *able* to keep on living for the past half millennium. And yet he knew that he must not, *must not* even start the process with this one girl who, to him, was the jewel lying on the dungheap of humanity.

To all appearances, he was perfectly in control, icy and precise, distant and disinterested.

The truth was that he was going out of his mind.

That night, after making sure that Elena had food and water and was safely locked into the Prius, Damon called down a damp fog and began to weave his darkest wards. These were announcements to any sisters or brothers of the night who might come upon the car that the girl inside it was under Damon's protection; and that Damon would hunt down and flay alive anyone who even disturbed the girl's rest . . . and then he'd get around to *really* punishing the culprit. Damon then flew a few miles south as a crow, found a dive with a pack of werewolves drinking in it and a few charming barmaids serving them, and brawled and bled the night away.

But it wasn't enough to distract him – not nearly enough. In the morning, returning early, he saw the wards around the car in tatters. Before he could panic, he realised that Elena had broken them from the inside.

There had been no warning to him because of her peaceful intent and innocent heart.

And then Elena herself appeared, coming up the bank of a stream, looking clean and refreshed. Damon was stricken speechless by the very sight of her. By her grace, by her beauty, by the unbearable closeness of her. He could smell her freshly washed skin, and couldn't help deliberately breathing in more and more of her unique fragrance.

He didn't see how he could put up with another day of this.

And then Damon suddenly had an Idea.

"Would you like to learn something that would help you to control that aura of yours?" he asked as she passed him, heading for the car.

Elena threw him a sidelong glance. "So you've decided to talk to me again. Am I supposed to faint with joy?"

"Well – that would always be appreciated—"

"Would it?" she said sharply, and Damon realised that he had underestimated the storm he had brewed inside this formidable girl.

"No. Now, I'm being serious," he said, fixing his dark gaze on her.

"I know. You're going to tell me to become a vampire to help control my Power."

"No, no, *no*. This has nothing to do with being a vampire." Damon refused to be drawn into an argument and that must have impressed Elena, because finally she said, "What is it, then?"

"It's learning how to circulate your Power. Blood circulates, yes? And Power can be circulated, too. Even humans have known that for centuries, whether they call it life-force or *chi* or *ki*. As it is, you're simply dissipating your Power into the air. That's an aura. But if you learn to circulate it, you can build it up for some really big release, and you can be more inconspicuous as well."

Elena was clearly fascinated. "Why didn't you tell me before?"

Because I'm stupid, Damon thought. Because to vampires it's as instinctive as breathing is to you. He lied unblushingly. "It takes a certain level of competence to accomplish."

"And I can do it now?"

"I think so." Damon put slight uncertainty in his voice.

Naturally, this made Elena even more determined. "Show me!" she said.

"You mean right now?" He glanced around. "Someone might drive by—"

"We're off the road. Oh, please, Damon? Please?" Elena looked at Damon with the huge blue eyes that altogether too many males had found irresistible. She touched his arm, trying once more to make some kind of contact, but when he automatically drew away, she continued, "I really do want to learn. You can teach me. Just show me once, and I'll practise."

Damon glanced down at his arm, felt his good sense and his will wavering. *How does she do that?*

"All right." He sighed. There were at least three or four billion people on this dust mote of a planet that would give anything to be with this warm and eager, yearning Elena Gilbert. The problem was that he happened to be one of them – and that she clearly didn't give a damn for him.

Of course not. She had dear Stefan. Well, he would see if his princess was still the same when – if – she managed to free Stefan and get out of their destination alive.

Meanwhile, Damon concentrated on keeping his

voice face, and aura all dispassionate. He'd had some practice at that. Only five centuries' worth, but it added up.

"First I have to find the place," he told her, hearing the lack of warmth in his voice, the tone that was not merely dispassionate but actually cold.

Elena's expression didn't flicker. She could be dispassionate, too. Even her deep-blue eyes seemed to have taken on a frosty glint. "All right. Where is it?"

"Near where the heart is, but more to the left. He touched Elena's sternum, and then moved his fingers to the left.

Elena fought back both tension and a shiver – he could see it. Damon was probing for the place where the flesh became soft over bone, the place most humans assumed their heart was because it was where they could feel their heart beating. It should be right around . . . *here* . . .

"Now, I'll run your Power through one or two circulations, and when you can do it by yourself – that's when you'll be ready to really conceal your aura."

"But how will I know?"

"You'll know, believe me."

He didn't want her to ask questions, so he simply held up one hand in front of her – not touching her flesh or even her clothing – and brought her life-force in synchronisation with his. There. Now, to set the process off. He knew what it would feel like to Elena: an electric shock, starting at the point where he had first touched her and quickly spreading warmth through her body.

Then, a rapid montage of sensations as he went through a practice rotation or two with her. Up towards him, to her eyes and ears, where she would suddenly find she could see and hear much better, then down her spine and out to her fingertips, while her heartbeat quickened and she felt something like electricity in her palms. Back up her arm and down the side of her body, at which point a tremor would set in. Finally, the energy would sweep down her magnificent leg all the way to her feet, where she would feel it in her soles, curling her toes, before coming back around to where it had started near her heart.

Damon heard Elena gasp faintly when the shock first hit her, and then felt her heartbeat race and her eyelashes flicker as the world suddenly became much lighter to her; her pupils dilating as if she were in love, her body going rigid at the tiny sound of some rodent in the grass – a sound she would never have heard without Power directed to her ears. And so, all around her body, once, and then again, so she could get a feel for the process. Then he let her go.

Elena was panting and exhausted; and *he'd* been the one expending energy. "I'll never – be able – to do that alone," she gasped.

"Yes, you will, in time and with practice. And when you can do it, you'll be able to control all your Power."

"If you . . . say so." Elena's eyes were shut now, her lashes dark crescents on her cheeks. It was clear that she'd been pushed to her limit. Damon felt the temptation to draw her to him, but suppressed it. Elena had made it clear that she didn't want him embracing her.

I wonder just how many boys she didn't push away, Damon thought abruptly, bitterly. That surprised him a little, the bitterness. Why should he care how many boys had handled Elena? When he made her his Princess of Darkness, they would both go hunting for human prey – sometimes together, sometimes alone. He wouldn't be jealous of her *then*. Why should he care how many romantic encounters she'd had now?

But he found that he *was* bitter, bitter and angry enough that he answered without warmth, "I do say you will. Just practise doing it alone."

In the car, Damon managed to stay annoyed with Elena. This was difficult, as she was a perfect travelling companion. She didn't chatter, didn't try to hum or – thank fortune – sing along with the radio, didn't chew gum or smoke, didn't backseat drive, didn't need too many rest stops, and *never* asked "Are we there yet?"

As a matter of fact, it was difficult for anyone, male or female, to stay annoyed at Elena Gilbert for any length of time. You couldn't say she was too exuberant, like Bonnie, or too serene, like Meredith. Elena was just sweet enough to offset her bright, active, ever-scheming mind. She was just compassionate enough to make up for her self-confessed egotism, and just skewed enough to ensure that no one would ever call her normal. She was intensely loyal to her friends and just forgiving enough that she herself considered almost no one an enemy – kitsune and Old Ones of the vampire kind excepted. She was honest and frank and loving, and of course she had a dark streak in her that her friends simply called wild, but that Damon recognised for what it really was. It compensated for the naive, soft, ingenuous side of her nature. Damon was very sure that he didn't need any of those qualities in her, especially right now.

Oh, yes . . . and Elena Gilbert was just gorgeous enough to make any of her negative characteristics completely irrelevant.

But Damon was determined to be annoyed and *he* was strong-willed enough that he could usually choose his mood and stick to it, appropriate or not. He ignored all of

Elena's attempts at conversation, and eventually she gave up trying to make them. He kept his mind pinned to the dozens of boys and men whom the exquisite girl beside him must have bedded. He knew that Elena, Caroline and Meredith had been the "senior" members of the quartet when they had all been friends, while little Bonnie had been the youngest and had been considered a bit too naive to be fully initiated.

So why was he with Elena now? he found himself asking sourly, wondering for just the slightest second if Shinichi was manipulating him as well as taking his memories.

Did Stefan ever worry about her past – especially with an old boyfriend, Mutt, still hanging around, willing to give his very life for her? Stefan must not, or he'd have put a stop – no, how could Stefan put a stop to *anything* Elena wanted to do? Damon had seen the clash of their wills, even when Elena had been a child mentally just after returning from the afterlife. When it came to Stefan and Elena's relationship, Elena was definitely in control. As humans said: *She wore the trousers in the family*.

Well, soon enough she could see how she liked wearing harem trousers, Damon thought, laughing silently, although his mood was darker than ever. The sky over the car darkened further in response, and wind ripped summer leaves from branches before their time. Cat's paws of rain dotted the windshield, and then came the flash of lightning and the echoing sound of thunder.

Elena jumped slightly, involuntarily, every time the thunder let loose. Damon watched this with grim satisfaction. He knew she knew that he could control the weather. Neither of them said a single word about it.

She won't beg, he thought, feeling that quick savage

pride in her again and then feeling annoyance with himself for being so soft.

They passed a motel, and Elena followed the blurry electric signs with her eyes, looking over her shoulder until it was lost in darkness. Damon didn't want to stop driving. Didn't dare stop, really. They were headed into a really nasty storm now, and occasionally the Prius hydroplaned, but Damon managed to keep it under control – barely. He enjoyed driving in these conditions.

It was only when a sign proclaimed that the next place of shelter was over a hundred miles away that Damon, without consulting Elena, swung into a flooding driveway and stopped the car. The clouds had let loose by then; the rain was coming down in bucketfuls; and the room Damon got was a small outbuilding, separated from the main motel.

The solitude suited Damon just fine.

CHAPTER
8

As they hastened from the car to the secluded motel room, Elena had to put pressure on her legs to keep them steady under her. As soon as the door to the room slammed shut, with the storm more or less outside and her own stiff and aching body inside, she headed for the bathroom without even turning on a light. Her clothes and hair and feet were all damp.

The fluorescent lights of the bathroom seemed too bright after the darkness of the night and the storm. Or maybe it was the beginning of her learning to circulate her Power.

That had certainly been a surprise. Damon hadn't even been touching her, but the shock she had felt still reverberated inside her. And as for the feeling of having her Power manipulated from outside her body, well, there just weren't words. It had been a breathtaking experience, all right. Even now just thinking about it made her knees tremble.

But it was more clear than ever that Damon wanted

nothing to do with her. Elena confronted her own image in the mirror and winced. Yes, she looked like a drowned rat that had been dragged backward a mile through the gutter. Her hair was damp, turning its silky waves into tiny wisps of curls all around her head and face; she was as white as an invalid, and her blue eyes were staring out of the pinched and exhausted face of a child.

For just a moment she remembered being in even worse shape a few days – yes, it was only days – ago, and having Damon treat her with the utmost gentleness, as if her bedraggled appearance had meant nothing to him. But those memories had been taken from Damon by Shinichi, and it was too much to hope that that might have been his real state of mind. It had been . . . whim . . . like all his other whims.

Furious at Damon – and at herself for the prickling behind her eyes she felt – Elena turned away from the mirror.

The past was the past. She had no idea why Damon had suddenly decided to start jerking away from her touch, or to look at her with the hard cold eyes of a predator. Something had caused him to hate her, to barely be able to sit in the car with her. And whatever it was, Elena had to learn to ignore it, because if Damon left, she would have no chance of finding Stefan.

Stefan. At last her trembling heart could find rest in thinking of Stefan. He wouldn't care what she looked like: his sole concern would be for her well-being. Elena shut her eyes as she turned on the hot water in the tub and stripped off her clammy clothes, basking in her imagination of Stefan's love and approval.

The motel had provided a small plastic bottle of bublebath, but Elena left it alone. She'd brought her own translucent-gold bag of vanilla bath crystals in her duffel bag, and this was the first chance she'd had to use it.

Carefully, she shook about a third of the beribboned bag's crystals into the rapidly filling tub and was rewarded with a steamy blast of vanilla, which she drew into her lungs gratefully.

A few minutes later, Elena was shoulder deep in hot water covered with a vanilla-scented foam. Her eyes were shut and the warmth was soaking into her body. The softly disintegrating salts were easing away all pain.

These weren't ordinary bath salts. They had no medicinal smell, but they'd been given to her by Stefan's landlady, Mrs Flowers, who was a genteel elderly white witch. Mrs Flowers's herbal recipes were her speciality, and right now Elena would swear that she could feel all the tension of the last few days being actively sucked out of her body and gently soothed away.

Oh, this was just what she had needed. Elena had never appreciated a bath like this before.

Now, there's just one thing, she told herself firmly, as she inhaled breath after delicious breath of vanilla steam. You asked Mrs Flowers for bath salts that would relax you, but you *cannot* fall asleep here. You'll drown, and you already know what *that* feels like. Been there, done that, didn't even have to buy the shroud.

But even now Elena's thoughts were dimmer and more fragmented, as the hot water continued to relax her muscles, and the vanilla scent swirled around her head. She was losing continuity, her mind drifting off into daydreams . . . She was giving herself to the heat and the luxury of not having to do anything at all . . .

She was asleep.

In her dream, she was moving briskly. It was only half-light, but she could tell somehow that she was skimming downward through deep grey mist. What worried her was that she seemed to be surrounded by arguing voices, and they were arguing about *her*.

"A second chance? I've spoken to her about it."

"She won't remember anything."

"It doesn't matter whether she remembers. Everything will remain inside her, if unawakened."

"It will germinate inside her . . . until the time is right."

Elena had no idea what any of it meant.

And then this mist was thinning, and clouds were making way for her, and she was drifting down, more and more slowly, until she was deposited gently on a ground covered with pine needles.

The voices were gone. She was lying on a forest floor, but she wasn't naked. She was wearing her prettiest nightgown, the one with real Valenciennes lace. She was listening to the tiny night sounds all around her when suddenly her aura reacted in a way that it never had before.

It told her someone was coming. Someone who brought a sense of safety in warm earthen hues, in soft rose colours and deep, blue violets that enfolded her even before the person arrived. These were . . . someone's . . . feelings about herself. And behind the love and soothing concern she experienced, there were deep forest greens, shafts of warm gold, and a mysterious tinge of translucency, like a waterfall that sparkled as it fell and foamed like diamonds around her.

Elena, a voice whispered. *Elena*.

This was so familiar. . . .

Elena. Elena.

She *knew* this. . . .

Elena, my angel.

It meant love.

Even as Elena was sitting up and turning in her dream, she was holding out her arms. This person belonged with her. He was her magic, her solace, her best-beloved. It didn't matter how he'd gotten there, or what had happened before. He was her soul's eternal mate.

And then . . .

Strong arms holding her tenderly . . .

A warm body close to hers . . .

Sweet kisses . . .

Many, many times . . .

This familiar feeling as she melted into his embrace . . .

He was so gentle, but almost fierce in his love for her. He had vowed not to kill, but he would kill to save her. She was his most precious thing in all the world . . . Any sacrifice would be worth it if she were safe and free. His life meant nothing without her, so he would gladly give it, laughing and kissing his hand to her with his last breath.

Elena breathed in the wonderful autumn-leaves scent of his sweater and was comforted. Like a baby, she allowed herself to be soothed by simple familiar odours, by the feeling of her cheek against his shoulder and the wonder of the two of them breathing together in synchronicity.

When she tried to put a name to this miracle, it was at the front of her mind.

Stefan . . .

Elena didn't even need to look up at his face to know that Stefan's leaf-green eyes would be dancing like the waters of a small pond ruffled by wind and sparkling with a thousand different points of light. She buried her head in his neck, afraid somehow to let go of him, although she couldn't remember why.

I don't know how I got here, she told him non-verbally.

In fact, she didn't remember anything before this, before awakening to his call, only jumbled images.

It doesn't matter. I'm with you.

Fear seized her. *This isn't . . . just a dream, is it?*

No dream is just a dream. And I'm with you always.

But how did we get here?

Shhh. You're tired. I'll hold you up. On my life, I swear it. Just rest. Let me hold you just once.

Just once? But . . .

But now Elena felt worried and dazed, and she had to let her head fall backward, had to see Stefan's face.

She tilted her chin back and found herself meeting laughing eyes of an infinite darkness in a chiselled, pale and proudly handsome face.

She almost cried out in horror.

Hush. Hush, angel.

Damon!

The dark eyes that met hers were full of love and joy. *Who else?*

How dare *you – how did you get here?* Elena was more and more confused.

I don't belong anywhere, Damon pointed out, suddenly sounding sad. *You know I'll always be with you.*

I do not; I do not *– give Stefan back to me!*

But it was too late. Elena was aware of the sound of water trickling and of tepid liquid sloshing around her. She woke up just in time to keep her head from going underwater in the bathtub.

A dream . . .

She felt much more flexible and easy in her body, but she couldn't help feeling saddened by the dream. It hadn't been an out-of-body experience, either – it had been a simple, crazy, mixed-up dream of her own.

I don't belong anywhere. I'll always be with you.

Now what was gibberish like that supposed to mean?

But something inside Elena trembled, even as she remembered it.

She hastily changed – not into a Valenciennes lace nightgown, but into a grey and black sweat suit. When she emerged, she was feeling overtired and prickly and ready to start a fight if Damon gave any sign of having picked up on her sleeping thoughts.

But Damon didn't. Elena saw a bed, managed to focus on it, stumbled towards it and collapsed, flopping down on pillows that sank unsatisfactorily beneath her head. Elena liked her pillows firm.

For a few moments she lay, savouring her after-bath sensations, as her skin gradually cooled – and her head cooled as well. As far as she could tell, Damon was standing in exactly the same position as he had taken up when they'd entered the room.

And he was still as silent as he had been since the morning.

Finally, to get it over with, she spoke to him. And being Elena, she went straight to the heart of the problem.

"What's wrong, Damon?"

"Nothing." Damon stared out the window, pretending to be engrossed in something beyond the glass.

"What nothing?"

Damon shook his head. But somehow, his turned back eloquently conveyed his opinion of this motel room.

Elena examined the room with the too-bright vision of someone who has forced their body beyond its limits. She contemplated beige walls, beige carpet, a beige armchair, a beige desk and, of course, a beige bedspread. Even Damon couldn't reject a room on the grounds that it doesn't match his basic black, she thought, and then: oh, I'm tired. And bewildered. And scared.

And . . . incredibly stupid. There's only one bed in here. I'm lying on it.

"Damon . . ." With an effort, she sat up. "What do you want? There's a chair. I can sleep on the chair."

He half turned, and she saw in the movement that he wasn't annoyed or playing games. He was furious. It was all there in the faster-than-the-human-eye-could-follow assassin's spin and the complete muscular control that stilled it almost before it had begun.

Damon with his sudden movements and his frightening stillness. He was looking out the window again, body poised as always for . . . something. Right now it looked poised to jump through glass to get outside.

"Vampires don't need sleep," he said in a voice icier and more controlled than she'd heard since Matt had left them.

That gave her the energy to get off the bed. "You know I know that's a lie."

"Take the bed, Elena. Go to sleep." But his voice was the same. She would have expected a flat, weary command. Damon sounded more tense, more controlled than ever.

More shaken than ever.

Her eyelids sank. "Is this about Matt?"

"No."

"Is it about Shinichi?"

"*No!*"

Aha.

"It is, isn't it? You're afraid that Shinichi will get past all your defences and possess you again. Aren't you?"

"Go to bed, Elena," Damon said tonelessly.

He was still shutting her out as completely as if she weren't there. Elena got mad.

"What does it take to show you that I trust you? I'm travelling all alone with you, without any idea where we're really going. I'm trusting you with Stefan's *life*." Elena was behind Damon now, on the beige carpet which smelled like . . . nothing, like boiled water. Not even like dust.

Her words were the dust. There was something about them that sounded hollow, wrong. They were the truth – but they weren't getting through to Damon . . .

Elena sighed. Touching Damon unexpectedly was always a tricky business, with all the risks of setting off murderous instinct by accident, even when he wasn't possessed. She reached out, now, very carefully, to put her fingertips on the elbow of his leather jacket. She spoke as precisely and unemotionally as she could.

"You also know that I have other senses now than the usual five. How many times do I have to say it, Damon? I *know* it wasn't you torturing me and Matt last week." Despite herself, Elena heard a certain pleading in her own voice. "I know that you've protected me on this trip when I was in danger, even killing for me. That means – a lot to me. You may say you don't believe in the human sentiment of forgiveness, but I don't think you've forgotten it. And when you know that there is nothing to forgive in the first place—"

"This has absolutely nothing to do with last week!"

The change in his voice – the force in it – hit Elena like a whiplash. It hurt . . . and it frightened her. Damon was serious. He was also under some dreadful strain, not completely unlike that of fighting off Shinichi's possession, but different.

"Damon . . ."

"Leave me alone!"

Now, where have I heard something like that

before? Befuddled, her heart pounding, Elena groped through memories.

Oh, yes. Stefan. Stefan when they had first been in his room together, when he was afraid to love her. When he was sure he would cause her to be damned if he showed he cared.

Could Damon be *that* much like the brother he always mocked?

"At least turn around and talk with me face-to-face."

"Elena." It was a whisper, but it sounded as if Damon couldn't summon up his usual silky menace. "Go to bed. Go to hell. Go anywhere, but *stay away from me*."

"You're so good at that, aren't you?" Elena's own voice was cold now. Recklessly, angrily, she moved in even closer. "At pushing people away. But I know that you haven't fed this evening. There's nothing else you want from me, and you can't do the starving-martyr bit half as well as Stefan—"

Elena had spoken knowing that her words were guaranteed to incite a response of some kind, but Damon's usual response to this sort of thing was to lounge against something and pretend not to have heard.

What happened instead was completely outside the range of her experience.

Damon whirled, caught her precisely, held her locked in an unbreakable grip. Then, with a swoop of his head like a falcon on a mouse, he kissed her. He was more than strong enough to hold her still without hurting her.

The kiss was hard and long and for quite a while Elena resisted out of sheer instinct. Damon's body was cool against hers, which was still warm and damp from the bath. The way he was holding her – if she put enough pressure on those particular points, it would hurt her possibly seriously. And then – she knew – he would release her. But did she really know what she knew? Was she prepared to break a bone to test it?

He was stroking her hair, which was so unfair, curling the ends and crushing them in his fingers . . . just hours after he'd taught her to feel things to the tips of her hair. He knew her weak spots. Not just every woman's weak spots. He knew hers; he knew how to make her want to cry out in pleasure and how to soothe her.

There was nothing to do but test her theory and maybe break a bone. She would *not* submit when she had not invited him. She would *not*!

But then she remembered her curiosity about the little boy and the great stone boulder, and she deliberately opened her mind to Damon's. He fell into the trap of his own making.

As soon as their minds connected there were something like fireworks. Explosions. Rockets. Stars going nova. Elena set her mind to ignoring her body and began looking for the boulder.

It was deep, deep inside the most locked-off part of his brain. Deep in the eternal darkness that slept there. But Elena seemed to have brought a searchlight with her. Wherever she turned, dark festoons of cobwebs fell and heavy-looking stone arches crumbled and fell to the ground.

"Don't worry," Elena found herself saying. "The light won't do that to *you*! You don't have to live down here. I'll show you the beauty of the light."

What am I saying? Elena wondered even as the words left her lips. How can I promise him – and maybe he likes living here in the dark!

But in the next second she had come much closer to the little boy, close enough to see his pale, wondering face.

"You came again," he said, as if it were a miracle. "You said you would come, and you did!"

That brought down all Elena's barriers at once. She knelt, and pulling the chains to their utmost length, took him on her lap. "Are you glad that I came back?" she asked gently. She was already stroking his hair smooth.

"Oh, yes!" It was a *cry*, and it frightened Elena almost as much as it pleased her. "You're the nicest person I've ever – the most beautiful thing I ever—"

"Hush," Elena told him, "hush. There's got to be some way to warm you up."

"It's the iron," the child said humbly. "Iron keeps me weak and cold. But it has to be iron; otherwise he wouldn't be able to control me."

"I see," Elena said grimly. She was beginning to get a grasp on what kind of relationship Damon had with this little boy. For a moment, on a hunch, she took two lengths of iron in her hands and tried to tear them apart. Elena had super-light here; why not superpowers? But all that happened was that she twisted and turned the length for nothing, and finally cut the web of her finger against an iron burr.

"Oh!" The boy's huge dark eyes fixed on the dark bead of blood. He stared as if he were fascinated – and afraid.

"Do you want it?" Elena held out the hand to him uncertainly. What a poor scrap of a creature to be coveting other people's blood, she thought. He nodded timidly as if he were sure she'd be angry. But Elena just smiled and he reverently held her finger and took the whole globe of blood at once, closing his lips like a kiss.

As he lifted his head, he seemed to have a tinge more colour in his pale face.

"You told me Damon keeps you here," she said, holding him again and feeling heat being sucked from her into his cold body. "Can you tell me why?"

The child was still licking his lips, but he turned his face towards her immediately and said, "I'm the Warden of Secrets. But" – sadly – "the Secrets have gotten so big that even I don't know what they are."

Elena followed the motion of his head from his own small limbs to the iron chain to the huge, metallic ball. She felt a sinking inside herself and a deep pity for such a small warden. And she wondered what on earth could be inside that great stone sphere that Damon was guarding so intently.

But she didn't get the chance to ask.

CHAPTER

9

Even as Elena opened her mouth to speak, she could feel herself lifted as if in a hurricane. For a moment she clung to the boy who was being torn from her grasp, then she just had time to shout, "I'll be back," and to hear his reply, before she was pulled into the ordinary world of baths and manipulation and motel rooms.

"I'll keep our secret!" That was what the little boy had cried to her at the last moment.

And what could that mean but that he would keep their rendezvous from the real (or "ordinairy") Damon?

A moment later Elena was standing in a dingy motel room, and Damon was clutching her upper arms. As he released her, Elena could taste salt. Tears were flowing freely down her cheeks.

It didn't seem to make any difference to her attacker. Damon seemed to be at the mercy of raw desperation. He was shaking like a little boy the first time he kissed his first love. That's what's driving the control away, Elena thought fuzzily.

As for herself, she felt as if she might faint.

No! She had to stay conscious.

Elena pushed and twisted, hurting herself deliberately against the apparently unbreakable grip that held her.

It held.

The possessor? Shinichi again, sneaking into Damon's mind and making him do things—

Elena fought harder, pushed herself until she actually could have screamed with pain. She whimpered once—

The hold broke.

Somehow Elena knew that Shinichi wasn't involved in this. The true soul of Damon was a little boy held in chains for God-knew-how-many centuries, who had never known warmth and closeness but who still had a tearful appreciation for them. The child who was chained to the rock surrounding was one of Damon's deepest secrets.

And now Elena was trembling so hard she wasn't sure she could stand up, and she was wondering about the child. Was he cold? Was he crying like Elena? How could she tell?

She and Damon were left staring at each other, both breathing hard. Damon's sleek hair was mussed, making him look as rakish as a buccaneer. His face, always so pale and self-composed, was flushed with blood. His eyes dropped to watch Elena automatically massaging her wrists. She could feel pins and needles now: she was getting back some circulation. Once he'd looked away, he couldn't seem to look her in the eye again.

Eye contact. All right. Elena recognised a weapon, groping for a chair and finding the bed unexpectedly close behind her. She didn't have many weapons right now; and she needed to use all of them.

She sat, giving in to the weakness in her body, but

she kept her eyes on Damon's face. His mouth was swollen. And that was . . . unfair. Damon's pout was a part of his most basic artillery. He had always had the most beautiful mouth she'd ever seen on anyone, man or woman. The mouth, the hair, the half-drooping lids, the heavy lashes, the delicacy of his jawline . . . unfair, even to someone like Elena, who'd long ago gotten past interest in a person because of some accident of beauty.

But she'd never seen *that* mouth swollen, the perfect hair disordered, the eyelashes trembling because he was looking everywhere except at her and trying not to show it.

"Was *that* . . . what you've been thinking about while you've been refusing to talk to me?" she asked, and her voice was almost steady.

Damon's sudden stillness was perfection like all his other perfections. No breathing, of course. He stared at a spot in the beige carpet that by rights ought to have broken into flames.

Then, finally, he lifted those huge dark eyes to hers. It was so hard to tell anything about Damon's eyes because the iris was almost the same colour as the pupil, but Elena had a feeling that at this moment they were dilated so far as to be *all* pupil. How could eyes as dark as midnight trap and hold light? She seemed to see in them a universe of stars.

Damon said softly, "Run."

Elena felt her legs tense. "Shinichi?"

"No. You should run now."

Elena felt her thigh muscles relax slightly and was grateful not to have to try to prove that she could run – or even crawl – at this exact instant. But her fists clenched.

"You mean this is just you being a bastard?" she said. "Have you decided to hate me again? Did you enjoy—"

Damon whirled again, stillness into motion faster than her eyes could track it. He hit the frame of the window, once, pulling the punch almost completely at the last instant. There was a crash and then a thousand little echoes as the glass showered like diamonds against the darkness outside.

"That might ... bring some people to help you." Damon wasn't trying to make the words seem more than an afterthought. Now that he was turned away from her, he didn't seem to care about keeping up appearances. Fine tremors ran through his body.

"This late, in this storm, this far away from the office – I doubt it." Elena's body was catching up with the adrenalin spurt that had allowed her to fight her way out of Damon's grip. She was tingling all over and she had to work to keep it from turning into outright shaking.

And they were back to square one, with Damon staring into the night and her staring at his back. Or, at least, that was where he wanted them to be.

"You could have just asked," she said. She didn't know if this was possible for a vampire to understand. She still hadn't taught Stefan. He went without things that he wanted because he didn't understand about asking. In all innocence and with all good intentions, Stefan left things until *she*, Elena, was forced to ask *him*.

Damon, she thought, didn't usually have that problem. He took whatever he wanted as casually as if picking items off a grocery store shelf.

And right now he was laughing silently, which meant that he was truly stricken.

"I'll take that as an apology," Elena said softly.

Now Damon was laughing out loud, and Elena felt a chill. Here she was, trying to help him, and—

"Do you think," he broke into her thoughts, "that *that* was all I wanted?"

Elena felt herself freeze again as she mulled this over. Damon could easily have taken her blood while he held her immobile. But – of course – that wasn't all he wanted from her. Her aura . . . she knew what it did to vampires. Damon had been protecting her all along from other vampires who might see it.

The difference, Elena's native honesty told her, was that she didn't give a damn about any of the others. But Damon was different. When he kissed her she could feel the difference inside her. Something she had never felt before . . . until Stefan.

Oh, God – was this really her. Elena Gilbert, betraying Stefan by the simple act of not running away from this situation? Damon was being a better person than she was; he was telling her to take the temptation of her aura away from him.

So that she could start the torture anew tomorrow.

Elena had been in many circumstances where she'd judged that it was best for her to leave before things got too hot. The problem here was that there was nowhere that she could go *to* without turning up the heat – putting herself in greater danger. And, incidentally, losing her chance to find Stefan.

Should she have gone with Matt? But Damon had said they couldn't get into this Dark Dimension place, not two humans by themselves. He'd said they needed him with them. And Elena still had some doubts as to whether Damon would take the trouble to even drive to Arizona, much less search for Stefan, if she wasn't with him every step of the way.

Besides, how could Matt have protected her on the dangerous road she and Damon were following? Elena knew that Matt would die for her – and that's just what he would do, too, if they came up against vampires or werewolves. Die. Leaving Elena facing her enemies alone.

Oh, yes, Elena knew what Damon did each night when she slept in the car. He put some kind of dark spells around her, signing them with his name, sealing them with his seal, and they kept random creatures of the night away from the car until morning.

But their greatest enemies, the kitsune twins, Shinichi and Misao, they had brought with them.

Elena thought about all this before raising her head to look Damon in the eyes. Eyes which, at that moment, reminded her of those of a ragged child chained to a rock.

"You're not going to leave, are you?" he whispered.

Elena shook her head.

"You're really not afraid of me?"

"Oh, I'm afraid." Again Elena felt that inward shiver. But she was flying somewhere now, she had set the course, and there was no way that she could stop. Especially not when he looked at her like that. It reminded her of the fierce joy, the almost reluctant pride he always showed when they took down an enemy together.

"I won't become your Princess of Darkness," she told him. "And you know that I could never give up Stefan."

A ghost of his old mocking smile touched his lips. "There's plenty of time to convince you to my way of thinking on those matters."

No need, Elena thought. She knew that Stefan would understand.

But even now, when it seemed the whole world was

whirling around her, something rose up in Elena to challenge Damon. "You say it's not Shinichi. I believe you. But is all this because – of what Caroline said?" She could hear the sudden hardness in her own voice.

"Caroline?" Damon blinked as if thrown off his stride.

"She said that before I met Stefan I was just a—" Elena found it impossible to get the last word out. "That I was . . . promiscuous."

Damon's jaw hardened and his cheeks flushed quickly – as if he'd been struck from an unexpected direction. "That girl," he muttered. "She's already fixed her destiny and if it were anyone else I might be inclined to take some pity. But she goes . . . beyond . . . she's . . . beyond . . . any propriety . . ." As he spoke his words slowed, and a look of bewilderment clouded his face. He was gazing at Elena and she knew he could see the tears standing in her eyes, because he reached up to brush them away with his fingers. As he did, however, he stopped dead in midmotion, and, his face suddenly bemused, he brought one of his hands up to his lips, tasting her tears.

Whatever they tasted like to him, he didn't seem to believe it. He brought the other hand up to his lips as well. Elena was openly staring at him now; he should have been put out of countenance – but he wasn't. Instead a kaleidoscope of expressions passed over his face, too quickly for her human eyes to catch them all. But she did see astonishment, disbelief, bitterness, more astonishment, and then finally a kind of joyful shock and a look almost as if there were tears in his own eyes.

And then Damon laughed. It was a quick, self-mocking laugh, but it was genuine, euphoric, even.

"Damon," Elena said, still blinking back tears – it had all happened that fast – "what is *wrong* with you?"

"Nothing's wrong, everything's right," he said, while raising a scholarly finger. "You should never try to fool a vampire, Elena. Vampires have many senses humans don't – and some we don't even know we have until we need them. It's taken me long enough to realise what I know about you. Because, of course, everyone was telling me one thing, and my own mind was telling me something else. But I've figured it out, at last. I know what you really are, Elena."

For half a minute Elena sat in shocked silence. "If you do, then I might as well tell you right now that *no one* will believe you."

"Maybe not," Damon said, "especially if they're human. But vampires are programmed to recognise the aura of a maiden. And *you* are unicorn bait, Elena. I don't know or care how you got your reputation. I was fooled by it myself for a long time, but I've finally found the truth." Suddenly he was bending over her so that she could see nothing but him, his fine hair brushing her forehead, his lips close to hers, his dark eyes, fathomless, capturing her gaze.

"Elena," he whispered. "This is your secret. I don't know how you've managed it, but . . . you're a virgin."

He leaned in toward her, his lips just brushing hers, sharing his deliberate breaths with hers. They stayed like that for a long, long time, Damon seeming enthralled to be able to give Elena something from his own body: the oxygen that both she and he needed, but acquired in different ways. For many humans, the stillness of their bodies, the silence, and the sustained eye contact, for neither of them had shut their eyes, might have been too much. It might have felt as if they had plunged themselves into their partner's personalities too far, that they were losing definition and becoming an ethereal part of each other before one kiss had even been completed.

But Elena was floating on air: on the breath that Damon gave her – and in the literal sense. If Damon's strong, long, slender hands had not held her shoulders, she would have escaped his grip entirely.

Elena knew that there was another way that he could keep her down. He could Influence her to let gravity have its way with her. But so far, she had felt not the slightest touch of attempted Influence. It was as if he still wanted to give her the honour of choice. He would not seduce her by any of his many accustomed methods, the tricks of domination learned over half a millennium of nights.

Only the breathing, which was coming more and more quickly, as Elena felt her senses begin to swim and her heart began to pound. Was she truly sure that Stefan wouldn't mind this? But Stefan had given her the greatest honour possible by trusting in her love and her judgement. And she was beginning to feel Damon's true self, his overwhelming need for her; his vulnerability because that need was becoming like an obsession to him.

Without attempting to Influence her, he was still spreading great soft dark wings all around her so that there was nowhere to run, nowhere to escape. Elena felt herself begin to swoon with the intensity of the passion they had wrought between them. As a final gesture, not of repudiation, but of invitation, she arched her head back, exposing to him her bare throat, and let him feel her longing.

And as if great crystal bells were ringing in the distance, she felt his jubilation at her voluntary surrender to the velvet darkness that was overtaking her.

She never felt the teeth that broke her skin and claimed her blood. Before that happened she was seeing stars. And then the universe was swallowed up in Damon's dark eyes.

CHAPTER

10

The next morning Elena got up and dressed quietly in the motel room, grateful for the extra space. Damon was gone, but she had expected that. He usually got his breakfast early while they were on the road, preying on waitresses at all-night truck stops or early-morning diners.

She was going to discuss that with him someday, she thought as she put the packet of ground coffee in the little two-cup percolator the motel provided. It smelled good.

But more urgently, she needed to talk to *someone* about what had happened last night. Stefan was her first choice, of course, but she'd found that out-of-body experiences weren't just to be had for the asking. What she needed to do was call Bonnie and Meredith. She *had* to talk to them – it was her right – but now, of all times, she *couldn't*. Intuitively, she felt that any contact between her and Fell's Church might be bad.

And Matt had never checked in. Not once. She had no

idea where he was on the road, but he had better be in Sedona on time, that was all. He had deliberately cut off all communication between them. Fine. As long as he showed up when he had promised.

But . . . Elena *still* needed to talk. To express herself.

Of course! She was an idiot! She still had her faithful companion that never said a word, and never kept her waiting. Pouring herself a cup of scalding black coffee on the way, Elena dug her diary out of the bottom of her duffel bag and opened it to a fresh, clean page. There was nothing like a fresh page and an ink pen that ran smoothly to start her writing.

Fifteen minutes later there was a rattle at one window and a minute later Damon was stepping through. He had several paper bags with him and Elena felt unaccountably pleased and homey. She had provided coffee, which was rather good even if it came with dried cream substitute, and Damon had supplied . . .

"Gasoline," he said triumphantly, raising his eyebrows significantly at her as he set the bags on the table. "Just in case they try to use plants against us. No, thanks," he added, seeing she was standing with a full cup of coffee held in his direction. "I had a garage mechanic while I was buying this. I'll just go wash my hands."

And he disappeared, walking right past Elena.

Walking right past her, without a glance, even though she was wearing her only clean pair of clothes left: jeans and a subtly coloured top that looked white at first glance and only in the brightest light revealed that it was ethereally rainbow-shaded.

Without a single look, Elena thought, feeling a strange sensation that somehow her life had just lapped itself.

She started to throw the coffee away but then decided she needed it herself and drank it in a few scalding gulps.

Then she went and stood by her diary, reading over the last two or three pages.

"Are you ready to go?" Damon was shouting over the sound of running water in the bathroom.

"Yes – in just a minute." Elena read the diary pages from the previous entry, and began skimming the one before that.

"We might as well go straight west from here," Damon shouted. "We can make it in one day. They'll think it's a feint for one particular gate and search all the small ones. Meanwhile we'll go on heading for the Kimon Gate and be days ahead of anyone tracking us. It's perfect."

"Uh-huh," Elena said, reading.

"We ought to be able to meet Mutt tomorrow – maybe even this evening; depending on what kind of trouble they cause."

"Uh-huh."

"But first I wanted to ask you: do you think it's a coincidence that our window is broken? Because I always put wards on them at night and I'm sure—" He passed a hand over his forehead. "I'm sure that I must have done that last night, as well. But something got through and broke the window and got away without a trace. That was why I bought all the gasoline. If they try something with trees, I'll blast them all back to Stonehenge."

And half the innocent residents of the state, Elena thought grimly. But she was in a state of such shock that not much could make an impression on top of it.

"What are you doing now?" Damon was clearly ready to get up and going.

"Getting rid of something I don't need," Elena said, and flushed the toilet, watching the torn-up bits of her diary swirl round and round before disappearing.

"I wouldn't worry about the window, though," she said, coming back into the bedroom and slipping her shoes on. "And don't get up for a minute, Damon. I've got to talk to you about something."

"Oh, come on. It can wait until we're on the road, can't it?"

"No, it can't, because we've got to pay for that window. You broke it last night, Damon. But you don't remember doing it, do you?"

Damon stared at her. She could tell that his first temptation was to laugh. His second temptation, to which he gave in, was to think that she was nuts.

"I'm serious," she said, once he had gotten up and started to pace towards the window with a distinct look of wanting to be a crow flying out of it. "Don't you dare go anywhere, Damon, because there's more."

"More stuff I did that I don't remember?" Damon lounged against the wall in one of his old, arrogant poses. "Maybe I smashed a few guitars, kept the radio on until four A.M.?"

"No. Not necessarily things from – last night," Elena said, looking away. She couldn't look at him. "Other things, from other days—"

"Like maybe I've been trying to sabotage this trip all along," he said, his voice laconic. He eyed the ceiling and sighed heavily. "Maybe I've done it just to be alone with you—"

"*Shut up, Damon!*"

Where had that come from? Well, she knew that, of course. From her feelings about last night. The problem was that she also had to get some other things settled – seriously, if he would take them. Come to think of it, that might be a better way to go about this.

"Do you think that your feelings about Stefan – well,

have changed at all recently?" Elena asked.

"*What?*"

"Do you think" – oh, this was so difficult looking into black eyes the colour of endless space. Especially when last night they had been full of myriads of stars – "do you think that you've come to think of him differently? To honour his wishes more than you used to do?"

Now Damon was openly examining her, just as she was examining him.

"Are you serious?" he said.

"Completely," she said, and, with a supreme effort, she sent her tears back where they were supposed to go.

"Something did happen last night," he said. He was looking intently at her face. "Didn't it?"

"*Something* happened, yes," Elena said. "It was – it was more of a—" She had to let out her breath, and with that almost everything went.

"Shinichi! *Shinichi, che bastardo! Imbroglione!* That thief! I'm going to kill him *slowly*!" Suddenly Damon was everywhere. He was beside her, his hands on her shoulders; the next minute he was shouting imprecations out the window, then he was back, holding both her hands.

But only one word mattered to Elena. Shinichi. The kitsune with his black, scarlet-tipped hair, who had made them give up so much just for the location of Stefan's cell.

"*Mascalzone! Maleducato*—" Elena lost track of Damon's cursing again. So it was true. Last night had been completely stolen from Damon, taken from his mind as simply and completely as the interval when she had used Wings of Redemption and Wings of Purification on him. The latter he had agreed to. But last night – and what other things had the fox been taking?

To cut out an entire evening and night – and this evening and night in particular, implied that . . .

"He never shut down the connection between my mind and his. He still can reach inside me any time he chooses." Damon had finally stopped swearing, and stopped moving. He was sitting on the couch opposite the bed with his hands drooping between his knees. He looked singularly forlorn.

"Elena, you have to tell me. What did he take from me last night? Please!" Damon looked as if he might fall on his knees in front of her, without melodrama. "If – if – it was what I think—"

Elena smiled, although tears were still running down her face. "It wasn't – what *anyone* would think, exactly, I suppose," she said.

"But—"

"Let's just say that this time – was mine," Elena said. "If he's stolen anything else from you, or if he tries to do it in the future, then he's fair game. But this . . . will be my secret." Until maybe someday you break into your huge boulder of secrets, she thought.

"Until I tear it out of him, along with his tongue and his tail!" snarled Damon, and it was truly the snarl of an animal. Elena was glad it wasn't directed at her. "Don't worry," Damon added in a voice so chilling that it was almost more frightening than the animal fury. "I *will* find him, no matter where he tries to hide. And I *will* take it from him. I might just take his entire little furry hide off with it. I'll make you a pair of mittens out of it, how's that?"

Elena tried to smile and did a pretty good job. She was just coming to terms with what had happened herself, although she didn't believe for a minute that Damon would really leave her alone on the subject until he forced the memory back out of Shinichi. She realised that on some level she was punishing Damon for what Shinichi had done, and that was wrong. I promise *no one* will know about last night, she told herself. Not until Damon does. I won't even tell Bonnie and Meredith.

This made things a lot harder on her, and therefore probably more equitable.

As they were cleaning up the debris from Damon's most recent fit of fury, he suddenly reached up to brush a stray tear from Elena's cheek.

"Thank you—" Elena began. Then she stopped. Damon was touching his fingers to his lips.

He looked at her, startled and a little disappointed. Then he shrugged. "Still unicorn bait," he said. "Did I say that last night?"

Elena hesitated, then decided that his words didn't fall within the crucial time limits of secrecy.

"Yes, you did. But – you won't give me away, will you?" she added, suddenly anxious. "I've promised my friends not to say anything."

Damon was staring at her. "Why should I say anything about anybody? Unless you're talking about the little redheaded one?"

"I told you; I'm not saying *anything*. Except that obviously Caroline isn't a virgin. Well, with all the ruckus about her being pregnant—"

"But you remember," Damon interjected, "I came to Fell's Church before Stefan did; I just lurked in the shadows longer. The way you talked—"

"Oh, I know. We liked boys and boys liked us, and we already had reputations. So we just talked any way we felt like talking. Some of it may have been true, but a lot of it you could take two ways – and then of course you know how *boys* talk—"

Damon knew. He nodded.

"Well and so pretty soon everyone was talking about us as if we'd done *everything* with *everyone*. They even wrote stuff about it in the paper and the yearbook and on the bathroom walls. But we had a little poem, too, and sometimes we even wrote it with our signatures on it. How did it go?" Elena cast her mind back a year, two years, more. Then she recited:

"Just because you heard it, doesn't make it true.
Just because you read it, doesn't make it so.
The next time that you hear it, it may be about you.
Don't think that you can change their minds,
  just 'cause you know – you know!"

As Elena finished, she looked at Damon, suddenly feeling the urgent need to get to Stefan. "We're almost there," she said. "Let's hurry."

CHAPTER

11

Arizona was as hot and barren a state as Elena had imagined. She and Damon drove directly to the Juniper Resort, and Elena was depressed, if not surprised, to see that Matt was not checked in.

"It can't have taken him longer than us to get here," she said, as soon as they'd been shown up to their rooms. "Unless – oh, God, Damon! Unless Shinichi caught him somehow."

Damon sat down on a bed and regarded Elena grimly. "I guess I hoped I wouldn't have to tell you this – that the jerk would at least have the courtesy to tell you himself. But I've been tracking his aura ever since he left us. It's been getting steadily farther away – in the direction of Fell's Church."

Sometimes, really bad news takes a while to sink in.

"You mean," Elena said, "that he's not going to show up here at all?"

"I mean that, as the crow flies, it wasn't all that far from where we got the cars to Fell's Church. He went in that direction. And he didn't come back."

"But why?" Elena demanded, as if logic could somehow conquer fact. "Why would he go off and leave me? Especially, why would he go to Fell's Church, where they're looking for him?"

"As for why he'd leave: I think he got the wrong idea about you and me – or maybe the right idea a little early" – Damon raised his eyebrows at Elena and she threw a pillow at him – "and decided to let us have some privacy. As for why Fell's Church . . ." Damon shrugged. "Look, you've known the guy longer than I have. But even I can tell he's the Galahad type. The *parfait gentil* knight, *sans peur et sans reproche*. If I had to say I'd say he went to meet Caroline's charges."

"Oh, *no*," Elena said, going to the door as a knock sounded. "Not after I told him and told him—"

"Oh, *yes*," Damon said, assuming a slight crouching position. "Even with your sage advice ringing in his ears—"

The door opened. It was Bonnie. Bonnie, with her petite frame, her curly strawberry hair, her wide, soulful brown eyes. Elena, in a state to disbelieve the evidence of her *own* eyes, and still not through with the argument with Damon, shut the door on her.

"Matt's going to get *lynched*," Elena almost screamed, vaguely annoyed that some knocking was going on somewhere.

Damon uncrouched. He passed Elena on the way to the door, said, "I think you'd better sit down," and then sat her down by putting her in a chair and holding her there until she stopped trying to get up again.

Then he opened the door.

This time it was Meredith knocking. Tall and willowy, with her hair falling in dark clouds around her shoulders,

Meredith radiated the intention to go on knocking until the door stayed open. Something happened inside Elena, and she found that she could get her mind around more than one subject at once.

It was Meredith. And Bonnie. In Sedona, Arizona!

Elena leaped up from the chair where Damon had put her and flung her arms around Meredith, saying incoherently, "You came! You came! You knew I couldn't call you, so you came!"

Bonnie edged around the embrace and said to Damon in an undertone, "Is she back to kissing everyone she meets?"

"Unfortunately," Damon said, "no. But be prepared to be squeezed to death."

Elena turned on him. "I heard that! Oh, Bonnie! I just can't believe you two are really *here*. I wanted to talk to you so much!"

Meanwhile, she was hugging Bonnie, and Bonnie was hugging her, and Meredith was hugging both of them. Subtle velociraptor sisterhood signals were being passed from one to another at the same time – an arched eyebrow *here*, a slight nod *there*, a frown and shrug ending with a sigh. Damon didn't know it, but he had just been accused, tried, acquitted, and restored to duty – with the conclusion that extra surveillance was necessary in the future.

Elena snapped out of it first. "You must have met with Matt – he had to tell you about this place."

"He did, and then he sold the Prius and we sort of packed on the run and got plane tickets here and we've been waiting – we didn't want to miss you!" Bonnie said breathlessly.

"I don't suppose that would have been just about two days ago that you bought your tickets here," Damon asked the ceiling wearily as he lounged with an elbow on Elena's chair.

"Let me see—" Bonnie began, but Meredith said flatly, "Yes it was. What? It made something happen to you?"

"We were trying to keep things slightly ambiguous for the enemy," Damon said. "But as it turns out, it probably didn't matter."

No, Elena thought, because Shinichi can reach inside your brain whenever he wants and try to take away your memories and all you can do is try to fight him off.

"But it does mean that Elena and I should start off right away," Damon continued. "I have to do an errand first. Elena should pack. Take as little as you can, just the absolute essentials – but include food for two or three days."

"You said . . . starting *now*?" Bonnie breathed, and then she sat down abruptly on the floor.

"It makes sense, if we've already lost the element of surprise," Damon replied.

"I can't believe you two came to say goodbye to me while Matt watches over the town," Elena said. "That is so *sweet*!" She smiled radiantly before adding, in her own mind, *And so dumb!*

"Well—"

"Well, I still have an errand," Damon said, waving without turning around. "Let's say we'll leave here in half an hour."

"Stingy," Bonnie complained, when the door was safely shut behind him. "That might have only given us a few minutes to talk before we start."

"I can pack in less than five minutes," Elena said sadly, and then got tangled up in Bonnie's previous sentence. " *'Before* we *start'*?"

"I can't pack just essentials at all," Meredith was

fretting quietly. "I couldn't store everything on my mobile, and I have no idea when I'll be able to recharge the batteries. I've got a suitcase of stuff on *paper*!"

Elena was looking back and forth at them nervously. "Um, I'm pretty sure I'm the one who's supposed to be packing," she said. "Because I'm the only one going . . . right?" Another look back and forth.

"As if we would let you set off into some other universe without us!" Bonnie said. "You *need* us!"

"Not another universe; only another dimension," Meredith said. "But the same principle applies."

"But – I can't let you come with me!"

"Of course you can't. I'm older than you," Meredith said. "You don't 'let' me do anything. But the truth is that we have a mission. We want to find Shinichi's or Misao's star ball if we can. If we could do that we think we could stop most of the stuff going on in Fell's Church immediately."

"Star ball?" Elena said blankly, while somewhere in the depths of her mind, an uneasy image stirred.

"I'll explain later."

Elena was shaking her head. "But – you left Matt to deal with whatever supernatural stuff is going on? When he's a fugitive and has to hide from the police?"

"Elena, even the police are scared of Fell's Church now – and frankly, if they put him in custody in Ridgemont it might be the safest place for him. But they're not going to do that. He's working with Mrs Flowers and they're *good* together; they're a solid team." Meredith stopped to take a breath, and seemed to be considering how to say something.

Bonnie said it for her in a very small voice. "And I was *no* good, Elena. I'd started – well, I started to get hysterical and see and hear things that weren't there – or at least to imagine them and maybe even make them come true. I was scaring myself out of my mind, and I think I actually was putting people in danger. Matt's too practical to do that." She dabbed at her eyes. "I know the Dark Dimension is pretty bad, but at least I won't be able to put houses full of innocent people in danger."

Meredith nodded. "It was all . . . going bad with Bonnie there. Even if we hadn't wanted to come with you I would have had to get her out. I don't want to be overly dramatic, but I believe that the demons there were after her. And that since Stefan's gone, Damon may be the only one who can keep them away. Or maybe you can help her, Elena?"

Meredith . . . overly dramatic? But Elena could see the fine tremors running under Meredith's skin, and the light sheen of perspiration on Bonnie's forehead that was dampening her curls.

Meredith touched Elena's wrist. "We haven't just gone AWOL or anything. Fell's Church is a war zone now; it's true, but we didn't leave Matt without allies. Like Dr Alpert – she's logical – she's the best country doctor there is – and she might even convince somebody that Shinichi and the malach are real. But besides all that, the parents have taken over. Parents and psychiatrists and newshounds. And they make it almost impossible to work openly anyway. Matt's not at any disadvantage."

"But – in just a week—"

"Take a look at this week's Sunday paper."

Elena took the *Ridgemont Times* from Meredith. It was the biggest paper in the area of Fell's Church. A banner headline read:

POSSESSION IN THE 21ST CENTURY?

Under the headline were many lines of grey print, but what really caught the eye was a photo of a three-way fight between girls, all of whom seemed to be undergoing seizures or contortions impossible to the human body. The expressions of two of the girls were simply those of pain and terror, but it was the third girl who froze the blood in Elena's veins. Her body was humped so that her face was upside down, and she was looking directly at the camera with her lips skinned back from her teeth. Her eyes – there was just no other way to put it – were demonic. They weren't rolled back in her head or malformed or anything. They weren't glowing eerily red. It was all in the expression. Elena had never seen eyes that made her sick to her stomach before.

Bonnie said quietly, "Do you ever sort of slip and get that feeling like, 'Oh, whoops, there goes the whole universe'?"

"Constantly, since meeting Stefan," Meredith said. "No offence meant, Elena. But the point is that all this has happened in just a couple of days; from the minute the adults who knew that there was something *really* going on got together."

Meredith sighed and ran fingers with perfectly manicured nails through her hair before continuing. "Those girls are what Bonnie calls possessed in the modern sense. Or maybe they're possessed by Misao – female kitsune are supposed to do that. But if we could just find these things called star balls – or even one – we could force *them* to clean all this up."

Elena put the newspaper down so she wouldn't have to see those upside-down eyes staring into hers. "And while all this is happening, what is your boyfriend doing during the crisis?"

For the first time, Meredith looked genuinely relieved. "He may be on his way as we speak. I've written to him about everything that's happening, and he was actually the one who said to get Bonnie out." She flashed a glance of apology at Bonnie, who simply lifted her hands and face to the heavens. "And as soon as he's finished with his work on some island called Shinmei no Uma, he's coming to Fell's Church. This kind of thing is Alaric's speciality, and he doesn't get spooked easily. So even if we're gone for *weeks*, Matt will have a backup."

Elena threw her own hands up in a gesture similar to Bonnie's. "There's just one thing you'd better know before we start. *I* can't help Bonnie. If you're counting on me to do any of the things I did when we fought Shinichi and Misao last time – well, I can't. I've tried over and over, as hard as I could, to do all my wings attacks. But nothing has ever come of it."

Meredith said slowly, "Well, then, maybe Damon knows something—"

"Maybe he does, but, Meredith, don't push him right now. Not right this minute. What he knows for certain is that Shinichi can reach in and take his memories – and who knows, maybe even possess him again—"

"That lying kitsune!" Bonnie spat out, sounding almost proprietory. As if, Elena thought, Damon was her boyfriend. "Shinichi *swore* he wouldn't—"

"And he swore he'd leave Fell's Church alone, too. The only reason I have any faith at all in the clues that Misao gave me about the fox key, is that she was taunting me. She never thought we'd do a deal, and so she wasn't trying to lie or be too clever – I *think*."

"Well, that's why we're here with you, to get Stefan out," Bonnie said. "And if we're lucky, to find the star balls that will let us control Shinichi. Right?"

"Right!" Elena said fervently.

"Right," Meredith said solemnly.

Bonnie nodded. "Velociraptor sisterhood for ever!"

They laid their right hands over one another's quickly, forming a three-spoked wheel. It reminded Elena of the days when there were four spokes.

"And what about Caroline?" she asked.

Bonnie and Meredith consulted each other with their eyes. Then Meredith shook her head. "You don't want to know. *Really*," she said.

"I can take it. *Really*," Elena said in almost a whisper. "Meredith, I've been dead, remember? Twice."

Meredith was still shaking her head. "If you can't look at that picture, you shouldn't hear about Caroline. We went to see her twice—"

"*You* went to see her twice," Bonnie interrupted. "The second time I fainted and you left me by the door."

"And I realised I could have lost you for good, and I've apologised—" Meredith broke off when Bonnie put a hand on her arm and gave her a little push.

"Anyway, it wasn't exactly a visit," Meredith said. "I went running into Caroline's room ahead of her mom and found her inside her nest – never mind what that is – eating something. When she saw me, she just giggled and went on eating."

"And?" Elena said, when the tension got to be too much for her. "What was it?"

"I think," Meredith said bleakly, "that it was worms and slugs. She would stretch them up and up and they'd squirm before she bit them. But that wasn't the worst. Look, you had to have been here to appreciate it, but she just smirked at me, and said in this thick voice, 'Have a bite?' and suddenly my mouth was filled with this wriggling mass – and it was going down my throat. So I was sick, right there on her carpet. Caroline just started laughing, and I ran down again and picked Bonnie up and ran out and we never went back. But . . .

halfway down the path to the house, I realised Bonnie was suffocating. She had the – the worms and things – in her mouth *and* her nose. I know CPR; I managed to get most of them out before she woke up vomiting. But—"

"It was an experience I would really rather not have again." The very lack of expression in Bonnie's voice said more than any tone of horror could.

Meredith said, "I've heard that Caroline's parents have moved out of that house, and I can't say I blame them. Caroline's over eighteen. All I can add is that everybody's sort of praying that somehow the werewolf blood will win out in her, because that seems at least to be less horrible than the malach or the – the demonic. But if it doesn't win out . . ."

Elena rested her chin on her knees. "And Mrs Flowers can deal with this?"

"Better than Bonnie can. Mrs Flowers is glad to have Matt around; like I said, they're a solid team. And now that she has finally spoken to the human race of the twenty-first century, I think she likes it. And she's been practising the craft constantly."

"The craft? Oh—"

"Yeah, that's what she calls witchcraft. I have no idea whether she's any good at it or not, because I don't have anything to compare her to – or with—"

"Her poultices work like magic!" Bonnie said firmly just as Elena said, "Her bath salts certainly work."

Meredith smiled faintly. "Too bad she isn't here instead of us."

Elena shook her head. Now that she had reconnected with Bonnie and Meredith she knew she could never go into the Darkness without them. They were more than her hands; they were so much more to her . . . and here they were, each prepared to risk their life for Stefan and for Fell's Church.

At that moment, the door to the room opened. Damon walked in, carrying a couple of brown paper bags in one hand.

"So everybody's said bye-bye nicely?" he asked. He seemed to have trouble looking at either of the two visitors, so he stared particularly hard at Elena.

"Well – not really. Not as such," Elena said. She wondered if Damon was capable of throwing Meredith out a fifth-storey window. Best to break it easily to him, by degrees . . .

"Because we're going with you," Meredith said, and Bonnie said, "We forgot to pack, though."

Elena slid quickly so that she was between Damon and the others. But Damon just stared at the floor.

"It's a bad idea," he said very softly. "A very, very, very bad idea."

"Damon, don't Influence them! Please!" Elena waved both hands at him in a gesture of urgency, and Damon raised one of his hands in a gesture of negation – and somehow their hands brushed each other's – and tangled.

Electric shock. But a nice one, Elena thought – although she didn't really have time to think it. She and Damon were both trying desperately to get their hands back to themselves, but didn't seem to be able to. Little shockwaves were running from Elena's palm all through her body.

Finally, the disentanglement worked and then they both turned, in guilty unison, to look at Bonnie and Meredith, who were staring at them with enormous eyes. Suspicious eyes. Eyes that belonged in faces saying "*Aha!* What have we here?"

There was a long moment when no one moved or spoke.

Then Damon said seriously, "This isn't some kind of pleasure trip. We're going because there's no other choice."

"Not alone, you're not," Meredith said in a neutral tone. "If Elena goes, we all go."

"We know it's a bad place," Bonnie said, "but we are *definitely* going with you."

"Besides, we have our own agenda," Meredith added. "A way to cleanse Fell's Church of the harm Shinichi has done – and is still doing."

Damon shook his head. "You don't understand. You won't *like* it," he said tightly. He nodded at her mobile. "No electric power in there. Even owning one of those is a crime. And the punishment for just about any crime is torture and death." He took a step toward her.

Meredith refused to back away, her dark gaze fixed on his.

"Look, you don't even realise what you have to do just to get in," Damon said bleakly. "First, you need a vampire – and you're lucky to have one. Then you'll have to do all sorts of things you won't like—"

"If Elena can do it, we can do it," Meredith interrupted quietly.

"I don't want either of you to get hurt. I'm going in because it's for Stefan," Elena said hastily, speaking partly to her friends and partly to the innermost core of her being, which the shockwaves and pulses of electricity had reached at last. Such a strange, melting, throbbing sweetness for something that had started out as a shock. Such a fierce shock for simply touching another person's hand . . .

Elena managed to tear her eyes away from Damon's

face and tune back into the argument that was going on.

"You're going in for Stefan, yes," Meredith was saying to her, "and we're going in with you."

"I'm telling you, you won't *like* it. You'll live to regret it – if you live, that is," Damon was saying flatly, his expression dark.

Bonnie simply gazed up at Damon with her brown eyes wide and pleading in her small heart-shaped face. Her hands were clasped together at the base of her throat. She looked like a picture on a Hallmark card, Elena thought. And those eyes were worth a thousand logical arguments.

Finally, Damon looked back at Elena. "You're probably taking them to their deaths, you know. You, I could probably protect. But you *and* Stefan, *and* your two little teenage girlfriends . . . *I can't.*"

Hearing it put that way was a shock. Elena hadn't quite thought of it like that. But she could see the determined set of Meredith's jaw and the way Bonnie had gone up a little on her toes to try to look bigger.

"I think it's already been decided," she said quietly, aware that her voice shook.

There was a long moment as she stared into Damon's dark eyes, and then suddenly he flashed his 250-kilowatt smile at all of them, shut it off almost before it had begun, and said, "I see. Well, in that case, I have another errand. I may not be back for quite a while, so feel free to use the room—"

"Elena should come to our room," Meredith said. "I have a lot of material to show her. And if we can't take much with us, we'll have to go over it all tonight—"

"Then let's say we meet back here at dawn," Damon said. "We'll set off for the Demon Gate from here. And remember – don't bring money; it isn't any good there.

And this is *not* a vacation – but you'll get that idea soon enough."

With a graceful, ironic gesture, he handed Elena her bag.

"The *Demon* Gate?" Bonnie said as they went to the elevator. Her voice shook.

"Hush," said Meredith. "It's only a name."

Elena wished she didn't know so well when Meredith was lying.

CHAPTER

12

Elena checked the edges of the hotel room's draperies for signs of dawn. Bonnie was curled up, drowsing in a chair by the window. Elena and Meredith had been up all night, and now they were surrounded by scattered printouts, newspapers, and pictures from the Internet.

"It's already spread beyond Fell's Church," Meredith explained, pointing to an article in one of the papers. "I don't know if it's following ley lines, or being controlled by Shinichi – or is just moving on its own, like any parasite."

"Did you try to contact Alaric?"

Meredith glanced at Bonnie's sleeping figure. She spoke softly, "That's the good news. I'd been trying to get him for ever, and I finally managed. He'll be arriving in Fell's Church soon – he just has one more stop first."

Elena drew her breath in. "One more stop that's more important than what's going on in that town?"

"That's why I didn't tell Bonnie about him coming. Or Matt either. I knew they wouldn't understand. But – I'll give you one guess as to what kind of legends he's following up in the Far East." Meredith fixed dark eyes on Elena's.

"Not . . . it is, isn't it? *Kitsune?*"

"Yes, and he's going to a very ancient place where they were supposed to have destroyed the town – just as Fell's Church is being destroyed. Nobody lives there now. That name – Unmei no Shima – means the Island of Doom. Maybe he'll find something important about fox spirits there. He's doing some kind of multicultural independent study with Sabrina Dell. She's Alaric's age, but she's already a famous forensic anthropologist."

"And you're not jealous?" Elena said awkwardly. Personal issues were difficult to talk about with Meredith. Asking her questions always felt like prying.

"Well." Meredith tipped back her head. "It isn't as if we have any formal engagement."

"But you never told anybody about all this."

Meredith lowered her head and gave Elena a quick look. "I have now," she said.

For a moment the girls sat together in silence. Then Elena said quietly, "The Shi no Shi, the kitsune, Isobel Saitou, Alaric and his Island of Doom – they may not have anything to do with each other. But if they do, I'm going to find out what it is."

"And I'm going to help," Meredith said simply. "But I had thought that after I graduated . . ."

Elena couldn't stand it any more. "Meredith, I promise, as soon as we get Stefan back and the town calmed down, we'll pin Alaric down with Plans A through Z," she said. She leaned forward and kissed Meredith's cheek. "That's a velociraptor sisterhood oath, OK?"

Meredith blinked twice, swallowed once, and

whispered, "OK." Then, abruptly, she was her old efficient self again. "Thank you," she said. "But cleaning up the town might not be such an easy job. It's already heading towards mass chaos there."

"And Matt *wanted* to be in the middle of it all? Alone?" Elena asked.

"Like we said, he and Mrs Flowers are a solid team," Meredith said quietly. "And it's what he's chosen."

"Well," Elena said drily, "he may turn out to have the better deal in the end, after all."

They went back to the scattered papers. Meredith picked up several pictures of kitsune guarding shrines in Japan.

"It says they're usually depicted with a 'jewel' or key." She held up a picture of a kitsune holding a key in its mouth at the main gate of the Fushimi Shrine.

"Aha," Elena said. "Looks like the key's got two wings, doesn't it?"

"Exactly what Bonnie and I thought. And the 'jewels' . . . well, take a close look." Elena did and her stomach lurched. Yes, they were like the "snow globe" orbs that Shinichi had used to create unbreakable traps in the Old Wood.

"We found they're called *hoshi no tama*," Meredith said. "And that translates to 'star balls'. Each kitsune puts a measure of their power into one, along with other things, and destroying the ball is one of the only ways to kill them. If you find a kitsune's star ball, you can control the kitsune. That's what Bonnie and I want to do."

"But how do you *find* it?" Elena asked, excited by the idea of controlling Shinichi and Misao.

"Sa . . ." Meredith said, pronouncing the word "sah" like a sigh. Then she gave one of her rare brilliant smiles. "In Japanese, that means: 'I wonder; hmm; wouldn't

want to comment; my gosh, golly, I really couldn't say.'
We could use a word like that in English."

Despite herself, Elena giggled.

"But, then, other stories say that kitsune can be killed
by the Sin of Regret or by blessed weapons. I don't know
what the Sin of Regret is, but—" She rummaged in her
luggage, and came up with an old-fashioned but
serviceable-looking revolver.

"Meredith!"

"It was my grandpa's – one of a pair. Matt's got
the other one. They're loaded with bullets blessed by
a priest."

"What priest would bless *bullets*, for God's sake?"
Elena demanded.

Meredith's smile turned bleak. "One that's seen what's
happening in Fell's Church. You remember how Caroline
got Isobel Saitou possessed, and what Isobel did to
herself?"

Elena nodded. "I remember," she said tautly.

"Well, do you remember how we told you that
Obaasan – Grandma Saitou – used to be a shrine maiden?
That's a Japanese priestess. *She* blessed the bullets for us,
all right, and specifically for killing kitsune. You should
have seen how spooky the ritual was. Bonnie almost
fainted again."

"Do you know how Isobel is doing now?"

Meredith shook her dark head slowly. "Better but – I
don't think she even knows about Jim yet. That's going
to be very tough on her."

Elena tried to quell a shudder. There was nothing
but tragedy in store for Isobel even when she got well.
Jim Bryce, her boyfriend, had spent only one night
with Caroline, but now had Lesch-Nye disease – or so
the doctors said. In that same dreadful night that Isobel

had pierced herself everywhere, and cut her tongue so that it forked, Jim, a handsome star basketball player, had eaten away his fingers and his lips. In Elena's opinion they were both possessed and their injuries were only more reasons why the kitsune twins had to be stopped.

"We'll do it," she said aloud, realising for the first time that Meredith was holding her hand as if Elena were Bonnie. Elena managed a faint but determined smile for Meredith. "We'll get Stefan out and we'll stop Shinichi and Misao. We *have* to do it."

This time it was Meredith who nodded.

"There's more," she said at last. "You want to hear it?"

"I need to know everything."

"Well, every single source I checked agrees that kitsune possess girls and then lead boys to destruction. What kind of destruction depends on where you look. It can be as simple as appearing as a will-o'-the-wisp and leading you into a swamp or off a cliff, or as difficult as shapeshifting."

"Oh, yes," Elena said tightly. "I knew that from what happened to you and Bonnie. They can look exactly like someone."

"Yes, but always with some small flaw if you have the wits to notice it. They can never make a perfect replicate. But they can have up to nine tails, and the more tails they have, the better at everything they are."

"Nine? Terrific. We've never even *seen* a nine-tailed one."

"Well, we may get to yet. They're supposed to be able to cross over freely from one world to another. Oh, yes. And they're specifically in charge of the 'Kimon' Gate between dimensions. Want to guess what that translates to?"

Elena stared at her. "Oh, no."

"Oh, yes."

"But why would Damon take us all the way across the country, just to get in through a Demon Gate that's run by fox spirits?"

"Sa . . . But when Matt told us you were headed to someplace near Sedona, that was really what decided Bonnie and me."

"Great." Elena ran her hands through her hair and sighed. "Anything else?" she asked, feeling like a rubber band that had been stretched to its utmost.

"Only this, which ought to really bake your cookies after all we've been through. Some of them are good. Kitsune, I mean."

"Some of them are good – good what? Good fighters? Good assassins? Good liars?"

"No, really, Elena. Some of them are supposed to be like gods and goddesses who sort of test you, and if you pass the test they reward you."

"Do you think we should count on finding one like that?"

"Not really."

Elena dropped her head to the coffee table where Meredith's printouts were scattered. "Meredith, seriously, how are we going to deal with them when we go through that Demon Gate? My Power is about as reliable as a low battery. And it's not just the kitsune; it's all the different demons and vampires – Old Ones, too! What are we going to *do*?"

She raised her head and looked deeply into the eyes of her friend – those dark eyes that she had never been able to classify as this colour or that.

To her surprise, Meredith instead of looking sober, tossed back the dregs of a Diet Coke and smiled.

"No Plan A yet?"

"Well . . . maybe just an idea. Nothing definite yet. What about you?"

"A few that might qualify for Plans B and C. So what we're going to do is what we always do – try our best and fall all over ourselves and make mistakes until you do something brilliant and save us all."

"Merry" – Meredith blinked. Elena knew why – she hadn't used that diminutive for Meredith for more years than she could remember. None of the three girls liked pet names or used them. Elena went on very seriously, holding Meredith's eyes, "There's nothing I want more than to save everybody – everybody – from these kitsune bastards. I'd give my life for Stefan and all of you. But . . . this time it may be somebody else who takes the bullet."

"Or the stake. I know. Bonnie knows. We talked about it while we were flying here. But we're still with you, Elena. You have to know that. We're all with you."

There was only one way to reply to that. Elena gripped Meredith's hand in both of hers. Then she let out her breath, and, like probing an aching tooth, tried to get news on a sore subject. "Does Matt – did he – well, how was Matt when you left?"

Meredith glanced at her sideways. Not much got past Meredith. "He seemed OK, but – distracted. He would go off into these fits where he'd just stare at nothing, and he wouldn't hear you if you spoke to him."

"Did he tell you why he left?"

"Well . . . sort of. He said that Damon was hypnotising you and that you weren't – weren't doing all you could to stop him. But he's a boy and boys get jealous—"

"No, he was right about what he saw. It's just that I've – gotten to know Damon a little better. And Matt doesn't like that."

"Um-hm." Meredith was watching her from under lowered eyelids, barely breathing, as if Elena was a bird that mustn't be disturbed or she'd fly away.

Elena laughed. "It's nothing *bad*," she said. "At least I don't think so. It's just that . . . in some ways Damon needs help even more than Stefan did when he first came to Fell's Church."

Meredith's eyebrows shot up, but all she said was, "Um-*hm*."

"And . . . I think that really Damon's a lot more like Stefan than he lets on."

Meredith's eyebrows stayed up. Elena finally looked at her. She opened her mouth once or twice and then she just stared at Meredith. "I'm in trouble, aren't I?" she said helplessly.

"If all this comes from less than one week riding in a car with him . . . then, yes. But we have to remember that women are Damon's speciality. And he thinks he's in love with you."

"No, he really is—" Elena began, and then she caught her lower lip between her teeth. "Oh, God, this is *Damon* we're talking about. I *am* in trouble."

"Let's just watch and see what happens," Meredith said sensibly. "He's definitely changed, too. Before, he would have just told you that your friends couldn't come – and that was it. Today he struck around and listened."

"Yes. I just have to – to be on my guard from now on," Elena said a little unsteadily. How was she going to help the child inside Damon without getting closer to him? And how would she explain all she might need to do to Stefan?

She sighed.

"It'll probably be all right," Bonnie muttered sleepily. Meredith and Elena both turned to look at her and Elena felt a chill go up her spine. Bonnie was sitting propped up, but her eyes were shut and her voice was indistinct. "The real question is: what will Stefan say about that night at the motel with Damon?"

"*What?*" Elena's voice was sharp and loud enough to awaken any sleeper. But Bonnie didn't stir.

"*What* happened *what* night at *what* motel?" Meredith demanded. When Elena didn't answer immediately, she caught Elena's arm and swung her so that they were face-to-face.

At last Elena looked at her friend. But her eyes, she knew, gave away nothing.

"Elena, what's she talking about? *What happened with Damon?*"

Elena still kept her face perfectly expressionless, and used a word she'd learned just that night. "Sa . . ."

"Elena, you're impossible! You're not going to *dump* Stefan after you rescue him, are you?"

"No, of *course* not!" Elena was hurt. "Stefan and I belong together – for ever."

"But still you spent a night with Damon where *something* happened between you."

"Something . . . I guess."

"*And that something was?*"

Elena smiled apologetically. "Sa . . ."

"I'll get it out of *him*! I'll put him on the defensive . . ."

"You can make a Plan A and Plan B and all," Elena said. "But it won't help. Shinichi took his memories away. Meredith, I'm sorry – you don't know how sorry. But I swore that nobody would ever know." She looked up at the taller girl, feeling tears pool in her eyes. Can't you just – once – let me leave it that way?"

Meredith sank bank. "Elena Gilbert, the world is lucky there is only one of you. You are the . . ." She paused, as if deciding whether to say the words or not. Then she said, "It's time to get to bed. Dawn is going to come early and so is the Demon Gate."

"Merry?"

"What now?"

"Thank you."

CHAPTER

13

The Demon Gate.

Elena glanced over her shoulder at the backseat of the Prius. Bonnie was blinking sleepily. Meredith, who'd gotten much less sleep but heard much more alarming news, was looking like a razor blade: keen, sharp as ice, and ready.

There was nothing else to see except Damon with his paper bags on the seat beside him, driving the Prius. Out the windows, where an arid Arizona dawn should be blinding its way across the horizon, was nothing but fog.

It was frightening and disorienting. They had taken a small road off Highway 179 and, gradually, the fog had crept in, sending tendrils of mist around the car, and finally engulfing it whole. It seemed to Elena that they were being deliberately cut off from the old ordinary world of McDonald's and Target, and were crossing a border into a place they weren't meant to know about, much less go.

There was no traffic in the other direction. None at all.

And as hard as Elena peered out of her window, it was like trying to look through fast-moving clouds.

"Aren't we going too fast?" Bonnie asked, rubbing her eyes.

"No," Damon said. "It would be – a remarkable coincidence – if anyone else were on the same route at the same time we are."

"It looks a lot like Arizona," she said, disappointed.

"It may *be* Arizona, for all I know," Damon replied. "But we haven't crossed the Gate yet. And this isn't anywhere in Arizona you could just accidentally walk into. The path always has its little tricks and traps. The problem is that you never know what you'll be facing.

"Now listen," he added, looking at Elena with an expression she had gotten to know. It meant: I'm not joking around; I'm talking to you as an equal; I'm *serious*.

"You've gotten very good at showing only a human-sized aura," Damon said. "But that means that if you can learn one more thing before we go in, you can actually *use* your aura, make it do you some good when you want it to, instead of just hiding it until it pops up out of control and lifts three-thousand-pound cars."

"Like what kind of good?"

"Like what I'm going to show you. First of all just relax and let me control it. Then, little by little, I'll slacken the controls and you'll take them up. By the end, you should be able to send your Powers to your eyes – and see much better; to your ears – and hear much better; to your limbs – and move much more quickly and precisely. All right?"

"You couldn't have taught me this before we started on this little excursion?"

He smiled at her, a wild, reckless smile that made her smile, too, even if she didn't know what it was about. "Until you showed how well you could control your aura throughout the path – the way here – I didn't think you were ready," he said bluntly. "Now I do. There are things in your mind just waiting to be unlocked. You'll understand when we unlock them."

And we unlock them – with what? A kiss? Elena thought suspiciously.

"No. No. And that's the other reason you've got to learn this. Your telepathy is getting out of hand. If you don't learn how to keep from projecting your thoughts, you'll never make it past the checkpoint at the Gate as a human."

Checkpoint. That sounded ominous. Elena nodded and said, "All right; what do we do?"

"What we did before. Like I said, relax. Try to trust me."

He put his right hand just to the left of her breastbone, not touching the cloth of her deep-gold top. Elena could feel herself flushing, and she wondered what Bonnie and Meredith must think of this if they were watching.

And then Elena felt something else.

It wasn't cold; it wasn't heat, but it was something like the furthest extremities of both of them. It was pure Power. It would have knocked her over if Damon hadn't been holding her by the arm with his other hand. She thought, he's using his own Power to prime mine, to do something—

—something that *hurt*—

No! Elena tried, vocally and telepathically, to tell Damon that the Power was too much, that it hurt. But Damon ignored her pleas even as he ignored the tears that spilled onto her cheeks. His Power was leading hers now, painfully, throughout her body. It was in her bloodstream, dragging her own Power behind it like a comet's tail. It was forcing her to take the Power to different parts of her body and let it build and build there, not letting her exhale it, not letting her move it on.

I'm going to burst—

All this time her eyes had been fixed on Damon's, broadcasting her feelings to him: from indignant anger to shock to agonised pain – and now . . . to . . .

Her mind exploded.

The rest of her Power went on circling, without causing any pain. Each new breath she drew added more Power to it, but it simply circulated through her bloodstream, not increasing her aura, but increasing the Power that was inside her. After two or three more quick breaths she realised that she was doing it effortlessly.

Now Elena's Power wasn't simply sliding around smoothly inside her, looking from the outside like any other human's. It was also filling several burst swollen nodes inside her and where it did that, it changed things.

She realised that she was looking at Damon with round eyes. He might have told her about how this would feel, rather than letting her go into it blind.

You really are a total bastard, aren't you? Elena thought, and, amazingly, she could feel Damon receive the thought, and could feel his automatic response, which was pleased agreement, rather than otherwise.

Then Elena forgot about him in the dawning of a new understanding. She was realising that she could keep circulating her Power inside her, and even build it higher and higher, getting ready for a truly explosive burst, and show *nothing* of what it was doing on the surface.

And as for the nodes . . .

Elena looked around her at what a few minutes ago had been barren wilderness. It was like taking bullets of light through both her eyes. She was dazzled; she was enthralled. Colours seemed to come to life in a painful glory. She felt that she could see much farther than she ever had, on and on into the desert, and at the same time, she could distinguish Damon's pupils from his irises.

Why, they're both black, but different shades of black, she thought. Of course, they go together – Damon would never have irises that didn't complement his pupils. But the irises are more velvety, where his pupils are more silky and shiny. And yet it's a velvet that can hold light inside it – almost like the night sky with stars – like those kitsune star balls that Meredith told me about.

Right now those pupils were wide and set unyieldingly on her face, as if Damon didn't want to miss a moment of her reaction. Suddenly, the corner of his lip quirked in a faint smile.

"You did it. You learned to channel your Power to your eyes." He spoke in a bare whisper that she could never have detected before.

"And to my ears," she whispered back, listening to the amazing symphony of tiny sounds around her. High in the air, a bat squeaked on a frequency too high for any ordinary human ear to notice. As for the fall of grains of sand around her, they formed something like a tiny concerto as they struck rock and bounced with a tiny ping before falling to the ground below.

This is amazing, she told Damon, hearing the smugness in her own telepathic voice. *And I can talk to you this way any time now?* She would have to watch out for that – telepathy threatened to reveal more than she might want to send to a recipient.

It's best to be careful, Damon agreed, confirming her suspicions. She'd sent more than she'd meant to.

But Damon – can Bonnie do this, too? Should I try to show her?

"Who knows?" Damon replied aloud, making Elena wince. "Teaching humans how to use Power isn't exactly my forte."

And what about my different Wings Powers? Will I be able to control them, now?

"About those I have absolutely no idea. I've never seen anything like them." Damon looked thoughtful for a moment and then shook his head. "I think you'd need someone with more experience than I have to learn to control those." Before Elena could say anything else, he added, "We'd better get back to the others. We're almost at the Gate."

"And I suppose I shouldn't be using telepathy then."

"Well, it is a rather obvious giveaway—"

"But you'll teach me later, won't you? As much as you know about controlling Power?"

"Maybe your boyfriend should be doing that," Damon said almost roughly.

He's afraid, Elena thought, trying to keep her thoughts hidden under a wall of white noise so that Damon wouldn't pick them up. He's just as afraid that he'll reveal too much to me as I am afraid of him.

CHAPTER

14

"**A**ll right," Damon said as he and Elena reached Bonnie and Meredith. "Now comes the hard part."

Meredith looked up at him. "*Now* comes . . .?"

"Yes. The really hard part." Damon had finally unzipped his mysterious black leather bag. "Look," he said in a bare murmur, "this is the actual Gate that we have to get through. And while we're doing it, you can have all the hysterics you want because you're supposed to be captives." He pulled out a number of pieces of rope.

Elena, Meredith, and Bonnie had drawn together in an automatic show of velociraptor sisterhood.

"What," Meredith said slowly, as if to give Damon the final benefit of some lingering doubt, "are those ropes for?"

Damon put his head to one side in an oh-come-on gesture. "They're for tying your hands."

"For *what*?"

Elena was amazed. She had never seen Meredith so obviously angry. She herself couldn't even get a word in.

Meredith had walked up and was looking at Damon from a distance of about four inches.

And her eyes are *grey*! some distant part of Elena's mind exclaimed in astonishment. Deep, deep, deep, clear grey grey. All this time I've thought they were brown, but they're not.

Meanwhile Damon was looking faintly alarmed at Meredith's expression. A T. rex would have looked alarmed at Meredith's expression, Elena thought.

"And you expect us to walk around with our hands tied up? While *you* do what?"

"While I act as your master," Damon said, suddenly rallying with a glorious smile that was gone almost before it was there. "The three of you are my slaves."

There was a long, *long* silence.

Elena waved the entire pile of objects away with a gesture. "We won't do that," she said simply. "We won't. There has to be some other way—"

"Do you want to rescue Stefan or not?" Damon demanded suddenly. There was a searing heat in the dark eyes he had fixed on Elena.

"Of course I do!" Elena flashed back, feeling heat in her cheeks. "But not as a slave, dragged along behind you!"

"That's the only way humans get into the Dark Dimension," Damon said flatly. "Tied or chained, as a vampire's or kitsune's or demon's property."

Meredith was shaking her head. "You never told us—"

"I told you that you wouldn't like the way in!"

Even while answering Meredith, Damon's eyes never left Elena. Underneath his outward coldness, he seemed to be pleading with her to understand, she thought. In the old days, she thought, he'd have just lounged against a wall and raised his eyebrows and said, "Fine; I didn't want to go anyway. Who's for a picnic?"

But Damon did want them to go, Elena realised. He was desperate for them to go. He just didn't know any honest way of conveying that. The only way he knew was to—

"You have to make us a promise, Damon," she said, looking him directly in the eyes. "And it has to be before we make the decision to go or not."

She could see the relief in his eyes, even if to the other girls it might seem as if his face was perfectly cold and impassive. She knew he was glad she wasn't saying that her previous decision was final, and that was that. "What promise?" Damon asked.

"You have to swear – to give your word – that no matter what we decide now or in the Dark Dimension, you won't try to Influence us. You won't put us to sleep by mind control, or nudge us to do what you want. You won't use *any* vampire tricks on our minds."

Damon wouldn't be Damon if he didn't argue. "But, look, suppose the time comes when you want me to do that? There are some things there that it might be better for you to sleep through—"

"Then we'll tell you we've changed our minds, and we'll release you from the promise. You see? There's no downside. You just have to swear."

"All right," Damon said, still holding her gaze. "I swear I won't use any kind of Power on your minds; I won't Influence you in any way, until you ask me to. I give my word."

"Right." At last Elena broke the stare down with the tiniest of smiles and nods. And Damon gave her an almost imperceptible nod in return.

She turned away to find herself looking into Bonnie's

searching brown gaze.

"Elena," Bonnie whispered, tugging on her arm. "Come here for a sec, OK?" Elena could hardly help it. Bonnie was strong as a small Welsh pony. Elena went, casting a powerless look over her shoulder at Damon as she did.

"What?" she whispered when Bonnie finally stopped dragging her. Meredith had come along as well, figuring it might be sisterhood business. "Well?"

"Elena," Bonnie burst out, as if unable to hold the words back any longer, "the way you and Damon act – it's different than it used to be. You didn't used to . . . I mean, what *really* happened between you two when you were alone together?"

"This is hardly the time for that," Elena hissed. "We're having a big problem here, in case you hadn't noticed."

"But – what if—"

Meredith took up the unfinished sentence, pushing a dark lock of hair out of her eyes. "What if it's something Stefan doesn't like? Like 'what happened with Damon when you were alone in the motel that night'?" she finished, quoting Bonnie's words.

Bonnie's mouth fell open. "What motel? What night? *What happened?*" she almost shrieked, causing Meredith to try to quiet her and get bitten for her pains.

Elena looked at first one and then the other of her two friends – the two friends who had come to die with her if necessary. She could feel her breath come short. It was so unfair, but . . . "Can we just discuss this later?" she suggested, trying to convey with her eyes and eyebrows *Damon can hear us!*

Bonnie merely whispered, "What motel? What night? What—"

Elena gave up. "*Nothing* happened," she said flatly.

"Meredith is only quoting *you*, Bonnie. You said those words last night while you were asleep. And maybe sometime in the future you'll tell us what you're talking about, because *I don't know*."

She finished by looking at Meredith, who just raised one perfect eyebrow. "You're right," Meredith said, completely undeceived. "The English language could use a word like 'sa'. It would make these conversations so much shorter, for one thing."

Bonnie sighed. "Well, then, I'll find out for myself," she said. "You may not think I can, but I *will*."

"OK, OK, but meanwhile does anyone have anything helpful to say about Damon's rope stuff?"

"Such as, do we tell him where to stuff it?" Meredith suggested under her breath.

Bonnie was holding a length of rope. She ran a small, fair-skinned hand over it.

"I don't think this was bought in anger," she said, her brown eyes unfocusing and her voice taking on the slightly eerie tone it always did when she was in trance. "I see a boy and a girl, over a counter at a hardware store – and she's laughing, and the boy says, 'I'll bet you anything that you're going to school next year to be an architect,' and the girl gets all misty-eyed, and says, yes, and—"

"And that's all the psychic spying I care to hear today." Damon had come right up to them without making a sound. Bonnie jumped violently, and almost dropped the rope.

"Listen," Damon continued harshly, "just a hundred metres away is the final crossing. Either you wear these and you *act* like slaves or you don't get in to help Stefan. Ever. That's *it*."

Silently, the girls conferred with their eyes. Elena

knew that her own expression said clearly that she wasn't asking either Bonnie or Meredith to go with her, but that she herself was going if it required crawling behind Damon on her hands and knees.

Meredith, looking directly into Elena's eyes, slowly shut her own and nodded, letting out her breath. Bonnie was nodding her head already, resigned.

In silence, Bonnie and Meredith let Elena tie their wrists in front of them. Elena then let Damon tie her wrists and thread a long rope between the three of them, as if they were a chain gang of prisoners.

Elena could feel a flush coming up from below her chest to burn in her cheeks. She couldn't meet Damon's eyes, not this way, but she knew without asking that Damon was thinking about the time that Stefan had dismissed him from his apartment like a dog, in front of just this audience, plus Matt.

Vengeful cad, Elena thought as hard as she could in Damon's direction. She knew the last word would hurt the most. Damon prided himself on being a gentleman . . .

But "gentlemen" don't go into the Dark Dimension, Damon's voice in her head said mockingly.

"All right," Damon added aloud, and took the lead rope in one hand. He started walking briskly into the darkness of the cave, the three girls crowding and stumbling behind him.

Elena would never forget that brief journey, and she knew neither Bonnie nor Meredith would either. They walked across the shallow opening of the cave and into the small opening in the back, which gaped like a mouth. It took some manoeuvring to get the three of them into it. On the other side the cavern flared out again, and they were in a large cavern. At least that was what

Elena's enhanced senses told her. The everlasting fog had returned and Elena had no idea which way they were going.

Only a few minutes later a building reared up out of the thick fog.

Elena didn't know what she had been expecting from the Demon Gate. Possibly huge ebony doors, carved with serpents and encrusted with jewels. Maybe a rough-hewn, weathered colossus of stone, like the Egyptian pyramids. Perhaps even some sort of futuristic energy field that flickered and flashed with blue-violet lasers.

What she saw instead looked like a ramshackle depot of some kind, a place for holding and shipping goods. There was an empty pen, heavily fenced, topped with barbed wire. It stank, and Elena was glad that she and Damon had not channelled power to her nose.

Then there were people, men and women in fine clothes, each with a key in one hand, murmuring something before opening a door in one side of the building. The same door – but Elena would bet anything that they weren't all going to the same place, if the keys were like the one she had briefly "borrowed" from Shinichi's house a week or so ago. One of the ladies looked as if she were dressed for a fancy masquerade, with fox ears that blended into her long auburn hair. It was only when Elena saw under her ankle-length dress the swishing of a fox tail that she realised that the woman was a kitsune making use of the Demon Gate.

Damon hastily – and none too gently – led them to the other side of the building, where a broken-hinged door opened into a dilapidated room that, strangely, seemed larger on the inside than on the outside. All sorts of things were being bartered or sold here: many looked as if they had to do with the management of slaves.

Elena, Meredith and Bonnie looked at one another, round-eyed. Obviously, people bringing wild slaves in from the outside considered torture and terror all in a day's work.

"Passage for four," Damon said briefly to the slump-shouldered but heavyset man behind the counter.

"Three savages all at once?" The man, eyes devouring what he could see of the three girls, turned to look at Damon suspiciously.

"What can I say? My job is also my hobby." Damon stared him straight in the eyes.

"Yeh, but . . ." The man laughed. "Lately we bin gettin' maybe one or two a month."

"They're legally mine. No kidnappings. Kneel," Damon added casually to the three girls.

It was Meredith who got it first and sank to the ground like a ballet dancer. Her dark, dark grey eyes were focused on something no one but she could see. Then Elena somehow untangled the single syllable from the others. She focused her mind on Stefan and pretended she was kneeling to kiss him on his prison pallet. It seemed to work; she was down.

But Bonnie was up. The most dependent, the softest, the most innocent member of the triumvirate found that her knees had gone solid.

"Redheads, eh?" the man said, eyeing Damon sharply even as he smirked. "Maybe you'd better buy a little tingler for that one."

"Maybe," Damon said tightly. Bonnie just looked at him blankly, looked at the girls on the ground and then threw herself into a prostrate position. Elena could hear her sobbing softly. "But I've found that a firm voice and a disapproving look actually work better."

The man gave up and slumped again. "Passage for

four," he grunted and reached up and pulled on a dirty bell rope. By this time Bonnie was weeping in fear and humiliation, but no one seemed to notice, except the other girls.

Elena didn't dare to try to comfort her telepathically; that wouldn't fit in with the aura of a "normal human girl" at all, and who knew what traps or devices might be hidden here in addition to the man who kept undressing them over and over with his eyes? She just wished she could call up one of her Wings attacks, right here in this room. That would wipe the smug look off the man's face.

A moment later, something else wiped it off as completely as she could have desired. Damon leaned across the counter and whispered something to him that turned the slumped man's leering face a sickly colour of green.

Did you hear what he said? Elena communicated this to Meredith using her eyes and eyebrows.

Meredith, her own eyes crinkling, positioned her hand in front of Elena's abdomen, then made a twisting, ripping motion.

Even Bonnie smiled.

Then Damon led them to wait outside the depot. They had only been standing a few minutes when Elena's new vision spotted a boat gliding silently through the mist. She realised that the building must be on the very bank of a river, but even with Power directed solely to her eyes she could barely make out where the non-reflective land gave way to shining water, and even with Power directed solely to her ears she could barely hear the sound of swift deep water running.

The boat stopped – somehow. Elena couldn't see any anchor dropped or anything to fasten it to. But the fact was that it did stop, and the slumped man put down a plank, which stayed in place as they boarded: first Damon, and then his bevy of "slaves".

On board, Elena watched Damon wordlessly offer six pieces of gold to the ferryman – two for each human who presumably wouldn't be coming back, she thought.

For a moment she was lost in the memory of being very young – only three or so, she must have been – and sitting on her father's lap while he read to her from a wonderfully illustrated book about the Greek myths. It told about the ferryman, Charon, who took spirits of the deceased over the river Styx to the land of the dead. And her father telling her that the Greeks put coins on the eyes of those who died so they could pay the ferryman . . .

There's no coming back from this journey! she thought suddenly and violently. No escape! They might as well be truly dead . . .

Strangely, it was horror that saved her from this morass of terror. Just as she lifted her head, perhaps to scream, the dim figure of the ferryman turned from his duties briefly as if to look back over the passengers. Elena heard Bonnie's shriek. Meredith, shaking, was frantically and illogically reaching for the bag in which her gun was stowed. Even Damon didn't seem to be able to move.

The tall spectre in the boat had no face.

He had deep depressions where his eyes should be, a shallow hollow for a mouth, and a triangular hole where his nose should have protruded. The uncanny horror of it, on top of the stink from the depot pens, was simply too much for Bonnie, and she slumped sideways, limp against Meredith, in a faint.

Elena, in the midst of her terror, had a moment of revelation. In the dim, moist, dripping twilight, she had forgotten to stop trying to use all her senses to their fullest. She was undoubtedly better able to see the inhuman face of the ferryman than, say, Meredith. She could also *hear* things, like the sounds of long-dead miners tapping at the rock above them, and the scurrying of enormous bats or cockroaches or something, *inside* the stone walls all around them.

But now, Elena suddenly felt warm tears on her icy cheeks as she realised that she had completely underestimated Bonnie for as long as she'd known about her friend's psychic powers. If Bonnie's senses were permanently open to the kinds of horrors Elena was experiencing now, it was no wonder that Bonnie lived in fear. Elena found herself promising to be a hell of a lot more tolerant the next time Bonnie faltered or started screaming. In fact, Bonnie deserved some kind of an award for keeping a grip on sanity this far, Elena decided. But Elena didn't dare do any more than gaze at her friend, who was completely unconscious, and swear to herself that from now on Bonnie would find a champion in Elena Gilbert.

That promise and the warmth of it burned like a candle in Elena's mind, a candle she pictured held by Stefan, the light of it dancing in his green eyes and playing over the planes of his face. It was just enough to keep her from losing her own sanity on the rest of the journey.

By the time the boat docked – at a place just slightly more travelled than the one where they had embarked – all three of the girls were in a state of exhaustion brought on by prolonged terror and wrenching suspense.

But they hadn't really used the time to think over the words "Dark Dimension" or to imagine the number of ways its darkness might be manifested.

"Our new home," Damon said grimly. Watching him

instead of the landscape, Elena realised from the tension in his neck and shoulders that Damon was not enjoying himself. She'd thought he'd be heading into his own particular paradise, this world of human slaves, and torture for entertainment, whose only rule was self-preservation of the individual ego. Now she realised that she had been wrong. For Damon this was a world of beings with Powers as great or greater than his own. He was going to have to claw out a foothold here among them, just like any urchin on the street – except that he couldn't afford to make any mistakes. They needed to find a way not just to live, but to live in luxury and mingle with high society, if they were to have any chance to rescue Stefan.

Stefan – no, she couldn't allow *herself* the luxury of thinking about him at that time. Once she started she would become undone, begin to demand ridiculous things, like that they go round to the prison, just to stare at it, like a junior high kid with a crush on an older boy, who just wanted to be driven "by *his* house" to worship it. And then what would that do to their plans for a jailbreak later? Plan A was: *don't make mistakes*, and Elena would stick to that until she found a better one.

That was how Damon and his "slaves" came to the Dark Dimension, through the Demon Gate. The smallest one needed to be revived with water in the face before she could get up and walk.

CHAPTER

15

Hurrying behind Damon, Elena tried not to look either to the left or the right. She could see too much of what to Meredith and Bonnie must have appeared to be featureless darkness.

There were depots on either side, places where slaves were obviously brought to be bought or sold or transported later. Elena could hear the whimpers of children in the darkness and if she hadn't been so frightened herself, she would have rushed off looking for the crying kids.

But I can't do that, because I'm a slave now, she thought, with a sense of shock that ran up from her fingertips. I'm not a real human being any more. I'm a piece of property.

She found herself once again staring at the back of Damon's head and wondering how on earth she had talked herself into this. She understood what being a slave meant – in fact she seemed to have an intuitive understanding of it that surprised her – and it was Not a Good Thing to Be.

It meant that she could be . . . well, that anything could be done to her and it was no one's business but that of her owner. And her owner (*how* had he talked her into this again?) was Damon, of all people.

He could sell all three girls – Elena, Meredith and Bonnie – and be out of here in an hour with the profits.

They hurried through this area of the docks, the girls with their eyes on their feet to prevent themselves from stumbling.

And then they crested a hill. Below them, in a sort of crater-shaped formation, was a city.

The slums were on the edges, and crowded almost up to where they were standing. But there was a chicken-wire fence in front of them, which kept them isolated even while allowing them a bird's-eye view of the city. If they had still been in the cave they had entered, this would have been the greatest underground cavern imaginable – but they weren't underground any more.

"It happened sometime during the ferry ride," Damon said. "We made – well – a twist in space, say." He tried to explain and Elena tried to understand. "You went in through the Demon Gate, and when you came out you were no longer in Earth's Dimension, but in another one entirely." Elena only had to look up at the sky to believe him. The constellations were different; there was no Little or Big Dipper, no North Star.

Then there was the sun. It was much larger, but much dimmer than Earth's, and it never left the horizon. At any moment about half of it showed, day and night – terms which, as Meredith pointed out, had lost their rational meaning here.

As they approached a gate made of chicken wire

that would finally let them out of the slave-holding area, they were stopped by what Elena would later learn was a Guardian.

She would learn that in a way, the Guardians were the rulers of the Dark Dimension, although they themselves came from another place far away and it was almost as if they had permanently occupied this little slice of Hell, trying to impose order on the slum king and feudal lords who divided the city among themselves.

This Guardian was a tall woman with hair the colour of Elena's own – true gold – cut square at shoulder length, and she paid no attention at all to Damon but immediately asked Elena, who was first in line behind him, "Why are you here?"

Elena was glad, very glad, that Damon had taught her to control her aura. She concentrated on that while her brain hummed at supersonic speed, wondering what the right response to this question was. The response that would leave them free and not get them sent home.

Damon didn't train us for this, was her first thought. And her second was, no, because he's never been here before. He doesn't know how everything works here, only some things.

And if it looked as if this woman was going to try to interfere with him, he might just go crazy and attack her, a helpful little voice added from somewhere in Elena's subconscious. Elena doubled the speed of her scheming. Creative lying had once been a sort of speciality of hers, and now she said the first thing that popped into her head and got a thumbs-up: "I gambled with him and lost."

Well, it sounded good. People lost all sorts of things when they gambled: plantations, talismans, horses, castles, bottles of genii. And if it turned out not to be enough of a reason, she could always say that that was just the start of her sad story. Best of all, it was in a way, true. Long ago she'd given her life for Damon as well as for Stefan, and Damon had not exactly turned over a new leaf as she'd requested. Half a leaf, maybe. A leaflet.

The Guardian was staring at her with a puzzled look in her true blue eyes. People had stared at Elena all her life – being young and very beautiful meant that you fretted only when people didn't stare. But the puzzlement was a bit of a worry. Was the tall woman reading her mind? Elena tried to add another layer of white noise at the top. What came out was a few lines of a Britney Spears song. She turned the psychic volume up.

The tall woman put two fingers to her head like someone with a sudden headache. Then she looked at Meredith.

"Why . . . are you here?"

Usually Meredith didn't lie at all, but when she did she treated it as an intellectual art. Fortunately, she also never tried to fix something that wasn't broken. "The same for me," she said sadly.

"And you?" The woman was looking at Bonnie, who was looking as if she were going to be sick again.

Meredith gave Bonnie a little nudge. Then she stared at her hard. Elena stared at her harder, knowing that all Bonnie had to do was mumble "Me, too." And Bonnie was a good "me, too-er" after Meredith had staked out a position.

The problem was that Bonnie was also either in trance, or so close to it that it didn't matter.

"Shadow Souls," Bonnie said.

The woman blinked, but not the way you blink when someone says something totally unresponsive. She blinked in astonishment.

Oh, God, Elena thought. Bonnie's got their password or something. She's making predictions or prophesying or whatever.

"Shadow ... souls?" the Guardian said, watching Bonnie closely.

"The city is full of them," Bonnie said miserably.

The Guardian's fingers danced over what looked like a palmtop computer. "We know that. This is the place they come."

"Then you should stop it."

"We have only limited jurisdiction. The Dark Dimension is ruled by a dozen factions of overlords, who have slumlords to carry out their orders."

Bonnie, Elena thought, trying to cut through Bonnie's mental haze even at the cost of the Guardian hearing her. *These are the* police.

At the same moment, Damon took over. "She's the same as the others," he said. "Except that she's psychic."

"No one asked your opinion," the Guardian snapped at him, without even glancing in Damon's direction. "I don't care what kind of bigwig you are down there" – she jerked her head contemptuously at the city of lights – "you're on my turf behind this fence. And I'm asking the little redhaired girl: is what he is saying the truth?"

Elena had a moment of panic. After all they'd been through, if Bonnie blew it now . . .

This time Bonnie blinked. Whatever else she was trying to communicate, it was true that she was the same as Meredith and Elena. And it was true that she was psychic. Bonnie was a terrible liar when she had too much time to think about things, but to this she could say without hesitation, "Yes, that's true."

The Guardian stared at Damon.

Damon stared back as if he could do it all night. He

was a champion out-starer.

And the Guardian waved them away.

"I suppose even a psychic can have a bad day," she said, then added to Damon, "Take care of them. You realise that all psychics have to be licenced?"

Damon, with his best *grand seigneur* manner, said, "Madam, these are not professional psychics. They are my private assistants."

"And I'm not a 'Madam'; I'm addressed as 'Your Judgement.' By the way, people addicted to gambling usually come to horrible ends here."

Ha, ha, Elena thought. If she only knew what *kind* of gamble we all are taking . . . well, we'd probably be worse off than Stefan is right now.

Outside the fence was a courtyard. There were litters here, as well as rickshaws and small goatcarts. No carriages, no horses. Damon got two litters, one for himself and Elena and one for Meredith and Bonnie.

Bonnie, still looking confused, was staring at the sun. "You mean it never finishes rising?"

"No," Damon said patiently. "And it's setting here, not rising. Perpetual twilight in the City of Darkness itself. You'll see more as we move along. Don't touch that," he added, as Meredith moved to untie the rope around Bonnie's wrists before either of them got on the litter. "You two can take the ropes off in the litter if you draw the curtains, but don't lose them. You're still slaves, and you have to wear something symbolic around your arms to show it – even if it's just matching bracelets. Otherwise I get in trouble. Oh, and you'll have to go veiled in the city."

"We – *what*?" Elena flashed a look of disbelief at him.

Damon just flashed back a 250-kilowatt smile and

before Elena could say another word, he was drawing gauzy sheer fabrics from his black bag and handing them out. The veils were of a size to cover an entire body.

"But you only have to put it on your head or tie it on your hair or something," Damon said dismissively.

"What's it made of?" Meredith asked, feeling the light silky material, which was transparent and so thin that the wind threatened to whip it from her fingers.

"How should I know?"

"It's different colours on the other side!" Bonnie discovered, letting the wind transform her pale-green veil into a shimmering silver. Meredith was shaking out a dramatic deep-violet silk into a mysterious dark blue dotted with a myriad of stars. Elena, who had been expecting her own veil to be blue, found herself looking up at Damon. He was holding a tiny square of cloth in a clenched fist.

"Let's see how good you've gotten," he murmured, nodding her closer to him. "Guess what colour."

Another girl might only have noticed the sloe-black eyes and the pure, carven lines of Damon's face, or maybe the wild, wicked smile – somehow wilder and sweeter than ever here, like a rainbow in the middle of a hurricane. But Elena also made note of the stiffness in his neck and shoulders – places where tension built up. The Dark Dimension was already taking its toll on him, psychically, even as he mocked it.

She wondered how many soundings of Power by the merely curious he was having to block each second. She was about to offer to help by opening herself up to the eldritch world, when he snapped, "Guess!" in a tone that didn't make it a suggestion.

"Gold," Elena said instantly, surprising herself. When she reached to take the golden square from his hand a powerful, pleasurable feeling of electric current shot from her palm up her arm and seemed to skewer her straight through the heart. Damon clung to her fingers briefly as she took the square and Elena found she could still feel electricity pulsing from his fingertips.

The underside of her veil blew out white and sparkling as if set with diamonds. God, maybe they *were* diamonds, she thought. How could you tell with Damon?

"Your wedding veil, perhaps?" Damon murmured, lips close to her ear. The rope around Elena's wrists had come very loose and she stroked the diaphanous fabric helplessly, feeling the tiny jewels on the white side cool to the touch of her fingers.

"How did you know you'd need all this stuff?" Elena asked, with bruising practicality. "You didn't know everything, but you seemed to know enough."

"Oh, I did research in bars and other places. I found a few people who'd been here and had managed to get out again – or who had gotten kicked out." Damon's wild grin grew even wilder. "At night while you were asleep. At a little hidden store, I got *those*." He nodded at her veil, and added, "You don't have to wear that over your face or anything. Press it to your hair and it will cling to it."

Elena did so, wearing the gold side out. It fell to her heels. She fingered her veil, already able to see the flirtatious possibilities in it, as well as the dismissive ones. If only she could get this damned rope off her wrists . . .

After a moment, Damon retreated back into the persona of the imperturbable master and said, "For all our sakes, we ought to be strict about these things. The slum lords and nobility who run this abominable mess they call the Dark Dimension know that it's only two days away from revolution at any time, and if we add anything to the balance they're going to Make a Public Example of Us."

"All right," Elena said. "Here, hold my string and I'll get on the litter."

But there wasn't much point in the rope, not once they were both sitting in the same litter. It was carried by four men – not big men, but wiry ones, and all of the same height, which made for a smooth ride.

If Elena had been a free citizen, she would never have allowed herself to be carried by four people whom (she assumed) were slaves. In fact, she would have made a big noisy fuss over it. But that talk she'd had with herself at the docks had sunk in. *She* was a slave, even if Damon hadn't paid anyone to buy her. She didn't have the right to make a big noisy fuss about *anything*. In this crimson, evil-smelling place she could imagine that her fuss might even make problems for the litter bearers themselves – make their owner or whoever ran the litter-bearing business punish them, as if it were their fault.

Best Plan A for now: Keep Mouth Shut.

There was plenty to see anyway, now that they had passed on a bridge over bad-smelling slums and alleys full of tumbledown houses. Shops began to appear, at first heavily barred and made of unpainted stone, then more respectable buildings, and then suddenly they were winding their way through a bazaar. But even here the stamp of poverty and weariness appeared on too many faces. Elena had expected, if anything, a cold, black, antiseptic city with emotionless vampires and fire-eyed demons walking the streets. Instead, everyone she saw looked human, and they were selling things – from medicines to food and drink – that vampires didn't need.

Well, maybe the kitsune and the demons need them, Elena reasoned, shuddering at the idea of what a demon might want to eat. On the street corners were hard-faced, scantily clad girls and boys, and tattered, haggard people holding pathetic signs: A MEMORY FOR A MEAL.

"What do they mean?" Elena asked Damon, but he didn't answer her immediately.

"This is how the free humans of the city spend most of their time," he said. "So remember that, before you start going on one of your crusades—"

Elena wasn't listening. She was staring at one of the holders of such a sign. The man was horribly thin, with a straggly beard and bad teeth, but worse was his look of vacant despair. Every so often he would hold out a trembling hand on which there was a small, clear ball, which he balanced on his palm, muttering, "A summer's day when I was young. A summer's day for a ten-geld piece." As often as not there was no one near when he said this.

Elena slipped off a lapis ring Stefan had given her and held it toward him. She didn't want to annoy Damon by getting out of the litter, and she had to say, "Come here, please," while holding the ring towards the bearded man.

He heard, and came to the litter quickly enough. Elena saw something move in his beard – lice, perhaps – and she forced herself to stare at the ring as she said, "Take it. Quickly, please."

The old man stared at the ring as if it were a banquet. "I don't have change," he moaned, bringing up his hand and wiping his mouth with his sleeve. He seemed about to drop to the ground unconscious. "I don't have change!"

"I don't want change!" Elena said through the huge swelling that had formed in her throat. "Take the ring. Hurry or I'll drop it."

He snatched it from her fingers as the litter bearers

started forward again. "May the *Guardians* bless you, lady," he said, trying to keep up with the litter bearer's trot. "Hear me who may! May *They* bless you!"

"You really shouldn't," Damon said to Elena when the voice had died away behind them. "He's not going to get a meal with that, you know."

"He was hungry," Elena said softly. She couldn't explain that he reminded her of Stefan, not just now. "It was *my* ring," she added defensively. "I suppose you're going to say he'll spend it on alcohol or drugs."

"No, but he won't get a meal with it, either. He'll get a banquet."

"Well, so much the—"

"In his imagination. He'll get a dusty orb with some old vampire's memory of a Roman feast, or someone from the city's memory of a modern one. Then he'll play it over and over as he slowly starves to death."

Elena was appalled. "Damon! Quick! I have to go back and find him—"

"You can't, I'm afraid." Lazily, Damon held up a hand. He had a firm grip on her rope. "Besides, he's long gone."

"How can he do that? How could anyone do that?"

"How can a lung cancer patient refuse to quit smoking? But I agree that those orbs can be the most addictive substances of all. Blame the kitsune for bringing their star balls here and making them the most popular form of obsession."

"Star balls? Hoshi no tama?" Elena gasped.

Damon stared at her, looking equally surprised. "You *know* about them?"

"All I know is what Meredith researched. She said that kitsune were often portrayed with either keys" – she raised her eyebrows at him – "or with star balls. And that myths say they can put some or all of their power in the ball, so that if you find it, you can control the kitsune. She and Bonnie want to find Misao's or Shinichi's star balls and have control over them."

"Be still, my unbeating heart," Damon said dramatically, but the next second he was all business. "Remember what that old guy said? A summer's day for a meal? He was talking about *this*." Damon picked up the little marble that the old man had dropped on the litter and held it to Elena's temple.

The world disappeared.

Damon was gone. The sights and sounds – yes, and the smells – of the bazaar were gone. She was sitting on green grass which rippled in a slight breeze and she was looking at a weeping willow that bent down to a stream that was copper and deep, deep green at once. There was some sweet scent in the air – honeysuckle, freesia? Something delicious that stirred Elena as she leaned back to gaze at picture-perfect white clouds rolling in a cerulean sky.

She felt – she didn't know how to say it. She felt young, but somewhere in her mind she knew that she was actually younger than this alien personality that had taken hold of her. Still, she felt excited that it was springtime and every golden-green leaf, every springy little reed, every weightless white cloud seemed to be rejoicing with her.

Then suddenly her heart was pounding. She had just caught the sound of a footfall behind her. In one springing joyous moment she was on her feet, arms held out in the extremity of her love, the wild devotion she felt for this . . .

. . . this young girl? Something inside the sphere user's brain seemed to fall back in bewilderment. Most of it, though, was taken up with cataloguing the perfections of the girl who had crept up so lightly in the waving grass: the clustering dark curls at her neck, the flashing green eyes below arching brows, the smooth glowing skin of her cheeks as she laughed with her lover, pretending to run away on feet as light as any elf's . . .!

Pursued and pursuer both fell down together on the soft carpet of long grass . . . and then things quickly got so steamy that Elena, the distant mind in the background, began wondering how on earth you made one of these things *stop*. Every time she put her hand to her temple, groping, she was caught and kissed breathless by . . . Allegra . . . that was the girl, Allegra. And Allegra was certainly beautiful, especially through this particular viewer's eyes. The creamy soft skin of her . . .

And then, with a shock just as great as she'd felt when the bazaar disappeared, it appeared again. She was Elena; she was riding on the litter with Damon; there was a cacophony of sounds around her – and a thousand different smells, too. But she was breathing hard and part of her was still resounding with John – that had been his name – with John's love for Allegra.

"But I *still* don't understand," she almost keened.

"It's simple," Damon said. "You put a blank star ball of the size you like to your temple and you think back to the time you want to record. The star ball does the rest." He waved off her attempted interruption and leaned forward with mischief in those fathomless black eyes of his. "Perhaps you got an especially *warm* summer day?" he said, adding suggestively, "These litters do have curtains you can draw closed."

"Don't be silly, Damon," Elena said, but John's feelings had sparked her own, like flint and tinder. She didn't want to kiss Damon, she told herself sternly. She wanted to kiss Stefan. But since a moment ago she had been kissing *Allegra*, it didn't seem as strong an argument as it could be.

"I don't think," she began, still breathless, as Damon reached for her, "that this is a very good . . ."

With a smooth flick of the rope, Damon untied her hands completely. He would have pulled it off both wrists, but Elena immediately half turned, supporting herself with that hand. She needed the support.

In the circumstances, though, there was nothing more meaningful – or more . . . exciting . . . than what Damon had done.

He hadn't drawn the curtains, but Bonnie and Meredith were behind them on their own litter, out of sight. Certainly out of Elena's mind. She felt warm arms around her, and instinctively nestled into them. She felt a surge of pure love and appreciation for Damon, for his understanding that she could never do this as a slave with a master.

We're both of us unmastered, she heard in her head, and she remembered that when cooling down most of her psychic abilities she had forgotten to set the volume on low for this one. Oh, well, it might just come in handy. . . .

But we both enjoy worship, she replied telepathically, and felt his laughter on her lips as he admitted the truth of it. There was nothing sweeter in her life these days than Damon's kisses. She could drift like this for ever, forgetting the outside world. And that was a good thing, because she had the feeling that there was much depression in the outside and not too much happiness. But if she could always come back to this, this welcome, this sweetness, this ecstasy . . .

Elena jerked in the litter, throwing her weight back so

fast that the men carrying it almost fell in a heap.

"You bastard," she whispered venomously. They were still psychically entangled, and she was glad to see that through Damon's eyes she was like a vengeful Aphrodite: her golden hair lifting and whipping behind her like a thunderstorm, her eyes shining violet in her elemental fury.

And now, worst of all, this goddess turned her face away from him. "Not one day," she said. "You couldn't even keep your promise for a single day!"

"I didn't! I didn't Influence you, Elena!"

"Don't call me that. We have a professional relationship now. I call you 'Master'. You can call me 'Slave' or 'Dog' or whatever you want."

"If we have the professional relationship of master and slave," Damon said, his eyes dangerous, "then I can just order you to—"

"Try it!" Elena lifted her lips in what really wasn't a smile. "Why don't you do that, and see just what happens?"

CHAPTER

16

Damon clearly decided to throw himself on the mercy of the court, and looked piteous and a little unbalanced, which he could easily do whenever he wanted. "I really didn't try to Influence you," he repeated, but then hastily added, "Maybe I can just change the subject for a while – tell you more about the star balls."

"That," Elena said in her most frosty voice, "might be a rather good idea."

"Well, the balls make recordings directly from your neurons, you see? Your neurons in your brain. Everything you've ever experienced is there in your mind somewhere, and the ball just draws it out."

"So you can always remember it and watch it over and over like a movie, too?" Elena said, twiddling with her veil to shade her face from him, and thinking that she would give a star ball to Alaric and Meredith before their wedding.

"No," Damon said rather grimly. "*Not* like that. For one thing, the memory is gone from you – these are kitsune toys we're talking about, remember? Once the star ball has taken it from your neurons, *you* don't remember a thing about the event. Second, the 'recording' on the star ball gradually fades – with use, with time, with some other factors nobody understands. But the ball gets cloudier, and the sensations weaker, until finally it's just an empty crystal sphere."

"But – that poor man was selling a day of his *life*. A wonderful day! I should think he would want to keep it."

"You saw him."

"Yes." Once again Elena saw the louse-ridden, haggard, grey-faced old man. She felt something like ice down her spine at the thought that he had once been the laughing, joyous, young John that she had experienced. "Oh, how sad," she said, and she wasn't talking about memory.

But, for once, Damon hadn't followed her thoughts. "Yes," he said. "There are a lot of the poor and the old here. They worked themselves free of slavery, or had a generous owner die . . . and then this is where they end up."

"But the star balls? Are they just made for poor people? The rich ones can just travel to Earth and see a real summer day for themselves, right?"

Damon laughed without much humour. "Oh, no, they can't. Most of them are *bound* here."

He said *bound* oddly. Elena ventured, "Too busy to go on vacation?"

"Too busy, too powerful to get through the wards protecting Earth from them, too worried about what their enemies will do while they're gone, too physically decrepit, too notorious, too dead."

"*Dead?*" The horror of the tunnel and the corpse-smelling fog seemed ready to envelop Elena.

Damon flashed one of his evil smiles. "Forgot that your boyfriend is *de mortius*? Not to mention your honourable master? Most people, when they die, go to another level than this – much higher or much lower. This is the place for the bad ones, but it's the upper level. Farther down – well, nobody wants to go there."

"Like Hell?" Elena breathed. "We're in Hell?"

"More like Limbo, at least where we are. Then there's the Other Side." He nodded towards the horizon where the lowering sun still sat. "The other city, which may have been where you went on your 'vacation' to the afterlife. Here they just call it 'The Other Side'. But I can tell you two rumours I heard from my informants. There, they call it the Celestial Court. And there, the sky is crystal blue and the sun is always rising."

"The Celestial Court . . ." Elena forgot that she was speaking aloud. She knew instinctively that it was the queens-and-knights-and-sorceresses kind of court, not a court of law. It would be like Camelot. Just saying the words brought up an aching nostalgia, and – not memories, but the tip-of-the-tongue feeling that memories were locked right behind a door. It was a door, however, that was securely locked, and all Elena could see through the keyhole were ranks of more women like the Guardians, tall, golden-haired and blue-eyed, and one – child-sized among the grown women – who glanced up, and, piercingly, from a long way off, met Elena's gaze directly.

The litter was moving out of the bazaar into more slums, which Elena took in with darting quick glances on either side of her, hiding in her veil. They seemed like any earthly slums, barrios or favella – only worse. Children, their hair turned red by the sun, crowded around Elena's litter, their hands held out in a gesture with universal meaning.

Elena felt a tearing at her insides that she had nothing of real value to give them. She wanted to build houses here, make sure these children had food and clean water, and education, and a future to look forward to. Since she had no idea how to give them any of these things, she watched them dash off with treasures such as her Juicy Fruit gum, her comb, her minibrush, her lip gloss, her water bottle and her earrings.

Damon shook his head, but didn't stop her until she began fumbling with a lapis and diamond pendant Stefan had given her. She was crying as she tried to disengage the clasp when suddenly the last bit of the rope around her wrist came up short.

"No more," Damon said. "You don't understand anything. We haven't even entered the city proper yet. Why don't you have a look at the architecture instead of worrying about useless brats who're likely to die anyway?"

"That's cold," Elena said, but she couldn't think of any way to make him understand, and she was too angry with him to try.

Still, she stopped fumbling with the chain and looked beyond the slums as Damon had suggested. There she could see a breathtaking skyline, with buildings that seemed meant to last for eternity, made of stones that looked the way the Egyptian pyramids and Mayan ziggurats must have looked when they were new. Everything, though, was coloured red and black by a sun now concealed by sullen crimson cloudbanks. That huge red sun – it gave the air a different look for different moods. At times it seemed almost romantic, glinting on a large river Elena and Damon passed, picking out a thousand tiny wavelets in the slow-moving water. At other times, it simply seemed alien and ominous, showing clearly on the horizon like a monstrous omen, tingeing the buildings, no matter how magnificent, the colour of blood. When they turned away from it, as the litter bearers moved down into the city where the huge buildings were, Elena could see their own long and menacing black shadow thrown ahead of them.

"Well? What do you think?" Damon seemed to be trying to placate her.

"I still think it looks like Hell," Elena said slowly. "I'd hate to live here."

"Ah, but whoever said that we should live here, my Princess of Darkness? We'll go back home, where the night is velvet black and the moon shines down, making everything silver." Slowly, Damon traced one finger from her hand, up her arm to her shoulder. It sent an inner shiver through her.

She tried holding the veil up as a barrier against him, but it was too transparent. He still flashed that brilliant smile at her, dazzling through the diamond-dotted white – well, shell pink, of course, because of the light – that was on her side of the veil.

"Does this place have a moon?" she asked, trying to distract him. She was afraid – afraid of him – afraid of herself.

"Oh, yes: three or four of them, I think. But they're very small and of course the sun never goes down, so you can't see them as well. Not . . . romantic." He smiled at her again, slowly this time, and Elena looked away.

And in looking, she saw something in front of her that captured her entire attention. In a side street a cart had overturned, spilling large rolls made out of fur and leather. There was a thin, hungry-looking old woman attached to the cart like a beast, who was lying on the ground, and a tall angry man standing over her, raining down blows with a whip on her unprotected body.

The woman's face was turned towards Elena. It was contorted in a grimace of anguish, as she tried ineffectually to roll into a ball, her hands over her stomach. She was naked from the waist up, but as the whip lashed into her flesh, her body from throat to waist was being covered by a coating of blood.

Elena felt herself swelling with Wing Powers, but somehow none would come. She willed with all her circulating life-force for something – *anything* – to break free from her shoulders, but it was no good. Maybe it had something to do with wearing the remains of slave bracelets. Maybe it was Damon, beside her, telling her in a forceful voice not to get involved.

To Elena, his words were no more than punctuation to the heartbeat pounding in her ears. She jerked the rope sharply out of his hands, and then scrambled out of the litter. In six or seven leaps she was beside the man with the whip.

He was a vampire, his fangs elongated at the sight of the blood before him, but never stopping his frenzied lashing. He was too strong for Elena to handle, but . . .

With one more step Elena was straddling the woman, both her arms flung out in the universal gesture of protection and defiance. Rope dangled from one wrist.

The slave owner was not impressed. He was already launching the next whiplash, and it struck Elena across the cheek and simultaneously opened a great gap in her thin summer top, slicing through her camisole and scoring the flesh underneath. As she gasped, the tail of the whip cut through her jeans as if denim were butter.

Tears formed involuntarily in Elena's eyes, but she ignored them. She had managed not to make a sound other than that initial gasp. And she still stood exactly where she had first landed in protection. Elena could feel the wind whip at her tattered blouse, while her untouched veil waved behind her, as if to protect the poor slave who had collapsed against the ruined cart.

Elena was still desperately trying to bring out any kind of Wings. She wanted to fight with real weapons, and she had them, but she couldn't force them to save either her or the poor slave behind her. Even without them Elena knew one thing. That bastard in front of her wasn't going to touch his slave again, not unless he cut Elena into pieces first.

Someone stopped to stare, and someone else came out of a shop, running. When the children who'd been trailing her litter surrounded her, wailing, a crowd of sorts gathered.

Apparently it was one thing to see a merchant beating his worn-out drab – the people around here must have seen that almost daily. But to see this beautiful new girl having her clothes slashed away, this girl with hair like golden silk under a veil of gold and white, and eyes that perhaps reminded some of them of a barely remembered blue sky – that was quite another thing. Moreover, the new girl was obviously a fresh barbarian slave who had clearly humiliated her master by tearing the lead ropes from his hands and was standing now with her sanctity veil made into a mockery.

Terrific street theatre.

And even given all of that, the slave owner was preparing for another stroke, raising his arm high and preparing to put his back into it. A few people in the crowd gasped; others were muttering indignantly. Elena's new sense of hearing, turned up high, could catch their whispering. A girl like *this* wasn't meant for the slums at all; she must have been destined for the heart of the city. Her aura alone was enough to show that. In fact, with that golden hair and those vivid blue eyes, she might even be a Guardian from the Other Side. Who knew?

The lash that was raised never descended. Before it could, there was a flash of black lightning – pure Power – that sent half the crowd scattering. A vampire, young in appearance and dressed in the clothing of the upper world, Earth, had made his way to stand between the golden girl and the slave owner – or rather to loom over the now cringing slave owner. The few in the crowd not stirred by the girl immediately felt their hearts pulse at the sight of *him*. He was the girl's owner, surely, and now he would see to the situation.

At that instant, Bonnie and Meredith arrived on the scene. They were reclining on their litter, decorously draped in their veils, Meredith in starry midnight blue and Bonnie in soft pale green. They could have been an illustration for *The Arabian Nights*.

But the moment they saw Damon and Elena, they most indecorously jumped off the litter. By now the crowd was so thick that working their way to the front required using elbows and knees, but in only seconds they were at Elena's side, hands defiantly unbound or trailing rope that hung defiantly free, veils floating in the wind.

When they did arrive beside Elena, Meredith gasped. Bonnie's eyes opened wide and stayed that way. Elena understood what they were seeing. Blood was flowing freely from the cut across her cheekbone and her blouse kept opening in the wind to reveal her torn and bloody camisole. One leg of her jeans was rapidly turning red.

But, drawn up into the protection of her shadow, was

a far more pitiful figure. And as Meredith raised Elena's diaphanous veil to help keep her blouse closed and once more enshroud her in decency, the woman herself raised her head, to look at the three girls with the eyes of a dumb and hunted animal.

Behind them, Damon said softly, "I shall quite enjoy this," as he lifted the heavy man into the air with one hand and then struck his throat like a cobra. There was a hideous scream, which went on and on.

No one tried to interfere, and no one tried to cheer the slave owner on to make a fight.

Elena, scanning the faces of the crowd, realised why. She and her friends had become used to Damon – or as used as you could become to his half-tamed air of ferocity. But these people were getting their first look at the young man dressed all in black, of medium height and slim build, who made up for his lack of bulging muscle with a supple and deadly grace. This was enhanced by the gift of somehow dominating all the space around him, so that he effortlessly became the focal point of any picture – the way a black panther might become the focal point if it were walking lazily down a crowded city street.

Even here, where menace and an aspect of outright evil were commonplace, this young man exuded a quality of danger that made people want to stay out of his line of sight, much less his way.

Meanwhile Elena and both Meredith and Bonnie were looking around for some sort of medical assistance, or even for something clean that would staunch wounds. After about a minute, they realised that it wasn't just going to appear, so Elena appealed to the crowd.

"Does anyone know a doctor? A healer?" she shouted. The audience merely watched her. They seemed loath to get involved with a girl who had obviously defied the black-clad demon now wringing the slave owner's neck.

"So you all think it's just fine," Elena shouted, hearing the loss of control, the disgust and fury in her own voice, "for a bastard like that to be whipping a starving pregnant woman?"

There were a few downcast eyes, a few scattered replies on the theme of "He was her master, wasn't he?" But one youngish man who had been leaning against a stopped wagon, straightened up. "Pregnant?" he repeated. "She doesn't look pregnant!"

"She is!"

"Well," the young man said slowly, "if that's true, he's only harming his own merchandise." He glanced nervously over to where Damon was now standing above the deceased slave owner, whose face was cast into a ghastly death grimace of agony.

This still left Elena with no help for a woman she was afraid was about to die. "Doesn't *anyone* know where I can find a doctor?" There were now mutterings in various tones from the crowd members.

"We might get further on if we could offer them some money," Meredith was saying. Elena immediately reached for her pendant, but Meredith was quicker, unfastening a fancy amethyst necklace from around her neck and holding it up. "This goes to whoever shows us a good doctor first."

There was a pause while everyone seemed to be assessing the reward and the risk. "Don't you have any star balls?" a wheezing voice asked, but a high, light voice cried, "That's good enough for *me*!"

A child – yes, a genuine street urchin – darted to the front of the crowd, grabbed Elena's hand and pointed, saying, "Dr Meggar, right up the street. It's only a couple of blocks; we can walk it."

The child was wrapped in a tattered old dress, but that might only be to keep warm, because he or she was also wearing a pair of trousers. Elena couldn't even figure out whether it was a boy or a girl until the child gave her an unexpectedly sweet smile and whispered, "I'm Lakshmi."

"I'm Elena," Elena said.

"Better hurry, Elena," Lakshmi said. "Guardians will get here soon."

Meredith and Bonnie had gotten the dazed slave woman to her feet, but she seemed to be in too much pain to understand if they meant to help her or kill her.

Elena remembered how the woman had huddled in the shadow of Elena's own body. She put a hand on the woman's bloody arm and said quietly, "You're safe now. You're going to be fine. That man – your . . . your master – is dead and I *promise* that nobody will hurt you again. I swear it."

The woman stared at her in disbelief, as if what Elena was saying was impossible. As if living without being beaten constantly – even with all the blood Elena could see old scars, some of them like cords, on the woman's skin – was something too far from reality to imagine.

"I *swear* it," Elena said again, not smiling, but grimly. She understood that this was a burden she was taking on for life.

It's all right, she thought, and realised that for some time now she had been sending her thoughts to Damon. *I know what I'm doing. I'm ready to be responsible for this.*

Are you sure? Damon's voice came to her, as uncertain as she'd ever heard him. *Because I'm sure as hell not going to take care of some old hag when you get tired of her. I'm not even sure I'm ready to deal with whatever it's going to cost me for killing that bastard with the whip.*

Elena turned to look at him. He was serious. *Well, then why did you kill him?* she challenged.

Are you joking? Damon gave her a shock with the vehemence and venom of his thought. *He hurt you. I should have killed him more slowly,* he added, ignoring one of the litter bearers who was kneeling beside him, undoubtedly asking what to do next. Damon's eyes, however, were on Elena's face, on the blood still flowing from her cut. *Il figlio de cafone,* Damon thought, his lips drawing back from his teeth as he looked down on the corpse, so that even the litter bearer scurried away on hands and knees.

"Damon, don't let him leave! Bring them all over here right now—" Elena began, and then, as there was a sort of universal gasp around her, she continued non-verbally, *Don't let the litter bearers leave. We need a litter to carry this poor woman to the doctor. And why is everyone staring at me?*

Because you're a slave, and you've just done things no slave should do and now you're giving me, *your master, orders.* Damon's telepathic voice was grim.

It's not an order. It's a – look, any gentleman would help a lady in distress, right? Well, there are four of us over here and one is more distressed than you want to look at. No, three are. I think I'm going to need some stitches, and Bonnie is about to collapse. Elena was striking methodically at weak points, and knew that Damon knew she was doing it. But he ordered one of the sets of litter bearers to come and pick up the slave woman and the other to take his girls.

Elena stuck with the woman and ended up in a litter with the curtains all closed around it. The smell of blood was a copper taste in her mouth, making her want to cry. Even she didn't want to look closely at the slave woman's injuries, but blood was running onto the litter. She found herself taking off her blouse and camisole and putting back only the blouse so that she could use the camisole to hold to a great diagonal slash across the woman's chest. Every time the woman raised dark-brown, frightened eyes to her, Elena tried to smile at her encouragingly. They were down deep somewhere in the trenches of communication, where a look and a touch meant more than words.

Don't die, Elena was thinking. Don't die, just as you have something to live for. Live for your freedom, and for your baby.

And maybe some of what she was thinking got through to the woman, because she relaxed against the litter cushions, holding on to Elena's hand.

CHAPTER

17

"**H**er name's Ulma," a voice said, and Elena looked down to find Lakshmi holding back the curtains of the litter with a hand over her head. "Everybody knows Old Drohzne and his slaves. He beats 'em until they pass out and then expects 'em to pick up his rickshaw and go on carrying a load. He kills five or six a year."

"He didn't kill this one," Elena murmured. "He got what he deserved." She squeezed Ulma's hand.

She was vastly relieved when the litter stopped and Damon himself appeared, just as she was about to start bargaining with one of the litter bearers to carry Ulma in their arms to the doctor. Without regard for his clothing, Damon still somehow managed to convey disinterest even as he picked up the woman – Ulma – and nodded to Elena to follow him. Lakshmi skipped around him and took the lead into an intricately patterned stone courtyard and then down a crooked hallway with some solid, respectable-looking doors. Finally, she knocked on one and a wizened man with a huge head and the faintest remnant of a wispy beard opened the door cautiously.

"I don't keep any *ketterris* here! No *hexen*, no *zemeral*! And I don't do love spells!" Then, peering short-sightedly, he seemed to focus on the little group.

"Lakshmi?" he said.

"We've brought a woman who needs help," Elena said shortly. "She's pregnant, too. You're a doctor, aren't you? A healer?"

"A healer of some limited ability. Come in, come in."

The doctor was hurrying into a back room. They all followed him, Damon still carrying Ulma. Once she arrived, Elena saw that the healer was in the corner of what looked like a crowded wizard's sanctuary, with quite a bit of voodoo and witch doctor thrown in.

Elena, Meredith and Bonnie glanced at one another nervously, but then Elena heard water splashing and realised that the doctor was in the corner because there was a basin of water there, and the healer was washing his hands thoroughly, rolling his sleeves up to his elbows and making a lot of frothy bubbles. He might call himself a "healer", yet he did understand basic hygiene, she thought.

Damon had put Ulma onto what looked like a clean white-sheeted examining table. The doctor nodded to him. Then, *tch-tch*ing, he pulled out a tray of instruments and set Lakshmi about fetching cloths to clean the cuts and staunch the profuse bleeding. He also opened various drawers to pull out strong-smelling bags and stood on a ladder to pull down clumps of herbs that were strung from the ceiling. Finally he opened a small box and took a pinch of snuff himself.

"Please hurry," Elena said. "She's lost a lot of blood."

"And you've lost not a little," the man said. "My name

is Kephar Meggar – and this would be Master Drohzne's slave, yes?" He peered at them, looking somehow as if he were wearing glasses, which he wasn't. "And you would be slaves, too?" He stared at the single rope Elena was still wearing, and then at Bonnie and Meredith, each wearing the same.

"Yes, but—" Elena stopped. Some infiltrator she was. She'd very nearly said "But not really; it's just to satisfy convention. She settled for saying, "But *our* master is very different from hers." They were very different, she thought. Damon didn't have a broken neck, for one thing. And for another, no matter how vicious and deadly he might be, he would never strike a woman, much less do something like this to one. He seemed to have some kind of internal block against it – except when he was possessed by Shinichi, and couldn't control his own muscles.

"And yet Drohzne allowed you to bring this woman to a healer?" The little man looked doubtful.

"No, he wouldn't have let us, I'm sure," Elena said flatly. "But please – she's bleeding and she's going to have a baby . . ."

Dr Meggar's eyebrows went up and down. But without asking anyone to leave while he treated her, he pulled out an old-fashioned stethoscope and listened carefully to Ulma's heart and lungs. He smelled her breath, and then gently palpated her abdomen below Elena's bloody camisole, all with a professional air, before tipping to her lips a brown bottle, from which she drank a few sips, then sank back, her eyes fluttering closed.

"Now," the little man said, "she's resting comfortably. She'll need quite a bit of stitching of course, and you could use a few stitches yourself, but that's as your master says, I suppose." Dr Meggar said the word *master* with a definite implication of dislike. "But I can almost promise you that she won't die. About her babe I don't know. It may come out marked as a result of this business – striped birthmarks, perhaps – or it may be perfectly all right. But with *food* and *rest*" – Dr Meggar's eyebrows went up and down again, as if the doctor would have liked to say this to Master Drohzne's face – "she should recover."

"Take care of Elena first, then," Damon said.

"No, *no*!" Elena said, pushing the doctor away. He seemed like a nice man, but obviously around here, masters were masters – and Damon was more masterful and intimidating than most.

But not, at this moment, to Elena. She didn't care about herself right now. She'd made a promise – the doctor's words meant that she might be able to keep it. That was what she cared about.

Up and down, up and down. Dr Meggar's eyebrows looked like two caterpillars on one elastic string. One lagged a little behind the other. Clearly, the behaviour he was seeing was abnormal, even liable to be punished by serious means. But Elena only noticed him peripherally, the way she was noticing Damon.

"*Help her*," she said vehemently – and watched the doctor's eyebrows shoot up as if they were aimed for the ceiling.

She'd let her aura escape. Not completely, thank God, but a blast had definitely discharged, like a flash of sheet lightning in the room.

And the doctor, who wasn't a vampire, but just an ordinary citizen, had noticed it. Lakshmi had noticed it; even Ulma stirred on the examining table uneasily.

I'm going to have to be a whole lot more careful, Elena thought. She cast a quick look at Damon, who was about to explode, himself – she could tell. Too many emotions, too much blood in the room, and the adrenalin of killing still pulsing in his bloodstream.

How did she know all that?

Because Damon wasn't perfectly in control, either, she realised. She was sensing things directly from his mind. Best to get him out of here quickly. "We'll wait outside," she said, catching his arm, to Dr Meggar's obvious shock. Slaves, even beautiful ones, didn't act that way.

"Go and wait in the courtyard then," the doctor said, carefully controlling his face and speaking to the air in between Damon and Elena. "Lakshmi, give them some bandages so they can staunch the young girl's bleeding. Then come back; you can help me."

"Just one question," he added as Elena and the others were walking out of the room. "How did you know that this woman is pregnant? What sort of spell can tell you that?"

"No spell," Elena said simply. "Any woman watching her should have known." She saw Bonnie flash her an injured look, but Meredith remained inscrutable.

"That horrible slaver – Drogsie, or whatever – was whipping her from the front," Elena said. "And look at those gashes." She winced, looking over two stripes that crossed Ulma's sternum. "In that case, any woman would be trying to protect her breasts, but this one was trying to cover her belly. That meant she was pregnant, and far along enough to be sure about it, too."

Dr Meggar's eyebrows drew down and together – and then he looked up at Elena as if peering over glasses. Then he nodded slowly. "You take some bandages and stop your own bleeding," he said – to Elena, not to Damon. Apparently, slave or not, she had won some kind of respect from him.

* * *

On the other hand, Elena seemed to have lost stature with Damon – or at least, he'd cut his mind off from hers quite deliberately, leaving her with a blank wall to stare at. In the doctor's waiting room, he waved an imperious hand at Bonnie and Meredith.

"Wait here in this room," he said – no, he ordered. "*Don't* leave it until the doctor comes out. *Don't* let anyone in the front door – lock it now, and keep it locked. Good. Elena is coming with me into the kitchen – that's the back door. I do not want to be disturbed by *anyone* unless an angry mob is threatening the house with arson, do you understand? Both of you?"

Elena could see Bonnie about to blurt out, "But Elena's still bleeding!" and Meredith was with her eyes and brows calling counsel on whether or not they needed to hold an immediate velociraptor sisterhood rebellion. They all knew Plan A for this: Bonnie would throw herself into Damon's arms, passionately weeping or passionately kissing him, whichever best fit the situation, while Elena and Meredith came at him from the sides and did – well, whatever had to be done.

Elena, with one flash of her own eyes, had categorically nixed this. Damon was angry, yes, but she could sense that it was more with Drohzne than with her. The blood had agitated him, yes, but he was used to controlling himself in bloody situations. And she needed help with her wounds, which had begun to hurt seriously, ever since she'd heard that the woman she had rescued would live, and might even have her baby. But if Damon had something on his mind, she wanted to know what it was – now.

With one last comforting glance at Bonnie, Elena followed Damon through the kitchen door. It had a lock on it. Damon looked at it and opened his mouth; Elena locked it. Then she looked up at her "master".

He was standing by the kitchen sink, methodically pumping water, with one hand clenched against his forehead. His hair hung over his eyes, getting splashed, getting wet. He didn't seem to care.

"Damon?" Elena said uncertainly. "Are you . . . all right?"

He didn't answer.

Damon? she tried telepathically.

I let you get hurt. I'm fast enough. I could have killed that bastard Drohzne with one blast of Power. But I never imagined you'd get hurt. His telepathic voice was at once filled with the darkest kind of menace imaginable and a strange, almost gentle, calm. As if he were trying to keep all the ferocity and anger locked away from her.

I couldn't even tell him – I couldn't even send words to him to tell him what he was. I couldn't think. He was a telepath; he would have heard me. But I didn't have any words. I could only scream – in my mind.

Elena felt a bit light-headed – a little more light-headed than she'd already been feeling. Damon was feeling this anguish – for her? He wasn't angry about her flagrantly breaking rules in front of crowds, maybe breaking their cover? He didn't mind looking *bedraggled*?

"Damon," she said. He'd surprised her into speaking out loud. "It – it – doesn't matter. It's not your fault. You would never even have let me do it—"

"But I should have known you wouldn't ask! I thought you were going to attack him, to jump on his shoulders and throttle him, and I was ready to help you do that, to take him down like two wolves taking down a big buck. But you're not a sword, Elena. Whatever you think, you're a shield. I should have known that you would take the next blow yourself. And because of me, you got—" His

eye drifted to her cheekbone and he winced.

Then he seemed to get a grip on himself. "The water is cold, but it's pure. We need to clean those slashes and stop that bleeding now."

"I don't suppose there's any Black Magic around," Elena said, half jokingly. This was going to hurt.

Damon, however, immediately began opening cupboards. "Here," he said after checking only three, triumphantly coming up with a half-full bottle of Black Magic. "Lots of doctors keep this as a medicine and anaesthetic. Don't worry; I'll pay him well."

"Then I think you should have some, too," Elena said boldly. "Come on, it'll do us both good. And it won't be the first time."

She knew that the last sentence would clinch it with Damon. It would be a way of getting back something that Shinichi had taken from him.

I'll get the whole of his memories back from Shinichi somehow, Elena decided, doing her best to screen her thoughts from Damon with white noise. I don't know how to do it, and I don't know when I'll get the chance, but *I swear I will. I swear.*

Damon had filled two goblets with the rich, heady-smelling wine and was handing one to Elena. "Just sip at first," he said, helpless but to fall into the role of instructor. "This is a good year."

Elena sipped, then simply gulped. She was thirsty and Clarion Loess Black Magic wine didn't have any alcohol – as such – in it. It certainly didn't taste like regular wine. It tasted like remarkably refreshing effervescent spring water that was flavoured with sweet, deep, velvety grapes.

Damon, she noticed, had forgotten to sip as well, and when he offered her a second glass to match his, she accepted willingly.

His aura sure had calmed down a lot, she thought, as he picked up a wet cloth and began, gently, to clean the cut that almost exactly followed the line of her cheekbone. It had been the one to stop bleeding first, but now he needed to get the blood flowing again, to cleanse it. With two glasses of Black Magic on top of no food since breakfast, Elena found herself relaxing against the back of the chair, letting her head drop back a little, and shutting her eyes. She lost track of time, as he stroked the cut smoothly. And she lost strict control of her aura.

When she opened her eyes it was in response to no sound, no visual stimulus. It was a blaze in Damon's aura, one of sudden determination.

"Damon?"

He was standing over her. His darkness had flared out behind him like a shadow, tall and wide and almost mesmerising. Definitely almost frightening.

"Damon?" she said again, uncertainly.

"We're not doing this right," he said, and her thoughts flashed at once to her disobedience as a slave, and Bonnie and Meredith's less serious infractions. But his voice was like dark velvet, and her body responded to it more accurately than her mind. It shivered.

"How . . . do we do it right?" she asked, and then she made the mistake of opening her eyes. She found that he was stooping over her as she sat on the chair, stroking – no, just touching – her hair so softly that she hadn't even felt it.

"Vampires know how to take care of wounds," he said confidently, and his great eyes that seemed to hold their own universe of stars caught and held her. "We can clean them. We can start them bleeding again – or stop them."

I've felt like this before, Elena thought. He's talked to

me like this before, too, even if he doesn't remember. And I – I was too frightened. But that was before . . .

Before the motel. The night when he'd told her to run, and she hadn't. The night that Shinichi had taken, just as he'd taken the first time they'd shared Black Magic together.

"Show me," whispered Elena. And she knew that something else in her mind was whispering too, whispering different words. Words that she would never have said if she had for a moment thought of herself as a slave.

Whispering, *I'm yours* . . .

That was when she felt his mouth lightly brush her mouth.

And then she just thought, *Oh!* and *Oh, Damon* . . . until he moved to gently touch her cheek with his silky soft tongue, manipulating chemicals first to make cleansing blood flow, and finally when the impurities had all been so softly swept away, to stop the blood and to heal the wound. She could feel his Power now, the dark Power that he had used in a thousand fights, to inflict hundreds of mortal wounds, being held tightly in check to concentrate on this simple, homely task, to heal the mark of a whiplash on a girl's cheek. Elena thought it was like being stroked with the petals of that Black Magic rose, its cool smooth petals gently sweeping away the pain, until she shivered in delight.

And then it stopped. Elena knew that she'd once again had too much wine. But this time she didn't feel sick. The deceptively light drink had gone to her head, making her tipsy. Everything had taken on an unreal, dreamlike quality.

"It will finish healing well now," Damon said, again touching her hair so softly that she could barely feel it.

But this time she did feel it, because she sent out fingers of Power to meet the sensation and enjoy every moment of it. And once again he kissed her – so lightly – his lips barely brushing hers. When her head fell back, though, he didn't follow, even when, disappointed, she tried to put pressure on the back of his neck. He simply waited until Elena thought things out . . . slowly.

We shouldn't be kissing. Meredith and Bonnie are right next door. How do I get myself in situations like this? But Damon isn't even trying to kiss . . . and we're supposed to be – oh!

Her other wounds.

They really hurt now. What cruel person had thought up a whip like that, Elena thought, with a razor-thin lash that cut so deeply it didn't even hurt at first – or not that much . . . but got worse and worse over time? And kept bleeding . . . we're supposed to be stopping the bleeding until the doctor can see me . . .

But her next wound, the one that burned like fire now, was diagonally across her collarbone. And the third was near her knee . . .

Damon started to get up, to get another cloth from the sink and cleanse the cut with water.

Elena held him back. "No."

"No? Are you sure?"

"Yes."

"All I want to do is cleanse it . . ."

"I know." She did know. His mind was open to hers, all its turbulent power running clear and tranquilly. She didn't know why it had opened to her like this, but it had.

"But let me advise you, don't go donating your blood to some dying vampire; don't let anyone sample it. It's worse than Black Magic—"

"Worse?" She knew he was complimenting her, but she didn't understand.

"The more you drink, the more you want to drink," Damon answered, and for a moment Elena saw the turbulence she had caused in those calm waters. "And the more you drink, the more Power you can absorb," he added seriously. Elena realised that she had never even thought of this as a problem, but it was. She remembered the agony it had been to try to absorb her own aura before she had learned how to keep it moving with her bloodstream.

"Don't worry," he added, still serious. "I know who you're thinking about." He made a move again to get a cloth. But without knowing it, he had said too much, presumed too far.

"*You* know who I'm thinking about?" Elena said softly, and she was surprised at how dangerous her own voice could sound, like the soft padding of heavy tigress feet. "Without asking me?"

Damon tried to finesse his way out. "Well, I assumed . . ."

"*No one* knows what I'm thinking about," Elena said. "Until I tell them." She moved and made him kneel to look at her, questioningly. Hungrily.

Then, just as it was she who had made him kneel, it was she who drew him to her wound.

CHAPTER

18

Elena came back to the real world slowly, fighting it all the way. She sank her nails into the leather of Damon's jacket, found herself wondering briefly if removing it would help, and then her mood was shattered again by that sound – a sharp, imperative knock.

Damon raised his head and snarled.

We *are* a pair of wolves, aren't we? Elena thought. Fighting nail and tooth.

But, another part of her mind supplied, that isn't stopping the knocking. He warned those girls . . .

Those girls! Bonnie and Meredith! And he'd said not to interrupt unless the house was on fire!

But, the doctor – oh, God, something's happened to that poor, wretched woman! She's dying!

Damon was still snarling, a trace of blood on his lips. It was only a trace, because her second wound had really been healed just as thoroughly as the first, the one across her cheekbone. Elena had no idea how long it had been since she had pulled Damon to her to kiss this cut. But now, with her blood in his veins and his pleasure interrupted, he was like an untamed black panther in her arms.

She didn't know whether she could stop him or even slow him down without using raw Power on him.

"Damon!" she said aloud. "Out there – those are our friends. Remember? Bonnie and Meredith and the healer."

"Meredith," Damon said, and again his lips peeled back, exposing terrifyingly long canines. He still wasn't in reality. If he saw Meredith now, he wouldn't be frightened, Elena thought – and, oh yes, she knew how her logical, thoughtful friend made Damon uneasy. They saw the world through such different eyes. She irked him like a pebble in his shoe. But right now he might deal with that unease in a way that would leave Meredith a savaged corpse.

"Let me go see," she said, as the knock came again – couldn't they *stop* that? Didn't she have enough to deal with?

Damon's arms merely tightened around her. She felt a flash of heat, because she knew that, even as he restrained her, he was holding back so much of his strength. He didn't want to crush her, as he could if he used a tenth of the power in his hard muscles alone.

The wave of feeling that washed over her made her shut her eyes briefly, helplessly, but she knew she had to be the voice of sanity here.

"Damon! They could be warning us – or Ulma may have died."

Death got through to him. His eyes were slits, the blood-red light from the kitchen shutters throwing bars of scarlet and black across his face, making him look more handsome – and more demonic – than ever.

"You'll stay here." Damon said it flatly, with no idea of being a "master" or a "gentleman". He was a wild beast protecting his mate, the only creature in the world that wasn't competition or food.

There was no arguing with him, not in this state. Elena would stay here. Damon would go to do whatever needed to be done. And Elena would stay for as long as he thought necessary.

Elena truly didn't know whose thoughts these last were. She and Damon were still trying to untangle their emotions. She decided to watch him and only if he really got out of control . . .

You don't want to see me out of control.

Feeling him snap from raw animal instinct to icy, perfect mental dominance was even scarier than the animal alone. She didn't know whether Damon was the sanest person she had ever met or just the one best able to cover up his wildness. She held her torn blouse together and watched as he moved with effortless grace to the door and then, suddenly, violently, wrenched it almost off its hinges.

No one fell; no one had been listening in on their private conversation. But Meredith stood, restraining Bonnie with one hand, and with the other hand raised, ready to knock again.

"Yes?" Damon said in glacial tones. "I thought I told you—"

"You did, and there is," Meredith said, interrupting *this* Damon in an unusual attempt to commit suicide.

"*There is what?*" Damon snarled.

"There's a mob outside threatening to burn the whole building down. I don't know if they're upset about Drohzne, or about us taking Ulma, but they're enraged about something, and they've got torches. I didn't want to interrupt Elena's – treatment – but Dr Meggar says they won't listen to him. He's a human."

"He used to be a slave," Bonnie added, wresting free of the chokehold that Meredith had on her. She looked up at Damon with streaming brown eyes, hands outstretched. "Only you can save us," she said, translating the message of her gaze aloud – which meant that things were really serious.

"All right, all right. I'll go take care of them. You take care of Elena."

"Of course, but—"

"No." Damon had either gone reckless with the blood – and the memories that were still keeping Elena from forming a coherent sentence – or he had somehow overcome all his fear of Meredith. He put a hand on each of her shoulders. He was only one and a half or two inches taller than she was, so he had no trouble holding her eyes. "You, personally, take care of Elena. Tragedies happen here every minute of the day: unforeseeable, horrible, *deadly* tragedies. I do *not* want one happening to Elena."

Meredith looked at him for a long moment, and for once didn't consult Elena with her eyes before answering a question involving her. She simply said, "I'll protect her," in a low voice that nevertheless carried. From her stance, from her tone, one could almost hear the unspoken addition, "with my life" – and it didn't even seem melodramatic.

Damon let go of her, strode out the door, and without a backward glance disappeared from Elena's sight. But his mental voice was crystalline in her mind: *You'll be safe if there is any way to save you. I swear it.*

If there was any way to save her. Wonderful. Elena tried to kickstart her brain.

Meredith and Bonnie were both staring at her. Elena took a deep breath, automatically sucked for a moment back into the old days, when a girl fresh from a hot date could expect a long and serious debriefing.

But all Bonnie said was, "Your face – it looks much better now!"

"Yes," Elena said, using the two ends of her blouse to tie a makeshift top around her. "My leg's the problem. We didn't – didn't finish it yet."

Bonnie opened her mouth, but closed it determinedly, which from Bonnie was a display of heroics similar to Meredith's promise to Damon. When she opened it again it was to say, "Take my scarf and tie it around your leg. We can fold it sideways and then tie a bow over the side that got hurt. That'll keep pressure on it."

Meredith said, "I think Dr Meggar has finished with Ulma. Maybe he can see you."

In the other room, the doctor was once again washing his hands, using a large pump to get more water into the basin. There were deeply red-stained cloths in a pile and a smell that Elena was grateful the doctor had camouflaged with herbs. Also in a large, comfortable-looking chair there sat a woman whom Elena did not recognise.

Suffering and terror could change a person, Elena knew, but she could never have realised how much – nor how much relief and freedom from pain could change a face. She had brought with her a woman who huddled until she was almost child-size in Elena's mind, and whose thin, ravaged face, twisted with agony and unrelenting dread, had seemed almost a sort of abstract drawing of a goblin hag. Her skin had been sickly grey in colour, her thin hair had scarcely seemed enough to cover her head, and yet it had hung down in strands like seaweed. Everything about her screamed out that she was a slave, from the iron bands around her wrists, to her nakedness and scarred, bloody body, to her bare and rusty feet. Elena could not even have told you the colour of the woman's eyes, for they had seemed as grey as the rest of her.

Now Elena was confronted by a woman who was perhaps in her early- to mid-thirties. She had a lean, attractive, somehow aristocratic face, with a strong, patrician nose, dark, keen-looking eyes, and beautiful eyebrows like the wings of a flying bird. She was relaxing in the armchair, with her feet up on an ottoman, slowly brushing her hair, which was dark with occasional streaks of grey that lent an air of dignity to the simple deep-blue housecoat she was wearing. Her face had wrinkles that lent it character, but overall one sensed a sort of yearning tenderness about her, perhaps because of the slight bulge in her abdomen, which she now gently laid a hand on. When she did this her face bloomed with colour and her whole aspect glowed.

For an instant Elena thought this must be the doctor's wife or housekeeper and she had a temptation to ask whether Ulma, the poor wreck of a slave, had died.

Then she saw what one cuff of the deep-blue housecoat could not quite conceal: a glimpse of an iron bracelet.

This lean dark aristocratic woman was Ulma. The doctor had worked a miracle.

A healer, he had called himself. It was obvious that, like Damon, he could heal wounds. No one who had been whipped as Ulma had could have come round to this state without some powerful magic. Trying to simply stitch up the bloody mess that Elena had brought in had obviously been impossible, and so Dr Meggar had healed her.

Elena had never experienced a situation like this, so she fell back upon the good manners that had been bred into her as a Virginian.

"It's nice to meet you, ma'am. I'm Elena," she said, and held out her hand.

The brush fell onto the chair. The woman reached out with both hands to take Elena's into hers. Those keen dark eyes seemed to devour Elena's face.

"You're the one," she said, and then, swinging her slippered feet off the ottoman, she went down on her knees.

"Oh, no, ma'am! Please! I'm sure the doctor told you to rest. It's best to sit quietly now."

"But you *are* the one." For some reason, the woman seemed to need confirmation. And Elena was willing to do anything to pacify her.

"I'm the one," Elena said. "And now I think you should sit down again."

Obedience was immediate, and yet there was a sort of joyful light about everything Ulma did. Elena understood it after only a few hours of slavery. Obeying when one had a choice was entirely different from obeying because disobedience could mean death.

But even as Ulma sat, she held out her arms. "Look at me! Dear seraph, goddess, Guardian – whatever you are: look at me! After three years of living as a beast I have become human again – because of you! You came like an angel of lightning and stood between me and the lash." Ulma began to weep, but they seemed to be tears of joy. Her eyes searched Elena's face, lingering on the scarred cheekbone. "But you're no Guardian; they have magicks that protect them and they never interfere. For three years, they never interfered. I saw all my friends, my fellow slaves, fall to *his* whip and *his* rage." She shook her head, as if physically unable to say Drohzne's name.

"I'm so sorry – so sorry. . . ." Elena was fumbling. She glanced back and saw that Bonnie and Meredith were similarly stricken.

"It doesn't matter. I heard your mate killed him on the street."

"I told her that," Lakshmi said proudly. She had entered the room without anyone noticing her.

"My mate?" Elena faltered. "Well, he's not my— I mean, he and I – we—"

"He's our master," Meredith said bluntly, from behind Elena.

Ulma was still looking at Elena with her heart in her eyes. "Every day, I will pray for your soul to ascend from here."

Elena was startled. "Souls can ascend from here?"

"Of course. Repentance and good deeds may accomplish it, and the prayers of others are always taken into consideration, I think."

You sure don't talk like a slave, Elena mused. She tried to think of a way to put it delicately, but she was confused and her leg hurt and her emotions were in turmoil. "You don't sound like – well, like what I'd expect from a slave," she said. "Or am I just being an idiot?"

She could see the tears form in Ulma's eyes.

"Oh, God! Please, forget I asked. Please—"

"No! There is no one I would rather tell. If you wish to hear how I came to this degraded state." Ulma waited, watching Elena – it was clear that Elena's least wish was to Ulma, a command.

Elena looked at Meredith and Bonnie. She couldn't hear any more noises of yelling outside on the street and the building certainly didn't seem to be on fire.

Fortunately, at that moment, Dr Meggar wandered

in again. "Everybody getting acquainted?" he asked, his eyebrows working in opposition now; one up, one down. He had the remnants of a bottle of Black Magic in his hand.

"Yes," Elena said, "but I was just wondering if we should be trying to evacuate or anything. Apparently there was a mob—"

"Elena's mate is going to give them something to think about," Lakshmi said with relish. "They've all gone to the Meeting Place to resolve the stuff about Drohzne's property. I bet *he'll* bash a few heads in and be back in no time," she added cheerfully, leaving no doubt as to *he* was. "Wish I was a boy so I could see it."

"You were braver than the boys; you were the one who led us here," Elena told her. Then she consulted Meredith and Bonnie with her eyes. It sounded as if the commotion had moved on elsewhere, and Damon was a master at getting himself out of commotions. He might also . . . *need* to fight, to rid himself of excess energy from Elena's blood. A commotion might actually be good for him, Elena thought.

She looked at Dr Meggar. "Will my – will our master be all right, do you think?"

Dr Meggar's eyebrows went up and down. "He'll probably have to pay Old Drohzne's relatives a blood price, but it shouldn't be too high. Then he can do what he likes with the old bastard's property," he said. "I'd say the safest place for you right now is here, away from the Meeting Place." He went on to enforce that opinion by pouring them all glasses – liqueur glasses, Elena noted – of Black Magic wine. "Good for the nerves," he said and took a sip.

Ulma smiled her beautiful, heartwarming smile at him, as he took the tray around. "Thank you – and thank you – and thank you," she said. "I won't bore you with my story—"

"No, tell us; tell us, please!" Now that there was no immediate danger to her friends or to Damon, Elena was eager to hear the tale. Everyone else was nodding.

Ulma flushed a little, but began sedately, "I was born in the reign of Kelemen II," she said. "I'm sure that means nothing to our visitors but much to those who knew him and his – indulgences. I studied under my mother, who became a very popular designer of fashions in fabrics. My father was a designer of jewellery almost as famous as she was. They had an estate on the outskirts of the city and could afford a house as fine as many of their wealthiest customers – though they were careful not to show the true extent of their wealth. I was the young Lady Ulma then, not Ulma the hag. My parents did their best to keep me out of sight, for my own safety. But . . ."

Ulma – Lady Ulma, Elena thought, stopped and took a deep sip of her wine. Her eyes had changed; she was seeing the past, and trying not to upset her listeners. But just as Elena was about to ask her to stop, at least until she felt better, she continued.

"But despite all their care . . . someone . . . saw me anyway and demanded my hand in marriage. Not Drohzne, he was just a furrier from the Outlands, and I never saw him until three years ago. This was a lord, a General, a demon with a terrible reputation – and my father refused his demand. They came on us in the night. I was fourteen when it happened. And that is how I became a slave."

Elena found that she was feeling emotional pain directly from Lady Ulma's mind. Oh, my God, I've done it again, she thought, hurriedly trying to tune down her psychic senses. "Please, you don't need to tell us this. Maybe another time . . ."

"I would like to tell you – *you* – so you will know what you have done. And I would prefer to say it only once. But if you do not wish to hear it—"

Politeness was warring with politeness here. "No, no, if you want – go ahead. I – I just want you to know how sorry I am." Elena glanced at the doctor, who was patiently waiting by the table for her with the brown bottle in his hands. "And if you don't mind, I'd like to get my leg . . . healed?" She was aware that she'd said the last word doubtfully, wondering how any one being could have the power to heal Ulma like this. She was not surprised when he shook his head. "Or stitched up, rather, while you talk, if you don't mind," she said.

It took several minutes to overcome Lady Ulma's shock and distress that she had left her saviour waiting, but at last Elena was on the table and the doctor was encouraging her to drink from the bottle, which smelled like cherry cough syrup.

Oh, well, she might as well try the Dark Dimension version of anaesthetic – especially since the stitching was bound to hurt, Elena thought. She took a sip from the bottle and felt the room reel around her. She waved away the offer of a second sip.

Dr Meggar undid Bonnie's ruined scarf, and then began to cut off her blood-soaked jeans leg above the knee.

"Well – you are so good to listen," Lady Ulma said. "But I knew you were good already. I will spare us both the painful details of my slavery. Perhaps it's enough to say that I was passed from one master to another over the years, always a slave, always going down. At last, as a joke, someone said, 'Give her to Old Drohzne. He'll squeeze the last use out of her if anyone can.' "

"God!" Elena said, and hoped that everyone would attribute it to the story and not to the bite of the cleansing solution the doctor was swabbing over her swollen flesh. Damon was so much better at this, she thought. I didn't even realise how lucky I was before. Elena tried not to wince as the doctor began to use his needle, but her grip on Meredith's hand tightened until Elena was afraid she was breaking bones. She tried to ease the grip, but Meredith squeezed back hard. Her long, smooth hand was almost like a boy's, but softer. Elena was glad to be able to squeeze as hard as she liked.

"My strength has been giving out on me lately," Lady Ulma said softly. "I thought it was that" – here she used a particularly crude expression for her owner – "that was leading me to death. Then I realised the truth." All at once radiance changed her face, so much that Elena could see what she must have looked like when she was in her teens and so beautiful that a demon would demand her as a wife. "I knew that new life stirred within me – and I knew that Drohzne would kill it if he had the chance—"

She didn't seem to recognise the expressions of astonishment and horror on the three girls' faces. Elena, however, had the feeling that she was groping through a nightmare, on the edge of a black crevasse, and that she would have to keep groping in the dark, around treacherous, unseen fissures in the ice in the Dark Dimension until she reached Stefan and got him free of this place. This casual reference to abomination wasn't the first of her steps around a crevasse, but it was the first she had recognised and counted.

"You young women are very new here," Lady Ulma said, as the silence stretched and stretched. "I did not mean to say anything out of place . . ."

"We're slaves here," Meredith replied, picking up a length of rope. "I think the more we learn the better."

"Your master – I've never seen anyone so quick to fight Old Drohzne before. Many people clucked their tongues, but that was all most dared to do. But your master—"

"*We* call him Damon," Bonnie put in pointedly.

It went right over Lady Ulma's head. "Master Damon – do you think he might keep me? After he pays the blood price to – to Drohzne's relatives, he will get first pick of all Drohzne's property. I am one of the few slaves he has not killed." The hope in the woman's face was almost too painful for Elena to look at.

It was only then that she consciously realised how long it had been since she'd seen Damon. How long should Damon's business be taking? She looked at Meredith anxiously.

Meredith understood exactly what the look meant. She shook her head helplessly. Even if they had Lakshmi take them to the Meeting Place, what could they do?

Elena bit back a wince of pain and smiled at Lady Ulma.

"Why don't you tell us about when you were a girl?" she said.

CHAPTER

19

Damon wouldn't have thought a sadistic old fool who whipped a woman to pieces for not being able to pull a cart meant for a horse would have any friends. And Old Drohzne, indeed, may not have had any. But that wasn't the issue.

Neither, strangely, was murder the issue. Murder was an everyday affair around the slums and the fact that Damon had initiated and won a fight was of no surprise to the inhabitants of these dangerous alleyways.

The issue lay in making off with a slave. Or perhaps it went deeper. The issue lay in how Damon treated his own slaves.

A crowd of men – all men, no women, Damon noticed – had indeed gathered in front of the doctor's building, and they did in fact have torches.

"Mad vampire! Mad vampire on the loose!"

"Drive him out here for justice to be done!"

"Burn the place down if they won't turn him out!"

"The elders say to bring him to them!"

This seemed to have the effect the crowd desired, clearing the streets of the more decent people and leaving only the bloody-minded sort who'd been hanging about at a loose end, and were only too glad of a fight. Most of them, of course, were vampires themselves. Most of them were *fit* vampires. But none of them, Damon thought, flashing a diamond-bright smile around the circle that was closing in on him, had the motivation of knowing that the lives of three young human girls depended on him – and that one of them was the jewel in the crown of humanity, Elena Gilbert.

If he, Damon, was torn to pieces in this fight, those three girls would lead lives of hell and degradation.

However, even this logic didn't seem to help him prevail as Damon was kicked, bitten, head-butted, punched, and stabbed with wooden daggers – the kind that slice vampire flesh. At first he thought he had a chance. Several of the youngest and fittest vampires fell prey to his cobra-quick strikes and his sudden strafes of Power. But the truth was that there were simply too many of them, Damon thought, as he snapped the neck of a demon whose two long tusks had already scored his arm almost through the muscle. And here came a huge vampire, clearly in training, with an aura that made Damon feel bile at the back of his throat. That one went down with a foot in the face, but he didn't stay down; he came up, clinging to Damon's leg and allowing several smaller vampires with wooden daggers to dart in and hamstring him. Damon felt black dismay as his legs went out from under him.

"Sunlight damn you," he grated through a mouthful of blood as another tusked, red-skinned demon punched him in the mouth. "Damn you all to the lowest hells . . ."

It was no good. Dully, still fighting, still using great

swaths of Power to maim and kill as many as he could, Damon realised this. And then everything became dreamlike and dazed – not like his dream of Elena, whom he seemed to see constantly in his side-eye, weeping. But dreamlike in a feverish, nightmare sense. He could no longer use his muscles efficiently. His body was battered and even as he healed his legs, another vampire scored a great cut across his back. He was feeling more and more as if he were in a nightmare where he could not move except in slow motion. At the same time, something in his brain was whispering for him to rest. Just rest . . . and it would all be over.

Eventually, the greater numbers bore him down, and somebody appeared with a stake.

"Good riddance to new rubbish," the stake bringer said, his breath reeking of stale blood, his leering face grotesque, as he used leprous-looking fingers to open Damon's shirt so as not to make a hole in the fine black silk.

Damon spat on him and had his face stamped on hard in return.

He blacked out for a moment and then, slowly, came back to pain.

And noise. The gleeful crowd of vampires and demons, drunk on cruelty, were all doing a stomping, rhythmic, improvised dance around Damon, roaring with laughter as they thrust imaginary stakes, working themselves into a frenzy.

That was when Damon realised that he was actually going to die.

It was a shocking realisation, even though he'd known how much more dangerous this world was than the one he'd recently left, and even in the human world he had only escaped death by a hair's-breadth more than once.

But now he had no powerful friends, no weaknesses in the crowd to exploit. He felt as if seconds were suddenly stretching into minutes, each one of incalculable worth. What was important? Telling Elena . . .

"Blind him first! Get that stick blazing!"

"I'll take his ears! Someone help me hold his head!"

Telling Elena . . . something. Something . . . sorry . . .

He gave up. Another thought was trying to break into his consciousness.

"Don't forget to knock out his teeth! I promised my girlfriend a new necklace!"

I thought I was prepared for this, Damon thought slowly, each word coming separately. But . . . not so soon.

I thought I'd made my peace . . . but not with the one person who mattered . . . yes, who mattered the most.

He didn't give himself time to think about that subject further.

Stefan, he sent out on the most powerful but clandestine jettison of Power he could manage in his foggy state. *Stefan, hear me! Elena's come for you – she'll save you! She has Powers that my death will let loose. And I am . . . I am . . . s—*

At that moment there was a stumbling in the dance around him. Silence descended on the drunken revellers. A few of them hastily bowed their heads or looked away.

Damon went still, wondering what could possibly have stopped the frenzied crowd in the very midst of their revelry.

Someone was walking toward him. The newcomer had long bronze hair that hung in separate unruly tangles down to his waist. He was naked to the waist, too, exposing a body that the strongest demon might envy. A chest that looked as if it had been carved out of gleaming bronze stone. Exquisitely sculpted biceps. Abs –

a perfect six pack. There was not a spare ounce of fat on his entire tall leonine frame. He wore unadorned black trousers with muscles rippling under them at every step.

All along one bare arm he had a vivid tattoo of a black dragon eating a heart.

Nor was he alone. He held no leash, but by his side was a handsome and uncannily intelligent-looking black dog that stood at alert attention every time he paused. It must have weighed close to two hundred pounds, but there was not an ounce of fat on it, either.

And on one shoulder he carried a large falcon.

It wasn't hooded as most hunting birds were on forays out of their mews. It also wasn't standing on anything padded. It gripped the bare shoulder of the bronze young man, digging its three front talons into the flesh and sending small streams of blood down his chest. He didn't seem to notice. There were similar, dried streams beside the fresh ones, undoubtedly from previous journeys. In the back, a single talon made a lonely red trail.

An absolute hush had fallen on the crowd and the last few demons between the tall man and the bloody, supine figure on the ground scrambled out of his way.

For a moment, the leonine man was still. He said nothing, did nothing, emitted no trace of Power. Then he nodded at the dog, which padded forward heavily and sniffed at Damon's bleeding arms and face. After that it sniffed at his mouth and Damon could see the hairs go up on its body.

"Good dog," said Damon dreamily as the moist, cool nose tickled his cheek.

Damon knew this particular animal and he knew also that it did not fit the popular stereotype of a "good dog". Rather, it was a hellhound who was used to taking vampires by the throat and shaking them until their arteries spouted blood six feet high into the air.

That kind of thing could keep you so occupied that having a stake slipped into your heart might seem an afterthought, Damon mused, holding perfectly still.

"*Arrêtez-le!*" said the bronze-haired youth.

The dog obediently backed off, never taking its shining black eyes off Damon's, who never took his own eyes off it until it was some feet away.

The bronze-haired youth glanced over the crowd briefly. Then he said with no particular vehemence, "*Laissez-le seul.*" Clearly, to the vampires no translation was necessary, and they began to edge away immediately. The unlucky ones were those who didn't edge fast enough and were still around when the bronze young man took another leisurely look about him. Everywhere he looked, he met downcast eyes and cringing bodies, frozen in the act of edging but apparently turned to stone now in an attempt not to attract attention.

Damon found himself relaxing. His Power was returning, allowing him to make repairs. He realised that the dog was going from individual to individual and sniffing at each one with interest.

When Damon was able to lift his head again, he smiled faintly at the newcomer. "Sage. Think of the devil."

The bronze man's brief smile was grim. "You compliment me, *mon cher*. You see? I'm blushing."

"I ought to have known you might be here."

"There is infinite space to wander, *mon petit tyran*. Even if I must do it alone."

"Ah, the pity. Tiny violins are playing—" Suddenly Damon couldn't do it any more. He just couldn't. Maybe it was because of being with Elena before. Maybe it was because this hideous world depressed him unutterably. But when he spoke again, his voice was entirely different. "I never knew I could feel so grateful. You've saved five lives, though you don't know it. Though how you stumbled on us . . ."

Sage crouched down, looked at him with concern. "What is it that has happened?" he said in a serious voice. "Is it that you hit your head? You know: news travels fast here. I heard you arrived with a harem—"

"That's true! He did!" Damon's ears caught a bare whisper of sound at the edge of the street where he'd been ambushed. *"If we take the girls hostage – torture them—"*

Sage's eyes met Damon's briefly. Clearly, he had heard the whisper as well. "Saber," he said to the dog. "Just the speaker." He jerked his head, once, in the direction of the whisper.

Instantly, the black dog jumped forward, and faster than it took for Damon to describe it in his own mind, had sunk his teeth into the throat of the whisperer, flipped him over once, causing a distinctive crack, and was bounding back, dragging the body between his legs.

The words: *Je vous ai informé au sujet de ceci!* blasted by on a surge of Power that made Damon wince. And Damon thought, yes, he did tell them before – but not what the consequences would be.

Laissez lui et ses amis dans la paix! Meanwhile, Damon was slowly getting up, only too glad to accept Sage's protection for himself and his friends.

"Well, that certainly should have done it," he said. "Why not come back and have a friendly drink with me?"

Sage peered at him as if he'd gone mad. "You know the answer to that is no."

"Why not?"

"I told you: no."

"That's not a reason."

"The reason I will not come back for a friendly drink . . . *mon ange* . . . is that we are not friends."

"We pulled some pretty scams together."

"*Il y a longtemps.*" Abruptly, Sage took one of Damon's hands. There was a deep and bloody scratch on it, which Damon hadn't got around to healing. Under Sage's gaze it closed, the flesh turned pink, and it healed.

Damon let Sage continue to hold the hand for a moment, and then, not ungently, retrieved it.

"Not such a *very* long time ago," he said.

"Away from you?" A sarcastic smile formed on Sage's lips. "We count time very differently, you and I, *mon petit tyran*."

Damon was full of befuddled cheer. "What's one drink?"

"Along with your harem?"

Damon tried to picture Meredith and Sage together. His mind baulked. "But you've made yourself responsible for them anyway," he said flatly. "And the truth is that none of them are mine. I give my word on that." He felt a twinge when he thought about Elena, but his word was true.

"Responsible for them?" Sage seemed to be reasoning it out. "You pledged to save them, then. But I only inherit your pledge if you die. But if you die . . ." The tall man made a helpless gesture.

"You have to live, to save Stefan and Elena and the others."

"I'd say no, but that would make you unhappy. So I'll say yes—"

"And if you don't perform, I swear I'll come back to haunt you."

Sage regarded him for a moment. "I don't think I've

ever been accused of being unable to perform before," he said. "But of course that was before I became *un vampire*."

Yes, Damon thought, the meeting of the "harem" and Sage was bound to be interesting. At least it would be if the girls discovered who Sage really was.

But maybe no one would tell them.

CHAPTER

20

Elena had seldom felt such relief as she did when she heard Damon's knock at Dr Meggar's door.

"What happened at the Meeting Place?" she asked.

"I never made it there." Damon explained about the ambush, while the others covertly studied Sage with varying degrees of approval, gratitude or sheer lust. Elena realised that she'd had too much Black Magic when she felt ready to pass out at several points – although she was sure that the wine had helped Damon to survive a mob attack which might otherwise have killed him.

They, in turn, explained Lady Ulma's story as briefly as possible. The woman was looking white and shaken by the end.

"I do hope," she said timidly to Damon, "that when you inherit Old Drohzne's property" – she paused to swallow – "that you'll decide to keep me. I know the slaves you brought with you are beautiful and young . . . but I can make myself very useful as a needlewoman and such. It's just my back that's lost its strength, not my mind . . ."

Damon was perfectly still for a moment. Then he walked over to Elena, who happened to be closest to him. He reached up, unclasped the last loop of rope that had been trailing from Elena's wrist, and threw it hard across the room. It whipped and wiggled like a snake. "Anyone else wearing one can do the same thing, as far as I'm concerned," he said.

"Except the throwing," Meredith said quickly, seeing the doctor's eyebrows clashing as he looked at the many breakable glass beakers stacked along the walls. But she and Bonnie lost no time in losing any final vestige of rope that was still trailing.

"I'm afraid mine are . . . permanent," Lady Ulma said, pulling the fabric away from her wrists to expose the welded-on iron bracelets. She looked ashamed at being unable to obey her new master's first command.

"Do you mind a moment of cold? I have enough Power to freeze them so they'll shatter," Damon said.

There was a soft sound from Lady Ulma. Elena thought she had never heard such desperation in any one human noise. "I could stand in snow to my neck for a year to get these awful things off," the Lady said.

Damon put his hands on either side of one bracelet and Elena could feel the rush of Power that emanated from him. There was a sharp cracking sound. Damon moved his hands and came up with two separate pieces of metal.

Then he did it again, on the other side.

The look in Lady Ulma's eyes made Elena feel more humble than proud. She had saved one woman from terrible degradation. But how many more remained? She would never know, or be able to save them all if she found out. Not with her Power in the state it was now.

"I think Lady Ulma really ought to get some rest," Bonnie said, rubbing her own forehead under tumbled strawberry curls. "And Elena, too. You should have seen how many stitches her leg took, Damon. But what do we do, go look for a hotel?"

"Use my house," said Dr Meggar, one eyebrow up and one down. Obviously, he had become enmeshed in this story, swept along by its sheer power and beauty – and brutality. "All I ask is that you don't destroy anything, and that if you see a frog, don't kiss it, and don't kill it. There are plenty of blankets and chairs and couches."

He wouldn't take a single link from the heavy gold chain Damon had brought to use as income in exchange.

"I . . . by rights I should help you all get ready for bed," Lady Ulma murmured faintly to Meredith.

"You're the worst hurt of all; you should get the best bed," Meredith replied tranquilly. "And *we* will help *you* get into it."

"The most comfortable bed . . . that would be in my daughter's old room." Dr Meggar fumbled with a ring of keys. "She married a porter – how I hated to see her go. And this young lady, Miss Elena, can have the old bridal chamber."

For an instant Elena's heart was torn by conflicting emotions. She was afraid – yes, she was very sure it was fear she felt – that Damon might sweep her up in his arms and make for the bridal suite with her. And on the other hand . . .

Just then Lakshmi looked up at her uncertainly. "Do you want me to leave?" she asked.

"Do you have anywhere to go?" Elena asked in turn.

"The street, I guess. I usually sleep in a barrel."

"Stay here. Come with me; a bridal bed sounds big

enough for two people. You're one of us, now."

The look Lakshmi gave her was one of sheer thunderstruck gratitude. Not at being given a place to stay, Elena understood. For the statement, *"You're one of us, now."* Elena could feel that Lakshmi had never been "one of" any group before.

Things were quiet until almost "dawn" the next "day", as the city's inhabitants called it, although the light hadn't varied all night.

This time a different sort of crowd had gathered outside the doctor's complex. It was mostly made up of elderly men wearing threadbare but clean robes – but there were a few old women, too. They were led by a silver-haired man who had a strange air of dignity.

Damon, with Sage as backup, went outside the doctor's complex and spoke to them.

Elena was dressed but still upstairs in the quiet bridal suite.

> *Dear Diary,*
> *Oh, God, I need help! Oh, Stefan – I need <u>you</u>. I need you to forgive me. I need you to keep me sane. Too much time around Damon and I'm completely emotional, ready to kill him or to . . . or to – I don't know. <u>I don't know!!!</u> We're like flint and tinder together – God! We're like gasoline and a flamethrower! Please hear me and help me and save me . . . from myself. Every time he even says my name . . .*

"Elena."

The voice behind Elena made her jump. She slammed

the diary shut and turned around.

"Yes, Damon?"

"How are you feeling?"

"Oh, great. Fine. Even my leg is b— I mean, I'm fine all over. How are you feeling?"

"I'm . . . well enough," he said, and he smiled – and it was a real smile, not a snarl twisted into something else at the last second, or an attempt to manipulate. It was just a smile, if a rather worried and sad one.

Elena somehow didn't notice the sadness until she remembered it later. She simply suddenly felt that she weighed nothing; that if she lost grip on herself she could be miles high before anyone could stop her – miles away, maybe even as far as this insane place's moons.

She managed a shaky smile of her own at him. "That's good."

"I came to talk to you," he said, "but . . . first—"

In another moment, somehow, Elena was in his arms.

"Damon – we can't keep on . . ." She tried to pull away gently. "We really can't keep doing this, you know."

But Damon didn't let go of her. There was something in the way he held her that half terrified her, and half made her want to cry with joy. She forced back the tears.

"It's all right," Damon said softly. "Go ahead and cry. We've got a situation on our hands."

Something in his voice frightened Elena. Not in the half-joyful way she'd been fearful a minute ago, but entirely frightened.

It's because *he's* afraid, she thought suddenly in wonderment. She had seen Damon angry, wistful, cold, mocking, seductive – even subdued, ashamed – but she had never seen him afraid of *anything*. She could hardly get her mind around the concept. Damon . . . frightened . . . for *her*.

"It's because of what I did yesterday, isn't it?" she asked. "Are they going to kill me?" She was surprised at how calmly she said it. She felt nothing except a vague distress and the desire to make Damon not afraid any more.

"No!" He held her at arm's length, staring. "At least not without killing me and Sage – and all the people in this house, too, if I know them." He stopped, seeming out of breath – which was impossible, Elena reminded herself. He's playing for time, she thought.

"But that's what they want to do," she said. She didn't know why she was so certain. Maybe she was picking up something telepathically.

"They have . . . made threats," Damon said slowly. "It's not the case of Old Drohzne really; I guess there are murders around here all the time and winner takes all. But apparently overnight word of what you did has been spreading. Slaves in nearby estates are refusing to obey their masters. This entire quarter of the slums is in turmoil – and they're afraid of what will happen if other sectors hear about it. Something has to be done as soon as possible or the whole Dark Dimension may just explode like a bomb."

Even as Damon spoke, Elena could hear the echoes of what he'd been told by the assembly who had come to Dr Meggar's door. *They* had been afraid, too.

Maybe this could be the start of something important, Elena thought, her mind soaring away from her own small problems. Even death wouldn't be too high a price to pay to free these wretched people from their demonic masters.

"But that's not what will happen!" Damon said, and Elena realised that she must be projecting her thoughts. There was genuine anguish in Damon's voice. "If we had planned things, if there were leaders who could stay here and oversee a revolution – if we could even *find* leaders strong enough to do it – then there might be a chance. Instead, *all* the slaves are being punished, everywhere that the word has spread. They're being tortured and killed on mere suspicion of sympathy with you. Their masters are making examples all over the city. And it's only going to get worse."

Elena's heart, which had been soaring on a dream of actually making a difference, came crashing down to the ground and she stared, horrified, into Damon's black eyes. "But we've got to stop that. Even if I have to die—"

Damon pulled her back in close to him. "You – and Bonnie and Meredith." His voice sounded hoarse. "Plenty of people saw the three of you together. Plenty of people now see all three of you as the troublemakers."

Elena's heart went cold. Maybe the worst thing was that she could see from a slave economy's point of view that if one incident of such insolence went unpunished and word of it spread . . . the tale would grow in the telling . . .

"We became famous overnight. We'll be legends tomorrow," she murmured, watching, in her mind, a domino toppling into another which hit another until a long string had fallen down spelling the word "Heroine".

But she didn't want to be a heroine. She had just come here to get Stefan back. And while she could have faced giving her life to stop slaves from being tortured and killed, she would herself kill anyone who tried to lay a hand on Bonnie or Meredith.

"They feel the same way," Damon said. "They heard what the congregation had to say." He held her arms hard as if trying to brace her. "A young girl named

Helena was beaten and hanged this morning because she had a similar name to yours. She was fifteen."

Elena's legs gave out, as so often they had done in Damon's arms . . . but never for this reason. He went with her. This was a conversation you had sitting on bare floorboards. "It wasn't your fault, Elena! You are what you are! People love you for what you are!"

Elena's pulse was hammering frantically. It was all so bad . . . but she had made it worse. By not thinking. By imagining that her life was the only one at stake. By acting before evaluating the consequences.

But in the same situation she would do it again. Or . . . with shame, she thought, I would do something like it. If I knew that I would put everyone I loved in danger I would have begged Damon to bargain with that slave-owner worm. Buy her for some outrageous price . . . if we had the money. If he would have listened . . . If another stroke of the whip hadn't killed Lady Ulma . . .

Suddenly her brain went hard and cold.

That is the past.

This is the present.

Deal with it.

"What can we do?" She tried to pull free and shake Damon; she was that frantic. "There must be something we can do now! They can't kill Bonnie and Meredith – and Stefan will die if we don't find him!"

Damon just held her more tightly. He was keeping his mind shielded from hers, Elena realised. This could either be good or bad. It might be that there was a solution he was reluctant to put to her. Or it could mean that the death of all three of the "rebel slaves" was the only thing the city leaders would accept.

"Damon." He was holding her much too tightly to get free, so Elena couldn't look him in the face. But she could visualise it, and she could also try to address him squarely, mind to mind.

Damon, if there's anything – *even any way we can save Bonnie and Meredith – you have to tell me. You have to. I order* you to!

Neither of them were in a mood to find that amusing or even to notice the "slave" giving orders to the "master". But at last Elena heard Damon's telepathic voice.

They say that if I take you back to Young Drohzne now and you apologise, that you can be let off with just six strokes of this. From somewhere Damon produced a pliant cane made of some pale wood. Ash, probably, Elena thought, surprised at how calm she was. *It's the one substance equally effective on everyone: even on vampires – even on Old Ones, which they undoubtedly have around here.*

But it has to be in public so that they can get the rumours started the other way. They think then that the turmoil will stop, if you – the one who started the disobedience – will admit your slave status.

Damon's thoughts were heavy, and so was Elena's heart. How many of her principles would she be betraying if she did this? How many slaves would she be condemning to lives of servitude?

Suddenly Damon's mental voice was angry. *We didn't come here to reform the Dark Dimension*, he reminded her, in tones that made Elena wince away. Damon shook her slightly. *We came to get Stefan, remember? Needless to say, we'll never have a chance to do that if we try to play Spartacus. If we start a war that we* know *we can't win. Even the Guardians can't win it.*

A light went on in Elena's mind.

"Of course," she said. "Why didn't I think of it before?"

"Think of what before?" Damon said desperately.

"We don't fight the war – now. I haven't even mastered my basic Powers, much less my Wings Powers. And this way they won't even wonder about them."

"Elena?"

"We come back," Elena explained to him excitedly. "When I can control all my Powers. And we bring allies with us – strong allies we'll find in the human world. It may take years and years but someday we come back and finish what we started."

Damon was staring at her as if she'd gone mad, but that didn't matter. Elena could feel Power coursing through her. This was one promise, she thought, that she would keep if it killed her.

Damon swallowed. "Can we talk about – about the present now?" he asked.

It was as if he had hit a bull's-eye.

The present. Now.

"Yes. Yes, of course." Elena looked at the ash cane contemptuously. "Of course, I'll do it, Damon. I don't want anyone else hurt because of me before I'm ready to fight. Dr Meggar is a good healer. If they allow me to come back to him."

"I honestly don't know," Damon said, holding her gaze. "But I do know one thing. You won't feel a single blow, I promise you that," he said quickly and earnestly, his dark eyes very big. "I'll take care of that; it'll all be channelled away. And you won't even see a trace of a mark by morning. But," he finished much more slowly, "you'll have to kneel to apologise to me, your owner, and to that filthy, scrofulous, abominable old—" Damon's imprecations carried him away for a moment so that he lapsed into Italian.

"To who?"

"To the leader of the slums, and possibly to Old Drohzne's brother, Young Drohzne, as well."

"OK. Tell them I'll apologise to as many Drohznes as they want. Tell them quick, in case we lose our chance."

Elena could see the look he gave her, but her mind was turned inward. Would she let Meredith or Bonnie do this? No. Would she allow it to happen to Caroline if by any means she could stop it? Again, no. No, no, no. Elena's feelings about brutality towards girls and women had always been exceedingly strong. Her feelings about the worldwide second-class citizenship of females had become remarkably clear since her return from the afterlife. If she had been returned to the world for any purpose, she had decided, helping to free girls and women from the slavery that many of them could not even see, was part of it.

But this wasn't just about a vicious slaveholder and faceless oppressed women and men. It was about Lady Ulma, and keeping her and her baby safe . . . and it was about Stefan. If she gave in, she would be just an impudent slave who caused a small ruckus in the road, but was firmly put back into her place by authorities.

Otherwise, if their party was scrutinised . . . if someone realised that they were here to release Stefan . . . if Elena was the one who caused the order to come: "Move him into stricter security – get rid of that silly kitsune-key thing . . ."

Her mind was ablaze with images of ways that Stefan could be punished, could be taken away, could be *lost* if this incident in the slums took on undue proportions.

No. She would not abandon Stefan now to fight a war that could not be won. But she wouldn't forget, either.

I'll come back for all of you, she promised. And then the story will have a different ending.

She realised that Damon still hadn't left. He was watching her with eyes as keen as a falcon's. "They sent me to bring you," he said quietly. "They never thought of a no for an answer." Elena could briefly feel the fierce rage of his fury at them and she took his hand and squeezed it.

"I'm coming back with you in the future, for the slaves," he said. "You know that, don't you?"

"Of course," said Elena, and her quick kiss became a longer kiss. She hadn't really absorbed what Damon had said about channelling away the pain. She felt she was due just one kiss for what she was about to endure, and then Damon stroked her hair and time meant nothing until Meredith knocked at the door.

The bloody-red dawn had taken on a bizarre, almost dreamlike quality by the time Elena was led to an open-air structure where the slumlords in charge of this area were seated on piles of once fine, now threadbare cushions. They were passing back and forth bottles and jewelled leather flasks filled with Black Magic, the only wine vampires could really enjoy, smoking hookahs and occasionally spitting into the darker shadows. This was regardless of the huge audience of street people dizzily attracted by word of a beautiful young human's public punishment.

Elena had been rehearsed in her lines. She was marched, gagged, hands manacled, before the hawking and spitting authorities. Young Drohzne was sitting in somewhat uncomfortable glory on a golden couch, and Damon was standing between him and the authorities, looking tense. Elena had never been so tempted to improvise a part since her junior play, when she had thrown a flowerpot at Petruchio and brought down the house in the last scene of *The Taming of the Shrew*.

But this was deadly serious business. Stefan's freedom, Bonnie's and Meredith's lives might depend upon it. Elena moved her tongue around inside her mouth, which was bone dry.

And, oddly, she found Damon's eyes, the man with the stick, uplifting her. He seemed to be telling her *courage and indifference* without using telepathy at all. Elena wondered if he himself had ever been in a similar situation.

She was kicked by one of her escorts and remembered where she was. She'd been loaned an "appropriate" costume from the discarded wardrobe of Dr Meggar's married daughter. It was pearl-coloured indoors, which meant it was mauve in the everlasting crimson sunlight. Most important, worn without its silken undershirt, its back plunged to below Elena's waistline, leaving her back completely bare. Now, in accordance with custom, she knelt in front of the elders, and bowed until her forehead rested on an ornate and very dirty carpet at the feet of the elders, but several steps lower. One of them spat on her.

There was excited, appreciative chattering, and ribaldry, and thrown missiles, mostly in the form of garbage. Fruit was too precious here to think of wasting. Dried excrement, however, was not, and Elena found the first tears coming to her eyes as she realised what she was being pelted with.

Courage and indifference, she told herself, not even daring to sneak a look up at Damon.

Presently, when the crowd was felt to have had its due playtime, one of the hookah-smoking civic elders stood up. He read words Elena couldn't understand from a creased scroll. It seemed to go on for ever. Elena, on her knees, with her forehead against the dusty carpet, felt as if she were smothering.

At last the scroll was put away and Young Drohzne leaped up and described in a high, almost hysterical voice, and flamboyant language, the story of a slave who attacked her own master (Damon, Elena noted mentally) to tear herself free of his supervision, and then attacked the head of his family (Old Drohzne, Elena thought) and his poor means of living, his cart, and his hopeless, impudent, slothful slave, and how all this had resulted in the death of his brother. To Elena's ears, at first, he seemed to be blaming Lady Ulma for the entire incident because she had fallen under her load.

"You all know the kind of slave I mean – she wouldn't bother to wave away a fly walking across her eye," he shrieked, appealing to the crowd, which responded with fresh insults and a renewed pelting upon Elena, since Lady Ulma wasn't there to punish.

At last, Young Drohzne finished recounting how this bold-faced hussy (Elena) who, wearing trousers like a man, had caught up his brother's own ne'er-do-well slave (Ulma) and had carried away this valuable property bodily away (all by myself? Elena wondered ironically) and had taken her to the home of a highly suspicious healer (Dr Meggar), who now refused to give her, the original slave, back.

"I knew when I heard this that I would never see my brother or his slave again," he cried, in the shrieking wail that he had somehow been able to maintain throughout the entire narrative.

"If the slave was so lazy, you should have been glad," a joker in the crowd called out.

"Nevertheless," said a very fat man whose voice reminded Elena irresistibly of Alfred Hitchcock's: the lugubrious delivery and the same pauses before important words, which served to make the mood more grim and entire business even more serious than anyone had heretofore thought. This was a man with power, Elena realised. The ribaldry, the pelting, even the hawking and spitting had fallen silent. The large man was undoubtedly the local equivalent of a "godfather" to these painfully poor residents of the slums. His word would be that which determined Elena's fate.

"And since then," he was saying slowly, crunching with every few words some irregularly shaped, golden-coloured sweetmeat from a bowl reserved for himself, "the young vampire Damien has made reparation – and most generously, too – for all the property damage." Here there was a long pause as he stared at Young Drohzne. "Therefore, his slave, Aliana, who started all this mischief will not be seized and put up for public auction, but will make her humble obeisance and surrender, here, and of her own will, receive the punishment she knows is her due."

Elena found herself dazed. She didn't know whether it was from all the smoke that had floated down to her level before curling away, but the words "put up for public auction" had sent a shock through her that almost led her to black out. She had had no idea that *that* could happen – and the pictures it brought to mind were extremely unpleasant. She also noticed her new alias, and Damon's. It was actually quite fortunate, she thought since it would be nice if Shinichi and Misao never heard about this little adventure.

"Bring the slave to us," the fat man concluded, and sat back down on a great pile of cushions.

Elena was lifted off her feet and roughly marched upward until she could see the man's gilded sandals, and remarkably clean feet, as she kept her eyes down in the manner of an obedient slave.

"Have you heard these proceedings?" The Godfather-type was still munching on his delicacies and a waft of breeze brought a heavenly smell to Elena's nose, and suddenly all the saliva she could ask for flooded to her dry lips.

"Yes, sir," she said, not knowing what title to give him.

"You address me as Your Excellence. And do you have anything to add in your defence?" the man asked, to Elena's astonishment. Her automatic response of: "Why ask me, since it's all been fixed up beforehand?" was stilled on her lips. This man was somehow *more* than any of the others she had met in the Dark Dimension – in fact, in her entire life. He listened to people. He would listen to me if I told him all about Stefan, Elena thought suddenly. But then, she thought, regaining her normal level-headedness, what could he do about it? Nothing, unless he could do some good *and* turn a profit out of it – or gain some power, or take down an enemy.

Still, he might make for an ally when she returned to level this place and freed the slaves.

"No, Your Excellence. Nothing to add," she said.

"And you are willing to prostrate yourself and beg my forgiveness and that of Master Drohzne?"

This was Elena's first scripted line. "Yes," she said, and she managed to get through her prefabricated apology clearly and with just the hint of a gulp at the end. Up close she could see flecks of gold on the large man's face, in his lap, in his beard.

"Very well. A penalty of ten ash rod strokes is laid upon this slave as an example to other mischief-makers. The punishment will be delivered by my nephew Clewd."

CHAPTER

21

Pandemonium. Elena whipped her head up, confused as to whether she was supposed to be the repentant slave any longer. The community leaders were all babbling at one another, pointing fingers, throwing up their hands. Damon had physically restrained the Godfather, who seemed to regard his part in the ceremony as concluded.

The crowd was hooting and cheering. It looked as if there would be another fight; this time between Damon and the Godfather's men, especially the one called Clewd.

Elena's head was whirling. She could catch only disjointed phrases.

"—only six strokes and promised me that *I* could administer—" Damon was shouting.

"—really think that these little flunkies tell the truth?" someone else – probably Clewd – was shouting back.

But isn't that exactly what the Godfather was, too? Just a bigger, more frightening and, undoubtedly, more efficient flunky who reported to someone higher up, and didn't cloud his mind with dope-smoke? Elena thought; and then ducked her head hastily as the fat man glanced towards her.

She could hear Damon again, this time clearly above the hubbub. He was standing by the Godfather. "I had believed that even here there was some honour once a bargain was struck." His voice made it obvious that he no longer thought negotiations were possible and that he was about to go on the attack. Elena tensed, horrified. She had never heard such open menace in his speaking voice.

"Wait." It was in the Godfather's lackadaisical tones, but it caused an instant of silence in the babble. The fat man, having removed Damon's hand from his arm, turned his head back toward Elena.

"I will waive, for my part, the participation of my nephew Clewd. Diarmund, or whoever you were, you are free to punish your own slave with your own tools."

Suddenly, surprisingly, the old man was brushing bits of gold out of his beard and speaking directly to Elena. His eyes were ancient, tired, and surprisingly discerning. "Clewd is a master at whipping, you know. He has his own little invention. He calls it the cat's whiskers and one blow can flay the skin from neck to hip. Most men die from ten lashes. But I'm afraid he'll be disappointed today." Then exposing surprisingly white and even teeth, the Godfather smiled. He extended to her the bowl of golden sweetmeats he'd been eating. "You might as well taste one before your Discipline. Go on."

Afraid to try one, afraid not to, Elena took one of the irregular pieces and popped it in her mouth. Her teeth crunched pleasantly. A walnut half! That's what the mysterious sweets were. A delicious half walnut dipped in some kind of sweet lemon syrup, with bits of hot pepper or something like that clinging to it, all gilded with that edible gold stuff. Ambrosia!

The Godfather was saying to Damon, "Do your own 'discipline', boy. But don't neglect to teach the girl how to cover her thoughts. She has too much wit to be wasted here in a slum-brothel. But then why do I not think she wishes to become a famous courtesan at all?"

Before Damon could answer or Elena look up from her genuflection, he was gone, carried by palanquin bearers to the only horse-drawn carriage Elena had seen in the slums.

By now the arguing, gesticulating civic leaders, egged on by Young Drohzne, had come to a sullen agreement. "Ten lashes, and she need not strip, and you may give them," they said. "But our final word is ten. The man who negotiated with you has no more power to argue."

Almost casually, one lifted by a tuft of hair a bodiless head. Absurdly, it was crowned with dusty leaves in anticipation of the banquet after the ceremony.

Damon's eyes flared with true rage that set objects around him vibrating. Elena could feel his Power like a panther rearing back against a leash. She felt as if she were speaking against a hurricane which cast every word back into her throat.

"I agree to it."

"What?"

"It's over, Da— Master Damon. No more yelling. I agree."

Now, as she prostrated herself on the carpets before Drohzne, there was a sudden keening of women and children and a fusillade of pellets aimed – sometimes badly – at the smirking slave owner.

The train of her dress was spread behind her like a bride's, the pearl overskirt making the underskirt a shimmering burgundy in the eternal red light. Her hair had fallen free of its high knot, making a cloud around her shoulders that Damon had to part with his hands. He was shaking. From fury. Elena didn't dare look at him, knowing that their minds would rush together. She was the one who remembered to say her formal speech before him and Young Drohzne so this entire farce would not have to be re-enacted.

Say it with feeling, her drama teacher, Ms Courtland, had always excoriated the class. If there was no feeling in you there could be none in the audience.

"Master!" Elena shouted in a voice that was loud enough to be heard above the women's lamentations. "Master, I am but a slave, not fit to address you. But I have trespassed and I accept my punishment eagerly – yea, eagerly, if it will restore to you but one hair's-breadth of the respectability you enjoyed before my unwonted evildoing. I beg you to punish this disgraced slave who lies like discarded offal in your gracious path."

The speech, which she had shouted in the unvarying glassy tones of someone who had been taught each word by rote, hadn't actually needed to be more than four words, "Master, I beg forgiveness." But no one seemed to have recognised the irony that Meredith had put into it, or to find it amusing. The Godfather had accepted it; Young Drohzne had already heard it once, and now it was Damon's turn.

But Young Drohzne wasn't finished yet. Smirking at Elena, he said, "Here's where you find out, Missy. But I want to see that ash rod before you use it!" —stumbling to Damon. A few practice swishes and blows to the cushions surrounding them (which filled the air with ruby-coloured dust) satisfied him that the rod was all that even he could want.

Mouth visibly watering, he settled on the gold couch, taking in Elena from head to toe.

And finally the time had come. Damon couldn't put it off any longer. Slowly, as if every step was part of a play that he hadn't rehearsed properly, he sidled alongside Elena to get an angle. Finally, as the gathered crowd became restless, and the women showed signs of losing themselves in drink, rather than in keening, he picked his spot.

"I ask forgiveness, my master," Elena said in her no-expression voice. If left to himself, she thought, he wouldn't even have remembered the necessities.

Now, indeed, was the time. Elena knew what Damon had promised her. She also knew that a lot of promises had been broken that day. For one thing, ten was almost twice six.

She wasn't looking forward to this.

But when the first blow came, she knew that Damon wasn't one of the promise-breakers. She felt a dull thud, and a numbness, and then, curiously, a wetness which had her glancing up through the latticework of boards above them for clouds. It was disconcerting to realise that the wetness was her own blood, spilled without pain, running down her side.

"Make her count them," Young Drohzne slurred in a snarl, and Elena said "One" automatically, before Damon could put up a fight.

Elena went on counting in the same clear, unaffected voice. In her mind she wasn't here, in this foul-smelling horrible gutter at all. She was lying with her elbows propped up to support her face, and looking down into Stefan's eyes – those spring-green eyes that would never be old, no matter how many centuries he accumulated. She was dreamily counting for him, and *ten* would be their signal to jump up and begin the race. It was raining gently, but Stefan was giving her a handicap, and soon, soon she would scramble off him and run away through lush green grass. She would make this a fair race and really put her muscle into it, but Stefan, of course, would catch her. Then they would go down on the grass together, laughing and laughing as if they were having hysterics.

As for the vague, far-off sounds of wolflike leers and drunken snarls, even they were gradually changing. It all had to do with some silly dream about Damon and an ash rod. In the dream, Damon was swinging hard enough to satisfy the most exacting of onlookers, and the blows, which Elena could hear in the increasing silence, sounded more than hard enough, and made her feel a bit nauseated when she reflected that they were the sound of her own skin splitting, but she felt no more than dull cuffs up and down her back. And Stefan was drawing up her hand to kiss!

"I'll always be yours," Stefan said. "We belong together every time you dream."

I'll always be yours, Elena told him silently, knowing he would get the message. I may not be able to dream of you all the time, but I am always with you.

Always, my angel. I'm waiting for you, Stefan said.

Elena heard her own voice say "Ten," and Stefan kissed her hand again and was gone. Blinking, bewildered, and confused by the sudden inrush of noises, she sat cautiously up, looking around.

Young Drohzne was hunched into himself, blind with fury, disappointment and more liquor than even he could stand up under. The wailing women had long ago gone silent, awed. The children were the only ones who still made any noise, climbing up and down on the boards, whispering to one another and running if Elena should happen to glance their way.

And then, with an entire lack of ceremony, it was over.

When Elena first stood up the world made a complete double circle around her and her legs folded. Damon caught her, and called to the few young men still conscious and inclined to look at him, "Give me a cape." It wasn't a request, and the best-dressed of the men, who seemed to have been slumming, tossed him a heavy cape, black, lined with greenish blue, and said, "Keep it. The performance – marvellous. Is it a hypnotist's act?"

"No performance," Damon snarled, in a voice that stopped the other slummers in the act of holding out business cards.

"Take them," Elena whispered.

Damon snatched up the cards in one hand, ungraciously. But Elena forced herself to toss the hair off her face and smile slowly, heavy-lidded, at the young men. They smiled somewhat timidly back.

"When you – ah – perform again . . ."

"You'll hear," Elena called to them. Damon was already carrying her back to Dr Meggar, surrounded by the inevitable entourage of children plucking at their cloaks. It was only then that it occurred to Elena to wonder why Damon had asked for a cloak from some strangers, when he, in fact, was already wearing one.

"They will be having ceremonies somewhere, now that there are this many of them," Mrs Flowers said in genteel distress as she and Matt sat and sipped herbal tea in the boarding-house parlour. It was dinnertime, but still quite light outside.

"Ceremonies to do *what*?" Matt asked. He had never made it to his parents' house since he'd left Damon and

Elena more than a week ago to come back to Fell's Church. He'd stopped by Meredith's house, which was on the edge of town, and she'd convinced him to come by Mrs Flowers's first. After the conversation the three of them had had with Bonnie, Matt had decided it was best to be "invisible". His family would be safer if no one knew that he was still in Fell's Church. He would live at the boarding-house, but none of the children who were making all the trouble would realise that. Then, with Bonnie and Meredith safely gone to meet Damon and Elena, Matt could be a sort of secret operative.

Now he almost wished he'd gone with the girls. Trying to be a secret operative in a place where all the enemies seemed to be able to hear and see better than you could, as well as to move much faster, hadn't turned out to be nearly as helpful as it had sounded. He spent reading most of the time the Internet blogs that Meredith had marked, looking for clues that might do them some good.

But he hadn't read of the need for any kind of ceremonies. He turned to Mrs Flowers as she thoughtfully sipped her tea.

"Ceremonies for what?" he repeated.

With her soft white hair and her gentle face and vague, amiable blue eyes, Mrs Flowers looked like the most harmless little old lady in the world. She wasn't. A witch by birth, and a gardener by vocation, she knew as much about black magic herbal toxins as about white magic healing poultices.

"Oh, doing generally unpleasant things," she replied sadly, staring into the tea leaves in her cup. "They're partly like pep rallies, you know, to get everyone all worked up. They probably also do some small black magic there. Some of it is by way of blackmail and brainwashing – they can tell any new converts that they are guilty now by reason of attending the meetings. They might as well give in and become fully initiated . . . that sort of thing. Very unpleasant."

"But what kind of unpleasant?" Matt persisted.

"I really don't know, dear. I never went to one of them."

Matt considered. It was almost 7:00, which was curfew for children under eighteen. Eighteen seemed to be the oldest that a child could be and become possessed.

Of course, it wasn't an official curfew. The sheriff's department seemed to have no idea of how to deal with the curious disease that was working its way through the young girls of Fell's Church. Scare them straight? It was the police that were frightened. One young sheriff had come tearing out of the Ryan house to be sick after seeing how Karen Ryan had bitten off the heads of her pet mice and what she had done with the rest of them.

Lock them away? The parents wouldn't hear of it, no matter how bad their child's behaviour was, how obvious it was that their kid needed help. Children who were towed off to the next town for an appointment with a psychiatrist sat demurely and spoke calmly and logically . . . for the entire fifty minutes of their appointment. Then, on their way back they took revenge, repeating everything their parents said in perfect mimicry, making startlingly real-sounding animal noises, holding conversations with themselves in Asian-sounding languages, or even resorting to the cliché but still chilling backward-talking routine.

Neither ordinary discipline nor ordinary medical science seemed to have an answer to the children's problem.

But what frightened parents the most was when their

sons and daughters would disappear. Early on, it was assumed that the children went to the cemetery, but when adults tried to follow them to one of their secret meetings, they found the cemetery empty – even down to Honoria Fell's secret crypt. The children seemed to have simply . . . vanished.

Matt thought he knew the answer to this conundrum. That thicket of the Old Wood still standing near the cemetery. Either Elena's powers of purification had not reached this far, or the place was so malevolent that it had been able to resist her cleansing.

And, as Matt knew well, the Old Woods were completely under the domination of the kitsune by now. You could take two steps into the thicket and spend the rest of your life trying to get out.

"But maybe I'm young enough to follow them in," he said now to Mrs Flowers. "I know Tom Pierler goes with them and he's my age. And then so were the ones who started it: Caroline gave it to Jim Bryce, who gave it to Isobel Saitou."

Mrs Flowers looked abstracted. "We should ask Isobel's grandmother for more of those Shinto wards against evil she blessed," she said. "Do you think you could do that sometime, Matt? Soon we'll have to ready ourselves for a barricade, I'm afraid."

"Is that what the tea leaves say?"

"Yes, dear, and they agree with what my poor old head says, too. You might want to pass the word on to Dr Alpert as well so she can get her daughter and grandchildren out of town before it's too late."

"I'll give her the message, but I think it's going to be pretty hard tearing Tyrone away from Deborah Koll. He's really stuck on her – hey, maybe Dr Alpert can get the Kolls to leave, too."

"Maybe she can. That would mean a few less children to worry about," Mrs Flowers said, taking Matt's cup to peer into it.

"I'll do it." It was weird, Matt thought. He had three allies now in Fell's Church and they were all women over sixty. One was Mrs Flowers, still vigorous enough to be up every morning taking a walk and doing her gardening; one was Obaasan – confined to bed, tiny and doll-like, with her black hair held up in a bun – who was always ready with advice from the years she had spent as a shrine maiden; and the last was Dr Alpert, Fell's Church's local doctor, who had iron-grey hair, burnished dark-brown skin, and an absolutely pragmatic attitude about everything, including magic. Unlike the police, she refused to deny what was happening in front of her, and did her best to help alleviate the fears of the children as well as to advise the terrified parents.

A witch, a priestess and a doctor. Matt figured that he had all his bases covered, especially since he also knew Caroline, the original patient in this case – whether it was possession by foxes or wolves or both, plus something else.

"I'll go to the meeting tonight," he said firmly. "The kids have been whispering and contacting each other all day. I'll hide in the afternoon someplace where I can see them going into the thicket. Then I'll follow, as long as Caroline – or, God help us, Shinichi or Misao – isn't with them."

Mrs Flowers poured him another cup of tea. "I'm very worried about you, Matt, dear. It seems to me to be a day of bad omens. Not the sort of day to take chances."

"Does your mom have anything to say about it?" Matt asked, genuinely interested. Mrs Flowers's mother had died sometime around the beginning of the 1900s, but that hadn't stopped her from communicating with her daughter.

"Well, that's just the thing. I haven't heard a word from her all day. I'll just try one more time." Mrs Flowers shut her eyes, and Matt could see her crepe-textured eyelids move around as she presumably looked for her mother or tried to go into a trance or something. Matt drank his tea and finally began to play a game on his mobile.

At last Mrs Flowers opened her eyes again and sighed. "Dear Ma*ma* (she always said it that way, with the accent on the second syllable) is being fractious today. I just can't get her to give me a clear answer. She does say that the meeting will be very noisy, and then very silent. And it's clear that she feels it will be very dangerous as well. I think I'd better go with you, my dear."

"No, no! If your mother thinks it's that dangerous I won't even try it," Matt said. The girls would skin him alive if anything happened to Mrs Flowers, he thought. Better to play it safe.

Mrs Flowers sat back in her chair, seeming relieved. "Well," she said at last, "I suppose I'd better get to my weeding. I have mugwort to cut and dry, too. And blueberries should be ripe by now, as well. How time flies."

"Well, you're cooking for me and all," Matt said. "I wish you'd let me pay you bed and board."

"I could never forgive myself! You are my guest, Matt. As well as my friend, I do so hope."

"Absolutely. Without you, I'd be lost. And I'll just take a walk around the edge of town. I need to burn off some energy. I wish—" He broke off suddenly. He'd started to say he wished he could shoot a few hoops with Jim Bryce. But Jim wouldn't be shooting hoops again – ever. Not with his mutilated hands.

"I'll just go out and take a walk," he said.

"Yes," said Mrs Flowers. "Please, Matt dear, be careful. Remember to take a jacket or windbreaker."

"Yes, ma'am." It was early August, hot and humid enough to walk around in swimming briefs. But Matt had been raised to treat little old ladies in a certain way – even if they were witches and in most things sharp as the X-acto knife he slipped into his pocket as he left the boarding-house.

He went outside, then, by a side route, down to the cemetery.

Now, if he just went over *there*, where the ground dipped down below the thicket, he'd have a good view of anyone going into the last remnant of the Old Wood while no one on the path below could see him from any angle.

He hurried toward his chosen hide noiselessly, ducking behind tombstones, keeping alert for any change in birdsong, which would indicate that the children were coming. But the only birdsong was the raucous shriek of crows in the thicket and he saw no one at all—

—until he slipped into his hideout.

Then he found himself face-to-face with a drawn gun, and, behind that, the face of Sheriff Rich Mossberg.

The first words out of the officer's mouth seemed to come entirely by rote, as if someone had pulled a string on a twentieth-century talking doll.

"Matthew Jeffrey Honeycutt, I hereby arrest you for assault and battery upon Caroline Beula Forbes. You have the right to remain silent—"

"And so do you," Matt hissed. "But not for long! Hear those crows all taking off at once? The kids are coming to the Old Wood! And they're close!"

Sheriff Mossberg was one of those people who never

stop speaking until they are finished, so by this time he was saying: "Do you understand these rights?"

"No, sir! *Mi ne komprenas* Dumbtalk!"

A wrinkle appeared between the sheriff's eyebrows. "Is that Italian lingo you're trying on me?"

"It's Esperanto – we don't have time! There they are – and, oh, God, *Shinichi*'s with them!" The last sentence was spoken in the barest of whispers as Matt lowered his head, peeking through the tall weeds at the edge of the cemetery without stirring them.

Yes, it was Shinichi, hand in hand with a little girl of maybe twelve. Matt recognised her vaguely: she lived up near Ridgemont. Now, what was her name? Betsy, Becca . . . ?

There was a faint anguished sound from Sheriff Mossberg. "My niece," he breathed, surprising Matt that he could speak so softly. "That, in fact, is my *niece*, Rebecca!"

"OK, just stay still and hang on," Matt whispered. There was a line of children following behind Shinichi just as if he were some sort of Satanic Pied Piper, with his red-tipped black hair shining and his golden eyes laughing in the late-afternoon sunlight. The children were giggling and singing, some of them in sweet nursery school voices, a remarkably twisted version of "Seven Little Rabbits". Matt felt his mouth go dry. It was agony to watch them march into the forest thicket, like watching lambs riding up a ramp into an abattoir.

He had to commend the sheriff for not trying to shoot Shinichi. That would really have caused all hell to break loose. But then, just as Matt's head was sagging in relief as the last of the children entered the thicket, he jerked it back up again.

Sheriff Mossberg was preparing to get up.

"No!" Matt grabbed his wrist.

The sheriff pulled away. "I have to go in there! He's got my niece!"

"He won't kill her. *They don't kill the children*. I don't know why, but they don't."

"You heard what sort of filth he was teaching them. He'll sing a different tune when he sees a semi-automatic Glock pistol aimed at his head."

"Listen," Matt said, "you've got to arrest me, right? I demand that you arrest me. *But don't go into that Wood!*"

"I don't see any proper Wood," the sheriff said with disdain. "There's barely room in that stand of oak trees for all those kids to sit down. If you want to be of some use in your life, you can grab one or two of the little ones as they come running out."

"Running out?"

"When they see me, they're going to scatter. Probably burst out in all directions, but some of 'em will take the path they used to go in. Now are you going to help or not?"

"*Not*, sir," Matt said slowly and firmly. "And – and, look – look, I'm *begging* you not to go in there! Believe me, I know what I'm talking about!"

"I don't know what kind of dope you're on, kid, but in fact I don't have time to talk any more right now. And if you try to stop me again" – he swung the Glock to cover Matt – "I'll cite you for another account of trying to obstruct justice. Get it?"

"Yeah, I get it," Matt said, feeling tired. He slumped back into the hide as the officer, making surprisingly little noise, slipped out and made his way down to the thicket. Then Sheriff Rich Mossberg strode in between the trees and was lost to Matt's field of vision.

Matt sat in the hide and sweated for an hour. He was

having trouble staying awake when there was a disturbance in the thicket and Shinichi came out, leading the laughing, singing children.

Sheriff Mossberg didn't come out with them.

CHAPTER

22

The afternoon after Elena's "discipline", Damon took out a room in the same complex where Dr Meggar lived. Lady Ulma stayed in the doctor's office until between them, Sage, Damon and Dr Meggar had healed her completely.

She never talked about sad things now. She told them so many stories about her childhood estate that they felt they could walk around it and recognise every room, vast though it was.

"I suppose it's home to rats and mice now," she said wistfully at the conclusion of one story. "And spiders and moths."

"But why?" Bonnie said, failing to see the signals that both Meredith and Elena were giving her not to ask.

Lady Ulma tipped her head back to look at the ceiling. "Because ... of General Verantz. The middle-aged demon who saw me when I was only fourteen. When he had the army attack my home, they slaughtered every living thing they found inside – except me and my canary. My parents, my grandparents, my aunts and uncles . . . my younger brothers and sisters. Even my cat sleeping on the window seat. General Verantz had me brought in front of him, just as I was, in my nightgown and bare feet, with my hair unbrushed and coming out of its braid, and beside him was my canary with the night-time cloth off its cage. It was still alive and hopping about as cheerful as ever. And that made everything else that happened seem worse somehow – and yet more like a dream, too. It's difficult to explain.

"Two of the general's men were holding me when they brought me before him. They were really propping me up more than keeping me from running, though. I was so young, you see, and everything kept fading in and out. But I remember exactly what the general said to me. He said, 'I told this bird to sing and it sang. I told your parents I wanted to give you the honour of being my wife and they refused. Now look over there. Will you be like the canary or your parents, I wonder?' And he pointed to a dim corner of the room – of course it was all torchlight then, and the torches had been put out for the night. But there was enough light for me to see that there was a heap of round objects, with thatch or grass at one side of them. At least that is what I first thought – truly. I was that innocent, and I believe shock had done something to my mind."

"Please," Elena said, stroking Lady Ulma's hand gently. "You don't have to keep on with this. We understand—"

But Lady Ulma didn't seem to hear the words. She said, "And then one of the general's men held up a sort of coconut with very long thatch at the top, braided. He swung it casually – and all of a sudden I saw it for what it really was. It was my mother's head."

Elena choked involuntarily. Lady Ulma looked around

at the three girls with steady, dry eyes. "I suppose you think me very callous for being able to talk about such things without breaking down."

"No, no—" Elena began hastily. She herself was shaking, even after tuning down her psychic senses to their least extent. She hoped Bonnie wouldn't faint.

Lady Ulma was speaking again. "War, casual violence, and tyranny are all I have known since my childhood innocence was crushed in that moment. It is kindness now that astounds me, that makes my eyes sting with tears."

"Oh, don't cry," begged Bonnie, throwing her arms around the woman impulsively. "Please don't. *We're* here for you."

Meanwhile Elena and Meredith were regarding each other with knitted eyebrows and quick shrugs.

"Yes, please don't cry," Elena put in, feeling faintly guilty, but determined to try Plan A. "But tell us, why did your family estate end up in such bad condition?"

"It was the fault of the general. He was sent to faraway lands to fight foolish, meaningless wars. When he left he would take most of his retinue with him – including slaves who were in favour at the moment. When he left once, three years after he had attacked our home, I was not in favour, and I was not chosen to be with him. I was lucky. His entire battalion was wiped out; the household members who went with him were taken captive or slaughtered. He had no heir and his property here reverted to the Crown, which had no use for it. It has lain unoccupied for all these many years – looted many times, no doubt, but with its true secret, the secret of the jewels, undiscovered . . . as far as I know."

"The Secret of the Jewels," Bonnie whispered, clearly

putting it all in capital letters, as if it were a mystery novel. She still had an arm around Lady Ulma.

"What secret of the jewels?" Meredith said more calmly. Elena couldn't speak for the delicious shivers that were running through her. This was like being part of some magical play.

"In my parents' day, it was common to hide your wealth somewhere on your estate – and to keep the knowledge of its hiding place strictly to the owners. Of course, my father, as a designer and trader in jewels, had more to hide than most people knew of. He had a wonderful room that seemed to me something like Aladdin's cave. It was his workshop, where he kept his raw gems as well as finished pieces that had been commissioned or that he designed for my mother or out of his imagination."

"And no one ever found that?" Meredith said. There was just the slightest tinge of scepticism in her voice.

"If anyone did, I never heard about it. Of course, they could have gotten the knowledge out of my father or mother, in time – but the general was not a meticulous and patient vampire or kitsune, but a rough and impatient demon. He killed my parents as he stormed through the house. It never occurred to him that I, a child of fourteen, might share the knowledge."

"But you did . . ." Bonnie whispered, fascinated, taking the story where it had to go.

"But I did. And I do now."

Elena gulped. She was still trying to stay calm, to be more like Meredith, to maintain a cool head. But just as she opened her mouth to be cool-headed, Meredith said, "What are we waiting for?" and jumped to her feet.

Lady Ulma seemed to be the most tranquil person there. She also seemed slightly bewildered and almost timid. "You mean that we should ask our master for an audience?"

"I mean that we should go out there and get those jewels!" Elena exclaimed. "Although, yes, Damon would be a big asset if there's anything that takes strength to lift. Sage, too." She couldn't understand why Lady Ulma wasn't more excited.

"Don't you see?" Elena said, her mind racing. "You can have your household back again! We can do our best to fix it up the way it was when you were a child. I mean, if that's what you want to do with the money. But I'd love, at least, to *see* the Aladdin's cave!"

"But – well," Lady Ulma seemed suddenly distressed. "I had meant to ask Master Damon for another favour – although the money from the jewels might help with that."

"What is it that you want?" Elena said as gently as she could. "And you don't need to call him Master Damon. He freed you days ago, remember?"

"But surely that was just a – a celebration of the moment?" Lady Ulma still looked puzzled. "He didn't make it official at the Servile Offices or anything, did he?"

"If he didn't it's because he didn't know!" Bonnie cried out at the same time as Meredith said, "We don't really understand the protocol. Is that what you need to do?"

Lady Ulma seemed able only to nod her head. Elena felt humble. She guessed that this woman, a slave for more than twenty-two years, must find true freedom difficult to believe in.

"Damon meant it when he said we were all free," she said, kneeling by Lady Ulma's chair. "He just didn't know all the things he had to do. If you tell us, we can tell him, and then we can all go to your old estate."

She was about to get up again, when Bonnie said, "Something's wrong. She isn't as happy as she was before. We have to find out what it is."

By opening her psychic perceptions a bit, Elena could tell that Bonnie was right. She stayed where she was, kneeling by Lady Ulma's chair.

"What is it?" she said, because the woman seemed to bare her soul most when she, Elena, asked the questions.

"I had hoped," Lady Ulma said slowly, "that Master Damon might buy . . ." She flushed, but struggled on. "Might find it in his heart to buy one more slave. The . . . the father of my child."

There was a moment of perfect silence, and then all three girls were talking, all three, Elena guessed, trying frantically to do what she herself was working at, which was not mentioning that she had assumed Old Drohzne was the father.

But of course he couldn't be, Elena scolded herself. She's *happy* about this pregnancy – and who could be happy to have a child by a disgusting monster like Old Drohzne? Besides, he didn't have a clue that she might be pregnant – and didn't care.

"It might be easier said than done," Lady Ulma said, when the babble of reassurances and questions had died down a little. "Lucen is a jeweller, a renowned man who creates pieces that . . . that remind me of my father's. He will be expensive."

"But we've got Aladdin's cave to explore!" Bonnie said gleefully. "I mean, you'll have enough if you sell off the jewellery, right? Or do you need more?"

"But that is Master Damon's jewellery," Lady Ulma said, seeming horrified. "Even if he did not realise it when he inherited all of Old Drohzne's property, he became my owner, and the owner of all my property . . ."

"Let's go get you freed and then we'll take things one step at a time," Meredith said in her firmest and most rational voice.

Dear Diary,

Well, I am writing to you still as a slave. Today we freed Lady Ulma, but decided that Meredith and Bonnie and I should remain "personal assistants". This is because Lady Ulma said Damon would seem odd and unfashionable if he didn't have several beautiful girls as courtesans.

There is actually an upside to this, which is that as courtesans we need to have beautiful clothes and jewellery all the time. Since I've been wearing the same pair of jeans ever since that b*st*rd Old Drohzne sliced up the pair I wore into this place, you can imagine that I'm excited.

But, truly, it's not just because of pretty clothes I'm excited. Everything that happened since we freed Lady Ulma and then went to her old estate has been a wonderful dream. The house was run down, and obviously the home of wild animals who used it as a lavatory as well as a bedroom. We even found the tracks of wolves and other animals upstairs, which led to the question of whether werewolves live in this world. Apparently they do, and some in very high positions under various feudal lords. Maybe Caroline would like to try a vacation here to learn about the real werewolves though — they're said to hate humans so much that they won't even have human or vampire (once human) slaves.

But back to Lady Ulma's house. Its foundation is of stone and it's panelled inside with hardwood, so the basic structure is fine. The curtains and tapestries are all hanging in shreds, of course, so it's sort of spooky to go inside with torches and see them dangling above and around you. Not to mention the giant spiderwebs. I hate spiders more than anything.

But we went inside, with our torches seeming like smaller versions of that giant crimson sun that always sits on the horizon, staining everything outside the colour of blood, and we shut the doors and lit a fire in a giant fireplace in what Lady Ulma calls the Great Hall. I think it's where you eat or have parties – it has an enormous table on a dais at one side, and a room for minstrels above what must be the dance floor. Lady Ulma said that this is where the servants all sleep at night, too (the Great Hall, not the minstrel gallery).

Then we went upstairs, where we saw – I swear – several dozen bedrooms with very large four-poster beds that are going to need new mattresses and sheets and coverlets and hangings, but we didn't stay to look around. There were bats hanging from the ceiling.

We headed for Lady Ulma's mother's workroom. It was a very large room where at least forty people could sit and sew the clothes that Lady Ulma's mother designed. But here's the exciting part!

Lady Ulma went to one of the wardrobes in the room and moved away all the tattered, moth-eaten clothes that were in it. And she pressed some different places at the back of the cupboard and the whole back of the cupboard slid out! Inside it was a very narrow stairway going straight down!

I kept thinking about Honoria Fell's crypt and wondering if some homeless vampire might have taken up residence in the room downstairs, but I knew that was silly because there were spiders' webs just inside the door. Damon still insisted that he go down first because he has the best eyesight in the dark, but I think the truth is that he was just curious to see what was down there.

We each followed him one at a time, trying to be careful with the torches, and . . . well, I can't find the right words for what we discovered. For just a few minutes I was disappointed because everything on the big table down there was dusty rather than sparkly, but then Lady Ulma began to gently brush jewels off with a special cloth and Bonnie found sacks and packages and she poured them out – and it was like pouring out a rainbow! Damon found a cabinet where there were drawers and drawers of necklaces, bracelets, rings, armlets, anklets, earrings, nose rings and hairpins and ornaments, too!

I couldn't believe what I was seeing. I poured out a pouch and found that I had a huge handful of glorious white diamonds dripping through my fingers, some of them as big as my thumbnail. I saw white pearls and black pearls, both smaller and perfectly matched, and huge and in marvellous shapes: almost as big as apricots with pink or golden or grey sheens to them. I saw sapphires the size of quarters, with stars you could see almost from across the room. I held handfuls of emeralds and peridots and opals and rubies and tourmalines and amethysts – and a lot *of lapis lazuli, for the discriminating vampire, of course.*

And the jewellery that was already made up was so beautiful it made my throat ache. I know Lady Ulma had a quiet little cry, but I think it was partly from happiness as we all kept complimenting her on her *jewels. In days she has gone from being a slave* who owned nothing to an incredibly rich woman who owns a house and all the means she would ever need to keep it up in style. We decided that even though she is going to marry her lover, it was best at first for Damon to buy him quietly and free him quietly, but to play "Head of the Household" for as long as we are here. During that time we will treat Lady Ulma as family, and will put the jeweller Lucen back to work until we leave, when he and Lady Ulma can quietly take Damon's place. The feudal lords around here are not demons any more, but vampires, and they have less objection to humans owning property.

Have I told you about Lucen? He's a wonderful artist with jewels! He has a burning need to create — in his early days as a slave he would create with mud and weeds, imagining that he was making jewellery. Then he got lucky and was apprenticed to a jeweller. He's felt sorry for Lady Ulma for so long, and loved her for so long, that it's like a little miracle that they are truly able to get together — and most importantly, as free citizens.

We were afraid that Lucen might not like the idea of us buying him as a slave and not freeing him until we leave, but he _never_ thought he'd be free — because of his talent. He's a slow, gentle, kind man, with a neat little beard and grey eyes that remind me of Meredith's. And he's so amazed at being treated decently and not worked around the clock that he would have accepted anything, just to be allowed to be near Lady Ulma. I guess he was an apprentice when her father was a jeweller, and he fell in love with her all those years ago, but he thought he would never, never _ever_ be able to be with her, because she *was a young lady of quality and he was a slave. They're so happy together!*

Every day Lady Ulma looks more beautiful, and younger. She asked permission from Damon to dye her hair all black, and he told her she could dye it pink if she liked, and now she just looks incredibly beautiful. I can't believe I ever thought of her as an old hag, but that's what agony and fear and hopelessness do to you. Every one of those grey hairs was from being a slave, with no property, no say in her future, no safety, no ability even to keep her children, if she had them.

I forgot to tell you the other upside of Meredith, Bonnie and I being "personal assistants" for a while. It's that we can employ a lot of poor women who make their living by sewing, and Lady Ulma actually wants to design and show them how to make our finest clothes. We told her that she could just relax, but she says all her life she's fantasised about being a designer like her mother and now she's dying to do it – with three completely different types of girl to dress. I'm dying to see what she'll come up with: she's already started sketching and tomorrow the man who sells fabric will come and she'll pick the materials.

Meanwhile Damon has hired about two hundred people (really!) to clean out Lady Ulma's estate, put up new wall hangings and curtains, refurbish the plumbing system, polish up the furniture that has kept nicely, and to get new furniture where things have fallen apart. Oh, and to plant ready-grown flowers and trees in the gardens and put in fountains and all kinds of stuff. With that many people working, we ought to be able to move in in just a matter of days.

All this has just one purpose, aside from making Lady Ulma happy. It's so that Damon and his "personal assistants" will be accepted by high society as the season of parties begins this year. Because I've kept the best for last. Both Lady Ulma and Sage could immediately identify the people in the riddles that Misao gave to us!

It just goes to prove what I thought before, that Misao never imagined that we'd actually make it here, or that we could get entrance to the places where they've hidden the two halves of the fox key.

But there's a very easy way to get invited into the houses we need to get into. If we're the newest, splashiest <u>nouveau riche</u> (sp?) around, and if we circulate the story that Lady Ulma has been restored to her rightful place, and if everyone wants to know about her – we'll get invited to parties! And that's how we get into the two estates we need to visit to look for the halves of the key that we need to free Stefan! And we're incredibly lucky, because this is the time of year when everyone begins to give parties, and both households we want to visit are having early celebrations: one is a gala, and one is a spring soirée to celebrate the first flowers.

I know my writing is shaky now. I'm shaky myself at the thought that we are actually going to look for the two halves of the fox key that will let us break Stefan out of his prison.

Oh, diary, it's late – and I can't – I can't write about Stefan. To be here in the same city with him, to know the direction to his prison . . . and yet to not be able to get to see him. My eyes are so blurred I can't see what I'm writing. I wanted to get some sleep to be ready for another day of running around, *supervising, and watching Lady Ulma's estate blossom like a rose – but now I'm afraid I'll just have nightmares about Stefan's hand slowly slipping out of mine.*

CHAPTER

23

That "night" they moved in, choosing the hour while the other estates they passed were darkened and quiet. Elena, Meredith and Bonnie each picked a room on the upper floor as a bedroom, all close together. Nearby was a luxurious bathing room, with a pale-blue and white marble floor and a unique pool shaped like a giant rose, fully large enough to swim in, heated by charcoal, with a cheerful-looking servant to tend it.

Elena was delighted with what happened next. Damon bought a number of slaves quietly, in a private sale from a respectable dealer, and then promptly freed them all and offered them wages and time off. Almost all the former slaves were only too happy to agree to stay, and only a few chose to leave or ran away, mostly women in search of their families. The others would remain and become Lady Ulma's staff once Damon, Elena, Bonnie, and Meredith left after freeing Stefan.

Lady Ulma, was given a "senior" room downstairs, although Damon almost had to use brute force to install her in it. He himself chose a room that was an office by day, since he wasn't likely to spend much of the night in the house anyway.

There was a slight embarrassment over that. Most of the staff knew of the ways of vampire masters, and the young girls and women who came to sew or who lived on the estate and cooked and cleaned seemed to expect some sort of rota to be worked out, with each of them taking turns at being donors.

Damon explained this to Elena, who quashed the idea before it could be implemented. She could tell that Damon was hoping for a steady stream of girls, ranging from flowerlike to red-cheeked and buxom, who would be glad to be "tapped" like beer kegs for the pretty bangles and baubles that were traditionally given.

Elena similarly disposed of the idea of hunting for hire. Sage had mentioned that there were even rumours of a possible Outside connection: a very advanced training course for Navy SEALs.

"And they can come out the world's only vampire seals," Elena had said sardonically, in front of a group of male slaves this time. "They can go out and bite sharks. Certainly you guys can go out and hunt some humans like a pair of owls hunting mice – just don't bother to come home afterwards, because the doors will be locked . . . permanently." She held Sage's gaze until her expression became a steely glare and he'd hastened off to do something else around the estate.

Elena didn't mind Sage's informal moving in with them. And after hearing how Sage had saved Damon from the mob that ambushed him on the way to the Meeting Place, she had determined in her own mind that if Sage ever wanted *her* blood, she would give it to him unhesitatingly. After a few days, when he had stayed around the house near Dr Meggar's and then moved with them into Lady Ulma's compound, she had wondered if her diminished aura and Damon's reticence weren't depriving him of something he should know about. So she'd thrown broader and broader hints at him, until once when he had doubled over, and then, with tears of laughter (but had it only been laughter?) in his eyes, had come over to her and said that the Americans had a saying, no? *You can lead a horse to water, but you cannot make it drink.* In his case, he said, you could lead a snarling black panther – her normal mental iconic image of Damon – to water, if you had electric cattle prods and elephant *ankusha*, but that afterward you'd be a fool to turn your back on it. Elena had laughed until she, too, cried, but had still pledged that if he wanted her blood, a reasonable share was his.

Now she simply felt glad to have him around. Her heart was too full already, with Stefan, Damon – and even Matt, despite his apparent desertion – for her to be in danger of falling for another vampire, no matter how terminally fit they were. She appreciated Sage as a friend and protector.

Elena was surprised at how much she came to rely on Lakshmi as each day passed. Lakshmi had begun as a sort of gofer, doing the running around that no one else wanted to, but more and more, she had become Lady Ulma's maid-in-waiting and Elena's source of information about this world. Lady Ulma was still officially bedridden, and having Lakshmi ready at any time of the day or night, to send messages, was wonderfully convenient. Too, she was someone that Elena could ask questions of that otherwise would get her eyed as if she were crazy. Did they need to buy plates or was food served on a large hunk of dried bread, which acted as a napkin for greasy fingers as well? (Plates had been recently introduced, along with forks, which were all the rage now.) How much were the men and woman of the household entitled to in wages (which had to be calculated from scratch, since no other household paid its slaves a geld, merely clothing them from a community uniform cache, and allowing them one or two "feast days" a year)? Young as she was, Lakshmi was both honest and bold and Elena was grooming her to become Lady Ulma's right hand, after Lady Ulma had become well enough to be the lady of the house.

CHAPTER

24

Dear Diary,
 It's the night before the night of our first party – or rather gala. But I don't feel very gala. I miss Stefan too much.
 I've been brooding about Matt, too. How he walked away, so angry at me, not even looking back. He didn't understand how I could . . . care for . . . Damon, and yet still love Stefan so much that it felt as if my heart was breaking.

Elena put down the pen and stared at her diary dully. The heartbreak manifested itself in actual physical pains in her chest that would have frightened her if she hadn't been sure of what it really was. She missed Stefan so desperately that she could hardly eat, could barely sleep. He was like a part of her mind that was constantly on fire, like a phanton limb that would never go away.

Not even writing in her diary would help tonight. All she could write about were painfully tantalising memories of the good times she and Stefan had shared together. How good it had been when she could just turn her head and know that she would *see* him – what a privilege that had been! And now it was gone, and in its place was racking confusion, guilt and anxiety. What was happening to him, right now, when she no longer had the privilege of turning her head and seeing him? Were they . . . hurting him?

Oh, God, if only . . .

If only I had made him lock all the windows to his room at the boarding-house . . .

If only I had been more suspicious of Damon . . .

If only I had guessed he had something on his mind that last night . . .

If only . . . if only . . .

It became a pounding refrain in time to her heart. She found herself breathing in sobs, her eyes tightly shut, clutching the rhythm to her and clenching her fists.

If I keep feeling this way – if I let it crush me enough – I'll become an infinitesimal point in space. I'll be crushed into nothingness – and even that will be better than needing him so much.

Elena lifted up her head . . . and stared down at her head, resting on her diary.

She gasped.

Once more her first reaction was to imagine death. And then, slowly, because she was stupefied by so many tears, she realised that she'd done it again.

She was out of her body.

This time she wasn't even aware of a conscious decision about where to go. She was flying, so fast that she couldn't tell which way she was going. It was as if she were being pulled, as if she were the tail of a comet that was rapidly shooting downward.

At one point she realised with familiar horror that she was passing through things, and then she was veering as if she were the end of the whip in a game of Crack the Whip and then she was catapulted into Stefan's cell.

She was still sobbing as she landed in the cell, unsure of whether she had solid form or gravity, and uncaring for the moment. The only thing she had time to see was Stefan, very thin but smiling in his sleep and then she was dumped onto him, into him, and still crying as she bounced, as lightly as a feather, and Stefan woke.

"Oh, can't you let me sleep for a few minutes in peace?" Stefan snapped, and added a couple of Italian words that Elena had never had reason to hear before.

Elena had an immediate fit of the Bonnies, sobbing so hard that she couldn't listen to – couldn't even *hear* – any comfort that was on offer. They were doing horrible things to him, and they were using *her* image, Elena's, to do them. It was all too awful. They were conditioning Stefan to *hate* her. She hated herself. *Everyone* in the whole *world* hated her—

"Elena! Elena, don't cry, love!"

Dully, Elena lifted herself up, getting a brief anatomical view of Stefan's chest before she was sobbing again, trying to wipe her nose on Stefan's prison uniform, which looked as if it could only be improved by anything she might do to it.

She couldn't, of course; just as she couldn't feel the arm that was trying to encircle her gently. She hadn't brought her body with her.

But she had, somehow, brought her tears, and a cold, cable-wire-tough voice inside herself said, *Don't waste them, idiot! Use those tears. If you're going to sob, sob over his face or his hands. And, by the way, everyone hates you.*

Even Matt hates you, and Matt likes everybody, the tiny

cruel, productive voice went on and Elena gave way to a fresh gale of sobbing, absently noting the effect of each teardrop. Each drop turned the white skin under it pink and the colour spread in ripples outward, as if Stefan were a pool, and she was resting on him, water on water.

Except that her tears were falling so fast that it looked like a rainstorm on Wickery Pond. And that only made her think about the time that Matt had fallen into the pond, trying to rescue a little girl who had fallen through the ice, and how Matt hated her now.

"Don't, oh don't; don't, lovely love," Stefan begged, so sincerely that anyone would have believed he meant it. But how could he? Elena knew what she must look like, face swollen and blotched by tears: no "lovely love" here! And he'd have to be mad to want her to stop crying: the teardrops were giving him new life wherever they touched his skin – and perhaps the storm inside him had done best, because his telepathic voice was strong and sure.

Elena, forgive me – oh, God, just give me one moment with her! Just a single moment! I can bear anything then, even the true death. Just one moment to touch her!

And perhaps God did look down for a moment in pity. Elena's lips were hovering over, quivering over, Stefan's, as if she could somehow steal a kiss like this as she used to when he was still asleep. But for just an instant it seemed to Elena that she felt warm flesh below hers and the flick of Stefan's lashes against her eyelids as his eyes flew open in surprise.

Instantly they both froze, eyes wide open, neither of them foolish enough to move in the slightest. But Elena couldn't help herself, as the flush of warmth from Stefan's lips sent a flush of warmth through her entire body. She melted into the kiss, and, while keeping her body carefully in the same position, felt her gaze go unfocused and her eyelids close.

As her lashes swept against something with substance, the moment swept quietly to an end. Elena had two choices: she could shriek and rail telepathically at *Il Signore* for only giving them what Stefan had asked for, or she could gather her courage and smile and maybe comfort Stefan.

Her better nature won out and when Stefan opened *his* eyes, she was leaning over him, pretending to be resting on her elbows and his chest, and smiling at him as she tried to straighten out her hair.

Relieved, Stefan smiled back at her. It was as if he could bear anything, as long as she was unhurt.

"Now, Damon would have been practical," she teased him. "He would have kept me crying, because in the end, his health would be the most important thing. And he'd have prayed for . . ." She paused and finally began laughing, which made Stefan smile. "I have no idea," Elena said finally. "I don't think Damon prays."

"Probably not," Stefan said. "When we were young – and human – the town priest walked with a cane that he seemed to enjoy using on young delinquent boys more than as a source of support."

Elena thought of the delicate child chained to the huge and heavy boulder of secrets. Was religion one of the things locked away, put behind doors closed one after another in secret there, like a chambered nautilus until almost everything he cared about was inside?

She didn't ask that of Stefan. Instead, she said, lowering her "voice" to the tiniest telepathic whisper, the barest disturbance of neurons in Stefan's receptive brain: *What other practical things can you think of that Damon might have thought of? Things relating to a jailbreak?*

"Well . . . for a jailbreak? The first thing I can think of is for you to know your way around the city. I was brought here blindfolded but since they don't have the *power* to take the curse off vampires and make them human, I still had all my senses. I'd say it's a city about the size of New York and Los Angeles combined."

"Big city," Elena noted, taking notes in her head.

"But fortunately the only bits that would interest us are in the south-western section. The city's supposed to be ruled by the Guardians – but they're from the Other Side and the demons and vampires here long ago realised that people were more afraid of *them* than the Guardians. It's set up now with about twelve to fifteen feudal castles or estates, and each of those estates has control of a considerable amount of land outside the city. They grow their own unique products and sell them in deals made here. For instance, it's the vampires who cultivate Clarion Loess Black Magic."

"I see," said Elena, who had no idea what he was talking about, except the Black Magic wine. "But all we really need to know is how to get to the Shi no Shi – your prison."

"That's true. Well, the easiest way would be to find the kitsune sector. The Shi no Shi is a cluster of buildings, with the largest one – the one without a top, although it's curved, and you may not be able to tell from the ground—"

"The one that looks like a coliseum?" Elena interrupted eagerly. "I get a sort of bird's-eye view of the city whenever I come here."

"Well, the thing that looks like a coliseum is a coliseum." Stefan smiled.

He really smiled; he's feeling well enough to smile, now, Elena rejoiced, but silently.

"So to get you in and out, we just head from below the coliseum to the gate back to our world," Elena said. "But to get you free there are – some things we need to collect – and those are probably going to be in different parts of the city." She tried to remember if she had ever described the twin fox key to Stefan or not. It was probably better not to do it if she hadn't already done it.

"Then I'd hire a native guide," Stefan said immediately. "I don't really know anything about the city, except what the guards tell me – and I'm not sure if I would trust them. But the little people – the ordinary ones – will probably know the things you want to know."

"That's a good idea," Elena said. She drew invisible designs with a transparent finger on his chest. "I think Damon really plans to do everything he can to help us."

"I honour him for coming," Stefan said, as if he were thinking things out. "He's keeping his promise, isn't he?"

Elena nodded. Deep, deep in her consciousness floated the thoughts: *His word to me that he would take care of you. His word to you that he would take care of me. Damon always keeps his word.*

"Stefan," she said, again in the innermost recesses of his mind, where she could share information – she hoped – in secret, "you should have seen him, really. When I did Wings of Redemption and every bad thing that had hardened him or made him cruel came undone. And when I did Wings of Purification and all the stone covering his soul came away in chunks. . . . I don't think you could imagine how he was. He was so perfect – and so new. And later when he cried . . ."

Elena could feel inside Stefan three layers of emotion succeed one another almost instantaneously. Disbelief that Damon could cry, despite all that Elena had been telling him. Then, belief and astonishment as he absorbed her pictures and her memories. And finally, the need to console her as she stared at a Damon forever trapped in penitence. A Damon that would never exist again.

"He saved you," whispered Elena, "but he wouldn't save himself. He wouldn't even bargain with Shinichi and Misao. He just let them take all his memories of that time."

"Maybe it hurt too much."

"Yes," said Elena, deliberately lowering her barriers so that Stefan could feel the hurt that the new and perfect creature she'd created had felt upon learning that he had committed acts of cruelty and treachery that – well, that would make the strongest soul flinch. "Stefan? I think he must feel very lonely."

"Yes, angel. I think you're right."

This time Elena thought a good deal longer before venturing, "Stefan? I'm not sure he understands what it's like to be loved." And while he thought out his response, she was on tenterhooks.

Then he said very softly, very slowly again, "Yes, angel. I think you're right."

Oh, she *did* love him. He always understood. And he was always most brave and gallant and trusting just when she needed him to be.

"Stefan? Can I stay again tonight?"

"Is it night-time, lovely love? You can stay – unless They come to take me somewhere." All at once Stefan was very solemn, holding her gaze. "But if They come – you'll promise me to leave then, won't you?"

Elena looked straight into his green eyes and said, "If that's what you want, I'll promise."

"Elena? Do you . . . do you keep your promises or not?" Suddenly, he sounded very sleepy, but the right kind of sleepy, not worn out, but someone who has been refreshed and is being lulled into a perfect slumber.

"I keep them close to me," Elena whispered. But I keep you closer, she thought. If someone came to hurt him, they would find out what a bodiless opponent could do. For instance, what if she just reached inside *their* bodies and managed to make contact for an instant? Long enough to squeeze a heart between her pretty white fingers? That would be something.

"I love you, Elena. I'm so glad . . . we kissed . . ."

"It's not the last time! You'll see! I swear it!" She dropped new healing tears down on him.

Stefan just smiled gently. And then he was asleep.

In the morning Elena woke up in her grand bedroom in Lady Ulma's house, alone. But she had another memory, like a pressed rose, to put away in its own special place inside her.

And somewhere, deep in her heart, she knew that these memories might be all she had of Stefan someday. She could imagine that these sweet-scented, fragile mementoes would be something to hold on to and cherish – if Stefan never came home.

CHAPTER
25

"**O**h, I just want to take a little peek," Bonnie moaned, looking at the forbidden sketchbook, the one in which Lady Ulma had drawn their high couture outfits for the first party, the one that would be held tonight. Beside it, just within reach, were some sample squares from bolts of fabric in shimmering satin, rippling silk, transparent muslin and soft, rich velvet.

"You'll get to try it on for the last fitting in an hour – this time with your eyes open!" Elena laughed. "But we can't forget that tonight isn't playtime. We'll have to dance some dances, of course—"

"Of course!" Bonnie repeated ecstatically.

"But our purpose there is to find the key. The first half of the double fox key. I just wish there was a star ball that showed the inside of tonight's house."

"Well, we all know pretty much about it; we can talk about it and try to imagine it," Meredith said.

Elena, who had been fiddling with the star ball from

the other house, now put the slightly cloudy orb down and said, "All right. Let's brainstorm."

"May I storm, too?" a low, modulated voice asked from the doorway. The girls all turned, rising at the same time to greet a smiling Lady Ulma.

Before taking a chair, she gave Elena a particularly heartfelt hug and kiss on the cheek and Elena couldn't help herself from comparing the woman as they had seen her at Dr Meggar's to the elegant lady she was now. Then, she had been hardly more than skin over bones, with the eyes of a timid wild creature under great strain, wearing a common housecoat, with men's bedroom slippers. Now, she reminded Elena of a Roman matron, with her face tranquil and beginning to fill out under a crown of glossy dark braids held back by jewelled combs. Her body was filling out, too, especially her belly, although she retained her natural grace as she took a seat on a velvet couch. She was wearing a saffron-coloured gown of raw silk, with an underskirt of fringed and shimmering apricot.

"We're so excited about the fitting tonight," Elena said, with a nod toward the sketchbook.

"I am as excited as a child, myself," Lady Ulma admitted. "I only wish I could do for you a tenth of what you have done for me."

"You have already," Elena said. "And if we can find the fox keys – it will only be because you helped us so much. And that – I can't tell you how much that means to me," she finished almost in a whisper.

"But you never thought I could help you when you defied the law for a ravaged slave. You simply wanted to save me – and you have suffered much for it," Ulma responded quietly.

Elena shifted uncomfortably. The cut running down

her face had left only a thin white scar along the cheekbone. Once – when she had first returned to Earth from the afterlife – she would have been able to wave the scar away with a simple wash of Power. But now, although she could channel her Power through her body, and use it to enhance her senses, she couldn't make it obey her will in any other way.

And once, she thought, imagining the Elena who had stood in Robert E. Lee High School's parking lot and drooled over a Porsche, she would have considered the marring of her face the greatest calamity of her life. But with all the accolades she had received, with Damon calling it her "white wound of honour," and her certainty that it would mean as little to Stefan as a scar on his cheekbone would mean to her, she had found she just couldn't take it very seriously.

I am not the same person I once was, she thought. And I'm glad.

"Never mind," she said, ignoring the pain down her leg that still throbbed at times. "Let's talk about the Silver Nightingale and her gala."

"Right," Meredith said. "What do we know about her? How did the clue go again, Elena?"

"Misao said, 'If I said that one of the halves was inside the silver nightingale's instrument, would that even give you an idea?' – or something like that," Elena repeated obediently. They all knew the words by heart but it was part of the ritual, every time they discussed it.

"And the 'Silver Nightingale' is the nickname for Lady Fazina Darley and everyone in the Dark Dimension knows it!" cried Bonnie, clapping her small hands in sheer delight.

"Indeed, that has long been her sobriquet, given to her when she first came here and began to sing and play on her harps strung with silver," Lady Ulma put in gravely.

"And harp strings need to be tuned, and they're tuned with keys," Bonnie continued excitedly.

"Yes." Meredith, in contrast, spoke slowly and thoughtfully. "But it's not a harp-tuning key we're looking for. They look like this." She put down on a table beside her an object made of smooth pale maple that looked like a very short T or, if held on its side, like a gracefully waving tree with one short horizontal branch. "I got that from one of the minstrels Damon hired."

Bonnie eyed the tuning key loftily. "It *might* be a harp-tuning key we're looking for," she insisted. "It might be used for both things, somehow."

"I don't see how," Meredith said doggedly. "Unless somehow they change shape when the two halves come together."

"Oh, my, yes," Lady Ulma said, as if Meredith had just made an obvious proposition. "If they are magical halves of a single key they will almost certainly change when the two halves come together."

"You see?" Bonnie said.

"But if they can be any sort of shape, then how the hell will we even know when we've found them?" Elena asked impatiently. All she cared about was finding what it took to save Stefan.

Lady Ulma fell silent, and Elena felt badly. She hated to use harsh language or even appear distressed in front of the woman who had lived a life of such subjection and horror since her early teens. Elena wanted Lady Ulma to feel safe, to be happy.

"Anyway," she said quickly, "we know one thing. It's *in* the Silver Nightingale's instrument. So whatever is inside Lady Fazina's harp, that has to be it."

"Oh, but—" Lady Ulma began, and then she stopped herself almost before the words were out.

"What is it?" Elena asked gently.

"Oh, nothing at all," Lady Ulma said hastily. "I mean, would you like to see your dresses now? This last fitting is really just to make sure every stitch is perfect."

"Oh, we'd love to!" Bonnie cried, at the same time making a dive for the sketchbook, while Meredith rang a bell pull that brought a servant hurrying in and hurrying away again to the sewing room.

"I only wish Master Damon and Lord Sage had agreed to let me create something for them to wear," Lady Ulma said mournfully to Elena.

"Oh, Sage is not going. And I'm sure Damon wouldn't have minded – as long as you designed him a black leather jacket, a black shirt, black jeans and black boots all exactly like the ones he wears every day. He'd have been happy to wear it then."

Lady Ulma laughed. "I see. Well, there will be enough fantastical styles worn tonight that he may change his mind for the future. Now let's draw the curtains on the windows all around. This gala is to be indoors, with gaslight only, so colours will show true."

"I wondered why it said 'indoors' on the invitations," Bonnie said. "I thought maybe it was because of rain."

"It's because of the sun," Lady Ulma said soberly. "That hateful crimson light, changing every blue to purple, every yellow to brown. You see, no one would wear aqua or green to an outdoor soirée – no, not even you, with that strawberry hair that cries out for it."

"I get it. I can see how having that sun hanging there every day would really get you down after a while."

"I wonder if you can," murmured Lady Ulma, and then she added hastily, "While we wait shall I show you what I have created for your tall friend who doubts me?"

"Oh, please, yes!" Bonnie held out the sketchbook.

Lady Ulma thumbed through it until she came to a page that seemed to please her. She took up pens and colouring pencils like a child eager to play with beloved toys again. "Here it is," she said, using the coloured pencils to add a line here and a curve there, but holding the book so that the three girls could see the design.

"Oh, my God!" cried Bonnie in genuine astonishment, and even Elena felt her eyes widening.

The girl in the sketch was definitely Meredith, with her hair half up and half down, but wearing a dress – such a dress! Black as ebony, strapless, it clung to the long slim figure perfectly sketched in the picture, emphasising the curves, enhancing them on top by what Elena learned was called a "sweetheart" neckline: one that made Meredith's front look like a Valentine's Day heart. It kept close to the body all the way to the knees where it suddenly flared out again, dramatically wide. "A 'mermaid' dress", Lady Ulma explained, satisfied with her sketch at last. "And here it is," she added as several sewing women entered, reverently holding the miraculous gown between them. Now the girls could see that the material was of plush black velvet dotted with tiny rectangular metallic golden flecks. It looked like midnight back home, Elena thought, with a thousand falling stars in the sky.

"And with it, you will wear these very large black onyx and gold earrings, these black onyx and gold combs to hold your hair up, and some lovely matching bracelets and rings Lucen has made just for this outfit," Lady Ulma continued. Elena realised that sometime in the last minutes Lucen must have entered the room. She smiled at him, and then her eyes dropped to the three-tiered tray he held. On the top tray, against an ivory background, were two black onyx and diamond bracelets, as well as a ring with a diamond in it that almost made her swoon.

Meredith was looking around the room as if she had stumbled into a private discussion and didn't know how to get out. Then she looked from the dress to the jewels to Lady Ulma again. Meredith was not one to lose her composure easily. But after a moment she simply went to Lady Ulma and hugged her fiercely, then went to Lucen and very gently put her hand on his forearm. It was clear that she couldn't speak.

Bonnie was studying the sketch with the eyes of a connoisseur now. "Those matching bracelets were made just for this dress, weren't they?" she said with a conspiratorial air.

To Elena's surprise Lady Ulma seemed uncomfortable. Then she spoke slowly. "The truth is . . . well, that Miss Meredith is . . . a slave. All slaves are required to wear some sort of symbolic bracelets when they travel outside their households." She turned her eyes down to the polished wooden floorboards. Her cheeks were flushed.

"Lady Ulma – oh, please, you can't think it matters to us?"

Lady Ulma's eyes flashed as she looked up. "Not matter?"

"Well," Elena said hautily, "it doesn't really matter . . . er, yet, because there's nothing to do about it, not now." Of course, the servants weren't in on the secrets of the Damon–Elena–Meredith–Bonnie relationship. Even Lady Ulma didn't see why Damon didn't free the three girls just in case "something should happen, may the Celestial Guardians forbid it". But the girls had formed a solid phalanx against it; it would be like jinxing their whole enterprise.

"Well, anyway," Bonnie was blathering, "I think the bracelets are beautiful. I mean she could hardly find anything more perfect for the dress, could she?" – striking at the professional sensibilities of the designer.

Lucen smiled modestly and Lady Ulma gave him a loving glance.

Meredith's face was still glowing. "Lady Ulma, I don't know how to thank you. I will wear this gown – and for tonight I will be someone I have never been before. Of course, you've drawn my hair up, or partly up. I don't usually wear it that way," Meredith finished weakly.

"You will tonight – up and high over that lovely wide brow of yours. This dress is to show off the charming curves of your bare shoulders and arms. It's a crime to cover them, day or night. And the hairstyle is to lay bare your exotic face instead of hiding it!" Lady Ulma said firmly.

Good, Elena thought. They've gotten her off the subject of symbolic slavery.

"You'll wear a touch of make-up as well – pale gold on your lids, and kohl to enhance and lengthen your lashes. A touch of golden lipstick, but no rouge; I don't believe in that for young girls. Your olive skin will complete the picture of a sultry maiden perfectly."

Meredith looked helplessly at Elena. "I don't usually wear make-up either," she said, but they both knew that she was beaten. Lady Ulma's vision would come to life.

"Don't call it a mermaid dress; she'll be a siren," Bonnie said enthusiastically. "But we'd better put a spell on it to keep all the vampire sailors away."

To Elena's surprise, Lady Ulma nodded solemnly. "My seamstress friend has sent a priestess today to bless all the garments and to keep you from being victimised by vampires, of course. If that meets with your approval?" She looked at Elena, who nodded.

"As long as they don't keep Damon out of the way," she added jokingly, and felt time freeze as Meredith and Bonnie immediately turned their eyes on her, hoping to catch something in Elena's expression that would give her away.

But Elena kept her expression neutral, as Lady Ulma continued, "Naturally, the restrictions would not apply to your— to Master Damon."

"Naturally," Elena said soberly.

"And now for the smallest beauty to go to the gala," Lady Ulma was saying to Bonnie, who bit her lip, blushing. "I have something very special for you. I don't know how long I've been yearning to work with this material. I've trudged by it in a shop window year after year, just aching to buy it and create with it. You see?" And the next set of sewing women came forward, holding a smaller, lighter frock between them, while Lady Ulma held up a sketch. Elena was already staring in amazement. The material was glorious – incredible – but especially clever was how it had been put together. The fabric was vivid peacock green-blue, with the most amazing hand stitching to represent a pattern of peacock eyes flaring up from the waist.

Bonnie's brown eyes had widened again. "This is for me?" she breathed, almost afraid to touch the material.

"Yes, and we're going to slick that hair of yours back until you look as sophisticated as your friend. Go ahead and try it on. I think you'll like the way this dress has come out." Lucen had retired and Meredith was already being carefully encased in the mermaid dress.

Bonnie happily began to strip.

* * *

Lady Ulma turned out to have been right. Bonnie loved the way she looked that evening. Right now she was being given the finishing touches, such as a delicate spray of citrus and rosewater; a fragrance made just for her. She stood before a giant silvered-glass mirror, just minutes before they were due to start off for the gala given by Fazina, the Silver Nightingale herself.

Bonnie turned a little, looking at the strapless, full-skirted dress in awe. Its bodice was made – or seemed to be made – entirely of the eyes of peacock feathers, arranged in a spray that was gathered together at her waist, showing off how tiny it was. There was another spray of larger feathers that pointed downward from the waist, front and back. The back actually had a small train of peacock feathers against emerald silk. In front, below the larger, downward pointing spray, a design worked in silver and gold, of stylised undulating plumes, all upside down, made its way to the bottom of the gown, which was edged with thin gold brocade.

As if this were not enough, Lady Ulma had had a fan made with real peacock eyes set in an emerald jade handle, with a tassel of softly clinking jade, citrine, and emerald charms at the bottom.

Around Bonnie's throat was a matching necklace of jade, inlaid with emerald, sapphire and lapis lazuli. And around each of her wrists were several emerald jade bracelets that clicked together whenever she moved, the symbol of her slavery.

But Bonnie's eyes could hardly linger on them, and she couldn't summon up a proper hatred of the bracelets. She was thinking of how a special hairdresser had come to "slick back" Bonnie's strawberry-coloured curls until, darkened into true red, they were plastered flat against her skull and held in place with jade and emerald clips. Her heart-shaped face had never looked so mature, so sophisticated. To emerald eyelids and kohl-darkened eyes, Lady Ulma had added a vivid red lipstick and had for once broken her rule and cleverly, wielding the brush herself, had added touches here and there of blusher so that Bonnie's translucent skin looked as if she were constantly colouring at some compliment. Delicately carved jade earrings with golden bells inside completed the ensemble, and Bonnie felt as if she were some Princess of the Ancient Orient.

"It's really some kind of miracle. Usually, I look like a pixie trying to dress up as a cheerleader or a flower girl," she confided, kissing Lady Ulma again and again, delighted to find that the lipstick stayed on her lips instead of transferring to her benefactress's cheeks. "But tonight I look like a young *woman*."

She would have kept on babbling, helpless to stop herself even though Lady Ulma already was trying to discreetly dab tears away from her eyes, except that at that moment Elena came in and she gasped.

Elena's dress had already been finished by the afternoon and so all Bonnie had seen of it was the sketch. But somehow that had failed to convey just what this dress would do for Elena.

Bonnie had secretly wondered if Lady Ulma were leaving too much to Elena's own natural beauty, and was hoping that Elena would be as excited about her own dress as everyone seemed to be about Bonnie's and Meredith's.

Now Bonnie understood.

"It is a called a goddess dress," Lady Ulma explained to the stunned silence in the room, as Elena walked in, and Bonnie dizzily thought that if goddesses *had* ever lived up on Mount Olympus, they would certainly have wanted to dress this way.

The trick of the dress lay in its very simplicity. It was made of milk-white silk, with a delicately pleated waist (Lady Ulma called the irregular tight pleating "ruching") which held two simple bodice panels that formed a V-neckline, showing off Elena's peach-blossom skin between them and behind them. These panels in turn were held at the shoulders by two carved clasps – gold inlaid with mother-of-pearl and diamonds. From the waist, the skirt fell straight in graceful, silken folds all the way to Elena's delicate sandals – again designed in gold, mother-of-pearl and diamonds. In the back, the two panels that clasped at the shoulder became straps and crossed over to once again meet at the pleated waist.

Such a simple dress, but so magnificent on the right girl.

At Elena's throat, an exquisitely designed golden and mother-of-pearl necklace in the stylised shape of a butterfly was inset with so many diamonds that it seemed to blaze with multicoloured fire each time she moved and they caught the light. She wore this over the lapis and diamond pendant Stefan had given her, since she had flatly refused to take the pendant off. It didn't matter. The butterfly covered the pendant completely.

On each wrist Elena wore a wide bracelet of gold and mother-of-pearl inset with diamonds, creations that they had found in the secret jewel room, obviously made to go with the necklace.

And that was all. Elena's hair had been brushed and brushed and *brushed* until it formed a silky golden tumble of waves that hung below her shoulders in back, and she was wearing a touch of rose-coloured lipstick. But her face, with its thick black eyelashes and lighter arched brows – and just now its look of excitement that parted her rose-coloured lips and brought brilliant colour to her cheeks – had been left entirely alone. Earrings that were just cascades of diamonds peeped through her gold tresses.

She's going to drive them crazy tonight, Bonnie thought, eyeing the daring dress with envy, but not with jealousy, instead rather revelling in the thought of the sensation Elena would make. She's wearing the simplest gown of any of us, but she still completely puts Meredith and me in the shade.

Yet Bonnie had never seen Meredith look better – or more exotic. She'd also never known what a stunning figure Meredith had, despite her friend's wide assortment of designer clothes.

Meredith shrugged when Bonnie told her this. She had a fan, too, black lacquer, that folded. Now she opened it and folded it shut again, tapping her chin thoughtfully.

"We're in the hands of a genius," she said simply. "But we can't forget what we're really here for."

CHAPTER

26

"**W**e have to keep our minds on saving Stefan," Elena was saying in the room Damon had taken over for his own, the old library in Lady Ulma's mansion.

"Where else would my mind be?" Damon said, never taking his eyes off her neck with its ornaments of mother-of-pearl and diamonds. Somehow the milk-white dress served to emphasise the slim soft column of Elena's throat, and Elena knew it.

She sighed.

"If we thought you really meant it, then we could all just relax."

"You mean be as relaxed as you are?"

Elena gave herself an inner shake. Damon might seem to be completely absorbed with one thing and one thing only, but his sense of self-preservation made sure that he was constantly on guard, and seeing not just what he wanted to see but everything that was around him.

And it was true that Elena was almost unbearably excited. Let the others think it was about her marvellous dress – and it *was* a marvellous dress, and Elena was profoundly grateful to Lady Ulma and her helpers for getting it done in time. What Elena was really excited about, though, was the chance – no, the certainty, she told herself firmly – that tonight she was going to find half of the key that would allow them to free Stefan. The thought of his face, of seeing him in the flesh was . . .

Was terrifying. Thinking about what Bonnie had said when she was asleep, Elena reached out for comfort and understanding, and somehow found that instead of holding Damon's hand, she was in Damon's arms.

The real question is: what will Stefan say about that night at the motel with Damon?

What would Stefan say? What was there to say?

"I'm frightened," she heard, and a minute too late, recognised her own voice.

"Well, don't think about it," Damon said. "It'll only make things worse."

But I've lied, Elena thought. You don't even remember it, or you'd be lying, too.

"Whatever happened, I promise I'll still be around for you," Damon said softly. "You've got my word on *that*, anyway."

Elena could feel his breath against her hair. "And on keeping your mind on the key?"

Yes, yes, but I haven't fed properly today. Elena started, then clasped Damon closer. For just an instant she'd felt, not merely a ravaging hunger, but a sharp pain that puzzled her. But now, before she could quite locate it in space, it was gone, and her connection to Damon had been abruptly cut off.

Damon.

"What?"

Don't shut me out.

"I'm not. I've just said all there is to say, that's all. You know I'll be looking for the key."

Thank you. Elena tried again. *But you can't just starve—*

Who said I was starving? Now Damon's telepathic connection was back, but something was missing. He was deliberately *holding* something back, and concentrating on assaulting her senses with something else – hunger. Elena could feel it rampaging in him, as if he were a tiger or wolf that had gone for days – for weeks – without making a kill.

The room did a slow spin around her.

"It's . . . all right," she whispered, amazed that Damon was able to stand and hold her at all, with his insides tearing at him that way. "Whatever . . . you need . . . take . . ."

And then she felt the most gentle probing at her throat of razor-sharp teeth.

She gave herself up to it, surrendering to the sensations.

In preparation for the Silver Nightingale's gala, where they would be searching for the first half of the double fox key to release Stefan, Meredith had been reading some of the hard copy she'd stuffed into her bag, from the huge amount of information she had downloaded from the Internet. She had done her best to describe everything that she'd learned to Elena and the others. But how could she be sure that she hadn't missed some vital clue, some vastly important thread of information that would make all the difference tonight between success and failure? Between finding a way to save Stefan and coming home defeated, while he languished in prison.

No, she thought, standing by a silvered mirror, almost

afraid to look at the exotic beauty she had become. No, we can't even think of the word *failure*. For the sake of Stefan's life, we *have* to succeed. And we have to do it without getting caught.

CHAPTER

27

Elena felt confident and just a little light-headed as they set out for the Silver Nightingale's gala. However, when the four of them arrived on litters – Damon with Elena, Meredith with Bonnie (Lady Ulma being forbidden by her doctor to go to any festivities while she was pregnant) – at the Honourable Lady Fazina's palatial home, she was struck with something like terror.

The house was truly a palace, in the best of story-telling tradition, she thought. Minarets and towers soared above them, probably painted in blue and lavish gilt, but turned lavender by the sunlight, and looking almost lighter than air. To complement the sunlight, torches had been lit on either side of the path of the litters up the hill and some chemical had been added – or some magic used – to make their lights shine in varying colours so that they changed from golden, to red, to purple, to blue, to green, to silver, and these colours shone true. They took Elena's breath away, as the only things that were not tinged with red in the whole world that she could see. Damon had brought a bottle of Black Magic with him and was almost too high-spirited – no pun intended, Elena thought.

As their litter stopped at the top of the hill, Damon and Elena were helped out and down a hallway that cut out much of the sunlight. Above them hung delicate, lighted paper lanterns – some larger than the litter they'd been in a moment ago – brightly lighted and fancifully shaped which gave a festive, playful air to a palace otherwise so magnificent that it was a little intimidating.

They passed by lighted fountains, some of which had surprises – like the line of magical frogs that constantly leaped from lily pad to lily pad: *plop, plop, plop*, like the sound of rain on a rooftop, or a huge gilded serpent that coiled among trees and over the heads of visitors, winding from there to the ground and then back up to the trees again.

Then again, it was the ground that would turn transparent with all manner of magical schools of fish, sharks, eels, and dolphins cavorting, while in the dim blue depths far below loomed the figure of a gigantic whale. Elena and Bonnie hurried quickly over this portion of the path.

It was clear that the owner of this estate could afford any kind of extravaganza her heart desired, and that above all things what she enjoyed the chiefest was music, for in each area, splendidly – sometimes bizarrely – dressed orchestra were playing, or there might be only one famous soloist, singing from a high gilded cage perhaps twenty-five feet above the ground.

Music . . . music and lights everywhere . . .

Elena herself, although thrilled by the sights, sounds, and glorious scents coming from huge banks of flowers as well as from the guests, both male and female, felt a slight fear like a small rock in her stomach. She had thought her dress and diamonds so elaborate when she had left Lady Ulma's estate. But now that she was here at Lady Fazina's . . . well, there were too many *rooms*, too many *people*, as fancifully and finely clad as herself and her sister "personal assistants". She was afraid that – well, that that woman over there, dripping jewels from her delicate three-tier diamond and emerald tiara to her delicate diamond-circled toes, made her own unadorned hair look dowdy or laughable, at such a grand affair.

Do you know how old she is? Elena almost jumped to hear Damon's voice in her head.

Who? Elena replied, trying at least to keep her envy – her worry – out of her telepathic voice. *And am I projecting that loudly?* she added in alarm.

Not all that loudly, but it never hurts to tune it down. And you know perfectly well "who": that giraffe you were eyeing, Damon replied. *For your information, she's about two hundred years older than I am, and she's trying to look around thirty, which is ten years younger than when she became a vampire.*

Elena blinked. *What are you trying to say?*

Send some Power to your ears, Damon suggested. *And stop worrying!*

Elena obediently increased slightly the Power to what she still thought of as her burst ear nodes, and conversations suddenly became audible all around her.

. . . oh, the goddess in white. She's just a child, but what a figure . . .

. . . yes, the one with the golden hair. Magnificent, isn't she?

. . . Oh, by Hades, look at that girl . . .

. . . Did you see the prince and princess over there? I wonder if they'd swap . . . or–or – do a quartet, dear?

This was more like what Elena was used to hearing at

parties. It gave her more confidence. It also, as she allowed her eyes to sweep more boldly across the opulently costumed crowed, caused her to feel a sudden surge of love and respect for Lady Ulma, who had designed and overseen the construction of three glorious dresses in only a week.

She's a genius, Elena informed Damon solemnly, knowing that through their mindlink he would see who she meant. *Look, Meredith already has a crowd around her. And . . . and . . .*

And she's not acting much like Meredith at all, Damon finished, sounding slightly uneasy.

Meredith didn't seem uneasy in the least. She had her face turned deliberately to show off a classical profile to her admirers, but it wasn't the profile of level-headed, serene Meredith Sulez at all. It was a sultry, exotic girl, who looked as if she might very well be able to sing the Habanera from *Carmen*. She had her fan open and was gracefully, languorously fanning herself. The soft but warm indoor lighting made her bare shoulders and arms gleam like pearl above the black velvet dress, which seemed even more mysterious and striking than it had back at home. In fact, it seemed to have stricken one devotee to the heart already; he was kneeling before her with a red rose in his hand, so hastily picked from one of the arrangements that a thorn had pricked him and blood welled from his thumb. Meredith didn't seem to have noticed. Both Elena and Damon felt for the young man, who was blond and extremely handsome. Elena felt sorry . . . and Damon felt hungry.

She certainly seems to have come out of her shell, ventured Damon.

Oh, Meredith *doesn't ever really come out,* Elena replied. *It's all playacting. But tonight I think it's the dresses that are doing it. Meredith is dressed like a siren, and so she's acting all sultry. Bonnie's dressed like a peacock and . . . look.*

She nodded down the long hallway that led to a huge room in front of them. Bonnie, dressed in what looked like real peacock feathers, had a crowd of her own followers – and that was just what they were doing: following. Bonnie's every movement was light and birdlike and her jade bracelets clinked together on her small rounded arms, her earrings chimed with each toss of her head, and her feet seemed to twinkle in golden sandals in front of her peacock train.

"You know, it's strange," Elena murmured, as they reached the large room and at last sound was muted so she could hear Damon's physical voice. "I didn't realise it, but Lady Ulma designed our dresses at different levels of the animal world."

"Hm?" Damon was looking at her throat again. But fortunately at that moment a handsome man dressed in formal Earth clothes – tuxedo, cummerbund, and so on – came by with Black Magic in large silver goblets. Damon drained his in one gulp and took another from the gracefully bowing waiter. Then he and Elena took seats – on the outside of the back row, even if this was a rudeness to their hostess. They needed to be free to manoeuvre

"Well, Meredith is a mermaid, which is the highest order, and she's acting like a siren. Bonnie is a bird, so that's the next highest order, and she *is* acting like a bird: watching all the boys display themselves while she keeps laughing. And I'm a butterfly – so I suppose I'll be a social butterfly tonight. With you beside me, I hope."

"How . . . cute," Damon said heavily. "But what exactly makes you think you're supposed to be a butterfly?"

"Well, the designs, silly," Elena said, and she lifted her mother-of-pearl and gold and diamond fan and gave him a tiny butterfly rap on the forehead with it. Then she opened it to show him a masterly sketch of the same design as her necklace on its front, decorated with tiny dots of diamond, gold, and mother-of-pearl where they would not be harmed by the folds.

"You see? A butterfly," she said, not displeased with the image.

Damon traced the outline with one long, tapering finger that reminded her so much of Stefan's that it hurt her throat, and stopped at six stylised lines above the head. "Since when do butterflies have hair?" His finger moved to two horizontal lines between the wings. "Or arms?"

"Those are legs," Elena told him, amused. "What kind of thing with arms and legs and a head has six hairs and wings?"

"A tipsy vampire," suggested a voice above them and Elena looked up, surprised to see Sage. "May I sit with you?" he asked. "I couldn't manage a shirt, but my fairy godmother did conjure up a vest."

Elena, laughing, scooted over a seat so that he could take the aisle seat by Damon. He was much cleaner than when she had last seen him working around the house, although his hair was still in long wild unruly curls. She noted however, that his fairy godmother had scented him with cedar and sandalwood, and provided him with Dolce & Gabbana jeans and vest. He looked . . . *magnifique*. There was no sign of his animals.

"I thought you weren't coming," Elena said to him.

"You can say that? Garbed as you are in celestial white and gold? You mentioned the gala; I took your wish as a command."

Elena giggled. Of course, everyone was treating her differently tonight. It was the dress. Sage, murmuring something about his latent heterosexuality, swore that the image on her necklace and fan was a phoenix. The very polite demon on her right, who had deep mauve skin and small, curling white horns, deferentially submitted that it looked to him like the goddess Ishtar, who had apparently sent him to the Dark Dimension a few millennia ago for tempting people to sloth. Elena made a mental note to ask Meredith whether this meant tempting them to eat sloths, which she knew were some kind of wild animal that didn't move around much, or something else.

Then Elena thought that Lady Ulma had called the dress a "goddess dress", hadn't she? It was certainly a dress you could only wear if your body was very young and very close to perfection, because there was no way to fit corsetry into it or even to drape it to minimise an unflattering feature. The only things under the dress were Elena's own firm young physique and a pair of scant, soft flesh-coloured lace underwear. Oh, and a spray of jasmine perfume.

So it's a goddess I feel like, she thought, thanking the demon (who stood and bowed). People were taking their seats for the Silver Nightingale's first performance. Elena had to admit to a longing to see Lady Fazina, and besides, it was too early to try for a restroom trip – Elena had already noticed that guards were posted at all the doors.

There were two harps on a dais in the middle of a great circle of chairs. And then suddenly everyone was on their feet and clapping, and Elena would have seen nothing, if the Lady Fazina had not chosen to walk down the same aisle Elena and Damon had taken. As it was, she paused right beside Sage to acknowledge the roar of acclamation, and Elena had a perfect view of her.

She was a lovely young woman, who to Elena's surprise looked hardly older than twenty, and was nearly as small as Bonnie. This diminutive creature obviously took her sobriquet very seriously: she was dressed entirely in a gown of silver mesh. Her hair was metallic silver, too, swept high in front and very short in back. Her train was barely attached to her, by two simple clasps at the shoulders. It floated horizontally behind her, constantly in motion, more like a moonbeam or a cloud than like real material until she got to the central dais and ascended it, then walked once around the tall uncovered harp, at which point the suspended part of the cape fell softly and gracefully to the floor in a semi-circle around her.

And then came the magic of the Silver Nightingale's voice. She began by playing the tall harp, which seemed even taller in comparison to her small body. She could make the harp sing under her fingers, coax it to cry like the wind or make music that seemed to descend from heaven in glissandos. Elena wept throughout her first song, even though it was sung in some foreign language. It was so piercingly sweet that it reminded Elena of Stefan, of the times they had been together, communicating by only the softest words and touches . . .

But Lady Fazina's most impressive instrument was her voice. Her tiny body could generate an extraordinary volume when she wanted it to. And as she sang one poignant, minor-tuned song after another, Elena could feel her skin break out into gooseflesh, and a trembling in her legs. She felt that at any moment she might fall to her knees as the melodies filled her heart.

When someone touched her from behind, Elena

started violently, brought back too quickly from the fantasy world the music had woven around her. But it was only Meredith, who despite her own love for music had a very practical suggestion for their group.

"I was going to say, why not start now, while everyone else is listening?" she whispered. "Even the guards are out of it. We agreed on two by two, yes?"

Elena nodded. "We're just having a look around the house. We may even find something while everyone is still *here*, listening, for nearly another hour. Sage, maybe you could sort of liaise between the two groups, telepathically."

"It would be my privilege, *Madame*."

The five of them set out into the Silver Nightingale's mansion.

CHAPTER

28

They walked right by the weeping door-guards. But very quickly, they discovered that while *almost* everyone was listening to Lady Fazina, in each room of the palace that was open to the public, a black-clad, white-gloved steward awaited, ready to give out information, and to keep a watchful eye on his lady's possessions.

The first room that gave them any kind of hope was Lady Fazina's Hall of Harpery, a room devoted entirely to the display of harps, from ancient, bowlike, single-stringed instruments, undoubtedly played by individuals who were similar to cave-dwellers, to tall, gilded, orchestral harps like the one Fazina was now playing, the music audible throughout the palace. Magic, Elena thought again. They seem to use it here instead of technology.

"Each kind of harp has a unique key to tune the strings," Meredith whispered, looking down the length of the hall. On each side the line of harps marched into the distance. "One of those keys might be *the* key."

"But how will we even know?" Bonnie was fanning herself lightly with her peacock feather fan. "What's the difference between a harp key and the fox key?"

"I don't know. And I've never heard of a key being kept *in* a harp, either. It would rattle around the sound box every time the harp shifted slightly," Meredith admitted.

Elena bit her lip. It was such a simple, reasonable question. She should feel dismayed, should be wondering how they could ever find one small half of a key in this place. Especially considering that the clue they had – that it was *in* the Silver Nightingale's instrument, suddenly seemed absurd.

"I don't suppose," Bonnie said a little giddily, "that the instrument is her voice, and that if we reach down her throat . . ."

Elena turned to look at Meredith, who was looking heavenward – or at whatever was above this hideous dimension. "I know," Meredith said. "No more drinks for birdbrain here. Although I suppose it's possible that they give out little silver whistles or instruments as favours – all big parties used to do that, you know – give you a gift."

"How," Damon said in a carefully expressionless tone, "would they possibly get the key into a favour for a party being given at least weeks away, and how could they ever hope to retrieve it? Misao might as well have told Elena, 'We threw the key away.'"

"Well," began Meredith, "I'm not at all sure that they did mean for the keys to be retrievable, even by them. And Misao could have meant 'You'd have to search all the garbage from the night of this gala' – or some other party Fazina performed at. I imagine she gets asked to play at a lot of other people's parties, too."

Elena hated bickering, even though she was a champion bickerer herself. But she was a goddess tonight. Nothing was impossible. If only she could *remember* . . .

Something like white lightning struck her brain.

For just an instant – one instant – she was back, struggling with Misao. Misao was in her fox form, biting and scratching – and snarling out a reply to Elena's question about where the two halves of the fox key were. *"As if you would understand the answers I could give. If I told you that one was inside the silver nightingale's instrument, would that give you any kind of idea?"*

Yes. *Those* had been the exact words, the *real* words that Misao had spoken. Elena heard her own voice, repeating the words distinctly now.

And then she felt something like an arc of lightning leave her mind – only to meet another's not far away. The next thing she knew her eyes were flying open in surprise because Bonnie was speaking in that blank toneless way she always did when making a prophecy:

"Each half of the fox key is shaped like a single fox, with two ears, two eyes, and a snout. The two fox key halves are gold and covered with gems – and their eyes are green. The key you seek is yet in the Silver Nightingale's instrument."

"Bonnie!" Elena said. She could see that Bonnie's knees were trembling, her eyes unfocused. Then they opened and Elena watched as confusion surged in to fill the blankness.

"What's going on?" Bonnie said, looking around to see everyone looking at *her.* "What – what happened?"

"You told us what the fox keys look like!" Elena couldn't help this exclamation – almost a shout of joy. Now that they knew what they were looking for they could free Stefan; they *would* free Stefan. Nothing would stop Elena now. Bonnie had just helped move this quest to an entirely different level.

But while she was quaking inside with joy at the prophecy, Meredith, in her own level-headed way, was taking care of the prophet. Meredith said quietly, "She's probably going to faint. Would you please . . ."

Meredith didn't have to ask further, for the vampires, Damon and Sage, were each quick enough to catch and support Bonnie on opposite sides. Damon was staring down at the diminutive girl in surprise.

"Thanks, Meredith," Bonnie said, and let out a breath, blinking. "I don't think I'll faint," she added, and then with a glance up at Damon through her lashes, "But it's probably just as well to make sure."

Damon nodded and got a better grip, looking serious. Sage turned half away, seeming to have something stuck in his throat.

"What did I say? I don't remember!"

And after Elena had solemnly repeated Bonnie's words it was *just* like Meredith to say, "You're sure now, Bonnie? Does that sound right?"

"*I'm* sure. I'm positive," Elena cut in. She *was* positive. The Goddess Ishtar and Bonnie had unlocked the past for her and shown her the key.

"All right. What if Bonnie and Sage and I take this room, and two of us can be distracting the steward, while the third looks in the harps for keys?" Meredith suggested.

"Right. Let's do it!" Elena said.

Meredith's plan proved to be more difficult in practice than it sounded. Even with two glorious young girls in the room and one terminally fit guy, the steward kept spinning in little circles and catching one or another of them handling and peering into a harp.

Naturally, the handling was strictly forbidden. It put the harps further out of tune and it could easily damage them, especially since the only way to make *absolutely* sure that a small golden key was not in a harp's sound box was to actually shake the harp and listen for rattling.

Worse, each of the harps was displayed in its own little nook, complete with dramatic lighting, a flamboyant painted screen behind it (most of them portraits of Fazina playing the harp in question) and a plush red rope across the front of the nook that said "Keep Out" as plainly as a sign.

In the end Bonnie, Meredith and Sage resorted to having Sage Influence the steward to be entirely passive – something he was only able to do for a few minutes of time, or the steward would notice the gaps in Lady Fazina's program. They would then each frantically search harps while the steward stood like a wax figure.

Meanwhile Damon and Elena were wandering the palace, looking through the rest of the mansion that was off-limits to visitors. If they found nothing, they intended to search the more available rooms as the gala continued.

It was dangerous work, this stealing in and out of darkened, cordoned-off – often locked – empty rooms: dangerous and strangely thrilling to Elena. Somehow, it seemed that fear and passion were more closely related than she had fully realised. Or at least, it seemed that way with her and Damon.

Elena couldn't help noticing and admiring little things about him. He seemed to be able to pick any lock with a single little implement he produced from inside his black jacket, the way other people produce fountain pens, and he had such a swift, graceful way of taking the pick out and putting it back in. Economy of motion, she knew, earned by living for around five centuries.

Also, no one could argue it: Damon seemed to keep his head in any situation, which made them a good pair right now when she was striding around like a goddess who could not be bound by the rules of mortals. This was even enhanced by the scares she got: shapes that looked like guards or sentries looming up at her turned out to be a stuffed bear, a slim cupboard and something Damon didn't allow her more than a glimpse of, but what looked like a mummified human. Damon wasn't fazed by any of them.

If I could just channel some more Power to my eyes, Elena thought, and things immediately brightened up. Her Power was obeying her!

God! I'll have to wear this dress for the rest of my life: it makes me feel so . . . powerful. So . . . unashamed. I'll have to wear it to college, if I ever get to college, to impress my professors; and to Stefan's and my wedding – just so people understand I'm not a slut; and – to the beach, just to give the guys something to ogle . . .

She stifled a giggle and was surprised to see Damon glance with mock reproach at her. Of course, he was as closely focused on her as she was on him. But it was a slightly different case, of course, because, to his eyes, she wore a big label with STRAWBERRY JAM written on it, tied around her neck. And he was getting hungry again. Very hungry.

Next time I'm going to see that you eat properly before you go out, she thought at him.

Let's worry about succeeding this time before we start planning for next time, he returned, with just the faintest firefly hint of his 250-kilowatt smile.

But it was all mixed in, of course, with a little of the

sardonic triumph that Damon always carried with him. Elena swore to herself that laugh at her as he might, beg her as he might, threaten or cajole as he might, she wouldn't give Damon the satisfaction of even one nip tonight. He could just pop the top off another jam pot, she thought.

Eventually, the sweet music of the concert was stilled and Elena and Damon dashed back to meet with Bonnie, Meredith and Sage in the Harpery Hall. Elena could have guessed the news by Bonnie's stance, even if she hadn't already known from Sage's silence. But the news was worse than Elena could have imagined: not only had the three found nothing in the Harpery Hall, but they had finally resorted to quizzing the steward, who could speak, if not move, under Sage's Influence.

"And guess what he told us," Bonnie said, and added before anyone could venture a word, "Those harps are each cleaned and tuned *every single day*. Fazina has, like, a whole army of servants for them. And anything, *anything* that didn't belong to a harp would be reported at once. And nothing has been! It just isn't there!"

Elena felt herself shrink from omniscient goddess to baffled human. "I was worried it would be like this," she admitted, sighing. "It would have been just too easy the other way. All right, Plan B. You mingle with the gala guests, trying to get a look at each room that's open to the public. Try to dazzle Fazina's consort and pump him for information. See if Misao and Shinichi have been here recently. Damon and I will keep looking in the rooms that are supposed to be closed off."

"That's so dangerous," Meredith said, frowning. "I'm afraid of what the penalty might be if you're caught."

"I'm afraid of what the penalty might be to Stefan if

we don't find this key tonight," Elena retorted shortly, and turned on her heel, leaving.

Damon followed her. They searched endless darkened rooms, now not even knowing whether they were looking for a harp or something else. First Damon would check if there were a breathing body inside the room (there might be a vampire guard, of course, but there wasn't much to do about that), then he picked the lock. Things were working seamlessly until they reached a room at the end of a long hall facing west – Elena had long since gotten lost in the palace, but she could unerringly tell west, because it was where the bloated sun hung.

Damon had picked the lock of this room and Elena had originally started forward eagerly. She searched the room, which contained, frustratingly, a silver-framed picture of a harp, but with nothing as bulky as the half of the fox key inside it, even when she had carefully used Damon's lock pick to unscrew the backing.

It was while she was placing this picture back on the wall that they both heard the thump. Elena winced, praying that none of the black-suited "security servants" who roamed the palace had heard the noise.

Damon quickly put a hand over her mouth and dialled the gaslight knob into darkness.

But they both could hear it now . . . footsteps approaching from outside in the hallway. Someone had heard the thump. The footsteps stopped outside the door and there was the distinct sound of an upper servant's discreet cough.

Elena whirled, feeling in that moment as if Wings of Redemption were within her reach. It would only require the slightest rise in adrenalin and she would have the security worker on his or her knees, sobbing in the penitence of a lifetime's work at evil. Elena and Damon would be gone before—

But Damon had another idea, and Elena was startled into going along with it.

When the door opened silently a moment later, the steward found a couple locked in such a tight embrace that they seemed not even to notice the intrusion. Elena could practically feel his indignation. The desire of a couple of guests to discreetly embrace in the privacy of Lady Fazina's many public rooms was understandable, but this was part of the private household. As he turned the lights up, Elena peeked at him out of the corner of her eye. Her psychic senses were open enough to catch his thoughts. He was going over the valuables in the room with an experienced but bored gaze. The exquisite miniature vase with the trailing roses picked out in rubies and emerald-encrusted vines; the magically preserved 5,000-year-old wooden Sumerian lyre; the twin pair of solid gold candlesticks in the shape of rearing dragons; the Egyptian funerary mask with its dark, elongated eyeholes seeming to watch out of its brilliantly painted features . . . all were here. It wasn't even as if her ladyship kept anything of great value here, but still, "This room is not part of the public display," he told Damon, who merely clasped Elena closer.

Yes, Damon seemed very determined to put on a good show for the steward . . . or something like that. But hadn't they already . . . done so? Elena's thoughts were losing coherency. The last thing . . . the very last thing that they could afford . . . was to . . . lose the chance of . . . finding the fox key. Elena started to pull away, and then realised that she mustn't.

Mustn't. Not couldn't. She was property, expensive property to be sure, decked out the way she was tonight, but Damon's to dispose of as he chose. While someone else was looking on, she must not seem to disobey her master's wishes.

Still, Damon was taking this too far . . . farther than he had ever taken liberties with her, although, she thought wryly, he didn't know that. He was caressing the skin left unprotected by the ivory goddess dress, her arms, her back, even her hair. He knew how she liked that, how she could somehow feel it when her hair was held and the ends caressed softly or gently crushed in a fist.

Damon! She was down to the last resort now: pleading. *Damon, if they detain us, or do anything to us that keeps us from finding the key tonight – when will we have another chance? . . .* She let him feel her desperation, her guilt, even the treacherous desire she had to forget everything and let each minute carry her further on this wave of ardor that he had created. *Damon, I'll . . . say it if you want. I'm . . . begging you.* Elena could feel her eyes prickling as tears flooded them.

No tears. Elena heard Damon's telepathic voice gratefully. There was something strange about it, though. It couldn't be starvation – he'd had her blood not much more than two hours ago. And it wasn't passion, for she could hear – and sense – that, all too clearly. Yet Damon's telepathic voice was so taut with control that it almost frightened her. More, she knew he could feel that it frightened her and that he chose to do nothing about it. No explanation. No exploration, either, she realised as she found that behind the control, his mind was entirely shut to her.

The only thing she could liken the feeling that she got from his steely control was *pain*. Pain that was just on the edge of the endurable.

But from what? Elena wondered helplessly.

What could cause him pain like that?

* * *

Elena couldn't waste their time on wondering what was wrong with Damon. She turned up the Power of her own hearing and began to listen at the doors before they entered.

It was while she was listening that suddenly a new idea solidified in Elena's mind, and she stopped Damon in a pitch-dark hallway and tried to explain to him what kind of room she was looking for. What, in modern days, would be called a "home office".

Damon, familiar with the architecture of great mansions, took her, after only a few false starts, into what was clearly a lady's writing room. Elena's eyes were by now as keen as his in the dimness as they searched by the light of a single candle.

While Elena was being frustrated after searching a remarkable desk with pigeonholes for secret drawers, and not finding any, Damon was checking the hallway.

"I hear someone outside," he said. "I think it's time to leave now."

But Elena was still looking. And – as her eyes raced across the room – she saw a small writing desk with an old-fashioned chair and an assortment of various pens, from ancient to modern, flaunting themselves from elaborate holders.

"Let's go while it's still clear," Damon murmured impatiently.

"Yes," Elena said distractedly. "All right . . ."

And then she saw.

Without an instant's hesitation she strode across the room to the desk and picked up a pen with a brilliant silver plume. It wasn't a genuine quill pen, of course; it was a fountain pen made to look elegant and old-fashioned – with a plume. The pen itself was curved to fit her hand, and the wood felt warm.

"Elena, I don't feel very . . ."

"Damon, shhh," Elena said, ignoring him, too absorbed in what she was doing to really hear. First: try to write. No go. Something was blocking the cartridge. Second: unscrew the fountain pen *carefully*, as if to refill its cartridge, while all the time her heart was clamouring in her ears and her hands were shaking. Keep moving slowly . . . don't miss anything . . . for God's sake don't let anything fall away and bounce in this dimness. The two parts of the pen parted in her hand . . .

. . . and onto the dark-green desk pad fell a small, heavy, curved piece of metal. It had just fit inside the widest part of the pen. She had it in her hand and was reassembling the pen before she could get a good look at it. But then . . . she *had* to open her hand and see.

The small crescent-shaped object dazzled her eyes in the light, but it was just like the description Bonnie had given Elena and Meredith. A tiny representation of a fox with a nominal body and a jewel-encrusted head that sported two flat ears. The eyes were two sparkling green stones. Emeralds?

"Alexandrite," Damon said in a bedroom whisper. "Folklore has it that they change colour in candlelight or firelight. They reflect the flame."

Elena, who had been leaning back against him, recalled with a chill the way Damon's eyes had reflected flame when he had been possessed: the blood-red flame of the malach – of Shinichi's cruelty.

"So," Damon demanded, "how did you do it?"

"This is really one of the two pieces of the fox key?"

"Well, it's hardly something that belongs in a fountain pen. Maybe it's a Crackerjack prize. But you went right to it the moment we entered the room. Even vampires need time to think, my precious princess."

Elena shrugged. "It's too easy, actually. When it was clear that all those harp keys were no goes, I asked myself what else was an instrument that you'd find in someone's house. A pen is a writing instrument. Then I just had to find out whether Lady Fazina had a study or writing room."

Damon let out a breath. "Hell's demons, you little innocent. You know what I've been looking for? Trap doors. Secret entries to dungeons. The only other instrument *I* could think of was an 'instrument of torture' and you'd be surprised at how many of them you'll find in this fair city."

"But not in *her* house!" Elena's voice rose dangerously, and they were both silent a moment to make up for it, listening, on tenterhooks, for any sound from the hallway.

There was none.

Elena let out her breath. "Quick! Where, where will it be safe?" She was realising that the one fault of the goddess dress was that there was absolutely no place to hide anything. She'd have to speak to Lady Ulma about that for next time.

"Down, down in the pocket of my jeans," Damon said, seeming to be as urgent and shaking as badly as she was. When he had jammed it deep into the recesses of his black Armani jeans he caught her by both hands. "Elena! Do you realise? We've done it. We've actually done it!"

"I know!" Tears were leaking out of Elena's eyes and all of Lady Fazina's music seemed to be swelling in one great, perfect chord. "We did it together!"

And then somehow – like all the other "somehows" that were getting to be a habit with them, Elena was in Damon's arms, sliding her own arms under his jacket to feel his warmth, his solidity. She wasn't surprised, either, to feel a double piercing at her throat when she dropped her head back: her lovely panther was really only a little tamed, and needed to learn a few basics of dating etiquette; such as you kiss before you bite.

He had said he was hungry earlier, she remembered, and she had ignored him, too enthralled by the silver pen to put the words together. But she put them together now, and understood – except why he seemed to be so exceptionally hungry tonight.

Maybe even . . . excessively hungry.

Damon, she thought gently, *you're taking a lot.*

She could feel no response but the raw hunger of the panther.

Damon, this could be dangerous . . . for me. This time Elena put as much Power as she could into the words she sent.

Still no response from Damon, but she was floating now, down into darkness. And that gave her the vague thread of an idea.

Where are you? Are you here? she called, picturing the little boy.

And then she saw him, chained to his boulder, curled up in a ball, with his fists covering his eyes.

What's wrong? Elena asked immediately, floating near to him, concerned.

He's hurting! He's hurting!

Are you hurt? Show me, Elena said instantly.

No! He's hurting you. He could kill you!

Husshh. Husshhh. She tried to cradle him.

We have to make him hear us!

All right, Elena said. She really was feeling odd and weak. But she turned, along with the child, and cried voicelessly: *Damon! Please! Elena says stop!*

And a miracle happened.

Both she and the child could feel it. The little sting of fangs being withdrawn. The stop of energy flow from Elena to Damon.

And then, ironically, the miracle began to take her away from the child, with whom she really wanted to speak.

No! Wait! she tried to tell Damon, clinging to the child's hands as hard as she could, but she was being catapulted back to consciousness as if by a hurricane. The darkness faded. In its place was a room, too bright, its one candle blazing like a police searchlight aimed directly at her. She shut her eyes and felt the warmth and heaviness of the corporeal Damon in her arms.

"I'm sorry! Elena, can you speak? I didn't realise how much—" There was something wrong with Damon's voice. Then she understood. Damon's fangs were unretracted.

Wha— Everything was wrong. They'd been so happy, but – but now her right arm felt wet.

Elena pulled away from Damon entirely, staring at her arms, which were red and with something that wasn't paint.

She was still too worked up to ask questions properly. She slipped behind Damon and pulled his black leather jacket off him. In the brilliant light she could see his black silk shirt marred by line after line of dried, partially dried, or just plain wet blood.

"Damon!" Her first reaction was horror without a touch of guilt or understanding. "What happened? Did you get in a fight? Damon, *tell me*!"

And then something in her mind presented her with a number. Since she had been a child, she had been able to count. In fact. she'd learned to count to ten before her first birthday. Therefore, she'd had seventeen full years of learning to count the number of irregular, deep, still-bleeding cuts in Damon's back.

Ten.

Elena looked down at her own bloody arms and at the goddess dress, which was now the horror dress because its pure milky whiteness was marred with brilliant red.

Red that should have been *her* blood. Red that must have felt like sword slashes into Damon's back as he channelled the pain and the marks of the Night of her Discipline from her to him.

And he carried me all the way home. The thought came swimming in from nowhere. Without a word about it. I would never have known . . .

And he still hasn't healed. Will he ever heal?

That was when she started screaming on all frequencies.

CHAPTER

29

Someone was trying to make her drink out of a glass. Elena's sense of smell was so acute that she could taste what was in the glass already – Black Magic wine. And she didn't want that! No! She spat it out. They couldn't *make* her drink.

"*Mon enfant*, it is for your own good. Now, drink it." Elena turned her head away. She felt the darkness and the hurricane rushing up to take her. Yes. That was better. Why wouldn't they leave her alone?

In the very deepest trenches of communication, a little boy was with her in the dark. She remembered him, but not his name. She held out her arms and he came into them and it seemed that his chains were lighter than they had been . . . when? Before. That was all she could remember.

Are you all right? she whispered to the child. Down here, deep in the heart of communion, a whisper was a shout.

Don't cry. No tears, he begged her, but the words

reminded her of something she couldn't bear to think of, and she put her fingers to his lips, gently silencing him.

Too loud, a voice from Outside came rumbling in. "So, *mon enfant*, you have decided to become *un vampire encore une fois.*"

Is that what is happening? she whispered to the child. *Am I dying again? To become a vampire?*

I don't know! the child cried. *I don't know anything. He's angry. I'm afraid.*

Sage won't hurt you, she promised. *He's already a vampire, and your friend.*

Not Sage . . .

Then who are you afraid of?

If you die again, I'll be wrapped in chains all over. The child showed her a pitiable picture of himself covered by coil after coil of heavy chains. In his mouth, gagging him. Pinning his arms to his sides and his legs to the ball. Moreover, the chains were spiked so that everywhere they dug into the child's soft flesh, blood flowed.

Who would do such a thing? Elena cried. *I'll make him wish he'd never been born. Tell me who's going to do this!*

The child's face was sad and perplexed. *I will,* he said sadly. *He will. He/I. Damon. Because we'll have killed you.*

But if it's not his fault . . .

We have to. We have to. But maybe I'll die, the doctor says . . . There was a definite lilt of hope in the last sentence.

It decided Elena. If Damon was not thinking clearly, then maybe she wasn't thinking clearly, she reasoned out slowly. Maybe . . . maybe she should do what Sage wanted.

And Dr Meggar. She could discern his voice as if through a thick fog. "—sake, you've been working all night. Give someone else a chance."

Yes . . . all night. Elena had not wanted to wake up

again, and she had a powerful will.

"Maybe switch sides?" someone – a girl – a young girl – was suggesting. Little in voice, but strong-willed, too. Bonnie.

"Elena . . . It's Meredith. Can you feel me holding your hand?" A pause, then very much louder, excitedly, "*Hey, she squeezed my hand! Did you see?* Sage, tell Damon to get in here quick."

Drifting . . .

". . . drink a little more, Elena? I know, I know, you're sick of it. But drink *un peu* for my sake, will you?"

Drifting . . .

"*Très bon, mon enfant! Maintenant*, what about a little milk? Damon believes you can stay human if you drink some milk."

Elena had two thoughts about this. One was that if she drank *any* more of *anything*, she might explode. Another was that she wasn't going to make any foolish promises.

She tried to speak but it came out in a thread of a whisper. "Tell Damon – I won't come up unless he lets the little boy free."

"Who? What little boy?"

"Elena, sweetie, all the little boys on this estate are free."

Meredith: "Why not let her *tell* him?"

Dr Meggar: "Elena, Damon is right here on the couch. You've both been very sick, but you're going to be fine. Here, Elena, we can move the examination table so you can talk to him. There, it's done."

Elena tried to open her eyes, but everything was ferociously bright. She took a breath and tried again. Still much too bright. And she didn't know how to dim her vision any more. She spoke with her eyes shut to the presence she felt in front of her: *I can't leave him alone again. Especially if you're going to load him with chains and gag him.*

Elena, Damon said shakily, *I haven't led a good life. But I haven't kept slaves before, I swear. Ask anyone. And I wouldn't do that to a child.*

You have, and I know his name. And I know that all he's made of is gentleness, and kindness, and good nature . . . and fear.

The low rumble of Sage's voice, ". . . agitating her . . ." the slightly louder murmur of Damon's: "I *know* she's off her head, but I'd still like to know the name of this little boy I'm supposed to have done this to. How does that agitate her?"

More rumbling, then: "But can't I just ask her? At least I can clear my name of these charges." Then, out loud: "Elena? Can you tell me what child I'm supposed to have tortured like this?"

She was so tired. But she answered aloud, whispering, "His name is Damon, of course."

And Meredith's own exhausted whisper, "Oh, my God. She was willing to die for a metaphor."

CHAPTER
30

VAMPIRE DIARIES

Matt watched Mrs Flowers go over Sheriff Mossberg's badge, holding it lightly in one hand and running her fingers over it with the other.

The badge came from Rebecca, Sheriff Mossberg's niece. It had seemed entirely a coincidence when Matt had almost run into her earlier that day. Then he'd noticed that she was wearing a man's shirt as a dress. The shirt had been familiar – a Ridgemont sheriff's shirt.

Then he had seen the badge still attached to it. You could say a lot of things about Sheriff Mossberg, but you couldn't imagine him losing his badge. Matt had forgotten all sense of gallantry and snatched at the little metal shield before Rebecca could stop him. He'd had a sick feeling in his stomach then, and it had only gotten worse since. Mrs Flowers's expression was doing nothing to comfort him.

"It wasn't in direct contact with his skin," she said softly, "so the images I get are hazy. But oh, my dear Matt" – she lifted shadowed eyes to his – "I am afraid."

She shivered, sitting at her kitchen table chair, where two mugs of hot spiced milk sat untouched.

Matt had to clear his throat and touch the scalding milk to his lips. "You think we need to go out to look."

"We *must*," said Mrs Flowers. She shook her head, with its soft, wispy white curls, sadly. "Dear Ma*ma* is most insistent, and I can feel it too; a great disturbance in this artifact."

Matt felt the faintest shade of pride tingeing his fear for having secured the "artifact" – and then he thought, yeah, robbing badges from the shirts of twelve-year-old girls is really something to be proud of.

Mrs Flowers's voice came from the kitchen. "You'd best put on several shirts and sweaters as well as a pair of these." She emerged sideways through the kitchen door, holding several long coats, apparently from the closet in front of the kitchen door, and several pairs of gardening gloves.

Matt jumped up to help her with the armfuls of coats and then went into a coughing fit as the smell of mothballs and of – something else, something spicy – surrounded him.

"Why do – I feel – like Christmas?" he said, forced to cough between each few words.

"Oh, now that would be Great-Aunt Morwen's clove preservation recipe," Mrs Flowers replied. "Some of these coats are from Mother's time."

Matt believed her. "But it's still warm out. Why should we wear coats at all?"

"For protection, dear Matt, for protection! These clothes have spells woven into the material to safeguard us from evil."

"Even the gardening gloves?" Matt asked doubtfully.

"Even the gloves," Mrs Flowers said firmly. She paused

and then said in a quiet voice, "And we'd better gather some flashlights, Matt dear, because this is something we're going to have to do in the darkness."

"You're kidding!"

"No, sadly, I am not. And we should get some rope to tie ourselves together. Under no circumstances must we enter the thicket of the Old Wood tonight."

An hour later, Matt was still thinking. He hadn't had any appetite for Mrs Flowers's hearty Braised Eggplant *au Fromage* dinner, and the wheels in his brain just wouldn't stop turning.

I wonder if this is how Elena feels, he thought, when she's putting together Plans A, B, and C. I wonder if she ever feels this *stupid* doing it.

He felt a tightening around his heart, and for the three-hundred-thousandth time since he'd left her and Damon, he wondered if he'd done the right thing.

It had to be right, he told himself. It hurt the worst, and that's the proof of it. Things that really, really hurt are the right thing to do.

But I just wanted to say goodbye to her. . . .

But if you'd said goodbye, you'd never have left. Face it, moron, as far as Elena goes you're the world's biggest loser. Ever since she found a boyfriend she liked better than you, you've been working like you were Meredith and Bonnie to help her keep him and keep away The Bad Guy. Maybe you should get you all little matching T-shirts saying: *I am a dog. I serve the Princess Ele—*

SMACK!

Matt leaped up, and landed crouching, which was more painful than it looked in movies.

Rattle-Smick!

It was the loose shutter on the other side of the room. That first bang had really been a slam, though. The exterior of the boarding-house was in pretty bad shape, and the wooden shutters there sometimes suddenly came free of their wintertime nails.

But was it really just a coincidence? Matt thought, as soon as his heart had stopped galloping. In this boarding-house where Stefan had spent so much time? Maybe somehow there were still remnants of his spirit around, tuned to what people thought within these halls. If so, Matt had just been given a solid whack to the solar plexus, from the way he felt.

Sorry, bud, he thought, almost saying it out loud. I didn't mean to trash your girl. She's under a lot of pressure.

Trash his girl?

Trash Elena?

Hell, he'd be the first person to knock out anybody who trashed Elena. Provided Stefan didn't use vampire tricks to get in front of him!

And what was it Elena always said? You can't be too prepared. You can't have too many subplans because, just as sure as God made a pesky shell around a peanut, your major plan was going to have some flaws.

That was why Elena also worked with as many people as possible. So what if C and D workers never needed to get involved. They were there if they were needed.

Thinking this, and with his head feeling a lot clearer than it had since he had sold the Prius and given Stefan's money to Bonnie and Meredith for plane fare plus, Matt went to work.

"And then we took a walk around the estate, and saw the apple orchard, and the orange orchard, and the cherry orchard," Bonnie told Elena, who was lying down, looking small and defenceless, in her four-poster bed, which had been hung with dusty-gold sheer panels, right now held back by heavy tassels in various shades of gold.

Bonnie was sitting comfortably in a gold upholstered chair that had been drawn to the bed. She had her small bare feet up on the sheets.

Elena was not being a good patient. She wanted to get up, she insisted. She wanted to be able to walk around. That would do her more good than all the oatmeal and steak and milk and five-times-a-day visits from Dr Meggar, who had come to live at the estate.

She knew what they were all really afraid of, though. Bonnie had blurted it all out in one long sobbing, keening wail one night when the little redhead had been on duty beside her.

"Y-you screamed and all the v-vampires heard it, and Sage just picked up Meredith and me like two kittens, one under each arm, and he ran to where the screaming was. But b-by then so many people had gotten to you *first*! You were unconscious but so was Damon, and somebody said, 'They-they've been attacked and I th-think they're *dead*!' And every-b-body was s-saying, 'Call the G-Guardians!' And I fainted, a little."

"Shhh," Elena had said kindly – and cannily. "Have some Black Magic to make it feel better."

Bonnie had had some. And some more. And then she'd gone on with the story. "But Sage must've known something because he said, 'Here, I'm a doctor, and I'm going to examine them.' And you would really believe him, the way he said it!"

"And then he looked at both of you, and I guess he knew right away what happened, because he said, 'Fetch a carriage! I need to take them t-to Dr Meggar, my colleague.' And the Lady Fazina herself came and said that they could have one of her carriages, and just send it back wh-whenever. She's sooooo *rich*! And then, we got you two out the back way because there were–were some *bastards* who said, let them die. They were real demons, white like snow, called Snow Women. And then, then, we were just in the carriage and, oh my God! Elena! Elena, you *died*! You stopped breathing twice! And Sage and Meredith just kept doing CPR on you. And I–I prayed so h-h-hard."

Elena, fully into the story by now, had cuddled her, but Bonnie's tears kept coming back.

"And we knocked at Dr Meggar's as if we were going to burst the door in – and – and someone told him – and he examined her and said, 'She needs a transfusion.' And I said, 'Take my blood.' Because remember in school when we both gave blood to Jody Wright and we were practically the only ones who could do it because we were the same kind? And then Dr Meggar got two tables ready like that" – Bonnie had snapped her fingers – "and I was so scared I could hardly hold still for the needle, but I did. I did, somehow! And they gave you some of my blood. And, meanwhile, you know what Meredith did? She let Damon bite her. She really did. And Dr Meggar sent the carriage back to the house to ask for servants who 'wanted a bonus' because th-that's what it's called here – and the carriage came back full. And I don't know how many Damon bit, but it was a lot! Dr Meggar said it was the best medicine. And Meredith and Damon and all of us talked and we convinced Dr Meggar to come here, I mean to live, and Lady Ulma is going to turn that whole building he was living in into a hospital for the poor people. And ever after that we've just been trying to get you well. Damon was fine the next morning. And Lady Ulma and Lucen and he – I mean it was their idea but he did it, sent this pearl to Lady Fazina – it was one that her father had never found a client rich enough to buy, because it's so big, like a good handful in size but irregular, that means with twists and turns, and a sheen like silver. They put it on a thick chain and sent it to her."

Bonnie's eyes had filled again. "Because she *saved* both you and Damon. Her carriage *saved* your lives." Bonnie had leaned forward to whisper, "And Meredith told me – it's a secret, but not from you – that being bitten isn't that bad. There!" And Bonnie, like the kitten she was, had yawned and stretched. "I would have been bitten next," she'd said almost wistfully, and quickly added, "but you needed my blood. Human blood, but mine especially. I guess they know all about blood types here because they can taste and smell the differences." Then she gave a little jump and said, "Do you want to look at the fox key half? We were so sure it was all over and we'd never ever find it, but when Meredith went in the bedroom to get bitten – and I promise that was all they did – Damon gave it to her and asked her to keep it. So she did and she took good care of it and it's in a little chest Lucen made out of something that looks like plastic but it's not."

Elena had admired the little crescent, but other than that there was nothing to do in bed but talk and read classical books or encyclopedias from Earth. They wouldn't even let her and Damon rest in the same room.

Elena knew why. They were afraid she wouldn't just talk to Damon. They were afraid that she would get near to him and smell his exotic familiar smell, made up of Italian bergamot, mandarin and cardamom, and that she would look up into his black eyes that could hold universes inside the pupils, and that her knees would go weak and she'd wake up a vampire.

They didn't know anything! She and Damon had been

safely exchanging blood for weeks before the crisis. If there was nothing to drive him out of sanity again, the way the pain had before, he would conduct himself like a perfect gentleman.

"Hm," Bonnie said, upon hearing this protest, pushing a tiny throw pillow around with toenails that had been painted silver. "I maybe wouldn't tell them that you've been exchanging blood so many times from the beginning. It might make them go 'Aha!' or something. You know, read something into it."

"There's nothing to read into. I'm here to collect my beloved Damon and Stefan is just helping me."

Bonnie looked at her with her brows knitted and her mouth pursed, but didn't venture a word.

"Bonnie?"

"Um-hm?"

"Did I just say what I thought I said?"

"Um-*hm*."

Elena, with one motion, gathered an armful of pillows and deposited them on her face. "Could you please tell chef that I want another steak and a big glass of milk?" she requested in a muffled voice from under the pillows. "I'm not well."

Matt had a new junk car. He was always able to get his hands on one when he really needed it. And now he was driving, in fits and starts, to Obaasan's house.

Mrs Saitou's house, he corrected himself hastily. He didn't want to tread on unfamiliar cultural customs, not when he was asking for a favour.

The door at the Saitous' was opened by a woman Matt had never seen before. She was an attractive woman, dressed very dramatically in a wide scarlet skirt – or maybe in very wide scarlet pants – she stood with her feet so far apart that it was hard to tell. She wore a white blouse. Her face was striking: two swaths of straight black hair and a smaller, neater swath of fringe that came to her eyebrows.

But the most striking thing of all about her was that she was holding a long curved sword, pointed directly at Matt.

"H-hi," Matt said, when the door swung open to reveal this apparition.

"This is a good house," the woman replied. "This is not a house of evil spirits."

"I never thought it was," Matt said, retreating as the woman advanced. "Honest."

The woman shut her eyes, seemed to be searching for something in her own mind. Then, abruptly, she lowered the sword. "You speak the truth. You mean no harm. Please come in."

"Thank you," Matt said. He'd never been so happy to have an older woman accept him.

"Orime," came a thin, feeble voice from upstairs. "Is that one of the children?"

"Yes, Hahawe," called the woman that Matt couldn't help thinking of as "the woman with the sword".

"Send him up, why don't you?"

"Of course, Hahawe."

"Ha ha – I mean 'Hahawe'?" Matt said, turning a nervous laugh into a desperate sentence as the sword swung by his midriff again. "Not Obaasan?"

The sword-woman smiled for the first time. "*Obaasan* means *grandmother*. *Hahawe* is one of the ways to say *mother*. But mother won't mind at all if you call her Obaasan; it's a friendly greeting for a woman of her age."

"OK," Matt said, trying his best to seem like an all-around friendly guy.

Mrs Saitou gestured him up the stairs and he peeped into several rooms before he found one with a large futon in the exact middle of a completely bare floor, and in it a woman who seemed so tiny and doll-like as not to be real.

Her hair was just as soft and black as the sword-woman's downstairs. It was put up or arranged somehow so that it lay around her like a halo as she lay on the bed. But the dark lashes on the pale cheeks were shut and Matt wondered if she had fallen into one of the sudden slumbers of the elderly.

But then quite abruptly, the doll-like lady opened her eyes and smiled. "Why, it's Masato-chan!" she said, looking at Matt.

Bad beginning. If she didn't even recognise that a blond guy wasn't her Japanese friend from about sixty years ago . . .

But then she was laughing, with her small hands in front of her mouth. "I know, I know," she said. "You're not Masato. He became a banker, very rich. Very thick. Especially in the head and the stomach."

She smiled at him again. "Sit down, please. You can call me Obaasan if you want, or Orime. My daughter was named for me. But life has been hard for her, as it was for me. Being a shrine maiden – *and* a samurai . . . it takes discipline and much work. And my Orime did so well . . . until we came here. We were looking for a town that would be peaceful and quiet. Instead, Isobel found . . . Jim. And Jim was . . . untrue."

Matt's throat swelled with the desire to defend his friend, but what defence could there be? Jim had spent one night with Caroline – at Caroline's pressing invitation. And he had become possessed and had brought that possession to his girlfriend Isobel, who had pierced her body grotesquely – among other things.

"We've got to get them," Matt found himself saying earnestly. "The kitsune who started it all – who started it with Caroline. Shinichi and his sister Misao."

"Kitsune." Obaasan was nodding her head. "Yes, I said there would be one involved from the very beginning. Let me see; I blessed some charms and amulets for your friends . . ."

"And some bullets. I just sort of filled my pockets," Matt said, embarrassed, as he spilled out a jumble of different calibres on the edge of her futon cover. "I even found some prayers on the Web about getting rid of them."

"Yes, you've been very thorough. Good." Obaasan looked at the hard copies he'd printed of the prayers. Matt squirmed, knowing that he had only been running down Meredith's To-Do list, and that the credit really belonged to her.

"I'll bless the bullets first and then I'll write out more amulets," she said. "Put the amulets wherever you need protection most. And, well, I suppose you know what to do with the bullets."

"Yes, ma'am!" Matt fumbled in his pockets for the last few, put them into Obaasan's outstretched hands. Then she chanted a long, elaborate prayer holding her tiny hands out over the bullets. Matt didn't find the incantation frightening, but he knew that as a psychic he was a dud, and that Bonnie had probably seen and heard things he couldn't.

"Should I aim for any particular part of them?" Matt asked, watching the old woman and trying to follow along on his own copy of the prayers.

"No, any part of the body or head will do. If you take out a tail, you'll make it weaker, but you'll enrage it, as well." Obaasan paused and coughed, a small dry old-lady cough. Before Matt could offer to run downstairs and get her a drink, Mrs Saitou entered the room with a tray and three cups of tea in little bowls.

"Thank you for waiting," she said politely as she knelt fluidly to serve them. Matt found with the first sip that the steaming green tea was much better than he'd expected from his few experiences at restaurants.

And then there was silence. Mrs Saitou sat looking at the teacup, Obaasan lay looking white and shrunken under the futon cover, and Matt felt a storm of words building up in his own throat.

Finally, even though good sense was counselling him not to speak, he burst out, "God, I'm so sorry about Isobel, Mrs Saitou! She doesn't deserve any of this! I just wanted you to know that I – I'm just so sorry, and I'm going to get the kitsune who's at the bottom of it. I promise you, I'll get him!"

"Kitsune?" Mrs Saitou said sharply, staring at him as if he'd gone mad. Obaasan looked on in pity from her pillow. Then, without waiting to gather up the tea things, Mrs Saitou jumped up and ran out of the room.

Matt was left speechless. "I – I—"

Obaasan spoke from her pillow. "Don't be too distressed, young man. My daughter, although a priestess, is very modern in her outlook. She would probably tell you that kitsune don't even exist."

"Even after – I mean how does she think Isobel—"

"She thinks that there are evil influences in this town, but of the 'ordinary, human' kind. She thinks Isobel did what she did because of the stress she was under, trying to be a good student, a good priestess, a good samurai."

"You mean, like, Mrs Saitou feels guilty?"

"She blames Isobel's father for much of it. He is a

'salaryman' back in Japan." Obaasan paused. "I don't know why I have told you all this."

"I'm sorry," Matt said hastily. "I wasn't trying to snoop."

"No, but you care about other people. I wish Isobel had had a boy like you instead of her daughter."

Matt thought of the pitiful figure he'd seen at the hospital. Most of Isobel's scars would end up invisible under her clothes – presuming she learned to speak again. Bravely, he said, "Well, I'm still up for grabs."

Obaasan smiled faintly at him, then put her head back down on the pillow – no, it was a wooden headrest, Matt realised. It didn't look very comfortable. "It's a great pity when there has to be strife between a human family and the kitsune," she said. "Because there are rumours that one of our ancestors took a kitsune wife."

"Say *what*?"

Obaasan laughed, again behind concealing fists. "*Mukashi-mukashi*, or as you say, long ago in the times of legend, a great Shogun became angry at all the kitsune on his estate for the mischief they made. For many long years they were up to all sorts of pranks, but when he suspected them of ruining the crops in the fields, that was it. He roused every man and woman in his household, and told them to take sticks and arrows and rocks and hoes and brooms and flush out all the foxes that had dens on his estate, even the ones between the attic and the roof. He was going to have every single fox killed without mercy. But the night before he did this, he had a dream in which a beautiful woman came and said she was responsible for all the foxes on the estate. 'And,' she said, 'while it is true that we make mischief, we repay you by eating the rats and mice and insects that really spoil the crops. Won't you agree to take your anger out just on me and execute me alone instead of all the foxes? I will come at dawn to hear your answer.'

"And she kept her word, this most beautiful of kitsune, arriving at dawn with twelve beautiful maidens as attendants, but she outshone all of them just as the moon outshines a star. The Shogun could not bring himself to kill her, and in fact asked for her hand in marriage, and married her twelve attendants to his twelve most loyal retainers as well. And it is said that she was always a faithful wife, and bore him many children as fierce as Amaterasu the sun goddess, and as beautiful as the moon, and that this continued until one day the Shogun was on a journey and he happened to accidentally kill a fox. He hurried home to explain to his wife that it hadn't been intentional, but when he arrived he found his household in mourning, for his wife had already left him, with all his sons and daughters."

"Oh, too bad," Matt muttered, trying to be polite, when his brain elbowed him in the ribs. "Wait. But if they *all* left . . ."

"I see you're an attentive young man," the delicate old woman laughed. "All his sons and daughters were gone . . . except the youngest, a girl of peerless beauty, although she was just a child. She said, 'I love you too much to leave you, dear father, even if I must wear a human shape all my life.' And that is how we are said to be descended from a kitsune."

"Well, these kitsune aren't just causing mischief or ruining crops," Matt said. "They're out to kill. And we have to fight back."

"Of course, of course. I didn't mean to upset you with my little story," Obaasan said. "I'll write out those amulets for you now."

It was as Matt was leaving that Mrs Saitou appeared at

the door. She put something into his hand. He glanced down at it and saw the same calligraphy that Obaasan had given him. Except that it was much smaller and written on . . .

"A Post-it Note?" Matt asked, bewildered.

Mrs Saitou nodded. "Very useful for slapping on the faces of demons or the limbs of trees or such." And, as he stared at her in complete amazement, "My mother doesn't know *all* there is to know about everything."

She also handed him a sturdy dagger, smaller than the sword she was still carrying, but very serviceable – Matt immediately cut himself on it.

"Put your faith in friends and your instincts," she said.

Slightly dazed, but feeling encouraged, Matt drove to Dr Alpert's house.

CHAPTER

31

"I'm feeling much better," Elena told Dr Meggar. "I'd like to take a walk around the estate." She tried not to bounce up and down on the bed. "I've been eating steak and drinking milk and I even took that vile cod liver oil you sent. Also I have a very firm grasp of reality: I'm here to rescue Stefan and the little boy inside Damon is a metaphor for his unconscious, which the blood we shared allowed me to 'see'." She bounced once, but covered it by reaching for a glass of water. "I feel like a happy puppy pulling at the leash." She exhibited her newly designed slave bracelets: silver with lapis lazuli inserts in fluid designs. "If I die suddenly, I am prepared."

Dr Meggar's eyebrows worked up and down. "Well, I can't find anything wrong with your pulse or your breathing. I don't see how a nice afternoon walk can hurt you. Damon's certainly up and walking. But don't you go giving Lady Ulma any ideas. She still needs months of bed rest."

"She has a nice little desk made from a breakfast

tray," Bonnie explained, gesturing to show size and width. "She designs clothes on that." Bonnie leaned forward, wide-eyed. "And you know what? Her dresses are *magic*."

"I wouldn't expect anything less," grunted Dr Meggar.

But the next moment Elena remembered something unpleasant. "Even when we get the keys," she said, "we have to plot the actual jailbreak."

"What's a jailbreak?" Lakshmi asked excitedly.

"It's like this – we've got the keys to Stefan's cell, but we still need to figure out how we're going to get into the prison, and how we're going to smuggle him out."

Lakshmi frowned. "Why not just go in with the line and take him out the gate?"

"Because," Elena said, trying for patience, "they won't let us just walk in and get him." She narrowed her eyes as Lakshmi put her head in her hands. "What're you thinking, Lakshmi?"

"Well, first you say that you're going to have the key in your hand when you go to the prison, then you act like they're not going to let him out of the prison."

Meredith shook her head, bewildered. Bonnie put a hand to her forehead as if it ached. But Elena slowly leaned forward.

"Lakshmi," she said, very quietly, "are you saying that if we have a key to Stefan's cell it's basically a pass in and out of prison?"

Lakshmi brightened up. "Of course!" she said. "Otherwise, what would a key be good for? They could just lock him in *another* cell."

Elena could hardly believe the wonder of what she had just heard, so she immediately began trying to poke holes in it. "That would mean we could go straight from Bloddeuwedd's party to the prison and just take Stefan out," she said with as much sarcasm as she could inject into her voice. "We could just show our key and they'd let us take him away."

Lakshmi nodded eagerly. "Yes!" she said joyfully, the sarcasm having gone right over her head. "And, don't be mad, OK? But I wondered why you never went to visit him."

"*We can visit him?*"

"Sure, if you make an appointment."

By now Meredith and Bonnie had come to life and were supporting Elena on either side. "How soon can we send someone to make an appointment?" Elena said through her teeth, because it was taking all her effort to speak – her entire weight was resting on her two friends. "*Who* can we send to make an appointment?" she whispered.

"I'll go," Damon said from the crimson darkness behind them. "I'll go tonight – give me five minutes."

Matt could feel that he had on his most cross and stubborn expression.

"C'mon," Tyrone said, looking amused. They were both gearing up for a trip into the thicket. This meant putting on two of the mothball-clove-recipe coats each and then using duct tape to fasten the gloves to the coats. Matt was sweating already.

But Tyrone was a good guy, he thought. Here Matt had come out of nowhere and said, "Hey, you know that bizarre thing you saw with poor Jim Bryce last week? Well, it's all connected to something even more bizarre – all about fox spirits and the Old Wood, and Mrs Flowers says that if we don't figure out what's going on, we're going to be in *real* trouble. And Mrs Flowers isn't just a batty old lady at the boarding-house, even though everybody says so."

"Of course she isn't," Dr Alpert's brusque voice had said from the doorway. She put down her black bag – still a country doctor, even when the town was in crisis – and addressed her son. "Theophilia Flowers and I have known each other a long time – and Mrs Saitou, too. They were both always helping people. That's their nature."

"Well—" Matt had seen an opportunity and jumped at it. "Mrs Flowers is the one who needs help now. Really, really needs help."

"Then what're you sitting there for, Tyrone? Hurry up and go help Mrs Flowers." Dr Alpert had ruffled her own iron-grey hair with her fingers, then ruffled her son's black hair fondly.

"I *was*, Mom. We were just leaving when you came in."

Tyrone, seeing Matt's grim horror-story of a car, had politely offered to drive them to Mrs Flowers's house in his Camry. Matt, afraid of a terminal blowout at some crucial moment, was only too happy to accept.

He was glad that Tyrone would be the lynchpin of the Robert E. Lee High football team in the coming year. Ty was the kind of guy you could count on – as witness his immediate offer of help today. He was a good sport, and absolutely straight and clean. Matt couldn't help but see how drugs and drinking had ruined not only the actual games, but the sportsmanship of the other teams on campus.

Tyrone was also a guy who could keep his mouth shut. He hadn't even peppered Matt with questions as they drove back to the boarding-house, but he did give a wolf whistle, not at Mrs Flowers, but at the bright-yellow Model T she was driving into the old stables.

"Whoa!" he said, jumping out to help her with a grocery bag, while his eyes drank in the Model T from fender to fender. "That's a Model T Fordor Sedan! This could be one beautiful car if—" He stopped abruptly and his brown skin burned with a sunset glow.

"Oh, my, don't be embarrassed about the Yellow Carriage!" Mrs Flowers said, allowing Matt to take another bag of groceries back through the kitchen garden and into the kitchen of the house. "She's served this family for nearly a hundred years, and she's accumulated some rust and damage. But she goes almost thirty miles an hour on paved roads!" Mrs Flowers added, speaking not only proudly, but with the somewhat awed respect owed to high-speed travel.

Matt's eyes met Tyrone's and Matt knew there was only one shared thought hanging in the air between them.

To restore to perfection the dilapidated, worn, but still beautiful car that spent most of its time in a converted stable.

"We could do it," Matt said, feeling that, as Mrs Flowers's representative, he should make the offer first.

"We sure could," Tyrone said dreamily. "She's already in a double garage – no problems about room."

"We wouldn't have to strip her down to the frame . . . she really rides like a dream."

"You're kidding! We could clean the engine, though: have a look at the plugs and belts and hoses and stuff. And" – dark eyes gleaming suddenly – "my dad has a power sander. We could strip the paint and repaint it the exact same yellow!"

Mrs Flowers suddenly beamed. "That was what dear Ma*ma* was waiting for you to say, young man," she said, and Matt remembered his manners long enough to introduce Tyrone.

"Now, if you had said, 'We'll paint her burgundy' or 'blue' or any other colour, I'm sure she would have objected," Mrs Flowers said as she began to make ham sandwiches, potato salad and a large kettle of baked beans. Matt watched Tyrone's reaction to the mention of "Mama" and was pleased: there was an instant of surprise, followed by an expression like calm water. His mother had said Mrs Flowers wasn't a batty old lady: therefore she wasn't a batty old lady. A huge weight seemed to roll off Matt's shoulders. He wasn't alone with a fragile elderly woman to protect. He had a friend who was actually a little bigger than he was to rely on.

"Now both of you, have a ham sandwich, and I'll make the potato salad while you're eating. I know that young men" – Mrs Flowers always spoke of men as if they were a special kind of flower – "need lots of good hearty meat before going into battle, but there's no reason to be formal. Let's just dig right in as things are done."

They had happily obeyed. Now they were preparing for battle, feeling ready to fight tigers, since Mrs Flowers's idea of dessert was a pecan pie split between the boys, along with huge cups of coffee that cleared the brain like a power sander.

Tyrone and Matt drove Matt's junker to the cemetery, followed by Mrs Flowers in the Model T. Matt had seen what the trees could do to cars and he wasn't going to subject Tyrone's whistle-clean Camry to the prospect. They walked down the hill to Matt and Sergeant Mossberg's hide, each of the boys giving a hand to help the frail Mrs Flowers over rough bits. Once, she tripped and would have fallen, but Tyrone dug the toes of his DC shoes into the hill and stood like a mountain as she tumbled against him.

"Oh, my – thank you, Tyrone dear," she murmured and Matt knew that "Tyrone dear" had been accepted into the fold.

The sky was dark except for one streak of scarlet as they reached the hide. Mrs Flowers took out the sheriff's badge, rather clumsily, due to the gardening gloves she was wearing. First she held it to her forehead, then she slowly drew it away, still holding it in front of her at eye-level. "He stood here and then he bent down and squatted here," she said, getting down in what was in fact the correct side of the hide. Matt nodded, hardly knowing what he was doing, and Mrs Flowers said without opening her eyes, "No coaching, Matt dear. He heard someone behind him – and whirled, drawing his gun. But it was only Matt, and they spoke in whispers for a while.

"Then he suddenly stood up." Mrs Flowers stood suddenly and Matt heard all sorts of alarming little pops and crackles in her delicate old body. "He went walking – striding – down into that thicket. That evil thicket."

She set off for the thicket as Sheriff Rich Mossberg had when Matt had watched him. Matt and Tyrone went hurrying after her, ready to stop her if she showed any signs of entering the remnant of Old Wood that still lived.

Instead, she walked around it, with the badge held to eye height. Tyrone and Matt nodded at each other and without speaking, each took one of her arms. This way they skirted the edge of the thicket, all the way around, with Matt going first, Mrs Flowers next, and Tyrone last. At some point Matt realised that tears were making their way down Mrs Flowers's withered cheeks.

At last, the fragile old woman stopped, took out a lacy handkerchief – after one or two tries – and wiped her eyes with a gasp.

"Did you find him?" Matt asked, unable to hold in his curiosity any longer.

"Well – we'll have to see. Kitsune seem to be very, very good at illusions. Everything I saw could have been an illusion. But" – she heaved a sigh – "one of us is going to have to step into the Wood."

Matt gulped. "That'll be me, then—"

He was interrupted. "Hey, no way, man. You know their ops, whatever they are. You've got to get Mrs Flowers out of this—"

"No, I can't risk just asking you to come over here and get hurt—"

"Well, what am I doing out here, then?" Tyrone demanded.

"Wait, my dears," Mrs Flowers said, sounding as if she were about to cry. The boys shut up immediately, and Matt felt ashamed of himself.

"I know a way that you both can help me, but it's very dangerous. Dangerous for the two of you. But perhaps if we only have to do it once, we can cut the risk of danger and increase our chance of finding something."

"What is it?" Tyrone and Matt said almost simultaneously.

A few minutes later, they were prepped for it. They were lying side by side, facing the wall formed by the tall trees and tangled underbrush of the thicket. They were not only roped together, but they had Mrs Saitou's Post-it Notes placed all over their arms.

"Now when I say 'three' I want you both to reach in and grab at the ground with your hands. If you feel something, keep hold of it and pull your arm out. If you don't feel anything, move your hand a little and then pull it out as fast as you can. And by the way," she added calmly, "if you feel anything trying to pull you in or immobilise your arm, yell and fight and kick and scream, and we'll help you to get out."

There was a long, long minute of silence.

"So basically, you think there are things all around on the ground in the thicket, and that we might get hold of them just by reaching in blindly," Matt said.

"Yes," Mrs Flowers said.

"All right," said Tyrone, and once again Matt glanced at him approvingly. He hadn't even asked *"What kind of things could pull us into the Wood?"*

Now they were in position and Mrs Flowers was counting "One, two, three," and then Matt had thrust his right arm in as far as it would go and was sweeping his arm while groping.

He heard a shout from beside him. "Got it!" And then instantly: *"Something's pulling me in!"*

Matt pulled his own arm out of the thicket before trying to help Tyrone. Something dropped down on it, but it hit a Post-it Note and it felt as if he'd been whacked by a piece of a Styrofoam.

Tyrone was thrashing wildly and had already been dragged in to his shoulders. Matt grabbed him by the waist and used all his strength to haul backward. There was a moment of resistance – and then Tyrone came popping out as if suddenly released like a cork. There were scratches on his face and neck, but none where the overcoats had covered him or where the Post-it Notes were.

Matt felt a desire to say "Thank you," but the two women who had made him amulets were far away, and he felt stupid saying it to Tyrone's coat. In any case, Mrs Flowers was fluttering and thanking people enough for three.

"Oh my, Matt, when that big branch came down

I thought your arm would be broken at least. Thank the dear Lord that the Saitou women make such excellent amulets. And, Tyrone dear, please take a swig out of this canteen—"

"Uh, I don't really drink much—"

"It's just hot lemonade, my own recipe, dear. If it weren't for both you boys, we wouldn't have succeeded. Tyrone, you found something, yes? And then you were caught and would never have been released if Matt hadn't been here to save you."

"Oh, I'm sure he'd've got out," Matt said hurriedly, because it must be embarrassing for anybody like The Tyreminator to admit they needed help.

Tyrone, however, just said soberly, "I know. Thanks, Matt."

Matt felt himself blush.

"But I didn't get anything after all," Tyrone said disgustedly. "It felt like a piece of old pipe or something—"

"Well, let's have a look," Mrs Flowers said very seriously.

She turned the strongest flashlight on the object Tyrone had risked so much to bring out of the thicket.

At first Matt thought it was a gigantic rawhide dog bone. But then an all-too-familiar shape made him look closer.

It was a femur, a human femur. The biggest bone in the body, the one from the leg. And it was still white. Fresh.

"It doesn't seem to be plastic," Mrs Flowers said in a voice that seemed very far away.

It wasn't plastic. Matt could see where little tiny bits had curled up and away from the exterior. It wasn't rawhide, either. It was . . . well, real. A real human leg bone.

But that wasn't the most horrifying thing; the thing that sent Matt spiralling out into darkness.

The bone was polished clean and marked with the imprints of dozens of tiny little teeth.

CHAPTER

32

Elena was radiantly happy. She had gone to sleep happy, only to wake up again happy, serene in the knowledge that soon – soon she would visit Stefan, and that after that – surely very soon – she would be able to take Stefan away.

Bonnie and Meredith weren't surprised when she wanted to see Damon about two things: one being who should go and two being what she was going to wear. What did surprise them were her choices.

"If it's all right," she said slowly at the beginning tracing a finger round and round on the large table in one of the parlours as everyone gathered the next morning, "I would like for just a few people to go with me. Stefan's been badly treated," she went on, "and he hates to look bad in front of other people. I don't want to humiliate him."

There was sort of a group blush at this. Or maybe it was a group flush of resentment – and then a group blush of culpability. With the western windows slightly open, so that an early-morning red light fell over everything, it was hard to tell. Only one thing was certain: everyone wanted to go.

"So I hope," Elena said, turning to look Meredith and Bonnie in the eye, "that none of you are hurt if I don't choose you to come with me."

That tells both of them they're out, Elena thought as she saw understanding blossom in both faces. Most of her plans depended on how her two best friends reacted to this.

Meredith gallantly stepped up to bat first. "Elena, you've been through hell – literally – and almost died doing it – to get to Stefan. You take with you the people who will do the most good."

"We realise it isn't a popularity contest," Bonnie added, swallowing, because she was trying not to cry. She *really* wants to go, Elena thought, but she understands. "Stefan may feel more embarrassed in front of a girl than a boy," Bonnie said. And she didn't even add *"even though we would never do anything to embarrass him,"* Elena thought, going around for a hug and feeling Bonnie's soft little birdlike body in her arms. Then she turned and felt Meredith's warm and slim hard arms, and as always felt some of her tension drain away.

"Thank you," she said, wiping tears from her eyes afterwards. "And you're right, I think it would be harder to face girls than boys in the situation he's in. Also it will be harder to face friends he already knows and loves. So I would like to ask these people to go with me: Sage, Damon and Dr Meggar."

Lakshmi leaped up as interested as if she had been chosen. "Where's he in jail?" she asked, quite cheerfully.

Damon spoke up. "The Shi no Shi."

Lakshmi's eyes became round. She stared at Damon

for a moment, and then she was bounding out the door, her shaken voice floating behind her: "I've got chores to do, master!"

Elena turned to look directly at Damon. "And what was *that* little reaction?" she asked in a voice that would have frozen lava at thirty metres.

"I don't know. Truly, I don't. Shinichi showed me kanji characters and said that they were pronounced 'Shi no Shi' and they meant 'the Death of Death' – as in lifting the curse of death from a vampire."

Sage coughed. "Oh, my trusting little one. *Mon cher idiot*. To not get a second opinion . . ."

"I did, actually. I asked a middle-aged Japanese lady at a library if the romaji – that's the Japanese words written out in our letters, meant the Death of Death. And she said yes."

"And you turned on your heel and walked out," Sage said.

"How do you know?" Damon was getting angry.

"Because, *mon cher*, those words mean many things. It all depends upon the Japanese characters first used – which you did *not* show her."

"I didn't have them! Shinichi wrote it in the air for me, in red smoke." Then in a kind of angry anguish: "*What other things do they mean?*"

"Well, they can mean what you said. They also could mean 'the new death'. Or 'the true death'. Or even – 'The Gods of Death'. And given the way Stefan has been treated . . ."

If stares had been stakes, Damon would have been a goner by now. Everyone was looking at him with hard, accusing eyes. He turned like a wolf at bay and bared his teeth at them in a 250-kilowatt smile. "In any case, I didn't imagine it was anything remarkably pleasant," he said. "I just thought it would help him to get rid of the curse of being a vampire."

"In any case," Elena repeated. Then she said, "Sage, if you would go and make sure that they'll let us in when we arrive, I would be enormously grateful."

"As good as done, *Madame*."

"And – let me see – I want everyone to wear something a little different to go visit him. If it's all right I'll go talk to Lady Ulma."

She could feel Bonnie's and Meredith's bewildered looks on her back as she left.

Lady Ulma was pale, but bright of eye when Elena was escorted into her room. Her sketchbook was open, a good sign.

It took only a few words and a heartfelt look before Lady Ulma said firmly, "We can have everything done in an hour or two. It's just a matter of calling the right people. I promise."

Elena squeezed her wrist very, very gently. "Thank you. Thank you – miracle worker!"

"And so I am to go as a penitent," Damon said. He was right outside Lady Ulma's door when Elena came out and Elena suspected him of some eavesdropping.

"No, that never even occurred to me," she said. "I just think that slave's clothing on you and the other guys will make Stefan less self-conscious. But why should you think I wanted to punish you?"

"Don't you?"

"You're here to help me save Stefan. You've gone through—" Elena had to stop and look in her sleeves for a clean handkerchief, until Damon offered her a black silk one.

"All right," he said, "we won't get into that. I'm sorry.

I think of things to say and then I just say them, no matter how unlikely I think they are, considering the person I'm speaking to."

"And don't you ever hear another little voice? A voice that says that people can be good, and may not be trying to hurt you?" Elena asked wistfully, wondering how loaded with chains the child was now.

"I don't know. Maybe. Sometimes. But, as that voice is generally wrong in this wicked world, why should I pay it any attention?"

"I wish sometimes you would just try," Elena whispered. "I might be in a better position to argue with you, then."

I like this position just fine, Damon told her telepathically and Elena realised – how did this *happen* over and over? – that they had melted into an embrace. Worse, she was wearing her morning attire – a long silky gown and a peignoir of the same material, both in the palest of pearly blues, which turned violet in the rays of the ever-setting sun.

I – like it too, Elena admitted, and felt shockwaves go through Damon from his surface, through his body, and deep, deep into that unfathomable hole that one could see by looking into his eyes.

I'm just trying to be honest, she added, almost frightened by his reaction. *I can't expect anyone else to be honest if I'm not.*

Don't be honest, don't be honest. Hate me. Despise me, Damon begged her, at the same time caressing her arms and the two layers of silk that were all that stood between his hands and her skin.

"But why?"

Because I can't be trusted. I'm a wicked wolf, and you're a pure soul, a snow-white newborn lamb. You mustn't let me hurt you.

Why should you hurt me?

Because I might – no, I don't want to bite you – I only want to kiss you, just a little, like this. There was revelation in Damon's mind-voice. And he did kiss so sweetly, and he always knew when Elena's knees were going to give out and picked her up before she could fall on the floor.

Damon, Damon, she was thinking, feeling very sweet herself because she knew she was giving him pleasure, when she suddenly realised.

Oh! Damon, please *let me go – I have to go have a fitting* right now!

Deeply flushed, he slowly, reluctantly put her down, grabbed her before she could fall, and put her down again.

I think I shall have to go have a fit right now as well, he told her earnestly as he stumbled out of the room, missing the door the first time.

Not a fit – a fitting! Elena called after him, but she never knew if he had heard. She was pleased, though, that he had let her go, without really understanding anything except that she was saying no. That was quite a bit of improvement.

Then she hurried in to Lady Ulma's room, which was filled with all sorts of people, including two male models, who had just been garbed in trousers and long shirts.

"Sage's clothes," said Lady Ulma, nodding at the large one, "and Damon's." She nodded at the smaller man.

"Oh, they're perfect!"

Lady Ulma looked at her with just the slightest doubt in her eyes. "These are made of genuine sacking," she said. "The meanest, lowest cloth in the slave hierarchy. Are you sure they will wear them?"

"They're wearing them or they aren't going at all," Elena said flatly and winked.

Lady Ulma laughed. "Good plan."

"Yes – but what do you think of my other plan?" Elena asked, genuinely interested in Lady Ulma's opinion, even while she blushed.

"My dear benefactress," Lady Ulma said. "I used to watch my mother put together such outfits . . . after I had turned thirteen, of course – and she told me that they always made her happy, for she was bringing joy to two at once, and that the purpose was nothing but joy. I promise you, Lucen and I will be done in no time. Now, should you not be getting ready?"

"Oh, yes – oh, I do love you, Lady Ulma! It's so funny that the more people you love, the more you want to love!" And with that Elena went running back to her own rooms.

Her maids-in-waiting were all there and all ready. Elena took the quickest, briskest bath of her life – she was keyed up – and found herself on a couch in the middle of a smiling, keen-eyed bunch, each neatly doing her job without interfering with the others.

There was a depilatory, of course – in fact one for each leg, one for her armpits and one for her eyebrows. While these women and the women with soft creams and unguents were at work, creating a unique fragrance for Elena, another one thoughtfully considered her face and body as a whole.

This woman touched up Elena's eyebrows to darken them, and gilded Elena's eyelids with metallic cosmetic paint before using something that added at least a quarter-inch to Elena's eyelashes. Then she extended Elena's eyes with exotic horizontal lines of kohl. Finally, she carefully made Elena's lips a rich glossy red that somehow gave the impression that they were continually puckered for a kiss. After this the woman sprinkled the faintest of iridescence all over Elena's body. Finally, a very large canary diamond that had been sent up from Lucen's jewellery bench was firmly cemented into her navel.

It was while the hairdressers were seeing to the last of the little curls on her forehead that the two boxes and a scarlet cape came from Lady Ulma's women. Elena thanked all her ladies-in-waiting and beauticians sincerely, paid them all a bonus that had them twittering, and then asked them to leave her alone. When they dithered, she asked them again, just as politely, but in louder tones. They went.

Elena's hands were trembling as she took out the outfit Lady Ulma had created. It was quite as decent as a bathing suit, but it *looked* like jewellery strategically placed on wisps of golden tulle. It all coordinated with the canary diamond: from the necklace to the armlets to the golden bracelets that denoted that, however expensively Elena was dressed, she was still a slave.

And that was it. She was going clad in tulle and jewellery, perfume and paint, to see her Stefan. Elena put the scarlet cloak on very, very carefully to avoid rumpling or smearing anything below, and slipped her feet into delicate golden sandals with very high heels.

She hurried downstairs and was exactly on time. Sage and Damon were wearing cloaks tightly closed – which meant that they were dressed in the sacking outfits underneath. Sage had had Lady Ulma's coach made ready. Elena settled her matching golden bracelets on her wrists, hating them because she *had* to wear them, pretty as they were against the white fur trim on her scarlet cloak. Damon held out a hand to help her into the coach.

"I get to ride inside? Does that mean I don't have to wear—" But, looking at Sage, her hopes were crushed.

"Unless we want to curtain all the windows," he said, "you're legally travelling outside without slave bracelets."

Elena sighed and gave her hand to Damon. Standing against the sun, he was a dark silhouette. But then, as Elena blinked in the light, he stared in astonishment. Elena knew he'd seen her gilded eyelids. His eyes dropped to her pursed-to-be-kissed lips. Elena blushed.

"I forbid you to order me to show you what's under the cloak," she said hastily. Damon looked thwarted.

"Hair in tiny curls all over your forehead, cloak that covers everything from neck to toes, lipstick like . . ." He stared again. His mouth twitched as if he were being compelled to fit it to hers.

"And it's time to go!" Elena caroled, hastily getting into the carriage. She felt very happy, although she understood why freed slaves would never wear anything like a bracelet again.

She was still happy when they reached the Shi no Shi – that large building that seemed to combine a prison with a training facility for gladiators.

And she was still happy as the guards at the large Shi no Shi checkpoint let them into the building without showing any signs of ill feeling. But then, it was hard to say if the cloak had any effect on them. They were demons: sullen, mauve-skinned, bullock-steady.

She noticed something that was at first a shock and then a river of hope inside her. The front lobby of the building had a door in one side that was like the door in the side of the depot/slaveshop: always kept shut; strange symbols above; people walking up to it in different costumes and announcing a destination before turning the key and opening the door.

In other words: a dimensional door. Right here in

Stefan's prison. God alone knew how many guards would be after them if they tried to use it, but it was something to keep in mind.

The guards on the lower floors of the Shi no Shi building, in what was most definitely a dungeon, had clear and obnoxious reactions to Elena and her party. They were some smaller species of demon – imps, maybe, Elena thought – and they gave the visitors a hard time over *everything*. Damon had to bribe them to be allowed in to the area where Stefan's cell was, to go in alone, without one guard per visitor, and to allow Elena, a slave, to go in to see a free vampire.

And even when Damon had given them a small fortune to get past these obstacles, they sniggered and made harsh guttural gurglings in their throats. Elena didn't trust them.

She was correct.

At a corridor where Elena knew from her out-of-body experiences they should have turned left, instead they went straight through. They passed another set of guards, who almost collapsed from sniggering.

Oh – God – are they taking us to see Stefan's dead body? Elena wondered suddenly. Then it was Sage who really helped her. He put out a large arm and bodily held her up, until she found her legs again.

They went on walking, deeper into what was a filthy and stinking stone-floored dungeon now. Then abruptly they turned right.

Elena's heart raced on before them. It was saying *wrong, wrong, wrong*, even before they got to the last cell in the line. The cell was completely different from Stefan's old cell. It was surrounded, not by bars, but by a sort of curlicued chicken wire that was lined with sharp spikes. No way to hand in a bottle of Black

Magic. No way to get the bottle top in position to pour into a waiting mouth on the other side. No room, even, to get a finger or the mouth of a canteen through for the cellmate to suck. And the cell itself wasn't filthy, but it was bare of everything except a supine Stefan. No food, no water, no bed to hide anything in, no straw. Just Stefan.

Elena screamed and had no idea if she screamed words or just a formless sound of anguish. She threw herself into the cell – or tried to. Her hands grabbed onto curls of steel as sharp as razor that caused blood to well up instantly wherever they touched, and then Damon, who had the fastest reactions, was pulling her back.

And then he just pushed past her and stared. He stared open-mouthed at his younger brother – a grey-faced, skeletal, barely breathing young man, who looked like a child lost in his rumpled, stained, threadbare prison uniform. Damon raised a hand, as if he'd forgotten the barrier already – and Stefan flinched. Stefan seemed not to know or recognise any of them. He peered more closely at the drops of blood left on the razor-sharp fencing where Elena had grasped it, sniffed, and then, as if something had penetrated the fog of his bafflement, looked around dully. Stefan looked up at Damon, whose cloak had fallen, and then, like a baby's, Stefan's gaze wandered on.

Damon made a choking sound and turned and, knocking anyone in his way aside, ran the other way down the corner. If he was hoping that enough guards would follow him that his allies could get Stefan out, he was wrong. A few followed, like monkeys, calling out insults. The rest stayed put, behind Sage.

Meanwhile, Elena's mind was churning and churning out plans. Finally she turned to Sage. "Use all the money we have plus this," she said, and she reached under her cloak for her canary diamond necklace – over two dozen thumb-sized gems – "and call to me if we need more. Get me half an hour with him. Twenty minutes, then!" – as Sage began to shake his head. "Stall them, somehow; get me *at least* twenty minutes. I'll think of something if it kills me."

After a moment Sage looked her in the eyes and nodded. "I will."

Then Elena looked at Dr Meggar pleadingly. Did he have something – did something exist – that would help?

Dr Meggar's eyebrows went down, then their inner sides went up. It was a look of grief, of despair. But then he frowned and whispered, "There's something new – an injection that's said to help in dire cases. I could try it."

Elena did her best not to fall at his feet. "Please! Please try it! *Please!*"

"It won't help beyond a couple of days—"

"It won't need to! We'll get him out by then!"

"All right." Sage had by now herded all the guards away, saying, "I'm a dealer in gems and there's something you all should see."

Dr Meggar opened his bag and took out of it a syringe. "Wooden needle," he said with a wan smile as he filled it with a clear red liquid from a vial. Elena had taken another syringe and she examined it eagerly as Dr Meggar coaxed Stefan by imitation to put his arm up to the bars. At last Stefan did as Dr Meggar wished – only to jump away with a cry of pain as a syringe was plunged into his arm and stinging liquid injected.

Elena looked at the doctor desperately. "How much did he get?"

"Only about half. It's all right – I filled it with twice the dose and pushed as hard as I could to get the" – some medical word Elena didn't recognise – "into him. I knew it would hurt him more, injecting that fast, but I accomplished what I wanted."

"Good," Elena said rapturously. "Now I want you to fill this syringe with my blood."

"Blood?" Dr Meggar looked dismayed.

"Yes! The syringe is long enough to go through the bars. The blood will drip out the other side. He can drink it as it comes out. It might save him!" Elena said every word carefully, as if speaking to a child. She desperately wanted to convey her meaning.

"Oh, Elena." The doctor sat down, with a clink, and took a hidden bottle of Black Magic out of his tunic. "I'm so sorry. But it's hard enough for me to get blood out of a vial. My eyes, child – they're ruined."

"But glasses – spectacles—"

"They're no good to me any more. It's a complicated condition. But you have to be very good to actually tap a vein in any case. Most doctors are pretty hopeless; I'm impossible. I'm sorry, child. But it's been twenty years since I was successful."

"Then I'll find Damon and have him open my aorta. I don't care if it kills me."

"*But I do.*"

This new voice coming from the brilliantly lighted cell in front of them made both the doctor and Elena jerk their heads up.

"Stefan! Stefan! Stefan!" Uncaring of what the razor fence would do to her flesh, Elena leaned over to try to hold his hands.

"No," Stefan whispered, as if sharing a precious secret. "Put your fingers *here* and *here* – on top of mine. This fence is only specially treated steel – it numbs my Power but it can't break my skin."

Elena put her fingers *there* and *there*. And then she was touching Stefan. Really touching him. After so long.

Neither of them spoke. Elena heard Dr Meggar get up and quietly creep away – to Sage, she supposed. But her mind was full of Stefan. She and he simply looked at each other, trembling, with tears quivering on their lashes, feeling very young.

And very close to death.

"You say I always make you say it first, so I'll confound you. I love you, Elena."

Teardrops fell from Elena's eyes.

"Just this morning I was thinking how many people there are to love. But really it's only because there's one in the first place," she whispered back to him. "One for ever. I love you, Stefan! I love you!"

Elena drew back for a moment and wiped her eyes the way all clever girls know how to do without ruining their make-up: by putting her thumbs beneath her lower lashes and leaning backward, scooping tears and kohl into infinitesimal droplets in the air.

For the first time she could *think*.

"Stefan," she whispered, "I'm so sorry. I wasted time this morning getting dressed up – well, dressed down – to show you what's waiting for you when we get you out. But now . . . I feel . . . like . . . ."

Now there were no tears in Stefan's eyes, either. "Show me," he whispered back eagerly.

Elena stood, and without theatrics, shrugged the cloak off. Shut her eyes, her hair in hundreds of kiss curls, little wispy spirals that were plastered around her face. Her gilded eyelids, waterproof, still gilded. Her only clothing the wisps of golden tulle with jewels attached to make it decent. Her entire body iridescent, perfection in the first bloom of youth that could never be matched or re-created.

There was a sound like a long sigh ... and then silence, and Elena opened her eyes, terrified that Stefan might have died. But he was standing up, clutching at the iron gate as if he might wrench it off to get to her.

"I get all this?" he whispered.

"All this for you. Everything for you," Elena said.

At that moment there was a soft sound behind her and she whirled to see two eyes shining in the dimness of the cell opposite Stefan's.

CHAPTER

33

To her surprise, Elena felt no anger, only a determination to protect Stefan if she could.

And then she saw that in the cell she'd assumed was empty, there was a kitsune.

The kitsune looked nothing like Shinichi or Misao. He had long, long hair as white as snow – but his face was young. He was wearing all white, too, tunic and breeches out of some flowing, silky material and his tail practically filled the small cell, it was so fluffy. He also had fox ears which twitched this way and that. His eyes were the gold of fireworks.

He was gorgeous.

The kitsune coughed again. Then he produced – from his long hair, Elena thought – a very, very small and thin-skinned leather bag.

Like, Elena thought, the perfect bag for one perfect jewel.

Now the kitsune took a pretend bottle of Black Magic (it was heavy and a pretend drink was delicious), and filled the little bag with it. Then he took a pretend syringe (he held it as Dr Meggar had and tapped it to get the bubbles out) and filled it from the little bag. Finally, he stuck the pretend syringe through his own bars and depressed his thumb, emptying it.

"I can feed you Black Magic wine," Elena translated. "With his little pouch I can hold it and fill the syringe. Dr Meggar could fill the syringe, too. But there's no time, so I'm going to do it."

"I—" began Stefan.

"*You* are going to drink as fast as you can." Elena loved Stefan, wanted to hear his voice, wanted to fill her eyes with him, but there was a life to be saved, and the life was his. She took the little pouch with a bow of thanks to the kitsune and left her cloak on the floor. She was too intent on Stefan to even remember how she was dressed.

Her hands wanted to shake but she wouldn't let them. She had three bottles of Black Magic here: her own, in her cloak, Dr Meggar's, and somewhere, in *his* cloak, Damon's.

So with the delicate efficiency of a machine, she repeated what the kitsune had shown her over and over. Dip, pull up lever, push through bars, squirt. Over and over and over.

After about a dozen of these Elena developed a new technique, the catapult. Filling the tiny bag with wine and holding it by the top until Stefan got his mouth positioned, and then, all in one motion, smashing the bag with her palm and squirting a fair amount straight into Stefan's mouth. It got the bars sticky, it got Stefan sticky; it would never have worked if the steel had been razor-sharp for *him*, but it actually forced a surprising amount down his throat.

The other bottle of Black Magic wine she put in the

kitsune's cell, which had regular bars. She didn't quite know how to thank him, but when she could spare a second, she turned to him and smiled. He was chugging the Black Magic straight from the bottle, and his face was set in an expression of cool, appreciative pleasure.

The end came too quickly. Elena heard Sage's voice booming, "It is no fair! *Elena* will not be ready! *Elena* has not had enough time with him!"

Elena didn't need an anvil dropped on her head. She shoved the last bottle of Black Magic wine into the kitsune's cell, she bowed for the last time and gave him back his tiny pouch – but with the canary diamond from her navel in it. It was the largest piece of jewellery she had left and she saw him turn it over precisely in long-nailed fingers and then rise to his feet and make a tiny bow to her. There was a moment for a mutual smile and then Elena was cleaning up Dr Meggar's bag, and pulling on her red cloak. Then she was turning to Stefan, jelly inside once more, gasping: "I'm so sorry. I didn't mean to make it a medical visit."

"But you saw the chance to save my life and just couldn't pass it up."

Sometimes the brothers were very much alike.

"Stefan, don't! Oh, I *love* you!"

"*Elena*." He kissed her fingers, pressed to the bars. Then, to the guards: "No, please, *please*, don't take her away! For pity's sake, give us one more minute! Just one!"

But Elena had to let go of his fingers to hold her cloak together. The last she saw of Stefan, he was pounding on the bars with his fists and calling, "Elena, I love you! Elena!"

Then Elena was dragged out of the hallway and a door shut between them. She sagged.

Arms went around her, helped her to walk. Elena got angry! If Stefan was being put back in his old lice-ridden cell – as she supposed he was, right about now – he was being made to walk. And these demons did nothing gently, she knew that. He was probably being driven like an animal with sharp instruments of wood.

Elena could walk, too.

As they reached the front of the Shi no Shi lobby Elena looked around. "Where's Damon?"

"In the coach," Sage answered in his gentlest voice. "He needed some time."

Part of Elena said, *"I'll give him time! Time to scream once before I rip his throat out!"* But the rest of her was just sad.

"I didn't get to say anything I wanted to say. I wanted to tell him how sorry Damon is; and how Damon's changed. He didn't even remember that Damon had been there—"

"He *talked* to you?" Sage seemed astonished.

The two of them, Sage and Elena, walked out of the final marble doors of the building of the Gods of Death. That was the name Elena had chosen for it in her own mind.

The carriage was at the kerb in front of them, but no one got in. Instead, Sage gently steered Elena a little distance from the others. There he put his large hands on her shoulders and spoke, still in that very soft voice,

"Mon Dieu, my child, but I do not want to say this to you. It is that I must. I fear that even if we get your Stefan out of jail by the day of Lady Bloddeuwedd's party that – that it will be too late. In three days he will already be . . ."

"Is that your medical opinion?" Elena said sharply, looking up at him. She knew her face was pinched and white and that he pitied her greatly, but what she wanted was an answer.

"I am not a medical man," he said slowly. "I am just another vampire."

"Just another Old One?"

Sage's eyebrows went up. "Now, what gave you that little idea?"

"Nothing. I'm sorry if I'm wrong. But will you please get Dr Meggar?"

Sage looked at her for a long minute more, then departed to get the doctor. Both men came back.

Elena was ready for them. "Dr Meggar, Sage only saw Stefan at the beginning, before you gave him that injection. It was Sage's opinion that Stefan would be dead in three days. Given the effects of the injection, do you agree?"

Dr Meggar peered at her and she could see the shine of tears in his short-sighted eyes. "It is possible – just possible – that if he has enough willpower, he could still be alive by then. But most likely . . ."

"Would it make any difference to your opinion if I said that he drank maybe a third of a bottle of Black Magic wine tonight?"

Both men stared at her. "Are you saying—"

"Is this just a plan you have now?"

"*Please!*" Forgetting about her cape, forgetting everything, Elena grasped Dr Meggar's hands. "I found a way to get him to drink about that much. Does it make a difference?" She squeezed the elderly hands until she could feel bone.

"It certainly should." Dr Meggar looked bewildered and afraid to hope. "If you really got that much into his system, he would be almost certain to live until the night of Bloddeuwedd's party. That's what you want, isn't it?"

Elena sank back, unable to resist giving his hands a little kiss as she let go.

"And now let's go tell Damon the good news," she said.

In the carriage, Damon was sitting bolt upright, his profile outlined against a blood-red sky. Elena got in and shut the door behind her.

With no expression at all, he said, "Is it over?"

"Over?" Elena wasn't really this dense, but she figured it was important that Damon be clear in his own mind as to what he was asking.

"Is he – dead?" Damon said wearily, pinching the bridge of his nose with his fingers.

Elena allowed the silence to go on for a few beats longer. Damon must know Stefan was not likely to actually die in the next half hour. Now that he wasn't getting instant confirmation of this his head snapped up.

"Elena, tell me! What happened?" he demanded, urgency in his voice. "*Is my brother dead?*"

"No," Elena said quietly. "But he's likely to die in a few days. He was coherent this time, Damon. Why didn't you speak to him?"

There was an almost palpable drawing-in on Damon's part. "What do I have to say to him that matters?" he asked harshly. " 'Oh, I'm sorry I almost killed you'? 'Oh, I hope you make it another few days'?"

"Things like that, maybe, if you lose the sarcasm."

"When *I* die," Damon said cuttingly, "I'm going to be standing on my own two feet and fighting."

Elena slapped him across the mouth. There wasn't room to get much leverage here, but she put as much Power behind the motion as she dared without risking breaking the carriage.

Afterward, there was a long silence. Damon was touching his bleeding lip, accelerating the healing, swallowing his own blood.

Finally he said, "It never even occurred to you that you are my slave, did it? That I'm your master?"

"If you're going to retreat into fantasy, that's your affair," Elena said. "Myself, I have to deal with the real world. And, by the way, soon after you ran away, Stefan was not only standing but laughing."

"Elena" – on a quick rising note. "You found a way to give him blood?" He grasped her arm so hard it hurt.

"Not blood. A little Black Magic. With two of us there, it would have gone twice as fast."

"There were three of you there."

"Sage and Dr Meggar had to distract the guards."

Damon took his hand away. "I see," he said expressionlessly. "So I failed him yet again."

Elena looked at him with sympathy. "You're completely inside the stone ball now, aren't you?"

"I don't know what you're talking about."

"The stone ball you stick anything that might hurt you inside. You even draw yourself inside it, although it must be very cramped in there. Katherine must be in there, I suppose, walled off in her own little chamber." She remembered the night at the hotel. "And your mother, of course. I should say, Stefan's mother. *She* was the mother you knew."

"Don't . . . my mother . . ." Damon couldn't even form a coherent sentence.

Elena knew what he wanted. He wanted to be held and soothed and told it was all right – just the two of them, under her cloak with her warm arms holding him. But he wasn't going to get it. This time she was saying no.

She had promised Stefan that this was for him, alone. And, she thought, she would keep to the spirit of that promise, if she hadn't kept to the letter, for ever.

As the week progressed, Elena was able to recover from the pain of seeing Stefan. Although none of them could speak about it except in choked, brief exclamations, they listened when Elena said that there was still a job to be done, and that if they managed to complete it well they would be able to go home soon – while if they did not complete it, Elena didn't care whether she went home or stayed here in the Dark Dimension.

Home! It had the sound of a haven, even though Bonnie and Meredith knew firsthand what kind of hell was lurking in Fell's Church for them. But somehow anything would be preferable to this land of bloody light.

With hope kindling interest in their surroundings, they were once again able to feel pleasure at the dresses Lady Ulma was having made for them. Designing was the one pursuit that the lady could still enjoy during her official bed rest, and Lady Ulma had been hard at work with her sketchbook. Since Bloddeuwedd's party would be an indoor/outdoor affair, all three dresses had to be carefully designed to be attractive both under candlelight and under the giant red sun's crimson rays.

Meredith's gown was deep metallic blue, violet in the sunlight, and it showed an entirely different side of the girl from the siren in the skin-tight mermaid dress who had attended Fazina's gala. It reminded Elena somehow of something an Egyptian princess would wear. Once again, it left Meredith's arms and shoulders bare, but the modest narrow skirt that fell in straight lines to her sandals, and the delicacy of the sapphire beads that adorned the shoulder straps served to give Meredith an unassuming look. That look was emphasised by Meredith's hair, which Lady Ulma dictated be worn down, and her face, which was bare of make-up except kohl around the eyes. At her throat, a necklace made of the very largest oval-cut sapphires formed an elaborate collar. She also had matching blue gems on her wrists and slender fingers.

Bonnie's dress was a little clever invention: it was made of a silvery material which took on a pastel tinge of the colour of the ambient lighting. Moonlight-coloured indoors, it shone a soft shimmering pink, almost exactly the colour of Bonnie's strawberry hair, when she was outside. It sported a belt, necklace, bracelets, earrings, and rings all of matching cabochon-cut white opals. Bonnie's curls were to be carefully pinned up and away from her face, in a daringly mussed-up mass, leaving her translucent skin to shine softly rose in the sunlight, and ethereally pale inside.

Once again, Elena's dress was the simplest and the most striking. Her gown was scarlet, the same colour under blood-red sun or indoor gas lamp. It was rather low cut, giving her creamy skin a chance to shine golden in the sunlight. Clinging close to her figure, it was slashed up one side to give her room to walk or dance. On the afternoon of the party Lady Ulma had Elena's hair carefully brushed into a tangled cloud that shimmered Titian outdoors, golden indoors. Her jewellery ranged from an inset of diamonds at the bottom of the neckline, to diamonds on her fingers, wrists and one upper arm, plus a diamond choker that fit over Stefan's necklace. All these would blaze as red as rubies in the sunlight, but would occasionally glint another startling colour, like a burst of mini-fireworks. Onlookers, Lady Ulma promised, would be dazzled.

"But I can't wear these," Elena had protested to Lady Ulma. "I might not get to see you again before we get Stefan – and from that moment we're on the run!"

"It's the same for all of us," Meredith had added quietly, looking at each of the girls in their "indoor" colours of silvery-blue, scarlet and opal. "We're all wearing the most jewellery we've ever worn indoors or out – but you might lose it all!"

"And you might need it all," Lucen had said quietly. "All the more reason for you each to have jewellery that you can trade for carriages, safety, food, whatever. It's simply designed, too – you can wrench out a stone and use it as payment, and the jewels are not in an elaborate setting that might not be to some collector's taste."

"In addition to which, they are all of the highest quality," Lady Ulma had added. "They are the most flawless examples of their kind we could get on such short notice."

At that point, all three girls had reached their limit, and rushed the couple – Lady Ulma on her enormous bed, sketchbook always beside her, and Lucen standing nearby – and cried and kissed and generally undid the beautiful jobs that had been done on their faces.

"You're like angels to us, do you know that?" Elena sobbed. "Just like fairy godparents or angels! I don't know how I can say goodbye!"

"Like angels," Lady Ulma had said then, wiping a tear from Elena's cheek. Then she grasped Elena, saying "Look!" and gestured to herself comfortably in bed, with a couple of blooming, dewy-eyed young women ready to attend to her wishes. Lady Ulma had then nodded at the window, out of which a small mill stream could be seen, and some plum trees, with ripe fruit blazing like jewels on the branches, and then with a sweep of her hand indicated the gardens, orchards, fields and forests on the estate.

Then she had taken Elena's hand and smoothed it over her own softly curving abdomen. "You see?" She had spoken almost in a whisper. "Do you see all of this – and can you remember how you found me? Which of us is an angel now?"

At the words "how you found me" Elena's hands had flown up to cover her face – as if she'd been unable to bear what memory showed her at that moment. Then she was hugging and kissing Lady Ulma again, and a whole new round of cosmetic-destroying embraces had begun.

"Master Damon was even kind enough to buy Lucen," Lady Ulma had said, "and you may not be able to picture it, but" – here she had looked at the quiet, bearded jeweller with eyes full of tears – "I feel for him as you feel for your Stefan." And then she had blushed and hidden her face in her hands.

"He's freeing Lucen today," Elena had said, dropping to her knees to rest her head against Lady Ulma's pillow. "And giving the estate to you irrevocably. He's had a lawyer – an advocate, you'd say – working on the papers all week with a Guardian. They're done now, and even if that hideous general should come back, he couldn't touch you. You have your home for ever."

More crying. More kissing. Sage, who had been innocently walking down the hallway, whistling, after a romp with his dog, Saber, had passed Lady Ulma's room and had been drawn in. "We'll all miss you, too!" Elena had wept. "Oh, thank you!"

Later that day, Damon had made good on all of Elena's promises, besides giving a large bonus to each member of the staff. The air had been full of metallic confetti, rose petals, music, and cries of farewell as Damon, Elena, Bonnie and Meredith had been carried to Bloddeuwedd's party – and away for ever.

"Come to think of it, why didn't Damon free *us*?" Bonnie asked Meredith as they rode in litters toward Bloddeuwedd's mansion. "I can understand that we needed to be slaves to get into this world, but we're in now. Why not make honest girls of us?"

"Bonnie, we're honest girls already," Meredith reminded her. "And I think the point is that we were never *real* slaves at all."

"Well, I meant: Why doesn't he free us so that everyone *knows* we're honest girls, Meredith, and you know it."

"Because you can't free somebody who's free already, that's why."

"But he could have gone through the ceremony," Bonnie persisted. "Or is it really hard to free a slave here?"

"I don't know," Meredith said, breaking at last under this tireless inquisition. "But I'll tell you why I *think* he doesn't do it. I *think* that it's because this way he's responsible for us. I mean, it's not that slaves can't be punished – we saw that with Elena." Meredith paused while they both shuddered at the memory. "But, ultimately, it's the slave *owner* that can lose their life over it. Remember, they wanted to stake Damon for what Elena did."

"So he's doing it for us? To protect us?"

"I don't know. I . . . suppose so," Meredith said slowly.

"Then – I guess we've been wrong about him in the past?" Bonnie generously said "we've" instead of "you've." Meredith had always been the one of Elena's group most resistant to Damon's charm.

"I . . . suppose so," Meredith said again. "Although it seems that everyone is forgetting that until recently Damon *helped* the kitsune twins to put Stefan here! And Stefan definitely hadn't done anything to deserve it."

"Well, of course *that's* true," Bonnie said, sounding relieved not to have been too wrong, and at the same time strangely wistful.

"All Stefan ever wanted from Damon was peace and quiet," Meredith continued, as if on more steady ground there.

"And Elena," Bonnie added automatically.

"Yes, yes – *and* Elena. But all Elena wanted was Stefan! I mean – all Elena *wants* . . ." Meredith's voice trailed off. The sentence didn't seem to work properly in the present tense any more. She tried again. "All Elena wants now is . . ."

Bonnie just watched her speechlessly.

"Well, whatever she wants," Meredith concluded, rather shaken, "she wants Stefan to be a part of it. And she doesn't want *any* of us to have to stay here – in this . . . this hellhole."

In another litter just beside them things were very quiet. Bonnie and Meredith were so used by now to travelling in closed litters that they hadn't even realised that another palanquin had drawn abreast of them and that their voices carried clearly in the hot, still afternoon air.

In the second litter, Damon and Elena both looked very hard at the silken curtains fluttering open.

Now, Elena, with an almost mad air of needing something to do, hurriedly unwound a cord and the curtains dropped into place.

It was a mistake. It closed Elena and Damon into a

surreal glowing red oblong, in which only the words that they had just heard seemed to have validity.

Elena felt her breath coming too quickly. Her aura was slipping. *Everything* was slipping sideways.

They don't believe that I only want to be with Stefan!

"Steady on," Damon said. "This is the last night. By tomorrow—"

Elena held up a hand to keep him from saying it.

"By tomorrow we'll have found the key and gotten Stefan and we'll be out of here," Damon said anyway.

Jinx, thought Elena. And sent up a prayer after it.

They rode in silence up toward Bloddeuwedd's grand mansion. For a surprisingly long time Elena didn't realise that Damon was trembling. It was a quick, involuntary shaken breath that alerted her.

"Damon! Dear – dear heaven!" Elena was stricken, at a loss, not for words, but for the right words. "Damon, look at me! *Why?*"

Why? Damon replied in the only voice he could trust not to tremble or crack or break. *Because – do you ever think of what's happening to Stefan while you're going to a party wearing splendid clothes, being carried along, to drink the finest wine and to dance – while he – while he—* The thought remained unfinished.

This is just what I needed right before being seen in public, Elena thought, as they reached the long driveway to Bloddeuwedd's home. She tried to call on all of her resources before the curtains were drawn and they were free to step out at the location of the second half of the key.

CHAPTER
34

I *don't think about those things*, Elena answered in the same way Damon had spoken and for the same reason. *I don't think because if I do I'll go insane. But if I go insane, what good will I be to Stefan? I couldn't help him. Instead I block it all out with walls of iron and I keep it away at any cost.*

"And you can manage that?" Damon asked, his voice shaking slightly.

"I can – because I have to. Remember in the beginning when we were arguing about the ropes around our wrists? Meredith and Bonnie had doubts. But they knew that I would wear handcuffs and crawl after you if that was what it took." Elena turned to look at Damon in the crimson darkness and added, "And you've given yourself away, time after time, you know." She slipped arms around him to touch his healed back, so that he would have no doubt about what she meant.

"That was for you," Damon said harshly.

"Not really," Elena replied. "Think about it. If you hadn't agreed to the Discipline, we might have run out of town, but we could never have helped Stefan after that. When you get down to it, everything, all you've done, you've done for Stefan."

"When you get down to it, I was the one who put Stefan here in the first place," Damon said tiredly. "I figure we're just about even now."

"How many times, Damon? You were possessed when you let Shinichi talk you into it," Elena said, feeling exhausted herself. "Maybe you need to be possessed again – just a little – so you remember how it feels."

Every cell in Damon's body seemed to flinch away from this idea. But aloud he just said, "There's something that everyone has missed, you know. About the archetypal story of how two brothers killed each other simultaneously, and became vampires because they'd dallied with the same girl."

"What?" Elena said sharply, shocked out of her tiredness. "Damon, what do you mean?"

"What I said. There's something you've all missed. Ha. Maybe even Stefan has missed it. The story gets told and retold, but nobody catches it."

Damon had turned his face away. Elena moved closer to him, just a bit, so he could smell her perfume, which was attar of roses that night. "Damon, tell me. Tell me, *please*!"

Damon started to turn towards her—

And it was at that moment that the liftmen stopped. Elena had only a second to wipe her face, and the curtains were being drawn.

Meredith had told them all the myth about Bloddeuwedd, which she'd got from a story-telling globe. All about how Bloddeuwedd had been made out of flowers and brought to life by the gods, and how she had betrayed her husband to his death, and how, in punishment, she had been doomed to spend each night from midnight to dawn as an owl.

And, apparently, there was something the myths didn't mention. The fact that she had been doomed to live here, banished from the Celestial Court into the deep red twilight of the Dark Dimension.

All things considered, it was logical that her parties started at six in the evening.

Elena found that her mind was jumping from subject to subject. She accepted a goblet of Black Magic from a slave as her eyes wandered.

Every woman and most of the men at the party were wearing clever attire that changed colour in the sun. Elena felt quite modest – after all, everything out of doors seemed to be pink or scarlet or wine-coloured. Downing her goblet of Magic, Elena was slightly surprised to find herself going into automatic party-mode behaviour, greeting people she'd met earlier in the week with cheek kisses and hugs as if she'd known them for years. Meanwhile she and Damon worked their way towards the mansion, sometimes with, sometimes against the tide of constantly moving people.

They made it up one steep set of white (pink) marble stairs, which sported on either side banks of glorious blue (violet) delphiniums and pink (scarlet) wild roses. Elena stopped here, for two reasons. One was to get a new goblet of Black Magic. The first had already given her a pleasant glow – although of course everything was constantly glowing here. She was hoping that the second cup would help her forget everything that Damon had brought up in the litter except the key – and help her remember what she'd been fretting over originally, before her thoughts had been hijacked by Bonnie and Meredith's talk.

"I expect the best way is just to *ask* someone," she told Damon, who was suddenly and silently at her elbow.

"Ask what?"

Elena leaned a little toward the slave who'd just supplied her with a fresh goblet. "May I ask – where is Lady Bloddeuwedd's main ballroom?"

The liveried slave looked surprised. Then, with his head, he made a gesture all around. "This plaza – below the canopy – has gained the name the Great Ballroom," he said, bowing over his tray.

Elena stared at him. Then she stared around her.

Under a giant canopy – it looked semi-permanent to her and was hung all around with pretty lanterns in shades that were enhanced by the sun – the smooth grass lawn stretched away for hundreds of yards on all sides.

It is bigger than a football field.

"What I'd like to know," Bonnie was asking a fellow guest, a woman who had clearly been to many of Bloddeuwedd's affairs and knew her way around the mansion, "is this: which room is the main ballroom?"

"Oh, my death, it depends on what you mean," the guest replied cheerfully. "Theah's the Great Ballroom out of doors – you *must* have seen it while climbing – the big pavilion? And then theah's the White Ballroom inside. That's lit with candelabras and has the curtains drawn all round. Sometimes it's called the Waltz Room, since all that is played in there is waltzes."

But Bonnie was still caught in horror a few sentences back. "There's a ballroom *outside*?" she said shakily, hoping that somehow she hadn't heard right.

"That's it, deah, you can see through that wall theah." The woman was telling the truth. You *could* see through the wall, because the walls were all of glass, one beyond another, allowing Bonnie to see what seemed to be an illusion done with mirrors: lighted room after lighted room, all filled with people. Only the last room on the bottom floor seemed to be made out of something solid. That must be the White Ballroom.

But through the opposite wall, where the guest was pointing – oh, yes. There was a canopy top. She remembered vaguely passing it. The other thing she remembered was . . .

"They dance on the grass? That – enormous field of grass?"

"Of course. It's all especially cut and rolled smooth. You won't trip over a weed or hummock of ground. Are you sure you're feeling quite well? You look rathah pale. Well" – the guest laughed – "as pale as anyone can look in this light."

"I'm fine," Bonnie said dazedly. "I'm just . . . fine."

The two parties met later and told each other of the horrors that they had unearthed. Damon and Elena had discovered that the ground of the outdoor ballroom was almost as hard as rock – anything that had been buried there before the ground was rolled smooth by heavy rollers would now be packed down in something like cement. The only place that anyone could dig there was around the perimeter.

"We should have brought a diviner," Damon said. "You know, someone who uses a forked stick or a pendulum or a bit of a missing person's clothing to home in on the correct area."

"You're right," Meredith said, her tone clearly adding *for once*. "Why *didn't* we bring a diviner?"

"Because I don't know of any," Damon said, with his

sweetest, most ferocious barracuda smile.

Bonnie and Meredith had found that the inside ballroom's flooring was rock – very beautiful white marble. There were dozens of floral arrangements in the room, but all that Bonnie had stuck her small hand into (as unobtrusively as possible) were simply cut flowers in a vase of water. No soil, nothing that could justify using the term "buried in".

"And besides, why would Shinichi and Misao put the key in water they knew would be thrown out in a few days?" Bonnie asked, frowning, while Meredith added,

"And how do you find a loose floorboard in marble? So we can't see how it could be buried there. By the way, I checked – and the White Ballroom has been here for years, so there's no chance that they dumped it under the building stones, either."

Elena, by now drinking her third goblet of Black Magic, said, "All right. The way we look at this is: one room scratched off the list. Now, we've already got half of the key – look how easy that was—"

"Maybe that was just to tease us," Damon said, raising an eyebrow. "To get our hopes up, before dashing them completely . . . here."

"That can't be," Elena said desperately, glaring at him. "We've come so far – farther than Misao ever imagined we would. We can find it. We *will* find it."

"All right," Damon said, suddenly deadly serious. "If we have to pretend to be staff and use pickaxes on that soil outdoors, we'll do it. But first, let's go through the entire house inside. That seemed to work well last time."

"All right," Meredith said, for once looking straight at him and without disapproval. "Bonnie and I will take the upstairs floors and you can take the downstairs ones –

maybe you can make something of that White Waltz Ballroom."

"All right."

They set to work. Elena wished that she could calm down. Despite most of three goblets of Black Magic oscillating inside her – or perhaps because of them – she was seeing certain things in new lights. But she must keep her mind on the quest – and only on the quest. She would do anything – *anything* – she told herself, to get the key. Anything for Stefan.

The White Ballroom smelled of flowers and was garlanded with large, opulent blooms in the midst of abundant greenery. Standing arrangements were placed to shield an area around a fountain into an intimate nook where couples could sit. And, although there was no visible orchestra, music poured into the ballroom, demanding a response from Elena's susceptible body.

"I don't suppose you know how to waltz," Damon said suddenly, and Elena realised that she had been swaying in time to the beat, eyes closed.

"Of course I do," Elena answered, a little offended. "We all of us went to Ms Hopewell's classes. That was the equivalent of charm school in Fell's Church," she added, seeing the funny side of it and laughing at herself. "But Ms Hopewell did love to dance, and she taught us every dance and movement she thought was graceful. That was when I was about eleven."

"I suppose it would be absurd for me to ask you to dance with *me*," Damon said.

Elena looked at him with what she knew were large and puzzled eyes. Despite the low-cut scarlet dress, she didn't *feel* like an irresistible siren tonight. She was too wrought up to feel the magic woven in the cloth, magic which she now realised was telling her she was a dancing flame, a fire elemental. She supposed that Meredith must feel like a quiet stream, flowing swiftly and steadily to her destination, but sparkling and glinting all the way. And Bonnie – Bonnie, of course was a sprite of the air, meant to dance as lightly as a feather in that opalescent dress, barely subject to gravity.

But abruptly Elena remembered certain glances of admiration she had seen directed towards herself. And now suddenly Damon was vulnerable? Yet he didn't imagine she would dance with him?

"Of course I would love to dance," she said, realising with a slight shock that she *hadn't* noticed before, that Damon was in flawless white tie. Of course, it was on the one night when it might hinder them, but it made him look like a prince of the blood.

Her lips quirked slightly at the title. Of the blood . . . oh, yes.

"Are you sure *you* know how to waltz?" she asked him.

"A good question. I took it up in 1885 because it was known to be riotous and indecent. But it depends on whether you are speaking of the peasant waltz, the Viennese Waltz, the Hesitation Waltz or—"

"Oh, come on, or we'll miss another dance." Elena grabbed his hand, feeling tiny sparks as if she'd stroked a cat's fur the wrong way, and pulled him into the swaying crowd.

Another waltz began. Music flooded into the room and lifted Elena almost off her feet as the small hairs on the back of her neck stood up. Her body tingled all over as if she had drunk some sort of celestial elixir.

It was her favourite waltz since childhood: the one she'd been brought up on. Tchaikovsky's *Sleeping Beauty* waltz. But some child part of her mind could never help but pairing the sweet sweeping notes that came after the thundering, electrifying beginning together with the words from the Disney movie version:

I know you; I danced with you once upon a dream . . .

As always, they brought tears to her eyes; they made her heart sing and her feet want to fly rather than dance.

Her dress was backless. Damon's warm hand was on her bare skin there.

I know, something whispered to her, why they called this dance riotous and indecent.

And now, certainly, Elena felt like a flame. *We were meant to be this way.* She couldn't remember if it was an old quote of Damon's or something new he was just barely whispering to her mind now. *Like two flames that join and merge into one.*

You're good, Damon told her, and this time she knew that it was him speaking and that it was in the present.

You don't need to patronise me. I'm too happy already! Elena laughed back. Damon was an expert, and not just at the precision of the steps. He danced the waltz as if it were still riotous and indecent. He had a firm lead, which of course Elena's human strength could not break. But he could interpret little signals of her own, about what she wanted and he obliged her, as if they were ice dancing, as if at any moment they might twirl and leap.

Elena's stomach was slowly melting and taking her other internal organs with it.

And it never once occurred to her to think what her high school friends and rivals and enemies would have thought of her melting over classical music. She was free of petty spite, petty shame over differences. She was through with labelling. She wished that she could go back to show everyone that she'd never meant it in the first place.

The waltz was over all too soon and Elena wanted to

push the Replay button and do it from the beginning again. There was a moment just when the music stopped where she and Damon were looking at each other, with equal exaltation and yearning and—

And then Damon bowed over her hand. "There is more to the waltz than just moving your feet," he said, not looking up at her. "There is a swaying grace that can be put into the movements, a leaping flame of joy and oneness – with the music, with a partner. Those are not matters of expertise. Thank you very much for giving me the pleasure."

Elena laughed because she wanted to cry. She never wanted to stop dancing. She wanted to tango with Damon – a real tango, the kind you were supposed to have to get married after. But there was another mission . . . a necessary mission that had to be completed.

And, as she turned, there were a whole crowd of *other* things in front of her. Men, demons, vampires, beastlike creatures. All of them wanted a dance. Damon's tuxedoed back was walking away from her.

Damon!

He paused but did not turn back. *Yes?*

Help me! We need to find the other half of the key!

It seemed to take him a moment to assess the situation, but then he understood. He came back to her, and taking her by the hand said in a clear, ringing voice, "This girl is my . . . personal assistant. I do not desire that she dance with anyone other than myself."

There was a restless murmuring at this. The kind of slaves that got taken to balls of this sort were not usually the kind that were forbidden to interact with strangers. But just then there was a sort of flurry at the side of the room, eventually pressing toward the opposite side where Damon and Elena were.

"What is it?" Elena asked, the dance and the key both forgotten.

"Who is it, I'd ask, rather," Damon replied. "And I'd answer: our hostess, Lady Bloddeuwedd herself."

Elena found herself crowding behind other people to get a glimpse of this most extraordinary creature. But when she actually saw the girl standing alone in the doorway to the ballroom, she gasped.

She was made out of flowers . . . Elena remembered. What would a girl made out of flowers look like?

She would have skin like the faintest blush of pink on an apple blossom, Elena thought, staring unashamedly. Her cheeks would be slightly deeper pink, like a dawn-coloured rose. Her eyes, enormous in her delicate, perfect face, would be the colour of larkspur, with heavy feathery black lashes that would make them droop half shut, as if she walked always half in a dream. And she would have yellow hair as pale as primroses, falling down almost to the floor, wound in braids that were themselves incorporated into thicker braids until the whole mass was brought together just above her delicate ankles.

Her lips would be as red as poppies, half open and inviting. And she would give off a scent that was like a bouquet of all the first blossoms of spring. She would walk as if swaying in the breeze.

Elena could only remember standing, gazing after this vision like the dozens of other guests around her. Just one more second to drink in such loveliness, her mind begged.

"But what was she wearing?" Elena heard herself say aloud. She could not remember either a stunning dress or a glimpse of lustrous apple-blossom skin through the many braids.

"Some sort of gown. It was made out of what else? Flowers," Damon put in wryly. "She was wearing a dress made of every kind of flower I've ever seen. I don't understand how they stayed put – maybe they were silk and sewn together." He was the only one who didn't seem dazzled by this vision.

"I wonder if she would talk to us – just a few words," Elena said. She was longing to hear the delicate, magical girl's voice.

"I doubt it," a man in the crowd answered her. "She doesn't talk much – at least until midnight. Say! It's you! How're you feeling?"

"Very well, thank you," Elena replied politely, and then quickly stepped back. She recognised the speaker as one of the young men who had forced their cards on Damon at the end of the Godfather's ceremony, the night of her Discipline.

Now she just wanted to get away unobtrusively. But there were too many of the men, and it was clear that they were not about to let her and Damon go.

"This is the girl I told you about. She goes into a trance and no matter how she's marked; she doesn't feel a thing—"

"—blood running down her sides like water and she never flinched—"

"They're a professional act. They go on the road . . ."

Elena was just about to say, coolly, that Bloddeuwedd had strictly forbidden this kind of barbarism at her party, when she heard one of the young vampires saying, "Don't you know, I was the one who persuaded Lady Bloddeuwedd to ask you to this get-together. I told her about your act and she was most interested to see it."

Well, scratch one excuse, Elena thought. But at least

be nice to these young men. They might be helpful somehow later.

"I'm afraid I can't do it tonight," she said quietly, so that they would be quiet themselves. "I'll apologise to Lady Bloddeuwedd directly, of course. But it just isn't possible."

"Yes, it is." Damon's voice, just behind her, astounded her. "It's quite possible – given that someone finds my amulet."

Damon! What are you saying?

Hush! What I have to.

"Unfortunately, about three and a half weeks ago I lost a very important amulet. It looks like this." He brought out the half of the fox key and let them all take a good look at it.

"Is that what you used to do the trick?" someone asked, but Damon was far too clever for that.

"No, many people saw me do the act just a week or so ago without it. This is a personal amulet, but with part of it missing, I simply don't feel like doing magic."

"It looks like a little fox. You're not a kitsune?" someone – too clever for their own good, Elena thought – asked next.

"It may look like that to you. It's actually an arrow. An arrow with two green stones at the arrowhead. It's a – masculine charm."

A female voice somewhere in the crowd said: "I shouldn't think you need any more masculine charm than you have right now!" and there was laughter.

CHAPTER

35

"**N**evertheless" – Damon's eyes took on a steely glint – "without the amulet my assistant and I will not perform."

"But – with it you will? I say, are you saying that you lost your amulet *here*?"

"As a matter of fact, yes. Just around the time the party arrangements were being set up." Damon flashed a beautiful, haunting smile at the young vampires and then turned it off suddenly. "I had no idea I would have your help, and I was trying to find a way to get an invitation. So I took a look around to see how the place would be laid out."

"Don't tell me it was before the grass was rolled," someone said apprehensively.

"Unfortunately, yes. And I was given a psychic message, which told me that the k— the amulet is *buried* somewhere here."

There was a chorus of groans from the crowd.

Then there were individual voices raised, pointing out

the difficulties: the rock-hardness of the rolled grass, the many ballrooms with their many floral arrangements in soil, the kitchen garden and flower gardens (which we haven't even seen yet, Elena thought).

"I realise the virtual impossibility of finding this," Damon said, taking the half of the fox key back into his hand and making it disappear neatly by passing it near Elena's hand, which was ready to receive it. She now had a special place for it – Lady Ulma had seen to that.

Damon was saying, "That is why I simply said no at the beginning. But you pressed me, and now I've given you the full answer."

There was some more grumbling, but then people began walking out in ones and twos and threes, talking about the best places to start looking.

Damon, they're going to destroy Bloddeuwedd's grounds, Elena protested silently.

Good. We'll offer all the jewels you three girls have on you, as well as all the gold I have on me, as a recompense. But what four people can't do, maybe a thousand can.

Elena sighed. *I still wish we'd had the chance to talk to Bloddeuwedd. Not just to hear her speak, but to ask her some questions. I mean what reason would a beautiful blossom like her have to protect Shinichi and Misao?*

Damon's telepathic answer was brief. *Well, let's try the top rooms, then. That was where she was headed, anyway.*

They found a case of crystal stairs – quite difficult to locate when all the walls were transparent, and frightening to ascend. Once on the second floor they looked for another one. Eventually Elena found it, by stumbling over the first step.

"Oh," she said, looking from the step, which now showed itself through a line of red across its front edge, to her shin, which showed the same damage. "Well, *it* may be invisible, but we aren't."

"It's not quite invisible." Damon was channelling Power to his eyes, she knew. She'd been doing the same – but these days she wondered which of them had more of her blood in them: him or her?

"Don't strain yourself, I can see the steps," he said. "Just shut your eyes."

"My eyes—" Before she could ask why she *knew* why and before she could scream he had picked her up, his body warm and solid and the only solid thing anywhere around. He headed up the stairs holding her so that her dress was out of the way of the blood droplets that fell freely into space.

For someone afraid of heights, it was a wild, terrifying ride: even though she knew Damon was in top condition and would not drop her and even though she was certain he could see where he was going. Still, left to herself and her own volition, she would never have made it farther than the first stair. As it was, she didn't even dare wiggle much in case she threw Damon off balance. She could only whimper and try to endure.

When, an eternity later, they reached the top, Elena wondered who would carry her down, or if she would be left here the rest of her life.

They were confronted by Bloddeuwedd, the most enchantingly inhuman creature Elena had yet seen. Enchanting . . . but odd. Was there not a slight primrose pattern to her hair in back and on the sides? Wasn't her face actually the *shape* of an apple-blossom petal as well as having the petal's faint bloom?

"You are in my private library," she said.

And, as if a mirror had cracked, Elena came free of the last of Bloddeuwedd's glamour.

The gods had made her out of flowers . . . but flowers

don't speak. Bloddeuwedd's voice was toneless and flat. It ruined the image of the flower-made girl completely.

"We're sorry," Damon said – naturally not at all out of breath. "But we'd like to ask you some questions."

"If you think I will help you, I will not," the flower-petal girl said in the same nasal tone. "I hate humans."

"But I am a vampire, as you have surely already discerned," Damon was beginning, laying the charm on thick, when Bloddeuwedd interrupted him. "Once a human, always a human."

"*I beg your pardon?*"

Damon's loss of control might have been the best thing that could have happened, Elena thought, trying to keep behind him. He was so clearly sincere about his scorn for humans that Bloddeuwedd softened a little.

"What did you come to ask?"

"Only if you had seen one of two kitsune lately: they're brother and sister and call themselves Shinichi and Misao."

"Yes."

"Or they might – I'm sorry? *Yes?*"

"The thieves came to my house at night. I was at a party. I flew back from the party and almost caught them. Kitsune are hard to catch, though."

"Where . . ." Damon swallowed. "Where were they?"

"Running down the front stairs."

"And do you remember the date that they were here?"

"It was the night that the grounds were made ready for this party. Stone rollers went over the grass. The canopy was erected."

Weird things to do at night, Elena thought, but then she remembered – again. The light was always the same.

But her heart was beating fast. Shinichi and Misao

could only have been here for one reason: to drop off half of the fox key.

And maybe drop it in the Great Ballroom, Elena thought. She watched dully as the entire outside of the library rotated, almost like a giant planetarium, so that Bloddeuwedd could pick out a globe and place it in some contraption that must make the music play in various rooms.

"Excuse me," Damon said.

"This is my private library," Bloddeuwedd said coldly against the swelling of the glorious ending to the *Firebird Suite*.

"Meaning now we must leave?"

"Meaning now I am going to kill you."

CHAPTER

36

"**W**hat?" shouted Damon over the music, while adding: *Run – go!* telepathically to Elena.

If it had merely been Elena's life, she would have been glad enough to die here with the thunderous beauty of *Firebird* all around her, rather than facing those steep, invisible steps alone.

But it wasn't just her life. It was Stefan's life, too. Still, the flower maiden didn't look particularly menacing, and Elena couldn't summon up enough adrenalin to try making it down that hideous stairway.

Damon, let's both go. We have to search the Great Ballroom outside. Only you're strong enough . . .

A hesitation. Damon would rather fight than face that enormous, impossible green field outside, Elena thought.

But Bloddeuwedd, despite her words, was now spinning the room around them again, so that she, at the edge of some invisible walkway, could find the exact orb she wanted.

Damon lifted Elena in his arms and said: *Shut your eyes.*

Elena not only shut her eyes, but put her hands over them as well. If Damon was going to drop her, she wasn't going to help matters by shouting "Look out!" as he did it.

The sensations themselves were sickening enough. Damon leaped from step to step like an ibex. He seemed barely to touch the steps in going down and Elena wondered – quite suddenly – if anything were after them.

If so, it was information she needed to know. She began to lift her hands and heard Damon whisper-snarl "Keep them shut!" in a voice that few people liked to argue with.

Elena peeked out between her hands, met Damon's exasperated eyes, and saw nothing following them. She clamped her hands back together and prayed.

If you were really a slave, you wouldn't last a day here, you know, Damon informed her, taking a final leap into space and then setting her down on invisible – but at least level – ground.

I wouldn't want to, Elena sent coldly. *I swear, I'd rather die.*

Be careful what you promise, Damon flashed his splendid smile down at her suddenly. *You may end up in other dimensions trying to fulfil your word.*

Elena didn't even try to one-up him. They were out, free, and racing through the glass house down to the stairs to the lower floor – a little tricky in her state of mind, but bearable – and finally out the door. On the grass of the Great Ballroom they found Meredith and Bonnie . . . and Sage.

He was actually in white tie as well, although his jacket strained at his shoulders. In addition, Talon was sitting on one – so the problem might be taken care of fairly soon, as she was ripping the material and drawing blood. Sage didn't seem aware of it. Saber was at his master's side, looking at Elena with eyes too thoughtful to be mere animal eyes, but without malice.

"Thank God you came back!" Bonnie cried, running to them. "Sage came and he has a marvellous idea."

Even Meredith was excited. "You remember how Damon said we should have brought a diviner? Well, we have two now." She turned to Sage. "Please tell them."

"As a rule, I don't take these two to parties." Sage reached down to scratch under Saber's throat. "But a little bird told me that you might be in trouble." His hand moved up to stroke Talon, ruffling the falcon's feathers slightly. "So, *dites-moi*, please: Just how much have you two been handling the half-key you *do* possess?"

"I touched it tonight and in the beginning, the night we found it," said Elena. "But Lady Ulma handled it and Lucen made a chest for it and we've all handled that."

"But outside the box?"

"I've held it and looked at it once or twice," said Damon.

"*Eh bien!* The kitsune smells should be much stronger on it. And kitsune have very distinctive smells."

"So you mean that Saber—" Elena's voice gave out for pure faintness.

"Can sniff out anything with the smell of kitsune on it. Meanwhile, Talon has very good eyesight. She can fly overhead and look for the glint of gold in case it's in plain sight somewhere. Now show them what they will be searching for."

Elena obligingly held out the crescent shaped half-key for Saber to sniff.

"*Voilà!* And Talon, now you take a good look." Sage backed away to what was, Elena supposed, Talon's optimal seeing distance. Then when he came back, he said, *"Commençons!"* and the black dog exploded away, nose to ground, while the falcon took off in grand, high, sweeping circles.

"So you think the kitsune were on this grass?" Elena asked Sage, as Saber began racing back and forth, nose still just above the grass – and then suddenly veered out onto the middle of the marble steps.

"But assuredly, they were here. You see how Saber runs, like a black panther, with his head low, and his tail straight? He has business in hand, him! He is hot on the scent."

I know someone else who gives off the same feeling, Elena thought as she glanced back at Damon, who stood with his arms folded, motionless, coiled like a spring, waiting for whatever news the animals would bring.

She happened to glance at Sage at the same moment, and she saw an expression on his face that – well, it was probably the same expression she'd been wearing a minute ago. He glanced at her and she blushed.

"Pardonnez-moi, Monsieur," she said, looking away quickly.

"Parlez-vous français, Madame?"

"Un peu," Elena said humbly – an unusual condition for her. "I can't really keep up a serious conversation. But I loved going to France." She was about to say something else, when Saber barked once, sharply, to attract attention and then sat bolt upright at the curb.

"They came or left in a carriage or litter," Sage translated.

"But what did they do in the house? I need a trail going the other way," Damon said, looking up at Sage with something like raw desperation.

"All right, all right. Saber! *Contremarche!"*

The black dog instantly turned around, put its nose to

the ground as if it afforded him the greatest delight, and began running back and forth across the stairs and the lawn that formed the "Great Ballroom" – now becoming pitted with holes as people took shovels, pickaxes and even large spoons to it.

"*Kitsune are hard to catch,*" Elena murmured into Damon's ear.

He nodded, glancing at his watch. "I hope we are, too," he murmured back.

There was a sharp bark from Saber. Elena's heart leaped in her chest.

"What?" she cried. "What is it?" Damon passed her, grabbed her hand, and dragged her in his wake.

"What has he found?" Elena gasped as they all reached the same point simultaneously.

"I don't know. It's not part of the Great Ballroom," replied Meredith. Saber was sitting up proudly in front of a bed of tall, clustering pale-lavender (deep-violet) hydrangeas.

"They don't look like they're doing too well," said Bonnie.

"And it's not below any of the upper ballrooms, either," Meredith said, stooping to get at Saber's height and then look up. "There's just the library."

"Well, I know one thing without a question," Damon said. "We're going to have to dig up this flower patch and I don't fancy asking Ms Larkspur-eyes-Now-I-have-to-kill-you for her permission."

"Oh, did you think they were larkspur, her eyes? Because I thought of bluebells, rahthah," said a guest behind Bonnie.

"Did she really say she had to kill you? But why?" another guest, nearer to Elena asked nervously.

Elena ignored them. "Well, let's put it this way, she's

certainly not going to like it. But it's the only clue we've got." *Except, I suppose, if the kitsune meant to leave it here, but then took off in a coach*, she added voicelessly to Damon.

"So that means the show can commence," cried one of the young vampire fans, stepping toward Elena.

"But I don't have my amulet back," Damon said flatly, moving in front of Elena like an impenetrable wall.

"But you will in minutes, surely. Look, couldn't some fellows backtrack with the dog to wherever the bad guys came from – came to the estate *from*, if you get me? And meanwhile we can be getting on with the show?"

"Can Saber do that?" Damon asked. "Follow a carriage?"

"With a fox in it? But of course. Actually, I could go with them," Sage said quietly. "I could make sure that these two enemies are caught if they are on the other end of the trail. Show them to me."

"These are the only shapes I know." Damon reached out two fingers and touched Sage's temple. "But, of course, they'll have more forms, possibly infinite ones."

"Well, they are not our priority, I assume. The, ah, amulet is."

"Yes," Damon said. "Even if you don't land a blow on them, get the key half and race back."

"So? Even more important than revenge," Sage said softly, shaking his head in wonder. Then he added quickly. "Well, I will wish us good luck. Any adventurous types who want to go with me? Ah, good, four – very well, five, *Madame* – is enough."

And he was gone.

Elena looked at Damon, who was looking back with blank, black eyes. "You really expect me to do – that – again?"

"All you need to do is stand there. I'll make sure you

lose as little blood as possible. And if you ever want to stop we can have a signal."

"Yes, but now I understand. And I can't handle it."

His face went cold suddenly. Shutting her out.

"You're not required to handle anything. Besides, isn't it enough if I say it's fair bargain for Stefan?"

Stefan! Elena's entire body went through some sort of elemental change. "Let me share it," she begged, and knew that she was begging and knew what Damon was going to say.

"Stefan is going to need you when we get out. Just make sure you can handle *that*."

Stop. Think. Don't bash his head in, Elena's brain told her. He's pushing your buttons. He knows how to do it. Don't let him push your buttons.

"I can handle both," she said. "Please, Damon. Don't treat me as if I were – one of your one-nighters, or even your Princess of Darkness. Talk to me as if I were Sage."

"Sage? Sage is the most frustrating, cunning—"

"I know. But you talk to him. And you used to talk to me, and now you're not. *Listen to me*. I can't bear to go through this scenario again. I'll scream."

"Now you're threatening—"

"No! I'm telling you what will happen. Unless you gag me, I'll scream. And scream. As I would scream for Stefan. I can't help it. Maybe I'm breaking down . . ."

"But don't you see?" Suddenly he had whirled around and taken hold of her hands. "We're almost at the end. You, who've been the strongest all along – you *can't* break down now."

"The strongest . . ." Elena was shaking her head. "I thought we were right there, on the verge of understanding each other."

"All right." His words came as hard chips of marble

now. "What if we do five?"

"Five?"

"Five strokes instead of ten. We'll promise to do the other five when the 'amulet' is found, but we'll run when we do find it."

"You would have to break your word."

"If it takes that—"

"No," she said flatly. "You say nothing. *I'll* tell them. I'm a liar and a cheat and I've always played with men. We'll see if I can't finally put my talents to good use. And there's no point in trying any of the other girls," she added, glancing up. "Bonnie and Meredith are wearing gowns that would fall right off if you slashed them. Only I have a bare back." She pirouetted in place to show off how her dress met only very high at the neck in a halter and very low in the back in a V.

"Then we're agreed." Damon had a slave refill his goblet and Elena thought: we're going to be the tipsiest act in history, if nothing else.

She couldn't help but shiver. The last time she had felt an inner trembling was from Damon's warm hand on her bare back as they danced. Now, she felt something much icier, just a draft of cold air perhaps. But it drew her mind to the feeling of her own blood running down her sides.

Suddenly Bonnie and Meredith were there beside her, forming a barricade between her and the increasingly curious and excited crowd.

"Elena, what's happened? They said a barbarian human girl was to be whipped—" began Meredith.

"And you just knew it had to be me," completed Elena. "Well, it's true. I don't see how I can get out of it."

"But what have you *done*?" Bonnie asked frantically.

"Been an idiot. Let some fraternity-type vampire boys

think that it was a sort of magic act," Damon put in. His face was still grim.

"That's a little unfair, isn't it?" Meredith asked. "Elena told us about the first time. It sounded as if they jumped to the conclusion that it was an act all by themselves."

"We should have denied it then. Now, we're stuck with it," Damon said flatly. Then, as if he were making an effort, "Oh, well, maybe we'll get what we came for, anyway."

"That was how we found out – some idiot came running down the steps yelling about an amulet with two green stones."

"It was all we could think of," Elena explained wearily. "It's worth it for Damon and I to do this if only we can find the other half of the key."

"You don't have to do it," Meredith said. "We can just leave."

Bonnie stared at her. "Without the fox key?"

Elena shook her head. "We've already been through all that. The unanimous decision was to do it this way. She looked around. "Now where are the guys that wanted to see it so much?"

"Looking in the field – that used to be a ballroom," Bonnie replied. "Or getting shovels – lots of 'em – from Bloddeuwedd's gardening compound. Ow! Why'd you pinch me, Meredith?"

"Oh, my, did *that* pinch? I meant to do *this*—"

But Elena was already striding away, as eager now as Damon was to get it over with. Half over with. I just hope he remembers to change into his leather jacket and black jeans, she thought. In white tie – the blood—

I won't let there be any blood.

The thought was sudden and Elena didn't know where it came from. But in the deepest reaches of her being, she thought: *he's been punished enough*. He was trembling in the litter. He thought about another person's well-being from minute to minute. It's enough now. Stefan wouldn't want him to be hurt any more.

She glanced up to see one of the Dark Dimension's small, misshapen moons moving visibly above her. This time the surrender she made to it was bright red, a feather shining in sullen crimson light. But she gave herself up to it unreservedly, body and soul, and it rested on the hallowed spring of eternal blood that was her womanhood. And then she knew what she had to do.

"Bonnie, Meredith, look: we're a triumvirate. We have to try to share this with Damon."

No one looked enthusiastic.

Elena, whose pride had been entirely broken from the moment she first saw Stefan in his cell, knelt down in front of them on the hard marble step. "I'm begging you—"

"Elena! Stop that!" Meredith gasped.

"Please get up! Oh, Elena—" Bonnie was a breath away from tears.

And so, it was small, soft-hearted Bonnie who turned the tide. "I'll try to teach Meredith how. But anyway, we'll at least share it between the three of us."

Hug. Kiss. A murmur into strawberry hair, "I know what you see in the dark. You're the bravest person I know."

And then, leaving a stunned Bonnie behind, Elena went to collect spectators for her own whipping.

CHAPTER

37

Elena had been tied, like someone in a B-movie who will soon be released, standing upright against a pillar. Digging on the field was still going on in a dilatory way as the vampires who had put her up to this fetched an ash stick they had brought, and allowed Damon to inspect it. Damon himself was moving in slow motion. Trying to find points to kibitz about. Waiting for the rattling of coach wheels that would tell him the carriage was back. Acting brisk, but inside feeling as sluggish as half-cooled lead.

I've never been a sadist, he thought. I've always tried to give pleasure – except in fights. But it should be me in that prison cell. Can't Elena see that? It's my turn beneath the lash now.

He had changed into his "magician clothes", taking as long as he dared without looking as if he wanted to put this off. And now there were somewhere between six and eight hundred creatures, waiting to see Elena's blood spill, to watch Elena's back cut and miraculously heal again.

All right. I'm as ready as I'll ever be to do this.

He came into his body, into the now of what was happening.

Elena swallowed. "Share the pain" she'd said – without in the least knowing how to do it. But here she was, like a sacrifice tied to a pillar, staring at Bloddeuwedd's house and waiting for the blows to come.

Damon was giving the crowd an introductory speech, talking gibberish and doing it very well. Elena found a particular window of the house to stare at. And then she realised that Damon was no longer speaking.

A touch of the rod against her back. A telepathic whisper.

Are you ready?

Yes, she said immediately, knowing that she wasn't. And then hearing, against dead silence, a swish through the air.

Bonnie's mind floating into hers. Meredith's mind flowing like a stream. The blow was a mere cuff, although Elena felt blood spill.

She could feel Damon's bewilderment. What should have been a sword slash was a mere slap. Painful, but definitely bearable.

And once again. The triumvirate portioned out the pain before Damon's mind could receive it.

Keep the triangle moving. And a third.

Two more to go. Elena allowed her gaze to wander over the house. Up to the second floor where Bloddeuwedd had to be enraged at what had become of her party.

One more to go. The voice of a guest coming back to her. "*That library. She has more orbs than most public libraries, and*" – with his voice dropping for a moment –

"they say she has all sorts of spheres up there. Forbidden ones. You know."

Elena hadn't known and still could still hardly imagine what might be forbidden *here*.

In her library, Bloddeuwedd, a single, lonely figure, moved in the brilliantly lighted great sphere to find a new orb. Inside the house music would be playing, different music in each different room. Outside, Elena could hear nothing.

The last blow. The triumvirate managed to handle it, allotting agonising pain amongst four people. At least, Elena thought, my dress was already as red as it could be.

And then it was over, and Bonnie and Meredith were quarrelling with some of the vampire ladies who wanted to help bathe the blood from Elena's back, showing it once again unblemished and perfect, glowing golden in the sunlight.

Better keep them away, Elena thought rather drowsily to Damon; *some of them may be compulsive nail-biters or finger-lickers. We can't afford for anyone to taste my blood and feel the life-force in it; not when I've gone through so much to conceal my aura.*

Although there was clapping and cheering everywhere, no one had thought to untie Elena's wrists. So she stood leaning against the pillar, gazing at the library.

And then the world froze.

All around her was music and motion. She was the still point in a turning universe. But she had to get moving, and fast. She yanked hard at her bonds, lacerating herself.

"Meredith! Untie me! Cut these ropes, quick!"

Meredith obeyed hastily.

When Elena turned, she knew what she would see. The face – Damon's face, bewildered, half resentful, half humble. It was good enough for her, right then.

Damon, we need to get to the—

But then they were engulfed by a riot. Well-wishers, fans, sceptics, vampires begging for "a tiny taste", gogglers who wanted to make sure that Elena's back was real and warm and unmarked. Elena felt too many hands on her body.

"Get away from her, damn you!" It was the primal savage roar of a beast defending its mate. People backed away from Elena, only to close in . . . very slowly and timidly . . . on Damon.

All right, Elena thought. I'll do it alone. I can do it alone. For Stefan, I can.

She shouldered her way through the crowd, accepting bunches of hastily dug-up flowers from admirers – and feeling more hands on her body. *"Hey, she really isn't marked!"* At last, Meredith and Bonnie helped her to get out – without them she would never have made it.

And then she was running, running into the house, not bothering to use the door that was near to Saber's barking place. She thought she knew what was there anyway.

On the first floor she spent a minute being bewildered before seeing a thin red line in nothingness. Her blood! See how many things it was good for? Right now it highlighted the first of the glass steps for her, the one she had stumbled into before.

And at that time, cradled in Damon's strong arms, she hadn't been able to imagine even crawling up these steps. Now she channelled all the Power she had into her eye nodes – and the stairs lit up. It was still terrifying. There were no handholds on either side, and she was woozy from excitement, fear, and loss of blood. But she forced herself up, and up, and up.

"Elena! I love you! Elena!"

She could hear the cry as if Stefan were beside her now.

Up, up, up . . .

Her legs ached.

Keep going. No excuses. If you can't walk, hobble. If you can't hobble, crawl.

She was crawling as she finally reached the top, the edge of the nest of the owl Bloddeuwedd.

At least it was still a pretty, if insipid-looking, maiden who greeted her. Elena realised at last what was wrong with Bloddeuwedd's looks. She had no animal vitality. She was, at heart, a vegetable.

"I am going to kill you, you know."

No, she was a vegetable with no heart.

Elena glanced around her. She could see outside from here, although in between was the dome that was made of shelves and shelves upon shelves of orbs, so everything was weirdly distorted.

There were no hanging creepers here, no flagrant displays of exotic, tropical blooms. But she was already in the centre of the room, in Bloddeuwedd's owl nest. Bloddeuwedd was nowhere near it; she was on the contraption that let her reach her star balls.

The key could only be buried in that nest.

"I don't want to steal from you," Elena promised, breathing hard. Even as she spoke, she plunged two arms into the nest. "Those kitsune played a trick on both of us. They stole something of mine and put the key to it in your nest. I'm just taking back what they put in."

"Ha! You – human slave! Barbarian! You dared to violate my private library! People outside are digging up my beautiful ballroom, my precious flowers. You think you're going to get away again this time, but you're not! *This time you're going to DIE!"*

It was an entirely different voice than the flat, nasal, but still maidenlike tones that had greeted Elena before. This was a powerful voice, a heavy voice . . .

. . . a voice to go with the size of the nest.

Elena looked up. She couldn't make anything of what she saw. An enormous fur coat in a very exotic pattern? Some huge stuffed animal's back?

The creature in the library turned towards her. Or rather, its head swivelled towards her, while its back remained perfectly still. It rotated its head sideways and Elena knew that what she was seeing was a face. The head was even more hideous and more indescribable than she could have imagined. It had a sort of single eyebrow which dipped from the edge of one side of its forehead down towards the nose (or where the nose should have been) and then went up again. The feature was like a gigantic V-shaped brow and below it were two huge round yellow eyes that often blinked. There was no nose or mouth like a human's, but instead there was a large, cruel, hooked black beak. The rest of the face was covered in feathers, mostly white, turning mottled grey at the bottom, where the neck seemed to be. It was also grey and white in two hornlike projections that shot up from the top of the head – like a demon's horns, Elena thought wildly.

Then, with the head still staring at her, the body turned towards, Elena.

It was the body of a sturdy woman, covered in white and grizzled feathers, Elena saw. Talons peeked out from under the lowest feathers.

"Hello," the creature said in a grating voice, its beak opening and closing to bite off the words. "I'm Bloddeuwedd, and I never let anyone touch my library. I am your death."

The words *Can't we at least talk about it first?* were on Elena's lips. She didn't want to be a hero. She certainly didn't want to take on Bloddeuwedd while searching for the key that *must* be here – somewhere.

Elena kept on trying to explain while frantically feeling inside the nest, when Bloddeuwedd extended wings that spanned the room and came at her.

And then, like a streak of lightning, something zipped between them, giving out a raucous cry.

It was Talon. Sage must have given the hawk orders when he left her.

The owl seemed to shrink a little – the better to attack, thought Elena.

"Please let me explain. I haven't found it yet, but there is something in your nest that doesn't belong to you. It's mine – and – and Stefan's. And the kitsune hid it the night you had to chase them off your estate. Do you remember that?"

Bloddeuwedd didn't answer for a moment. Then she showed that she had a simple, one-size-fits-all-situations philosophy.

"You set foot into my private quarters. You die," she said and this time when she swooped by Elena, Elena could hear the clack of her beak coming together.

Again something small and bright dove at Bloddeuwedd, aiming for her eyes. The great owl had to take her attention off Elena in order to deal with it.

Elena gave up. Sometimes you just needed help. "Talon!" she cried, unsure of how much human speech Talon understood. "Try to keep her occupied – just for a minute!"

As the two birds darted and wheeled and shrieked around her, Elena tried to search with her arms, while ducking when she needed to. But that great black beak was always too close. Once it sliced into her arm, but Elena was on an adrenalin high, and she hardly felt the pain. She kept searching without a pause.

Finally, she realised what she should have done from the beginning. She snatched up an orb from its transparent rack.

"Talon!" she called. "Here!"

The falcon dove down toward her and there was a snap. But afterwards Elena still had all her fingers and the *hoshi no tama* was gone.

Now, *now*, Elena truly heard a shriek of rage from Bloddeuwedd. The giant owl went after the hawk, but it was like a human trying to slap a fly – an intelligent fly.

"Give that orb back! It's priceless! Priceless!"

"You'll get it back as soon as I find what I'm looking for." Elena, mad with terror and soaked in hormones, climbed all the way inside the nest and began searching the marble bottom with her fingers.

Twice Talon saved her by dropping orbs with a crash to the ground as the huge owl Bloddeuwedd was headed toward Elena. Each time, the noise of the crash caused the owl to forget about Elena and try to attack the hawk. Then Talon snatched another orb and swept at great speed right under the owl's nose.

Elena was beginning to have a nightmare feeling that everything she had known just half an hour before was wrong.

She had been leaning against the canopy pole, exhausted, staring up into the library and the maiden who inhabited it and the words had simply flowed into her mind.

Bloddeuwedd's orb room . . .

Bloddeuwedd's globe room . . .

Bloddeuwedd's . . . star ball room . . .

. . . Bloddeuwedd's ballroom.

Two ways to take the same words. Two very different kinds of rooms.

It was just as she was remembering this that her fingers touched metal.

CHAPTER

38

"**T**alon! Uh – heel!" Elena shouted and began to race as fast as she could to get out of the room. This was strategy. Would the owl become even smaller so as to get through the door or would it destroy its sanctuary in order to stay on top of Elena?

It was a good strategy, but it didn't amount to much in the end. The owl shrank to dart through the door, and then resumed gigantic size to attack Elena as she ran down the stairs.

Yes, ran. With all of her Power channelled to her eyes, Elena leaped from step to step as Damon had before. Now there was no time for fear, no time for thinking. There was only time to turn over in her fingers a small, hard, crescent-shaped object.

Shinichi and Misao – they did make it into her nest.

There must be a ladder or something made of glass that even Damon couldn't see, in the flowerbed where Saber had stopped and barked. No – Damon *would* have seen it, so they must have brought their own ladder.

That's why their trail ended there. They climbed straight up into the library. And they ruined the flowers in the bed, which is why the new flowers weren't doing so well.

Elena knew from Aunt Judith, from her childhood, that transplanted flowers took a while to revive and perk up again.

Leap . . . jump . . . leap . . . I am a spirit of fire. I cannot miss a step. I am a fire elemental. Leap . . . leap . . . leap.

And then Elena was looking at level ground, trying not to leap into it, but a prisoner to her body which was already leaping. She fell hard enough to numb one side, but she kept hold of the precious crescent clenched in a deathgrip in her hand.

A gigantic beak smashed into glass where she had been a moment before she slid. Talons raked her back.

Bloddeuwedd was still after her.

Sage and his group of sturdy young male and female vampires travelled at the pace of a running dog. Saber could lead them, but only as fast as he himself could go. Fortunately few people seemed to want to instigate a fight with a dog that weighed as much as they did – that weighed more than many of the beggars and children they encountered as they reached the bazaar.

The children crowded around the carriage, slowing them further. Sage took the time to exchange an expensive jewel for a purse full of small change and he scattered the coins behind the carriage as they went, allowing Saber free rein.

They passed dozens of stalls and crossing streets, but Saber was no ordinary bloodhound. He had enough Power to confound most vampires. With perhaps only one or two of the key molecules stuck to his nasal membrane he could hunt down his goal. Where another dog might be fooled by one of the hundreds of similar kitsune trails they were travelling through, Saber examined and rejected each of them as being not *quite* the right shape, size, or sculpture.

There came a time, though, when even Saber seemed defeated. He stood in the centre of a six-way crossroads, regardless of traffic, limping slightly, and going in circles. He couldn't seem to choose a path.

And nor could I, my friend, Sage thought. We've come so far, but it's clear they went on farther. No way to go up or dig down . . . Sage hesitated, looking around the crimson-coloured wheel of roads.

And then he saw something.

Directly across from him, but to his left was a perfumery. It must sell hundreds of fragrances, and billions of scent molecules were deliberately being released into the air.

Saber was blind. Not blind in his keen liquid dark eyes. But where it mattered he was numbed and blinded by the billions of scents that were being blown up his nose.

The vampires in the carriage were calling to go on or go back. They had no sense of real adventure, them. They just wanted a nice show. And undoubtedly many had slaves who were recording the whipping for them so they could enjoy it at leisure at home.

At that moment a flash of blue and gold decided Sage. A Guardian! *Eh, bien* . . .

"Heel, Saber!"

Saber's head and tail drooped as Sage randomly picked one of the directions and had him race alongside the running vampire to get out of the thoroughfare and onto another street.

But then, miraculously, the tail went up again. Sage

estimated that there could not be even one molecule of the kitsune's scent left in Saber's nostrils now . . .

. . . but the memory of the scent . . . that was still there.

Saber was once again in hunting mode, with head down, tail straight, all his Power and intelligence concentrated on one goal and one goal only: to find another molecule that matched the three-dimensional memory of the one in his mind. Now that he was not blinded by the searing smell of all those different concentrated odours, he was able to think more clearly. And thinking alerted him to slip in between streets, causing a commotion behind him.

"What about the carriage?"

"Forget about the carriage! Don't lose sight of that guy with the dog!"

Sage, trying to keep up with Saber himself, knew when a chase was about to end. *Tranquillité!* he thought to Saber. He also barely whispered the word. He had never been certain if his animal friends were telepathic or not, but he liked to believe that they were, while behaving as if they were not. *Tranquillité!* he told himself.

And so, when the huge black dog with the shining dark eyes and the man ran up the steps to one particular ramshackle building, they did it silently. Then, as if he'd had a pleasant stroll in the country, Saber sat and looked at Sage in the face, laughing-panting. He opened and closed his mouth in a silent parody of a bark.

Sage waited for the young vampires to catch up with him before be opened the door. And, as he wanted the element of surprise, he didn't knock. Instead he smashed a fist with the Power of a sledgehammer through the door and groped for locks and chains and bolts. He could feel none. He did feel a knob.

Before opening the door, and going into who knew

what peril, he said to those behind him, "Any loot we take is the property of Master Damon. I am his foreman and it was only through my dog's skills that we have made it so far."

There was agreement, ranging from grumbling to indifferent.

"By the same token," Sage said, "whatever danger is in there, I face first. Saber! NOW!"

They burst into the room, nearly taking the door off its hinges.

Elena cried out involuntarily. Bloddeuwedd had just done what Damon would not, and lined her back with bloody furrows from her talons.

But even as Elena managed to find the glass door to the outside, she could feel other minds surging to help sustain her, to lift and share some of the pain.

Bonnie and Meredith were picking their way through huge shards of glass to get to her. They were screaming at the owl. And Talon, heroically, was attacking from above.

Elena couldn't stand it any longer. She had to see. She had to know that this metallic-feeling thing that she'd picked out of Bloddeuwedd's nest wasn't some bit of filthy rubbish. She had to know *now.*

Rubbing the tiny scrap of metal against the ill-fated scarlet dress, she took a moment to glance downward, to see crimson sunlight sparkle against gold and diamonds and two folded-back little ears and two bright-green alexandrite eyes.

The duplicate of the first fox key half, but facing the other way.

Elena's legs almost gave way underneath her.

She was holding the second half of the fox key.

Hurriedly, then, Elena brought up her free hand and plunged her fingers down into the carefully made little pocket behind the diamond insert. It concealed a tiny pouch, specially sewn there by Lady Ulma herself. In it was the first half of the fox key, replaced there as soon as Saber and Talon had finished with it. Now, as she shoved the second half-key into the pocket with the first, she was disconcerted to feel movement in the pouch. The two pieces of the fox key were – what, becoming one?

A black beak slammed into the wall beside her.

Without even thinking, Elena ducked and rolled to escape it. When her fingers flew back to make sure that the pouch was tied up and secure, she was astonished to feel a familiar shape resting inside.

Not a key?

Not a key!

The world was spinning wildly around Elena. Nothing mattered; not the object; not her own life. The kitsune twins had tricked them, had made fools of the idiot humans and the vampire who had dared to face up to them. There *was* no double fox key.

Still, hope refused to die. What was it Stefan used to say? *Mai dire mai* – never say never. Knowing what a chance she was taking, knowing she was a fool for taking it, Elena thrust her finger again into the pouch.

Something cool slipped onto one finger and stayed there.

She glanced down and for a moment was arrested by the sight. There, on her ring finger, gleamed a gold, diamond-encrusted ring. It represented two abstract foxes curled together, one facing each way. Each fox had two ears, two green alexandrite eyes and a pointed nose.

And that was all. Of what use was a trinket like this to Stefan? It bore no resemblance to the double-winged keys shown in the pictures of kitsune shrines.

As treasure, it was surely worth a million times less than what they had already spent to get it.

And then Elena noticed something.

A light shone from the eyes of one of the foxes. If she hadn't been staring at it so closely, or if she hadn't been by now in the White Waltz Ballroom, where colours showed true, she might not have noticed it. But the light was shining straight ahead of her as she turned her hand sideways. Now it was shining from four eyes.

It was shining in exactly the direction of Stefan's prison cell.

Hope rose up like a phoenix in Elena's heart, and took her soaring on a mental journey out of this labyrinth of glass rooms. The music playing was the waltz from *Faust*. Away from the sun, deep into the heart of the city, that was where Stefan was. And that was where the pale-green light from the fox's eyes was shining.

Riding high on hope, she turned the ring. The light winked out of both fox's eyes, but when she turned the ring so that the second fox was in line with Stefan's cell, it winked on.

Secret signals. How long could she have owned a ring like that and done nothing if she hadn't already *known* where Stefan's prison was?

Longer than Stefan had left to live, probably.

Now she only had to survive long enough to reach him.

CHAPTER

39

Elena waded into the crowd feeling like a soldier. She didn't know why. Maybe because she had thought of a quest and had managed to complete it and stay alive and bring back loot. Maybe because she bore honourable wounds. Maybe because above her there was an enemy who was still out for her blood.

Come to think of it, she thought, I'd better get all these non-combatants out of here. We can keep them in a safe house – well, a few dozen safe houses and—

What *was* she thinking? *Safe house* was a phrase from a book. She wasn't responsible for these people – idiots, mostly, who had stood, slavering, and watched her being whipped. But – despite that, maybe she should get them out of here.

"Bloddeuwedd!" she cried dramatically and pointed to a wheeling silhouette above. "Bloddeuwedd is free! She gave me these!" – pointing to the three lacerations on her back. "She'll go after you, too!"

At first most of the angry exclamation seemed to be

about the fact that Elena now had a marked back. Elena was in no mood to argue. There was only one person here she wanted to talk to now. Keeping Bonnie and Meredith close behind her, she called.

Damon! Damon it's me! Where are you?

There was so much telepathic traffic that she doubted he would hear her.

But finally, she caught a faint, *Elena?*

. . . Yes . . .

Elena, hold on to me. Think of holding me physically, and I'll take us to a different frequency.

Hold on to a voice? But Elena imagined holding on to Damon tightly, tightly, while she physically held Bonnie's and Meredith's hands.

Now can you hear me? This time the voice was much clearer, much louder.

Yes. But I can't see you.

But I see you. I'm coming to – WATCH OUT!

Too late, Elena's senses warned her of a huge shadow plummeting from above. She couldn't move quickly enough to get out of the way of a snapping, alligator-sized beak.

But Damon could. Leaping from somewhere, he gathered her and Bonnie and Meredith all in one great armful and leaped again, hitting grass and rolling.

Oh, God! Damon!

"Is anybody hurt?" he asked aloud.

"I'm fine," Meredith said quietly, calmly. "But I suspect I owe you my life. Thank you."

"Bonnie?" Elena asked.

I'm OK. I mean, "I'm OK. But Elena, your back—"

For the first time, Damon was able to turn Elena and see the wounds on her back. "I . . . did that? But . . . I thought . . ."

"Bloddeuwedd did that," Elena said sharply, looking upward for a circling shape in the deep red sky. "She just barely touched me. She has talons like knives, like steel. We have to go, now!"

Damon put both hands on her shoulders. "And come back when things have calmed down, you mean."

"And never come back! Oh, God, here she comes!"

Something out of the corner of her eye became baseball-sized in an instant, volleyball-sized in a second, human-sized in a moment. And then they were all scattering, leaping, rolling, trying to get away, except Damon, who seized Elena and shouted, "This is my slave! If you have any argument with her, you first argue with me!"

"And I am Bloddeuwedd, created by the gods, condemned to be a murderer every night. I'll kill you first, then eat her, the thief!" Bloddeuwedd called back in her raucous new voice. "Two bites is all it will take."

Damon, I need to tell you something!

"I'll fight you, but my slave is out of it!"

"First bite; here I come!"

Damon, we have to go!

A scream of primal pain and fury.

Damon was standing slightly crouched with a huge piece of glass held in his hand like a sword and great black drops of blood were dripping from where he had – oh, God! Elena thought – he'd put out one of Bloddeuwedd's eyes!

"YOU WILL ALL DIE! ALL!"

"Bloddeuwedd made a charge at a random vampire directly below her and Elena screamed as the vampire screamed. The black beak had caught him by one leg and was lifting him.

But Damon was running forward, jumping, slashing.

With a scream of fury, Bloddeuwedd took to the sky again.

Now everyone understood the danger. Two other vampires rushed to take their comrade from Damon, and Elena was glad that her friends were not responsible for another life. She had too much on her hands already.

Damon, I'm leaving now. You can come with me or not. I've got the key.

Elena sent the words on the frequency that they were more or less alone on, and she sent it without dramatics. She had no room for drama left. She'd been stripped of everything except the need to get to Stefan.

This time, she knew Damon heard her.

At first, she thought Damon was dying. That Bloddeuwedd had somehow come back and pierced him through his entire body, as with a spear made of light. Then she realised that the feeling was rapture, and two tiny child hands reached out of the light and clung to hers, allowing her to pull a thin, ragged, but laughing child away free.

No chains, she thought dizzily. *He's not even wearing slave bracelets.*

"My brother!" he told her. "My little brother's going to *live*!"

"Well, that's a fine thing," Elena said shakily.

"He's going to live!" A tiny frown line appeared. "If you hurry! And take good care of him! And—"

Elena put two fingers over his lips, very gently. "You don't need to worry about anything like that. You just be happy."

The little boy laughed. "I will! I *am*!"

"Elena!"

Elena came out of – well, she supposed it was a daze, although it had been more real than many other things she'd experienced recently.

"Elena!" Damon was trying desperately to restrain himself. *"Show me the key!"*

Slowly, majestically, Elena lifted her hand.

Damon's shoulders tensed, for – something – went down.

"It's a ring," he said dully. The slow and majestic bit hadn't worked on him at all.

"That's what I thought at first. It's a key. I'm not asking you, or seeing if you agree with me; I'm telling you. It's a key. The light from its eyes points to Stefan."

"What light?"

"I'll show you later. Bonnie! Meredith! We're leaving."

"YOU'RE NOT IF I SAY YOU'RE NOT!"

"Watch out!" screamed Bonnie.

The owl was diving again. And again, at the last second, Damon gathered the three girls and leaped. The owl's beak struck not grass nor shards of glass but the marble steps. They cracked. There was a scream of pain and another, as Damon, nimble as a dancer, slashed at the giant bird's one good eye. He got in a cut right above it. Blood began to fill the eye.

Elena couldn't stand any more. Ever since starting out on this journey with Damon and Matt, she had been a vial filling with anger. Drop by drop, with each new outrage, that anger had filled and filled the vial. Now her rage was about to fill it to overflowing.

But then . . . what would happen?

She didn't want to know. She was afraid she wouldn't survive it.

What she did know was that she couldn't watch any more pain and blood and anguish right now. Damon genuinely enjoyed fighting. Good. Let him. She was going to Stefan if she had to walk the whole way.

Meredith and Bonnie were silent. They knew Elena in this mood. She wasn't fooling around. And neither of them wanted to be left behind.

It was exactly at that moment that the carriage came rumbling up to the base of the marble stairs.

Sage, who obviously knew something about human nature, demonic nature, vampiric nature, and various kinds of bestial nature, jumped out of the carriage with two swords drawn. He also whistled. In a moment a shadow – a small one – came streaking to him out of the sky.

Last, slowly, stretching each leg like a tiger, came Saber, who immediately pulled back his lips to show an amazing number of teeth.

Elena leaped toward the carriage, her eyes meeting Sage's. *Help me*, she thought desperately. And his eyes said just as plainly, *Have no fear.*

Blindly, she reached behind her with both hands. One small, fine-boned, lightly trembling hand was thrust into hers. One slim, cool hand, hard as a boy's but with long tapering fingers grabbed her other one.

There was no one here to trust. No one to say goodbye to, or leave messages of goodbye with. Elena scrambled into the carriage. She got into the backseat, the farthest from the front, to accommodate incoming humans and animals.

And in they did come, like an avalanche. She had dragged Bonnie with her, and Meredith had followed, so that when Saber leaped into his accustomed place he landed on three soft laps.

Sage hadn't wasted a moment. With Talon clamped on his left wrist, he left just enough room for Damon's final spring – and a spring it was. Cracked and broken, oozing black fluid, Bloddeuwedd's beak hit the end of the marble stairs where Damon had been standing.

"Directions!" shouted Sage, but only after the horses were heading at a gallop – somewhere, anywhere, *away*.

"Oh, please don't let her hurt the horses," Bonnie gasped.

"Oh, please don't let her split this roof like cardboard," said Meredith, somehow able to be wry even when her life was in danger.

"Directions, *s'il vous plaît*!" roared Sage.

"The prison, of course," panted Elena. She felt that it had been a long time since she had been able to get enough air.

"The prison?" Damon seemed distracted. "Yes! The prison!" But then, he added, pulling up something like a pillowcase filled with billiard balls, "Sage, what are these?"

"Loot. Booty. Spoils! *Plunder!*" As the horses swung in a new direction, Sage's voice seemed to get more and more cheerful. "And look around your feet!"

"More pillowcases . . .?"

"I wasn't prepared for a big haul tonight. But things worked out well anyway!"

By now, Elena was feeling one of the pillowcases for herself. The case was, indeed, full of clear, sparkling hoshi no tama. Star balls. Memories. Worth . . .

Worthless?

"Priceless . . . although of course we don't know what's on them." Sage's voice changed subtly. Elena remembered the warning about "forbidden spheres". What, in the name of the yellow sun, could they possibly forbid down here?

Bonnie was the first to pick up a disc and put it to her temple. She did it so quickly, with such flashing, birdlike movements, that Elena couldn't stop her.

"What is it?" Elena gasped, trying to pull the star ball away.

"It's . . . poetry. Poetry I can't understand," said Bonnie crossly.

Meredith had also picked up a sparkling orb. Elena reached for her but once again she was too late.

Meredith sat as if in a trance for a moment, then grimaced and put the sphere down.

"What?" demanded Elena.

Meredith shook her head. She wore a delicate expression of distaste.

"*What?*" Elena almost yelled. Then as Meredith put the star ball by her feet, Elena lunged at it. She clapped it to her own temple and immediately was dressed in black leather from head to toe. There were two broad, square men in front of her, without a lot of muscle tone. And she could see all of their musculature because they were stark naked except for rags such as beggars wore. But they weren't beggars – they looked well fed and oily and it was clearly an act when one of them grovelled, "We have trespassed. We beg your forgiveness, O master!"

Elena was reaching to take the sphere off her temple (they stuck gently, if you put a little pressure there) and saying, "Why don't they use the space for something else?"

Something else was immediately all around her. A girl, in poor clothing, but not sacking. She looked terrified. Elena wondered if she were being controlled.

And Elena was the girl.

Pleasedon'tletitgetmepleasedon'tletitgetme—

Let what get you? Elena asked, but it was like watching a movie or book character while they were going into a lonely house in a howling storm and the music had turned eerie. The Elena who was walking in fear could not hear the Elena who was asking practical questions.

I don't think I want to see how this one comes out, she decided. She put the star ball back at Meredith's feet.

"Do we have three sacks?"

"Yes, ma'am, yes, ma'am; three sacks full."

Oh. That didn't work out very well. Elena was opening her mouth again, when Damon added quietly: "And one sack empty."

"Really? We do? Then let's all try to divide these. Anything – forbidden – goes in one sack. Weird stuff like Bonnie's poetry reading goes into another. Any news of Stefan – or of us – goes in the third. And nice things, like summer days, go in the fourth," Elena said.

"I think you are being optimistic, me," Sage said. "To expect to find an orb with Stefan on it so quickly—"

"Everybody, hush!" Bonnie said frantically. "This is Shinichi and Damon talking him into it."

Sage stiffened, as if taking a lightning bolt from the stormy sky, then he smiled. "Speak of the devil," he murmured. Elena smiled at him and squeezed his hand before taking another ball.

"This one seems to be some kind of legal stuff. I don't understand it. A slave must be taking it because I can see all of them." Elena felt her facial muscles tighten with hatred at the sight – even in a sort of dream – of Shinichi, the kitsune who had done so much harm. His hair was black, except for an irregular fringe around the edges, which made it look as if it had been dipped in red-hot lava.

And then, of course, Misao. Shinichi's sister – allegedly. This star ball must have been made by a slave, because she could see both of the twins and a lawyerly-looking man.

Misao, Elena thought. Delicate, deferential, demure . . . demonic. Her hair was the same as Shinichi's, but it was held up and back in a ponytail. You could see the demonic part if she raised her eyes. They were effervescent, golden, laughing eyes, just like her brother's; eyes that had never had a regret – except perhaps for not exacting enough revenge. They took no responsibility. They found anguish funny.

And then something odd happened. All three of the figures in the room suddenly turned around and looked straight at her. Straight at whoever had made the sphere, Elena corrected herself, but it still was disconcerting.

It was even more disconcerting when they continued to advance. Who am I? Elena thought, feeling half frantic with anxiety. Then she tried something she had never done before, or seen or heard of being done. She carefully extended her Power into the Self around the orb. She was Werty, a sort of lawyer's secretary. She/he took notes when important deals were done.

And Werty definitely didn't like the way things were going right now. The two clients and his boss closing in on him like this, in a way they never had before.

Elena pulled herself out of the clerk and put the ball down to one side. She shivered, feeling as if she'd been plunged into ice-cold water.

And then the roof crashed in.

Bloddeuwedd.

Even with her crippled beak, the huge owl tore off quite a bit of the roof of the carriage.

Everyone was screaming and no one was giving much good advice. Saber and Damon had both damaged her: Saber by raising right off the three soft laps he was sitting on and lunging straight up for Bloddeuwedd's feet. He had torn and shaken one before letting go to fall back into the carriage, where he almost slid off the back. Elena, Bonnie and Meredith grabbed at whatever portions of canine anatomy they could reach, and hauled the huge animal into the backseat again.

"Scoot over! Give him his own seat," wailed Bonnie, looking at the shreds of her pearl-coloured dress where Saber had taken off and ripped right through the gauzy material. He'd left red welts in his path.

"Well," Meredith said, "next time we'll request steel petticoats. But I really hope there isn't going to be a next time, anyway!"

Elena prayed fervently that she was right. Bloddeuwedd was skimming in from a lower angle now, undoubtedly hoping to snap off a few heads.

"Everybody grab wood. And spheres! Throw the spheres at her as she comes close to us." Elena was hoping that the sight of star globes – Bloddeuwedd's obsession – might slow her down.

At the same time Sage shouted, "Don't waste the star balls! Throw anything else! Besides, we're almost there. Hard left, then straightaway!"

The words gave Elena new hope. I have the key, she thought. The ring is the key. All I have to do now is get Stefan – and get all of us to the door with the keyhole. All in one building. I'm practically home.

The next sweep came in even lower. Bloddeuwedd, blind in one eye, with blood filling the other one, and her olfactory senses blocked by her own dried blood, was trying to ram the carriage and knock it over.

If she manages it, we'll be dead, Elena thought. And any who're still writhing like worms on the ground, she can pick off.

"*DUCK!*" She screamed the word both vocally and telepathically.

And then something like an airplane flew so close to her that she felt tufts of hair being pulled out, caught in its claws.

Elena heard a cry of pain from the front seat but didn't raise her head to see what it was. And that was good, for while the carriage suddenly slammed to a halt, the next instant a whirling, screaming, bird of death came searing out on the same course. Now Elena needed all of her attention, all her faculties, to avoid this monster that was buzzing them even lower.

"The carriage, she is finished! Get out! Run!" Sage's voice came rumbling to her.

"The horses," screamed Elena.

"Finished! Get out, damn you!"

Elena had never heard Sage swear before. She dropped the subject.

Elena never knew how she and Meredith did get out, tumbling over each other, trying to help and only getting in each other's way. Bonnie was already out, by virtue of the coach having hit a pole and sending her flying. Fortunately, it had sent her into a square of ugly but springy red clover, and she wasn't seriously injured.

"Ahhh, my bracelet – no, there it is," she cried, grabbing something glittering out of the clover. She cast a cautious look upward into the crimson night. "Now what do we do?"

"We run!" came Damon's voice. He came around the wreckage of the corner where they had fallen in a heap. There was blood on his mouth, on the previously immaculate white at his throat. It reminded Elena of those people who drank cow's blood as well as milk for nutrition. But Damon only drank from humans. He would never stoop to equine blood . . .

The horses will still be here and so will Bloddeuwedd, a

harsh voice explained in her head. *She would play with them; there would be pain. This way was quick. It was . . . a whim.*

Elena reached for his hands, gasping. "Damon! I'm *sorry*!"

"GET OUT OF HERE," Sage was roaring.

"We have to get to Stefan," Elena said, and grabbed Bonnie with her other hand. "Help guide me, please. I can't see the ring very well." Meredith, she trusted, would get to the Shi no Shi building on her own resources.

And then there was a nightmare of running and flinching and false alarms by a shaken Bonnie. Twice the horror from above came skimming straight towards them only to crash just in front of them, or a little to the side, breaking wood and tile road alike, throwing up clouds of dust. Elena didn't know about all owls, but Bloddeuwedd swooped down at an angle on her prey, then opened her wings and dropped at the last moment. Part of the worst thing about the giant owl was her silence. There was no rustling to warn them of where she might be. Something in her own feathers muffled the sound, so that they never knew when she was going to drop next.

In the end they had to crawl through all sorts of rubbish, going as fast as they could, holding wood, glass, anything sharp over their heads, as Bloddeuwedd made another pass.

And all the time Elena was trying to use her Power. It was not a Power she had used before, but she could feel its name shaping her lips. What she could not feel, could not force, was a connection between the words and the Power.

I'm useless as a heroine, she thought. I'm pathetic. They should have given these Powers to someone who already knew how to control such things. Or, no, they should have given them to someone and then given the someone a course on how to use them. Or – no—

"Elena!" Rubbish was flying in front of her, but then she was cutting left and somehow getting around it. And then she was on the ground and looking up at Damon, who had protected her with his body.

"Thank you," she whispered.

"Come on!"

"I'm sorry," she whispered and held out her right hand, with the ring on it, for him to take.

And then she doubled up, heaving with sobs. She could hear the flapping of Bloddeuwedd right above her.

CHAPTER

40

Matt and Mrs Flowers were in the bunker – the addition to the house that Mrs Flowers's uncle had put onto the back for woodwork and other hobbies. It had fallen into even more neglect than the rest of the house, being used as a storage space for things Mrs Flowers didn't know where else to put – such as Cousin Joe's folding cot and that old sagging couch that didn't match a stick of furniture inside any more.

Now, at night, it was their haven. No child or adult from Fell's Church had ever been invited inside. In fact, except for Mrs Flowers, Stefan – who'd helped move large furniture into it – and now Matt, no one had even been in for as long as Mrs Flowers could remember.

Matt clung to this. He had been, slowly but surely, reading through the material Meredith had researched and one precious excerpt had meant a lot to him and Mrs Flowers. It was the reason they were able to sleep at night, when the voices came.

> *The kitsune is often thought to be a sort of cousin to
> Western vampires, seducing chosen men (as most fox
> spirits take on a female form) and feeding directly on
> their chi, or life spirit, without the intermediary of
> blood. Thus one may make a case that they are bound
> by similar rules to the vampire. <u>For example, they
> cannot enter human dwellings without invitation</u> . . .*

And oh, the voices . . .

He was profoundly glad now that he'd taken Meredith
and Bonnie's advice and gone to Mrs Flowers's first
before going home. The girls had convinced him he'd
only be putting his parents in danger by facing up to the
lynch mob that awaited him, ready to kill him for
allegedly assaulting Caroline. Caroline seemed to have
found him at the boarding-house immediately, anyway,
but she never brought any kind of mob with her. Matt
thought that perhaps it was because that would have
been useless.

He had no idea what might have happened if the
voices had belonged to ex-friends long ago invited to his
house while he was at home.

Tonight . . .

"Come on, Matt," Caroline's voice, lazy, slow and
seductive, purred. It sounded as if she were lying down,
speaking into the crack under the door. "Don't be such a
spoilsport. You know you have to come out sometime."

"Let me talk to my mom."

"I can't, Matt. I told you before, she's undergoing
training."

"To be like you?"

"It takes a lot of work to get to be like me, Matt."
Suddenly Caroline's tone was not flirtatious any longer.

"I bet," Matt muttered, and added, "You hurt my

family and you're going to be sorrier than you can imagine."

"Oh, Matt! Come on, get real. Nobody is going to hurt anybody."

Matt slowly opened his hands to look at what he had clenched between them. Meredith's old revolver, filled with the bullets blessed by Obaasan.

"What is Elena's middle name?" he asked – not loudly, even though there were the sounds of music and dancing in Mrs Flowers's backyard.

"Matt, what are you talking about? What are you doing in there, making a family tree?"

"I asked you a simple question, Care. You and Elena played since you were practically babies, right? So what is her middle name?"

A flurry of activity. When Caroline finally answered he could clearly hear the whispered coaching, as Stefan had heard so long ago, just a beat before her words.

"If all you're interested in is playing games, Matthew Honeycutt, I'll go find someone else to talk to."

He could practically hear her flounce away.

But he felt like celebrating. He allowed himself a whole graham cracker and half a cup of Mrs Flowers's home-made apple juice. They never knew when they might be locked in here for good, with only the supplies they had, so whenever Matt went out of the bunker he brought back as many things as he could find that might be useful. A barbecue lighter and hairspray equalled a flame thrower. Jar after jar of Mrs Flowers's delicious preserves. Lapis rings in case the worst happened and they ended up with pointy teeth.

Mrs Flowers turned in her sleep on the couch. "Who was that, Matt dear?" she asked.

"Nobody at all, Mrs Flowers. You just go back to sleep."

"I *see*," Mrs Flowers said in her sweet-old-lady voice. "Well, if nobody at all comes back you might ask her her own mother's first name."

"I *see*," Matt said in his best imitation of her voice and then they both laughed. But underneath his laughter there was a lump in his throat. He had known Mrs Flowers a long time, too. And he was scared, scared of the time that it would be Shinichi's voice calling.

Then they were going to be in trouble for good.

"There it is," shouted Sage.

"Elena!" screamed Meredith.

"Oh, God!" screamed Bonnie.

The next instant, Elena was thrown, and something landed on top of her. Dully, she heard a cry. But it was different from the others. It was a choking sound of pure pain as Bloddeuwedd's beak thunked into something made of flesh. Me, Elena thought. But there was no pain.

Not . . . me?

There was a coughing sound above her.

"Elena – go – my shields – won't hold—"

"Damon! We'll go together!"

Hurts . . .

It was just the shadow of a telepathic whisper and Elena knew Damon didn't think she'd heard it. But she was circling her Power faster and faster, done with deception, caring only about getting those she loved out of danger.

I'll find a way, she told Damon. *I'll carry you. Fireman's lift.*

He laughed at that, giving Elena some hope that he wasn't dying. Now Elena wished she'd taken Dr Meggar in the carriage with them so he could use his healing powers on the injured—

—and then what? Leave him to the mercies of Bloddeuwedd? He wants to build a hospital here, in this world. He wants to help the children, who surely don't deserve all the evils that I've seen visited on them—

She shunted the thoughts aside. This was no time for a philosophical debate about doctors and their obligations.

It was time to run.

Reaching behind her, she found two hands. One was slick with blood so she reached farther, thanking her late mother for all the ballet lessons, all the children's yoga, and she grabbed the sleeve above it. And then she put her back into it and pulled.

To her surprise she hauled Damon up with her. She tried to heft him farther up on her back, but that didn't work. And then she even managed a wobbly step forward, and another—

And then Sage was there picking both of them up and they were going into the lobby of the building of the Shi no Shi.

"Everyone, get out! Get out! Bloddeuwedd's after us and she'll kill anything in her way!" Elena shouted. It was the strangest thing. She hadn't meant to shout. Hadn't formulated the words, except perhaps in the deepest parts of her subconscious. But she did shout them into the already frenzied lobby and she heard the cry taken up by others.

What she didn't expect was that they would run, not out into the street, but down towards the cells. She ought to have, of course, but she hadn't. And then she felt herself and Sage and Damon going down, down the way they had last night . . .

But was it really the right way? Elena clamped one hand over the other and saw, judging by foxlight, that they needed to head off to the right.

"WHAT ARE THOSE CELLS TO THE RIGHT OF US? HOW DO WE GET THERE?" she shouted to the young vampire gentleman next to her.

"That's Isolation and Mentally Disturbed," the vampire gentleman shouted back. "Don't go that way."

"I have to! Do I need a key?"

"Yes, but—"

"Do you have a key?"

"Yes, but—"

"Give it to me now!"

"I can't do that," he wailed in a way that reminded her of Bonnie at her most difficult.

"All right. Sage!"

"*Madame?*"

"Send Talon back to peck this man's eyes out. He won't give me the key to Stefan's ward!"

"As good as done, *Madame*!"

"W-wait! I cha-changed my mind. Here's the key!" The vampire fished through a ring of keys and handed one to her.

It looked like the other keys on his ring. Too much alike, Elena's suspicious mind said.

"Sage!"

"*Madame!*"

"Can you wait till I pass with Saber? I want him to tear the you-know-what off this guy if he's lied to me."

"Of course, *Madame*!"

"W-w-w-wait," gasped the vampire. It was clear that he was completely terrified. "I may – may have given you the wrong key – in this – this light—"

"Give me the right key and tell me anything I need to

know or I'll have the dog backtrack you and kill you," Elena said, and at that moment, she meant it.

"H-here." This time the key didn't look like a key. It was round, slightly convex, with a hole in the middle. Like a doughnut that's been sat on by a police officer, part of Elena's mind said, and began laughing hysterically.

Shut up, she told her mind sharply.

"Sage!"

"*Madame?*"

"Can Talon see the man I'm holding by the hair?" She had to go on tiptoe to grasp him.

"But of course, *Madame!*"

"Can she remember him? If I can't find Stefan I want her to show him to Saber so he can track him."

"Uh . . . ah . . . got it, *Madame!*"

A hand, dripping blood from the wrist, lifted a falcon high, at the same time as there was a serendipitous crash from the top of the building.

The vampire was almost sobbing. "Turn r-right at the n-next right. Use the k-key in the slot at h-head height to g-get into the corridor. There m-may be guards there. But . . . if – if you don't have a key to the individual cell you want – I'm sorry, but—"

"I do! I have the cell key and I know what to do after that! Thank you, you've been very kind and helpful."

Elena let go of the vampire's hair.

"*Sage! Damon! Bonnie! Look for a corridor, locked, going right. Then don't get swept away. Sage, hold Bonnie and have Saber bark like crazy. Bonnie, hold on to Meredith in front of the guys. The corridor leads to Stefan!*"

Elena never knew how much any one of her allies heard of this message, sent by voice and telepathy. But ahead she heard a sound that to her was like choirs of angels singing.

Saber was barking madly.

Elena would never have been able to stop by herself. She was in a raging river of people and the raging river was taking her right around the barrier made by four people, a falcon and a mad-seeming dog.

But eight hands reached out to her as she was swept by – and a snarling, snapping muzzle leaped ahead of her to divide the crowd. Somehow she was being run into, bruised, cradled, shoved and, grasped and grasping, forced all the way to the right wall.

But Sage was looking at that same wall in despair. "*Madame*, he tricked you! There is no keyhole here!"

Elena's throat went raw. She prepared to shout, "Saber, heel," and go after the vampire.

But then, just below her, Bonnie's voice said, "Of course there is. It's shaped like a circle."

And Elena remembered.

Smaller guards. Like imps or monkeys. Bonnie's size.

"Bonnie, take this! Shove it into the hole. Be careful! It's the only one we've got."

Sage immediately directed Saber to stand and snarl just ahead of Bonnie in the tunnel, to keep the stream of panicked demons and vampires from jostling her.

Carefully, solemnly, Bonnie took the large key, examined it, cocked her head, turned it in her hands – and placed it in the wall.

"Nothing's happening!"

"Try turning or pushing—"

Click.

The door slid open.

Elena and her group more or less fell into the corridor, while Saber stood between them and the herd pounding by, barking and snapping and leaping.

Elena, lying on the ground, legs entwined with who-knew-who-else's, cupped a hand around her ring.

The fox eyes shone straight ahead and a bit to the right.

They were shining into a cell ahead.

CHAPTER

41

"*Stefan!*" Elena screamed and knew that she sounded like a madwoman when she screamed it.

There was no answer.

She was running. Following the light. "Stefan! Stefan!"

An empty cell.

A yellowed mummy.

A pyramid of dust.

Somehow, subconsciously, she suspected one of these things. And any one would have caused her to run out to fight Bloddeuwedd with her bare hands.

Instead, when she reached the right cell, she saw a weary young man, whose face showed that he had given up all hope. He lifted a stick-thin arm, rejecting her utterly.

"They told me the truth. You were exported for aiding a prisoner. I'm not susceptible to dreams any more."

"Stefan!" She fell to her knees. "Do we have to go through this every single time?"

"Do you know how often they re-create you, *bitch?*"

Elena was shocked. More than shocked. But the next moment the hatred had faded from his face.

"At least I get to look at you. I had . . . I had a picture. But they took that, of course. They cut it up, very slowly, making me watch. Sometimes they made me cut it. If I didn't cut it, they would—"

"Oh, *darling*! Stefan, darling! *Look at me*. Listen to the prison. Bloddeuwedd is destroying it. Because I've stolen the other half of your key from her nest, Stefan, and I am not a dream. Do you see this? Did they *ever* show you this?" She held out the hand with the double fox ring on it. "Now – now – where do I put it?"

"You are warm. The bars are cold," Stefan said, clutching her hand and speaking as if reciting out of a children's book.

"Here!" Elena cried triumphantly. She didn't need to take the ring off. Stefan was holding her other hand, and this lock worked like a seal ring. She placed it straight into a circular depression in the wall. Then, when nothing happened, she turned it right. Nothing. Left.

The cell bars slowly began to lift into the ceiling.

Elena couldn't believe it and for an instant thought she was hallucinating. Then when she turned sharply to look at the ground she saw that the bars were already at least a foot above it.

Then she looked at Stefan, who was standing again.

Both of them fell back to their knees. They would have both gotten down and wriggled like snakes if necessary, the need to touch was so great. The horizontal struts on the bars made it impossible for them to hold hands as the bars lifted.

Then the bars were over the top of Elena's head and she was holding Stefan – *she was holding Stefan in her arms!* – appalled to feel bones under her hands, but *holding* him, and no one could tell her he was a hallucination or a dream, and if she and Stefan had to die together, then they would die together. Nothing mattered but that they not be separated again.

She covered the unfamiliar, bony face with kisses. Strange, no half-grown, gone-to-the-wild beard, but vampires didn't grow beards unless they had them when they became vampires.

And then there were other people in the cell. Good people. People laughing and crying and helping her create a makeshift litter out of stinking blankets and Stefan's pallet and no one screamed when lice jumped on them because everyone knew that Elena would have turned and ripped their throat out like Saber. Or rather, like Saber, but as Ms Courtland had always said, *with feeling*. To Saber it was just a job.

Then somehow – things had begun to become disconnected – Elena was watching Stefan's beloved face and gripping his litter, and running – he didn't weigh anything – up a different corridor than the one she'd fought and shouldered and pushed and floundered in on her way in. Apparently all the Shi no Shi's salmon had chosen the other corridor to swim up. Undoubtedly there was a safe place for them at the end on that side.

And even as Elena wondered how a face could be so pure, and handsome, and perfect, even when it looked almost like a skull, she was thinking, I can run and stoop. And she bent over Stefan and her hair made a shield around them, so that it was just the two of them inside it. The entire outside world was shut out, and they were alone, and she said in his ear: "Please, we need you to be strong. Please – for me. Please – for Bonnie. Please – for Damon. Plea—"

She would have gone on naming all of them, and

probably some over and over, but it was too much already. After his long deprivation, Stefan was in no mood to be contrary. His head darted up and Elena felt more than the usual pain because he was at the wrong angle, and Elena was *glad* because Stefan had struck a vein down its length and blood was flowing into his mouth in a steady stream.

They had to go a little more slowly now, or Elena would have tripped and coloured Stefan's face maroon like a demon's, but they were still jogging. Someone else was guiding them.

Then, very suddenly they stopped. Elena, eyes shut, mind locked on to Stefan's, would not have looked up for the world. But in a moment they were moving again, and there was a feeling of spaciousness all around Elena and she realised that they were in the lobby and she had to make sure everyone knew.

It's on the left side of us now, she sent to Damon. *It's close to the front. It's a door with all sorts of symbols above.*

I believe I'm familiar with the species, Damon sent back drily, but even he couldn't hide two things from her. One was that he was glad, actually glad to feel Elena's elation, and to know that it was he, in the main part, that had brought it about.

The other was simple. That if there was a choice between the life of himself and the life of his brother, he would give his own life. For Elena's sake, for his own pride.

For Stefan.

Elena didn't dwell on these secret things she had no right to know. She simply embraced them, let Stefan feel them in all their raw vibrancy, and made sure there was no feedback to tell Damon that Stefan knew. Angels were singing in heaven for her. Black Magic rose petals were scattering around her body. There was a release of doves and she felt their wings. She was happy.

But she was not safe.

She only learned it as she entered the lobby, but they were very lucky that the Dimensional Door was on the side it was. Bloddeuwedd had methodically destroyed the other side until it had collapsed into a mound that was nothing but splintered wood. Elena and Bloddeuwedd's feud might have started out as a quarrel between a hostess who thought her guest had broken the house rules and a guest who just wanted to run away, but it had become a war to the death. And given the way vampires, werewolves, demons and other folk down here in the Dark Dimension reacted, it had created a sensation. The Guardians had their hands full keeping people out of the building. Dead bodies lay strewn on the street.

Oh, God, the people! The poor people! Elena thought, as this at last came into her field of view. As for the Guardians, who were keeping this place clear and fighting Bloddeuwedd on her behalf – God bless you for that, Elena thought, envisioning a standing-room-only lobby as they tried to race with Stefan across the floor. As it was, they were alone.

"Now we need your key again, Elena," Damon's voice, just above her, said.

Elena gently pried Stefan off her throat. "Just for a moment, my darling. Just for a moment."

Looking at the door, Elena was confounded for several moments. There was a hole, but nothing happened when she put the ring in it and pushed, jammed, or twisted left or right. Out of the corner of her eye she saw some dark shadow above her, dismissed it as irrelevant, and then had it come screaming at her like a dive-bomber, steel talons reaching for her.

There was no roof. Bloddeuwedd's talons had methodically ripped it away.

Elena knew it.

Because somehow Elena suddenly saw the whole of the situation, not just her part in it, but as if she were someone outside her body, who understood many more things than puny little Elena Gilbert did.

The Guardians were here to prevent collateral damage. They could or would not stop Bloddeuwedd.

Elena knew that, too.

All the people running down the other corridor had been doing what an owl's prey normally does. They had been dashing for the bottom of their burrow. There was an enormous safe room there.

Somehow, Elena knew it.

But now, blurrily but definitely, Bloddeuwedd saw the ones she had been after in the first place, the nest robbers, the ones who had for ever put out one of her huge round orange far-seeing eyes, and cut her so deeply that the other eye was filling with blood.

Elena could feel it.

Bloddeuwedd could see they were the ones who had caused her to smash her beak. The criminals, the savages, the ones she would tear to pieces slowly, slowly, a limb at a time, switching from one to another as she clutched five or six in one set of claws, or as she watched them, unable to run from lack of limbs, writhing beneath her.

Elena could sense it.

Beneath her.

Right now ... they were directly beneath Bloddeuwedd.

Bloddeuwedd dove.

"Saber! Talon!" shouted Sage, but Elena knew that

there would be no distraction now. There would be nothing but killing and tearing, slowly, and screams echoing off the single lobby wall.

Elena could picture it.

"It won't open, damn it," shouted Damon. He was manipulating Elena's wrist to move the key in the hole. But no matter how he pulled or pushed, nothing happened.

Bloddeuwedd was almost upon them.

She accelerated, throwing telepathic images before her.

Sinew stretching, joints cracking, bone splintering . . .

Elena knew—

NOOOOO!

Elena's cup of rage ran over.

Suddenly she saw everything she needed to know in one great sweeping epiphany. But it was too late to get Stefan inside the door, so the first thing she shouted was *"Wings of Protection!"*

Bloddeuwedd, barely six feet away, slammed into a barrier that a nuclear missile could not have harmed. She slammed into it at the speed of a racing car and with the mass of a medium-sized aeroplane.

Horror exploded beak first against Elena's wings. They were clear green at the top, dotted with flashing emeralds, and shading into a dawn pink covered with crystals at the bottom. The wings enwrapped all six humans and two animals – and they did not move by one millimetre when Bloddeuwedd smashed into them.

Bloddeuwedd had made herself roadkill.

Shutting her eyes, and trying not to think of the maiden who had been made of flowers (and who had killed her husband! Elena told herself desperately) with dry lips, and wetness trickling down her cheeks, Elena turned back to the door. Put the ring in. Made sure it was flush.

And said, "Fell's Church, Virginia, USA, Earth. Near the boarding-house, please."

It was well after midnight. Matt was sleeping on the bunker's cot, while Mrs Flowers slept on the couch, when they were suddenly wakened by a thump.

"What on earth?" Mrs Flowers got up and stared out the window, which should have been dark.

"Be careful, ma'am," Matt said automatically, but couldn't help adding, "What is it?" – as always, expecting the worst and making sure the revolver with the blessed bullets was ready.

"It's . . . light," Mrs Flowers said helplessly. "I don't know what else to say about it. It's light."

Matt could see the light, throwing shadows on their bunker floor. There was no sound of thunder, and hadn't been since he woke up. Hastily he ran to join Mrs Flowers at the window.

"Did you ever . . . ?" exclaimed Mrs Flowers, lifting her hands and dropping them again. "Whatever could it mean?"

"I don't know, but I remember everybody talking about ley lines. Lines of Power in the ground."

"Yes, but those run along the surface of the earth. They don't point upward, like – like a fountain!" Mrs Flowers said.

"But I heard that wherever three ley lines come together – I think Damon said – they can form a Gate. A Gate to where they were going."

"Dear me," said Mrs Flowers. "You mean you think one of those Gateway things is out *there*? Maybe it's them, coming back."

"It couldn't be." The time Matt had spent with this particular old woman had made him not only respect her, but love her. "But I don't think we should go outside, anyway."

"Dear Matt. You are such a comfort to me," Mrs Flowers murmured.

Matt didn't really see how. It was all her stored food and water they were using. Even the fold-up bed was hers.

If he had been on his own he might have investigated this . . . extraordinary thing. Three spotlights shining out of the ground at an angle so that they met just about at the height of a human being. Bright lights. And getting brighter every minute.

Matt sucked in his breath. Three ley lines, huh? God, it was probably an invasion of monsters.

He didn't even dare to hope.

Elena didn't know if she had needed to say USA or Earth, or even if the door *could* take her to Fell's Church, or if Damon would have to give her the name of some gate that was close to it. But . . . surely . . . with all those ley lines . . .

The door opened, revealing a small room like an elevator.

Sage said quietly, "Can you four carry him if you have to fight, too?" And – after a second to unravel what this meant – three shrieks of protest, in three different feminine tones, came.

"No! Oh, please, no! Oh don't *leave* us!!" – Bonnie, begging.

"You're not coming home with us?" – Meredith, straight-from-the-shoulder.

"I *order* you to get in – and make it quick!" – Elena.

"Such a dominant woman," murmured Sage. "Ah, well, it seems the Great Pendulum has swung again. I am only a man. I obey."

"What? Does that mean you're coming?" Bonnie cried.

"It means I am coming, yes." Gently, Sage took Stefan's wasted body in his arms and stepped into the little cubicle inside the door. Unlike the first keys Elena had used today, this one seemed to work more like a voice-activated elevator . . . she hoped. After all, Shinichi and Misao had each only needed one key for themselves. Here, a number of people might want to go to the same place at once.

She hoped.

Sage back-kicked Stefan's old bedding away. Something rattled on the ground. "Oh—" Stefan reached helplessly for it. "It's my Elena diamond. I found it on the floor after . . ."

"Plenty more where that came from," Meredith said.

"It's important to him," Damon, who was already inside, said. Instead of crowding farther into the elevator, the little room that might disappear at any second, that might be gone for Fell's Church before he could turn back, he walked out into the lobby, looked closely at the floor, and knelt. Then, quickly, he reached down and then got up and hurried into the little room again.

"Do you want to hold it or shall I?"

"You hold it . . . for me. Take care of it."

Anyone who knew of Damon's track record, especially with regards to Elena or even an old diamond that had belonged to Elena, would have said Stefan had to be a madman. But Stefan wasn't mad.

He clasped his hand over his brother's that held the diamond.

"And I'll hold on to you," he said with a faint, wry smile.

"I don't know if anyone is interested," Meredith

said, "but there is a single button on the inside of this contraption."

"Push it!" cried Sage and Bonnie, but Elena cried more loudly, "No – *wait*!"

She'd spotted something. Across the lobby, the Guardians had been unable to stop a single, apparently unarmed citizen from entering the room and crossing the floor at a high-paced graceful glide. He must have been over six feet tall, wearing an entirely white tunic and breeches, which matched his long white hair, alert foxlike ears, and the long flowing silky tail that waved behind him.

"Shut the door!" bellowed Sage.

"Oh, *my*!" breathed Bonnie.

"Can someone tell me what the hell is going on?" snarled Damon.

"Don't worry. It's only a fellow prisoner. A silent fellow. Hey, you got out, too!" Stefan was smiling and that was enough for Elena. And the intruder was holding out something to him that – well, it couldn't be what it looked like, but it was getting quite close now and it *looked* like a bouquet of flowers.

"That *is* a kitsune, is it not?" Meredith asked, as if the world had gone mad around her.

"A prisoner—" said Stefan.

"A THIEF!" shouted Sage.

"Hush!" said Elena. "He can probably hear even if he can't speak."

By then the kitsune was upon them. He met Stefan's eye, glanced at the others and held out the bouquet, which was heavily sealed in plastic wrap and some kind of long stickers with magical-looking inscriptions on them.

"This is for Stefan," he said.

Everyone, including Stefan, gasped.

"Now I must deal with some tiresome Guardians." He sighed. "And you must press the button to make the room go, Beauty," he said to Elena.

Elena, who had momentarily been fascinated by the whisking of a fluffy tail around silken breeches suddenly blushed scarlet. She was remembering certain things. Certain things that had seemed very different . . . in a lonely dungeon . . . in the dark of artificially formed night . . .

Oh, well. Best to put a brave face on it.

"Thank you," she said, and pushed the button. The doors began to close. "Thank you again!" she added, bowing slightly to the kitsune. "I'm Elena."

"*Yoroshiku*. I am—"

The door shut between them.

"Is it that you have gone crazy?" Sage cried. "Taking a bouquet from a fox!"

"You're the one who seems to know him, *Monsieur* Sage," Meredith said. "What's his name?"

"I do *not* know his name! I *do* know he stole three-fifths of the Seine Cloister Treasure from me! I know that he is expert, but expert at cheating at the cards! Ahh!"

The last was not a cry of rage but an exclamation of alarm, for the little room was moving sideways, plunging downward, almost stopping, before it resumed its former steady motion.

"Will it really take us to Fell's Church?" Bonnie asked timidly, and Damon put an arm around her.

"It'll take us somewhere," he promised. "And then we'll see. We're a pretty able set of survivalists."

"Which reminds me," Meredith said. "I think Stefan looks better." Elena, who had been helping to buffer him from the dimensional elevator's motion, glanced up at her quickly.

"Do you really? Or is it just the light? I think he should be feeding," she said anxiously.

Stefan flushed, and Elena pressed fingers to her lips to stop them trembling. *Don't, darling*, she said voicelessly. *Every one of these people have been willing to give their life for you – or for me – for us. I'm healthy. I'm still bleeding. Please don't waste it.*

Stefan murmured, "I'll stop the bleeding." But when she bent to him, as she had known he would, he drank.

CHAPTER

42

By now Matt and Mrs Flowers couldn't ignore the blinding lights any more. They had to go outside.

But just as Matt opened the door there was – well, Matt didn't know what it was. Something blasted straight out of the ground and into the sky, where it got smaller and smaller, became a star, and disappeared.

A meteor that had gone through the Earth? But wouldn't that mean tsunamis and earthquakes and shockwaves and forest fires and maybe even the Earth ripping apart? If one meteor that hit the surface could kill off all the dinosaurs . . .

The light that had been shining upward had faded slightly.

"Well, bless my soul," said Mrs Flowers in a small, shaken voice. "Matt, dear, are you all right?"

"Yes, ma'am. But . . ." Matt's vocabulary couldn't stand the strain. "What the *hell* was it?"

And to his slight surprise, Mrs Flowers said, "My sentiments exactly!"

"Wait – there's something moving. Get back!"

"Dear Matt, be careful with that gun . . ."

"It's people! Oh, my God! *It's Elena.*" Matt abruptly sat down on the ground. He could only whisper now. "*Elena.* She's alive. *She's alive!*"

From what Matt could see, there were a group of people climbing and helping others climb out of a perfectly rectangular hole, perhaps five feet deep, in Mrs Flowers's angelica patch.

They could hear voices. "All right," Elena was saying, as she bent down. "Now grab my hands."

But the way she was dressed! A scrap of scarlet that showed all sorts of scratches and cuts on her legs. On top – well, the remains of the gown covered about what a bikini would. And she was wearing the largest, most sparkly costume jewellery that Matt had ever seen.

More voices, going on through Matt's shock.

"Be careful, yes? I will lift him to you—"

"I can climb out my own." – surely that was *Stefan*!

"You see?" Elena rejoiced. "He says he can climb out his own!"

"*Oui,* but perhaps one small lift—"

"This is hardly the time for machismo, little brother." And *that,* Matt thought, fingering the revolver, was Damon. Blessed bullets . . .

"No, I want – to do it myself – OK – got it. There."

"There! You see! He's better every second!" Elena carolled.

"Where's the diamond? Damon?" Stefan sounded anxious.

"I have it safe. Relax."

"I want to hold it. Please."

"More than you want to hold me?" Elena asked. There was a blur and then Stefan was lying back in her arms, while she said, "Easy, easy."

Matt stared. Damon was right behind them, almost as if he belonged there. "I'll watch the diamond," he said flatly. "You watch your girl."

"Excuse me – I'm sorry, but . . . could somebody *please* lift me out?" And that was Bonnie! Bonnie, sounding plaintive but not afraid or unhappy. Bonnie giggling! "Have we got all the sacks of star balls?"

"We've got all the ones from that house we found." And that was Meredith. Thank God. They'd all made it out. But despite his thoughts, his eyes were drawn again to one figure – the one who seemed to be supervising things – the one with golden hair.

"We *need* the star balls because any one of them might be—" she was beginning, when Bonnie cried out, "Oh, look! Look! It's Mrs Flowers and Matt!"

"Now, Bonnie, they'd hardly be waiting for us," Meredith put in.

"Where? Bonnie, where?" Elena demanded.

"If it's Shinichi and Misao in disguise I'm going to— Hey, Matt!"

"Will someone please tell *me* where?"

"Right there, Meredith!"

"Oh! Mrs Flowers! Um . . . I hope we didn't wake you."

"I have never had a happier awakening," Mrs Flowers said solemnly. "I can see what you have been through in the Dark Place. Your – er – lack of sufficient clothing . . ."

A sudden silence. Meredith glanced at Bonnie. Bonnie glanced at Meredith.

"I know these clothes and gems may seem a little too much . . ."

Matt found his voice. "Those jewels? They're *real*?"

"Oh, they're nothing. And we're all dirty . . ."

"Forgive me. We stink – which is my fault—" Stefan began, only to have Elena cut in.

"Mrs Flowers, Matt: Stefan's been a prisoner! All this time! Starved and tortured – oh, God!"

"Elena. Shhh. You got me back."

"We got you back. Now, I'll never let you go. Ever, ever."

"Easy, love. I really need a bath and—" Stefan stopped suddenly. "There're no iron bars! Nothing to shut off my Powers! I can . . ." He stepped away from Elena, who clung with one hand. There was a soft, silvery flash of light, like a full moon appearing and disappearing in their midst.

"Over here!" he said. "Anyone who doesn't want little beastly parasites, I can take care of you."

"I'm your girl," said Meredith. "I have a phobia about fleas, and Damon never even got me any flea powder. What a master!"

There was laughter at this, laughter Matt didn't understand. Meredith was wearing – well, it had to be costume jewellery, but still it *looked* like about a few million dollars' worth of sapphires.

Stefan took Meredith's hand. There was the same soft flash of light. And then Meredith stepped back saying, "Thanks."

Stefan's low response was, "Thank *you*, Meredith." Meredith's blue dress was at least in one piece, Matt observed.

Bonnie – whose dress had been slashed into starlight-coloured ribbons – was raising a hand. "Me too, please!"

Stefan took her hand, and it happened all over again. "Thank you, Stefan! Oooh! I feel so much better! I hated itching!"

"Thank *you*, Bonnie. I hated to think I was dying alone."

"Other vampires, take care of yourselves!" Elena said, as if she had a clipboard and were checking items off. "And, Stefan, please—" She held out her hands to him.

He knelt in front of her, kissed both her hands, then enshrouded them in the soft white light.

"But I'd still like a bath . . ." said Bonnie pleadingly, as the new vampire – the tall fit one – and Damon had each sparked a moonlight glow around themselves.

Mrs Flowers spoke up. "There are four working bathtubs in that house: in Stefan's room, in my room, in the rooms on either side of Stefan's. Be my guest. I'll put some bath salts in each right now." And then she added, holding her arms out to the whole ragged, bleeding, dirty bunch of them: "My house is yours, my dears."

There was a chorus of passionate "thank yous".

"I'll arrange a rota. For feeding Stefan, I mean. If you girls are willing," Elena added quickly, looking at Bonnie and Meredith. "He doesn't need much, just a little every hour until morning."

Elena still seemed very shy of Matt. Matt was very shy of her. But he stepped forward, empty hands held up to show that he was harmless. "Is it a rule that it's only girls? Because I've got blood, too, and I'm healthy as a horse."

Stefan quickly looked at him. "No rule about only girls. But you don't have to—"

"I want to help you."

"OK, then. Thank you, Matt."

The proper response seemed to be "Thank you, Stefan," but Matt couldn't think of anything until, "Thanks for taking care of Elena."

Stefan smiled. "Thank Damon for that. He and the others all helped me – and each other."

"We Also Walk Dogs – at least Sage does," Damon said slyly.

"Oh – that reminds me. I should use that de-parasiting trick on my two friends. Saber! Talon! Heel!" He added a whistle that Matt could never have imitated.

In any case, Matt was operating in a dream. A huge dog, almost as big as a pony, seemingly, and a falcon came out of the darkness.

"Now," the fit vampire said, and once again the soft light shone.

And then: "There. If you don't mind; I prefer to sleep out of doors with my friends. I am grateful for all your kindnesses, *Madame*, and my name is Sage. The hawk is Talon; the dog, Saber."

Elena said, "Dibs on Stefan's bath for Stefan and me, and Mrs Flowers's bath for the girls. You boys can work things out on your own."

"I," Mrs Flowers said gravely, "will be in the kitchen, making sandwiches." She turned to go.

That was when Shinichi arose from the earth above them.

Or rather when his face arose. It was clearly an illusion, but a terrifying and marvellous one. Shinichi actually seemed to be there, a giant, perhaps supporting the world on his shoulders. The black part of his hair blended in with the night, but the scarlet tips made a flaming halo around his face. Having come from a land that was dominated by a giant red sun, night and day, it was an odd sight.

Shinichi's eyes were red as well, like two small moons in the sky, and they focused on the group by Mrs Flowers's house.

"Hello," he said. "What, you look so surprised? You

shouldn't be. I really couldn't let you come back without popping up to say 'hello'. After all, it's been a long time – for some of you," the giant face said, grinning. "Also, of course, to share in the festivities – we've saved little Stefan, and, my, we even fought an oversized chicken to do it."

"I'd like to see you take Bloddeuwedd on, one on one, and get a secret key out of her nest, at the same time," Bonnie began indignantly, but stopped when Meredith squeezed her arm.

Sage, meanwhile was murmuring something about what his own "oversized chicken", Talon, would do if Shinichi were brave enough to show up in person.

Shinichi ignored all this. "Oh, yes, and the mental calisthenics you had to go through. Truly formidable. Well, never again will we mistake you for blunder-headed idiots who never really asked *why* my sister would give you any clues in the first place, much less clues that Outsiders could understand. I mean" – he leered – "why not just go and swallow the key in the first place, hmm?"

"You're bluffing," Meredith said flatly. "You underestimated us, plain and simple."

"Maybe," said Shinichi. "Or maybe it was something else entirely."

"You lost," said Damon. "I realise that may be an entirely new concept for you, but it's true. Elena has gained much more control over her Powers."

"But will they work here?" Shinichi smiled eerily. "Or will they suddenly disappear in the light of a pale-yellow sun? Or in the depths of true darkness?"

"Don't let him bait you, *Madame*," Sage shouted. "Your Powers come from a place he cannot enter!"

"Oh, yes, and the renegade. The Rebel's rebel son. I

wonder . . . what are you calling yourself this time? Cage? Rage? I wonder what these children will think when they learn who you *really* are?"

"It won't matter who he is," Bonnie cried. "We know that. We know that he's a vampire, but that he can be gentle and kind and he's saved us over and over again." She shut her eyes, but held her ground against the gale of Shinichi's laughter.

"So '*Madame*'," Shinichi mocked, "you think you have gained 'Sage'. But I wonder if you know what in chess we call a 'gambit' is? No? Well, I'm sure your intellectual friend will be glad to inform you."

There was a pause. Then Meredith said, with no expression at all, "A gambit is when a chess player sacrifices something – for instance, a pawn – deliberately – just to get something else. A position on the chessboard that they want, for instance."

"I knew you'd be able to tell them. What do you think of our first gambit?"

Another silence, then Meredith said: "I presume you mean you've given us back Stefan to achieve something better."

"Oh, if you only had golden hair – as your friend Elena has so generously displayed."

There were various exclamations on the theme of "Huh?" – most of them directed at Shinichi, but some at Elena.

Who promptly exploded. "You took Stefan's memories."

"Now, now, nothing so drastic, my dear. But a thirty-meld-a-session beautician – now, she was most cooperative."

Elena turned her gaze up at the giant face with a look of utter contempt. "You . . . *cad*."

"Oh, I'm stricken to the heart." But the thing was,

Shinichi's giant face did look stricken – angry and dangerous. "Between you, all such close friends: do you know how many secrets there are? Of course, Meredith is a mistress of secrecy, keeping her secrets from her friends all these years. You think you've already pumped her dry, but the best is yet to come. And then, of course, there is Damon's secret."

"Which if spoken of here and now will mean instant war," Damon said. "And you know, it's strange, but I got the feeling that you came here tonight to negotiate."

This time Shinichi's laughter really was a gale, and Damon had to leap behind Meredith to prevent her being knocked into the hole the elevator had made.

"Very gallant," Shinichi boomed again, shattering glass somewhere on Mrs Flowers's house. "But I really must be going. Shall I leave a synopsis of the prizes you still have to search for before your little company can look each other in the eye?"

"I think we already have them. And you are no longer welcome around this home," Mrs Flowers said coolly.

But Elena's mind was still working. Even standing here, knowing that Stefan needed her, she was searching for the reasons behind this: Shinichi's second gambit. Because she was sure that this was one.

"Where are the pillowcases?" she said in a sharp voice that frightened and bewildered half the group, and simply frightened the rest.

"I was holding one, but then I decided to hold on to Saber instead." – Sage.

"I had one, at the bottom of the hole, but I dropped it when somebody lifted me out." – Bonnie.

"I've still got one, although I don't understand what good—" Damon began.

"Damon!" Elena whirled to him. "Trust me! We've

got yours and Sage's safe – *what's happening to Bonnie's in the hole*?"

The moment she had said *"trust me"* Damon had dumped his pillowcase on top of Sage's, and by the time she was finished, he had leaped into the hole, which was still so bright with leylight as to hurt any vampire's eyes.

But Damon made no complaint. He said, "I have it safe now – no, wait! A root! A damned root is curled around one of the star balls! Someone toss me a knife, quick!"

While everyone else was slapping their pockets for knives, Matt did something that Elena couldn't believe. First he glanced down into the six-foot-deep hole while pointing – a revolver, was it? Yes, she recognised it as the twin of Meredith's. Then without trying to let himself down easily, he simply jumped as Damon had, into the hole.

"DON'T YOU WANT TO KNOW—" roared Shinichi, but no one was paying any attention to him.

Matt's jump didn't end lightly as Damon's had. It ended with a gasp and a stifled curse. But Matt didn't waste time; still on his knees, he handed the gun up to Damon.

"Blessed bullets – shoot it!"

Damon moved very fast. He didn't even seem to aim. But he must have clicked the safety off and aimed immediately, for the root was now streaking for the soft wall of the hole, its end wrapped tightly around something round.

Elena heard two shattering revolver shots; three. Then Damon stooped and picked up a vine-wrapped ball, medium-sized and crystal clear where its true surface could be seen.

"PUT THAT DOWN!" Shinichi's rage was beyond all measure. The two burning red spots of his eyes were like

flames – like moons of fire. He seemed to be trying to get them to comply by sheer volume. "I SAID, DON'T TOUCH THAT WITH YOUR FILTHY HUMAN HANDS!"

"Oh, my God!" gasped Bonnie.

Meredith said simply, "It's Misao's – it has to be. He'd gamble with his own; but not with hers. Damon, hand it up to me, along with the revolver. I bet it's not bulletproof." She knelt, reaching into the hole.

Damon, with a raised eyebrow, did as she said.

"Oh, God," Bonnie cried, from the edge of the hole. "Matt's sprained his ankle – at least."

"I TOLD YOU," roared Shinichi. "YOU'LL BE SORRY—"

"Here," Damon said to Bonnie, taking not the slightest notice of Shinichi. Without any more ado, he picked up Matt and floated up out of the hole. He deposited the fair-haired boy beside Bonnie, who looked at him with the wide brown eyes of utter confusion.

Matt, though, was a Virginian through and through. After swallowing only once, he got out a "Thank you, Damon."

"No problem, Matt," Damon said, and then "What?" as someone gasped.

"You remembered," Bonnie cried, "You remembered his— Meredith!" she broke off, looking at the tall girl. "The grass!"

Meredith, who had been examining the star ball with a strange expression, now tossed the revolver to Damon and tried with her free hand to tear away the grass that had twined around her feet and up her ankles already. But even as she did so, the grass seemed to leap upward and grab her hand, binding it to her feet. And now it was sprouting, growing, racing up her body towards the ball which she held high in the air.

At the same time, it was tightening around her chest, forcing air out of her lungs.

It all happened so fast that it was only when she gasped, "Somebody take th'ball," that the others leaped to her aid. Bonnie was the first to get there, tearing with her fingernails at the greenery that was squeezing Meredith's chest. But each blade was like steel, and she couldn't rip away even one of them. Neither could Matt or Elena. Meanwhile, Sage was trying to lift Meredith bodily – to pluck her from the earth – and having no more success than the rest.

Meredith's face, clearly visible in the light still shining from the hole, was going white.

Damon snatched the star ball from her fingers just before the tangled greenery running up her arm could reach it. He then began moving faster than the human eye could track, never stopping in any one place long enough for any plant to grasp him.

But still, the grass around Meredith was tightening. Now her face was turning blue. Her eyes were wide, her mouth open for a breath that would not come.

"Stop it!" Elena screamed at Shinichi. "We'll give you the star ball! Just let go of her!"

"LET GO OF *HER*?" Shinichi bellowed laughter. "MAYBE YOU'D BETTER LOOK TO YOUR OWN INTERESTS FIRST BEFORE ASKING ME A FAVOUR."

Wildly, Elena looked around – and saw that grass had almost completely enveloped a kneeling Stefan, who had been too weak to move as quickly as the others had.

And he had never made a sound to call attention to himself.

"*No!*" Elena's desperate scream almost drowned out Shinichi's laughter. "Stefan! No!" Even knowing it was futile, she threw herself at him and tried to rip the grass away from his thin chest.

Stefan simply gave her the faintest of smiles and shook his head sadly.

That was when Damon came to a stop. He held the star ball up toward Shinichi's lowering visage. "Take it!" he shouted. "Take the ball, damn you, but let the two of them *go*!"

This time the gale of Shinichi's laughter went on and on. A spiral of grass grew from a point beside Damon and an instant later had formed a hideous, shaggy green fist, which almost reached the star ball.

But—

"Not yet, my dears," gasped Mrs Flowers. She and Matt had come breathlessly from the boarding-house storage room – Matt limping badly – and they both held what looked like Post-it Notes in their hands.

The next thing Elena knew, Damon was moving at ferocious speed again, away from the fist, and Matt was slapping a bit of paper on the grass covering Stefan, while Mrs Flowers did the same to the greenery on Meredith.

As Elena watched in disbelief, the grass seemed to melt, dying away into hay-coloured blades that fell to the ground.

The next moment she was holding Stefan.

"Let's get inside, my dears," Mrs Flowers said. "It's safe in the storage room – the able help the wounded, of course."

Meredith and Stefan were taking great gasping breaths.

But Shinichi had the last word.

"Don't you worry," he said, strangely calm as if he realised he'd lost – for now. "I'll get that sphere back soon enough. You don't know how to use that kind of Power anyway! And besides all that, I'm going to tell you what you've been hiding from your so-called friends. Just a few secrets, yes?"

"The hell with your secrets," shouted Bonnie.

"Language, language! How about this: One of you has kept a secret all their life, and is doing so even now. One of you is a murderer – and I am not speaking of a vampire, or a mercy killing, or anything like that. And then there is the question of the true identity of Sage – good luck on your research there! One of you has already had their memory erased – and I don't mean Damon or Stefan. And what about the secret stolen kiss? And then there is the question of what happened the night of the motel, that it seems that nobody but Elena can recall. You might ask her sometime about her theories about Camelot. And then—"

That was when the sound as loud as Shinichi's giant-sized gales of laughter interrupted him. It tore through the face in the sky, leaving it drooping ridiculously. Then the face disappeared.

"What was that?"

"Who has the gun?"

"What kind of gun could do that to *him*?"

"One with blessed bullets," Damon said coolly, showing them the revolver, pointed down.

"You mean *you* did that?"

"Good for Damon!"

"Forget Shinichi!"

"He is a liar when it suits him, that I can tell you."

"I think," Mrs Flowers said, "that we can retire to the boarding-house now."

"Yeah, and let's go get our baths."

"Just one last thing." Shinichi's voice, giant-sized seemed to come from everywhere around them; from the sky, from the earth.

"You're really going to love what I have in mind next for you. If I were you, I'd start negotiating for that star ball right NOW." But his laughter was off and the muffled feminine sound behind him was almost like crying, as if Misao couldn't help herself.

"YOU'RE GOING TO *LOVE* IT!" Shinichi insisted in a roar.

CHAPTER
43

Elena had a feeling she couldn't quite describe. It wasn't letdown. It was . . . let*up*. For what seemed like most of her life she had been searching for Stefan.

But now she had him back again, quite safe and clean (he'd had a long bath while she insisted on scrubbing him gently with all sorts of brushes and pumice stones, and then a shower, and then a rather cramped shower with her). His hair was drying into the silky soft dark shock – a little longer than he usually kept it – that she knew. He hadn't had energy for frivolities like keeping his hair short and clean before. Elena understood that.

And now . . . there were no guards or kitsune around to spy on them. There was nothing to keep them from each other. They had been playful in the shower, splashing each other, Elena always making sure to keep her feet on the no-slip guard and ready to try to support Stefan's lanky weight. But they could not be playful now.

The shower's spray had been very helpful, too – at concealing the teardrops that kept flowing down Elena's cheeks. She could – oh, dear heaven – count and feel each one of his ribs. He was just bones and skin, her beautiful Stefan, but his green eyes were alive, sparkling and dancing in his pale face.

After they were dressed in nightclothes they simply sat on the bed for a little while. Sitting together, both breathing – Stefan had got into the habit from being around humans so much and, recently, from trying to eke out the small amount of nutrition he received – in synchronicity, and both *feeling* the other's warm body beside them . . . it was almost too much. Then, almost tentatively, Stefan groped for Elena's hand, and catching it, held it in both of his, turning it over wonderingly.

Elena was swallowing and swallowing, trying to make a start in a conversation, felt herself practically radiating bliss. Oh, I never want anything more, she thought, although she knew that soon enough she would want to talk, and to hold, and to kiss, and to feed Stefan. But if someone had asked her if she would have accepted just this, sitting together, communicating by touch and love alone, she would have accepted it.

Before she knew it, she was talking, words that came like bubbles out of molasses, only these were bubbles from her soul. "I thought that somehow I might lose this time. That I'd won so many times, and that this time something would teach me a lesson and you . . . wouldn't make it."

Stefan was still wondering over her hand, bending industriously to kiss each separate finger. "You call 'winning' dying in pain and sunlight to save my worthless life – and my even more worthless brother's?"

"I call this a better kind of winning," Elena admitted. "Any time we get to be together is winning. Any moment – even in that dungeon . . ."

Stefan winced, but Elena had to finish her thought. "Even there, to look in your eyes, to touch your hand, to know that you were looking at me and touching me – and that you were happy – well, that's winning, in my book."

Stefan lifted his eyes to hers. In the dim light, the green looked suddenly dark and mysterious. "And one more thing," he whispered. "Because I am what I am . . . and because your crowning glory isn't that glorious golden cloud of hair, but an aura that is . . . ineffable. Indescribable. Beyond any words . . ."

Elena had thought they would sit and simply gaze at each other, drowning in each other's eyes, but that wasn't happening. Stefan's expression had slipped and Elena realised how close to bloodlust – and to death – he still really was.

Hurriedly, Elena pulled her damp hair to one side of her neck, and then she leaned back, knowing Stefan would catch her.

He did this, but although Elena tilted her chin back, he tilted it down in his two hands to look at her.

"Do you know how much I love you?" he asked.

His entire face was masked now, enigmatic and strangely thrilling. "I don't think you do," he whispered. "I've watched and watched how you were willing to do anything, *anything* to save me . . . but I don't think you know how much that love has been building up, Elena . . ."

Delicious shivers were going down Elena's spine.

"Then you'd better show me," she whispered. "Or I might not believe that you mean it."

"I'll show you what I mean," Stefan whispered back. But when he bent down it was to kiss her softly. The feelings inside Elena – that this starving creature wanted to kiss her instead of going at once for her throat, reached a peak that she could not explain in thoughts or words, but only by drawing Stefan's head so that his mouth rested on her neck.

"Please," she said. "Oh, Stefan, *please.*"

Then she felt the quick sacrificial pains, and then Stefan was drinking her blood, and her mind, which had been fluttering around like a bird in a lighted room, now saw its nest and its mate and swooped up and up and up to at last reach unity with its best-beloved.

After that there was no need for clumsy things like words. They communicated in thoughts as pure and clear as shimmering gems, and Elena rejoiced because all of Stefan's mind was open to her, and none of it was walled off or dark and there were no boulders of secrets or chained and weeping children . . .

What! she heard Stefan exclaim voicelessly. *A child in chains? A mountain-sized boulder? Who could have that in their mind—*

Stefan broke off, knowing the answer, even before Elena's lightning-swift thought could tell him. Elena felt the clear green wave of his pity, spiced by the natural anger of a young man who has gone through the depths of hell, but untainted by the terrible black poison of hatred of brother for brother.

When Elena had finished explaining all she knew about Damon's mental processes, she said, *And I don't know what to do! I've done everything I could, Stefan, I've – I've even loved him. I gave him everything that wasn't yours alone. But I don't know if it's made even the slightest difference.*

He called Matt "Matt" instead of Mutt, Stefan interrupted.

Yes. I . . . noticed that. I'd kept asking him to, but it never seemed to matter.

It mattered this way: you managed to change him. Not many people can.

Elena wrapped him in a tight embrace, stopped, worried that it was too tight, and glanced at him. He smiled and shook his head. He was already looking like a person rather than a death camp survivor.

You should keep using it, Stefan said voicelessly. *Your influence over him is strongest.*

I will – without any artificial Wings, Elena promised. Then she worried that Stefan would think her too presumptuous – or too attached.

But one look at Stefan was enough to assure her that she was doing the right thing.

They clung to each other.

It wasn't as hard as Elena had imagined it would be – handing Stefan over to other humans to be bled. Stefan had a clean pair of pyjamas on, and the first thing he said to all three donors was, "If you get frightened or change your mind, just say so. I can hear perfectly well, and I'm not in bloodlust. And anyway, I'll probably sense it if you're not enjoying it before you do, and I'll stop. And finally – thank you – thank you all. I've decided to break my oath tonight because there's still some little chance that if I slept I wouldn't wake up tomorrow without you."

Bonnie was horrified and indignant and furious. "You mean you couldn't sleep *all that time* because you were afraid to – to . . . ?"

"I did fall asleep from time to time, but thank fortune – thank *God* – I always woke up again. There were times when I didn't dare move to conserve energy, but somehow Elena kept finding ways to come to me, and every single time she came, she brought me some kind of sustenance." He gave Elena a look that sent her heart spinning out of her chest and high into the stratosphere.

And then she set up a schedule, with Stefan being fed every hour on the hour, and then she and the others left the first volunteer, Bonnie, alone, so as to be more comfortable.

It was the next morning. Damon had already been out to visit Leigh, the antiques-seller's niece, who had seemed very glad to see him. And now he was back, to look with scorn at the slug-a-beds who were distributed all around the boarding-house.

That was when he saw the bouquet.

It was heavily sealed down with wards – amulets to help get it through the dimensional gap. There was something powerful in there.

Damon cocked his head to one side.

Hmm . . . I wonder what?

Dear Diary,

I don't know what to say. We're home.

Last night we each had a long bath . . . and I was half disappointed, because my favourite long-handled back-scrubbing brush wasn't there, and there was no star ball to make dreamy music for Stefan – and the water was LUKEWARM! And Stefan went to see if the water heater was turned on all the way and met Damon going to do the same thing! Only, they couldn't because we're home again.

But I woke up a couple of hours ago for a few minutes to see the most beautiful sight in the world . . . a sunrise. Pale pink and eerie green in the east, with night-time still full dark in the west. Then deeper rose in the sky, and the trees all wreathed in dew clouds. Then a shiny glory from the edge of the horizon and dark rose, cream, and even a green melon colour in the sky, Finally, a line of fire and in an instant all the colours change. The line becomes an arc, the western sky is deepest deepest blue, and then up comes the sun bringing warmth and light and colour to the green trees and the sky begins to become celestial blue — celestial just means heavenly, although somehow, I have a delicious shivery feeling when I say it. The sky becomes a gemlike, celestial, cerulean blue and the golden sun begins to pour energy, love, light and every good thing onto the world.

Who could not be happy to watch this while Stefan held her?

We who are so lucky as to be born into the light — who see it every day and never think about it, we're blessed. We could have been born shadow souls who live and die in crimson darkness, never even knowing that somewhere there is something better.

CHAPTER

44

Elena was wakened by shouting. She'd already once awakened to unbelievable bliss. Now she was awake again – but surely that was Damon's voice. *Shouting?* Damon didn't shout!

Throwing on a robe, she went dashing out the door and downstairs.

Raised voices – confusion. Damon was kneeling on the floor. His face was blue-white. There wasn't a plant in the room that could be strangling him.

Poisoned, was the next thing Elena thought and immediately her eyes darted around the room to see a spilled drink, a dropped plate, any sign that poison had done this. There was nothing.

Sage was clapping Damon on the back. Oh, God, could he have choked? But that was idiocy. Vampires didn't breathe, except for talking and building Power.

But then what was happening?

"You have to breathe," Sage was shouting in Damon's ear. "Take a breath, as if you were going to speak, but then hold on to it, as if for raising your Power. Think about your insides. Get those lungs working!"

The words only confused Elena.

"There!" cried Sage. "You see?"

"But it only lasts an instant. Then I need to do it again."

"But, yes, that is the point!"

"I tell you I'm dying and you laugh at me?" a dishevelled Damon shouted. "I'm blind, deaf, my senses are haywire – and you laugh!"

Dishevelled, thought Elena, bothered by something.

"Well." Sage seemed to be at least trying not to laugh. "Perhaps, *mon petit chou*, you should not have opened something that was not addressed to you?"

"I put wards all around me before I did it. The house was safe."

"But you were not – *breathe*! *Breathe*, Damon!"

"It looked completely harmless – and admit it – we were all going – to open it last night – when we got too tired!"

"But to do it alone, to open a present from a kitsune . . . that was foolish, yes?"

A choking Damon snapped, "Don't lecture me. Help me. Why am I muffled in cotton wool? Why can't I see? Or hear? Or smell – anything? I'm telling you I can't smell a thing!"

"You are fit and sharp as any human could be. You could probably defeat most vampires if you fought with one right now. But human senses are very few and very dull."

Words were swimming in Elena's head . . . opening things not addressed to you . . . bouquet from a kitsune . . . human . . .

Oh, my God!

Apparently, the same words were going through the mind of someone else, because suddenly a figure dashed in from the kitchen area. Stefan.

"You stole my bouquet? From the kitsune?"

"I was very careful—"

"Do you realise what you've done?" Stefan shook Damon.

"Ow. That hurts! Do you want to break my neck?"

"*That* hurts? Damon, you're in for a *world* of hurt! Do you understand? I talked to that kitsune. Told him the whole story of my life. Elena came to visit and he saw her practically . . . well, never mind – he saw her crying over me! Do . . . you . . . realise . . . what . . . you . . . have . . . *done*?"

It was as if Stefan had started climbing a series of steps, and that each one lifted him to a higher level of fury than the last. And here, at the top . . .

"I'll KILL YOU!" Stefan shouted. "You *took* it – my humanity! He gave it to me – *and you took it*!"

"You'll kill *me*? I'll kill *you*, you – you *bastard*! There was one flower in the middle. A black rose, bigger than I have ever seen. And it smelled . . . heavenly . . ."

"It's gone!" Matt reported, producing the bouquet. He displayed it. There was a gaping hole in the centre of the mixed flower arrangement.

Despite the hole, Stefan ran to it, and stuck his face into the bouquet, sucking in great heaving breaths of air. He kept coming up and snapping his fingers and each time lightning flared between his fingertips.

"Sorry, bud," Matt said. "I think it's gone."

Elena could see it all now. That kitsune . . . he was one of the good ones, like the stories Meredith had told them about. Or at least good enough to sympathise with Stefan's plight. And so, when he had gotten free, he had made up a bouquet – kitsune could do anything with plants, although surely this was a great feat, something like finding the secret of eternal youth ... to turn vampires into humans. And after Stefan had endured and endured and endured and should have finally gotten his reward ... right now ...

"I'm going back," Stefan shouted. "I'm going to find him!"

Meredith said quietly, "With or without Elena?"

Stefan stopped. He looked up at the stairway, and his eyes met Elena's.

Elena ...

We'll go together.

"No," Stefan shouted. "I would never put you through that. I'm not going after all. I'm just going to murder *you*!" He swung back on his brother.

"Been there, done that. Besides, I'm the one that's going to kill you, you bastard! You took my world away from me! I am a vampire! I'm not a" – some creative cursing – "human!"

"Well, you are now," Matt said. He was just barely not laughing out loud. "So I'd say you'd better get used to it."

Damon leaped at Stefan. Stefan didn't step aside. In an instant there was a ball of thrashing, kicking and punching, and cursing in Italian that made it sound as if there were at least four vampires fighting five or six humans.

Elena sat down helplessly.

Damon ... a human?

How were they going to deal with this?

Elena looked up to see that Bonnie had carefully made up a tray of all sorts of things that tasted good to humans, and that she'd undoubtedly done it for Damon before he had worked his way into hysteria.

"Bonnie," Elena said quietly, "don't give it to him yet. He'll just throw it at you. But perhaps later . . ."

"Later he *won't* throw it?"

Elena winced.

"How is Damon going to deal with being human?" she asked herself aloud.

Bonnie looked at the cursing, spitting ball of vampire/human fury.

"I'd say . . . kicking and screaming the whole way."

Just then Mrs Flowers came out of the kitchen. She had a huge mound of fluffy waffles stacked on several plates on a tray. She saw the rolling, swearing, snarling ball that was Stefan and Damon.

"Oh, my," she said. "Did something go wrong?"

Elena looked at Bonnie. Bonnie looked at Meredith. Meredith looked at Elena.

"You . . . could say so," gasped Elena.

And then the three of them gave way to it. Gales and gales of helpless laughter.

You've lost a powerful ally, said a voice in Elena's mind. Do you know that? Can you foresee the consequences? Today, when you have just come back from a world of Shinichis?

We'll win, Elena thought. We have to.

Also by Hodder Children's Books:

Coming soon . . .
Read the final thrilling book in the series:

Vampire Diaries: The Return – Midnight
L. J. Smith

*In Midnight, golden girl Elena Gilbert is back from the
Dark Dimension, but has she managed to save her
vampire boyfriend Stefan Salvatore from imprisonment?
And will there be consequences to the trio travelling
there?*

*Elena, Stefan and Damon are left reeling after a hugely
unexpected event, but they must focus on the task at hand:
Dealing with the demons that have taken over Elena's
hometown, Fell's Church. Can the trio find a happy
ending? MIDNIGHT takes Elena, Stefan, and Damon to
their darkest moments yet . . .*

NIGHT WORLD
Volume I
L.J. Smith

The Night World is a secret society of vampires, werewolves, witches and creatures of darkness – a place where it is too dangerous to fall in love . . .

Read the first compelling volume in the series:
SECRET VAMPIRE, DAUGHTERS OF DARKNESS AND ENCHANTRESS

In *Secret Vampire*, Poppy is dying. Her best friend, James can offer her eternal life – as a vampire. One kiss and she sees into his soul. But can she follow him into death . . . and beyond?

In *Daughters of Darkness*, there are three sisters with a secret, on the run from their cruel and ruthless brother. Can their new human friend Mary Lynette resist the powerful charm of their brother – and save the sisters and herself from a deadly fate at the hands of a werewolf?

In *Enchantress*, Blaise is irresistible. She's lethal. She bewitches boys for sport. Then she meets a boy who matters to her cousin, Thea. They become rivals in love. It's Thea's white magic against Blaise's black magic. They're both breaking the rules. But it's Thea who risks expulsion from the Night World . . .

NIGHT WORLD
Volume II
L.J. Smith

The Night World is a secret society of vampires, werewolves, witches and creatures of darkness – a place where it is too dangerous to fall in love . . .

Read the second compelling volume in the series:
DARK ANGEL, THE CHOSEN AND SOULMATE

In *Dark Angel*, Angel saves Gillian from death in the icy wilderness and then offers to make her the most popular girl at school. But what does he want in return?

In *The Chosen*, vampire killer Rashel is torn between her feelings for her soulmate Quinn, and her loathing for his thirst for human blood. She loves him, but is that enough?

In *Soulmate*, Hannah's true love – Lord of the Night World, has come back into her life and reignited her passion. But her joy is threatened by the return of an ancient enemy.

Coming Soon . . .

ISBN: 978 1 4449 0058 3

Countless teenage girls have been brutally murdered, and Scarlett and Rosie March know how they died – torn apart by werewolves. For Scarlett, the memories of a similar attack have left not just emotional scars, but physical ones. The sisters fight side by side to save others from the same fate.

When the mysterious and brooding Silas arrives he inadvertently causes a series of events that could endanger them all. As passion grows between Rosie and Silas, Scarlett uncovers some shocking secrets about Silas's family history that could tear the sisters apart – one way or another . . .